evolve

Vampire Stories of the New Undead

edited by

Nancy Kilpatrick

EDGE SCIENCE FICTION AND FANTASY PUBLISHING

AN IMPRINT OF HADES PUBLICATIONS, INC.

CALGARY

Edge Science Fiction and Fantasy Publishing
An Imprint of Hades Publications Inc.
P.O. Box 1714, Calgary, Alberta, T2P 2L7, Canada

Interior design by Brian Hades
Cover Illustration by John Kaiine
Evolve logo by Ryanne Hamilton
ISBN-13: 978-1-894063-33-3

EDGE Science Fiction and Fantasy Publishing and Hades Publications, Inc.
acknowledges the ongoing support of the Canada Council for the Arts and the
Alberta Foundation for the Arts for our publishing programme.

Alberta Foundation for the Arts   Canada Council   Conseil des Arts
                                         for the Arts   du Canada

Library and Archives Canada Cataloguing in Publication

Evolve : vampire stories of the new undead
    / Nancy Kilpatrick, editor.

ISBN 978-1-894063-33-3

1. Vampires--Fiction. 2. Horror tales, Canadian (English).
3. Fantasy fiction, Canadian (English). 4. Short stories,
Canadian (English). 5. Canadian fiction (English)—21st century.
I. Kilpatrick, Nancy

PS8323.H67E96 2010   C813'.087380806   C2010-900158-3

FIRST EDITION
(o-20100601)
Printed in Canada
www.edgewebsite.com

PRAISE FOR EVOLVE

"The premise behind Evolve is a simple one: just as humans have undergone a social evolution, from the time a caveperson picked up that thigh bone and smashed his/her neighbor over the head, so vampires have evolved from the somewhat crude lurkers of the 18th and 19th century. One of the results of such evolution is that the evolved ones bear only a slight resemblance to the original. Evolve is an excellent example of this, demonstrating changes that would have made these vampires unrecognizable to Ur-vampire Dracula."
— Michael Mirolla , Rover Arts

"I had thought that vampires were a dead horse, that we had done everything possible with them, imagined them in every conceivable way, and every 'new' vampire story was simply a re-telling of the older ones. I am pleased to say that this anthology has proved me wrong. The authors in Evolve have done the unthinkable – they have given life to vampires."
— Lyndsey Holder, Innsmouth Free Press

"I loved that the beginning opened with poetry and the end closed with yearning for more." — Tina, Blog With Bite

"The vampires in the anthology are not the sparkly kind, in case you are wondering, but instead pay a much closer homage to Dracula with a few modern twists. The stories feel both familiar and, at the same time, new." — Michell Plested

"Overall this is a collection that should not be ignored. Each story stands on it's own as a solid piece of fiction, but together you begin to see the nature of the modern Vampire myth."
— A Novel Approach

"I enjoyed this anthology quite a bit! I think there's a story in here for everyone. An eclectic mix." — VampChix

"With stories from genre veterans Kelley Armstrong and Tanya Huff, as well as a slew of newcomers, Evolve: Vampire Stories of the New Undead is a worthy anthology for vampire lovers."
— Quill and Quire

Limited Edition Available

If you collect limited editions of books, you need to check out the special "COFFIN" edition of *EVOLVE: Vampire Stories of the New Undead*.

Protected in a magnetically sealed miniature pine coffin; packaged in an open ended black bag; identified by a unique wax seal; and certified as an original; is a hardcover copy of *EVOLVE: Vampire Stories of the New Undead*.

Each of these "COFFIN" editions is identified by unique number: on the lid, the box and the book. Each book is signed by all of the authors, the cover artist, the editor and the publisher.

Only 50 copies of this limited edition are available. You must order your copy directly from the publisher. Limited to one copy per customer. We expect the COFFIN edition to sell out quickly. Act fast to avoid disappointment.

Limited "COFFIN" edition — $230.00 US plus shipping and taxes.

"If you're into vampires at all, this is a collection
of stories you'll love." — Lisa C.

Bram Stoker, my great grand uncle, spent seven years, 1890-1897 researching and writing his classic story *Dracula*. During those years, he was the personal secretary to Henry Irving and manager of Irving's Lyceum Theater in London. The Lyceum Company toured North America on two occasions, including stops in Montreal and Toronto. Some years later, Bram's brother Richard retired to B.C. and their nephew, my grandfather, relocated to Montreal.

Many traits of Bram's Count Dracula are now accepted as standard vampire characteristics, integral to the genre today. It is worth mentioning that Bram Stoker did not invent the characteristics, but rather gathered the attributes for his Count from earlier vampire fiction, folklore, and mythologies.

The intriguing vampires appearing in *evolve* all share a common link to the iconic character Dracula, which can be traced back to those special pages of Bram's notes for Dracula, housed in the Rosenbach Museum.

Dacre Stoker
Great grandnephew of Bram Stoker
Canadian Co-Author of *Dracula: The Un-Dead*

Contents

Introduction
Nancy Kilpatrick 1
Let the Night In
Sandra Kasturi 13
Learning Curve
Kelley Armstrong 15
Chrysalis
Ronald Hore 22
Mother of Miscreants
Jennifer Greylyn 35
Resonance
Mary E. Choo 47
The New Forty
Rebecca Bradley 63
Red Blues
Michael Skeet 72
The Drinker
Victoria Fisher 81
Sleepless in Calgary
Kevin Cockle 86
Come to Me
Heather Clitheroe 101
An Ember Amongst the Fallen
Colleen Anderson 109
Mamma's Boy
Sandra Wickham 124
The Morning After
Claude Bolduc (Translated by Sheryl Curtis) 128
All You Can Eat, All the Time
Claude Lalumière 136

Alia's Angel
   Rhea Rose 149
When I'm Armouring My Belly
   Gemma Files 157
A Murder of Vampires
   Bev Vincent 169
The Greatest Trick
   Steve Vernon 184
Soulfinger
   Rio Youers 197
Bend to Beautiful
   Bradley Somer 214
Evolving
   Natasha Beaulieu 219
How Magnificent is the Universal Donor
   Jerome Stueart 229
The Sun Also Shines On the Wicked
   Kevin Nunn 249
Quid Pro Quo
   Tanya Huff 260

Biographies 275

evolve

Vampire Stories of
the New Undead

Acknowledgments

The editor would like to thank her dear friends and her partner Hugues Leblanc for consistently supporting her work, as they always do, despite her moods. The writers herein were nothing but generous with their stories and most gracious about accepting editorial feedback. John Kaiine's art, which graces the cover, is an amazingly lovely work which we were lucky to get. Brian Hades has once again gone above and beyond and everyone in Canada should be grateful that such a magnificent publisher exists, one willing to take risks—the man is open to working with people obsessed with vampires!

Introduction
By Nancy Kilpatrick

I began editing this anthology when I was eleven years old. That's when I first encountered Dracula.

It was a dark and stormy night in Philadelphia, and for some reason I was allowed by the Powers That Were to stay up and watch the Late Show on TV, which always aired the old black and white horror movies from the 1930s.

The Late Show was then called Shock Theater and hosted by Roland, aka The Cool Ghoul, who began his career in Philly and was so popular that a New York station scooped him up and took him away. These were BC days—before cable—and a major city might have three local TV stations, if it was lucky. Cities were always snatching popular figures and Roland moved to the Big Apple, leaving Philadelphia TV destined to settle for its fifteen-minutes-of-fame via American Bandstand.

Roland — real name John Zacherley — was vampiric. He possessed hollowed out cheeks, a wild and crazy stare, wore the requisite Count Dracula duds, and had ongoing eerie conversations with My Dear, who dwelt in the coffin center stage that he frequently bent over to catch her replies—and which only he could hear—or, alternately, yelled at his lab assistant Igor, a voiceless chain-rattler offstage. "Where's Igor?" became a buzzphrase, printed on an oversized black and white button that I wish I still possessed!

During his terrifying tenure, Roland introduced many horror classics to an enthralled audience of mainly youth, of which I was one. I soon became a regular viewer, begging, wheedling, sneaking out to the old console TV in what felt like the middle of the night to catch the latest and greatest of Roland's offerings.

My favorite films were vampire movies. Especially *Dracula*. Enter Bela Lugosi. Exit Nancy's free will, or so it has often seemed over the years because vampires became an obsession.

As much as I loved Bela Lugosi's *Dracula* (1931), Carol Borland's *Mark of the Vampire* (1935), Gloria Holden's *Dracula's Daughter* (1936) Lon Chaney Jr's *Son of Dracula* (1943), these early vampires gave way over time to other, more modern filmatic bloodsuckers; clearly, the vampire was altering.

Somewhere around the time I hit puberty, Christopher Lee appeared in *Horror of Dracula* (1958), filling the screen with his particularly menacing version of Count Dracula's heavy control issues laced with dynamic sex appeal that started a series of films staring the *Tall, Dark and Gruesome* (the title of his autobiography) actor. Besides the series of vampire movies Lee appeared in, other Hammer Studio blood drinkers included, among others, *The Brides of Dracula* (1960), Ingrid Pitt as Elizabeth Bathory in *Countess Dracula* (1970); *Vampire Circus* (1972), *The Legend of the Seven Golden Vampires* (1974).

But Hammer wasn't the only studio doing vampires. *Black Sunday* (1960) starred the amazing Barbara Steele; *The Last Man on Earth* (1964), based on the Richard Matheson ground-breaking book *I Am Legend* (1954), starred the incomparable Vincent Price. (That book would see film three times to date); Polanski's *The Fearless Vampire Killers* (1967); Robert Quarry made a creepy *Count Yorga* (1970) and a sequel; the exquisite Delphine Seyrig created an arresting female vampire in *Daughters of Darkness* 1971); Shakespearean action and opera-trained singer William Marshall starred in *Blacula* (1972) and a sequel; the lovely and obscure film *Lemora* (1973); the intriguingly funny *Andy Warhol's Dracula* (1974) starred the delightful actor Udo Kier; the breathtakingly beautiful Werner Herzog remake *Nosferatu the Vampyre* (1977); and George Romero's *Martin* (1977), staring John Amplas, who I don't think we've seen much of since! And this is but a tiny list—there are plenty more vampire movies where these came from!

The pace picked up for vampire films in the 1980s, 1990s, and into the new millennium, forcing the undead into the modern age and allowing more sophisticated FX than had been available before this time: *The Hunger* (1983); *Fright Night* (1985); *Vamp* (1986); *The Lost Boys* (1987); *Near Dark* (1987); *Cronos* (1993); *Nadja* (1994); *The Addiction* (1995); *From Dusk to Dawn* (1996); *John Carpenter's Vampires* (1998); *Shadow of the Vampire* (2000); *Night Watch* (2004); *30 Days of Night* (2007); *Let the Right One In* (2008), to name only a handful.

The list goes on and I haven't even touched on major hits like *Salem's Lot* (1979); *Bram Stoker's Dracula* (1992); *Buffy the Vampire Slayer* (1992); *Interview With the Vampire* (1994); *Blade* (1998); *Underworld* (2003) and so many of the other big screen movies that we're all familiar with, films that document the vampire's evolution.

Over the years, whenever a new vampire movie hit the theaters, I was eager to see it. More than eager. In rep theaters, I tracked down the 1922 silent film *Nosferatu* by Murnau, and Carl Dreyer's 1932 classic *The Vampire*. Vampires in cinema became almost a necessity of life for me and I prided myself on having watched every single vampire movie ever made. That may not be so. According to Stephen Jones' listing of vampire cinema in *The Illustrated Vampire Movie Guide* (1993), there are some movies I've missed. But not many. Such is the nature of obsession.

Along with being a committed vampire film buff, I have always been an avid reader. In the early 1970s I began perusing vampire literature in earnest. Granted, until that time, there hadn't been much published. Once I got started, I went through early stories and novels fairly quickly.

The first short story published in English, "The Vampyre" (1819), by John Polidore, is based on a fragment penned by the infamous poet Lord Byron on that fateful weekend when these two men joined the poet Percy Bysshe Shelley, his soon-to-be wife Mary Wollstonecraft Godwin and her sister Claire Clairmont for a vacation by a lake in Switzerland. The guests, being *avant garde* types,

grew bored with the inclement weather and decided to
tell each other ghost stories. Mary Shelley came up with
Frankenstein, based on a dream, and Byron tossed in his
scribbled page which Polidore had the chutzpa to expand
on and publish under his own name. A lawsuit concerning
who owned the copyright followed. Polidore won.

Next up on my reading list was the first novel in English,
Varney the Vampire or, The Feast of Blood (1847), written by
Thomas Preskett Prest or James Malcolm Rhymer, take your
pick.

Following that I found the quasi-lesbian story *Carmilla*
(1872), the female vampire, by Irish writer Joseph Sheridan
le Fanu, then *Dracula* (1897), by Bram Stoker, another Irish
writer, who lived in London and may have based his now
famous Count loosely on the infamous Transylvania war-
lord Vlad Tepesh.

"The Vampyre" features a ruthless aristocratic vampire
count who preys on the sister of his 'friend'. *Varney the
Vampire* is another aristocratic count preying on young
women in their boudoirs. (It's worth noting that Varney
is repulsed by his actions and at the conclusion of the 1000
page opus hurls himself into the active volcano Vesuvius.)
Carmilla is an aristocratic countess looking to seduce nubile
young ladies in the social register and *Dracula*, as mentioned, was an aristocratic count from Transylvania, the
Carpathian Mountains to be exact, ready and willing to
explore London life.

There's a theme here. Early vampires in English literature were all of the upper crust. Interesting. Noteworthy.
And if vampires were still being written like that today,
you'd find Paris Hilton with a set of gold-plated fangs.

My reading soon incorporated other and often more
subtle early vampiric works, including poetry: "The Vam-
pire" (1748) by Heinrich August Ossenfelder; "The Giaour"
(1813) by Lord Byron; and Coleridge's "Christabel (1816).
Other early short fiction I tracked down included trans-
lations of "The Horla" (1887) by Guy de Maupassant; "La
Morte Amoureuse" (1836) by Theophile Gautier; and "The
Family of the Vourdalak" (1843) by Count Alexis Tolstoy.
And in English, "For the Blood is the Life" (1911) by F.
Marion Crawford. If you like vampire literature, every-

thing I've mentioned so far is worth a read or a view. The foundations of this sub-genre are fascinating.

Vampires survived the Penny Dreadfuls of the Victorian era, which catered to the sensationalism the general population craved, and found new life in the lurid 1930s pulp magazines without much wear and tear on the archetype. The creatures of the twentieth century then moved towards literate stories by exceptional writers: Robert Bloch's "The Cloak" (1939) and Fritz Leiber's classic "The Girl with the Hungry Eyes" (1949).

But all in all, not much was written up to the 1970s, with the notable exceptions of books based on the *Dark Shadows* TV series. The show featured Jonathan Frid as Barnabus Collins (1966-1971—and remade in 1991 starring Ben Cross in the role), which had a spin-off book series that saw publication beginning in the late 1960s, the forty-plus volumes mostly written by Dan Ross using the pen name of his wife Marilyn Ross, a romance writer. And a short series of *Vampirella* books, based on the skimpily-clad comic book character of the same name (1975-1976). Robert Lory wrote a series of novels in the mid-1970s featuring wheelchair bound Professor Harmon whose mental powers allow him to control Dracula by moving a sliver of wood that acts as a mini stake in or out of the Count's heart, depending on whether or not the vampire's services are required.

Lest I forget, besides *Dark Shadows*, television has produced a number of interesting vampire shows. *Kojak* starred Telly Savalas as the cop/vampire hunter in the 1973 to 1978 version, and in 2005 the single season *Kojak* starred Ving Rhames. *Forever Knight* was originally a television movie in 1989 that turned into a much-loved TV series in 1992 starring Geraint Wyn Davies as the vampire detective. Inspired by the movie *Buffy*, the TV series *Buffy the Vampire Slayer* (1997-2003) starred Sarah Michelle Geller. A five year spin-off based on one character *Angel* began in 1999. Other TV vampires have seen the light of day. *Kindred: The Embraced*, based on the Vampire Masquerade role-playing game, graced the tube for one year in 1996. The popular-with-vamp-fans *Moonlight*, starring Alex O'Loughlin as vampire PI Mick St. John, aired for one season in 2007-2008, pulled from the air even though it won a People's Choice Award. And *Blood Ties*, some of which was scripted by Canadian Tanya Huff who wrote the vampire novels from which the show was derived, had a two-season run in 2007-2008. Kyle Schmid played Henry Fitzroy, a vampire who writes romance novels and befriends former cop, now PI Vicki Nelson. Currently, three interesting shows are breathing life into the undead. From the US, the excellent *True Blood*, with a host of vampires immersed in rural southern life, the main one being Civil-War-soldier-brought-back-from-the-dead Bill Compton (played by Stephen Moyer) who is loved by the delightfully quirky Sookie Stackhouse (Canadian born Anna Paquin). Also from the U.S., the TV series based on L.J. Smith's book *The Vampire Diaries*, pitting vampire brothers Stefan and Damon (Paul Wesley and Ian Somerhalder) against one another for the love of Elena (raised-in-Canada Nina Dobrev), an intriguing high school girl who resembles someone from their past. And from the UK, the BBC's wonderful hit series *Being Human*, featuring twenty-something housemates who just happen to be a werewolf, a ghost, and a vampire (played by the handsome Aidan Turner).

It became clear to me that between 1975 and 1978, everything about vampires changed. Fred Saberhagen published *The Dracula Tape* (1975) which would be the start of a ten-book vampire series (to 2002). Stephen King published the stellar and terrifying vampire novel *Salem's Lot* (1975). Chelsea Quinn Yarbro published the innovative *Hotel Transylvania* (1978), which began her long and ongoing series featuring the Count St. Germain and spinoff books with two characters. And Anne Rice gave us the phenomenal *Interview With the Vampire* (1976) which, of course, led to a series of vampire novels and two films.

These four books feature the vampire in a new role and together they form the basis for the vampire as we know him/her today: Dracula as hero/rescuer; Vampire as evil mass-murderer; Vampire as sophisticate with moral values and in control of his hunger; Vampire as mentally manipulative and erotically charged.

The vampire had, yet again, evolved.

Since those ground-breaking titles, a *lot* of vampire fiction has been published. My library, bulging at nearly 2000 volumes, mostly fiction, attests to that fact. I have watched the vampire go from a lone resuscitated corpse hell-bent on biting family members, to beings that travel in packs that prey on anyone and everyone, to humorous creatures parodying themselves, to romantic sub-genre heroes that have appeared in everything from literary novels to Harlequin Romances to mysteries to erotica. Some vampires are ethereal by nature, others physical. Some rue their condition, others revel in it. Vampires are ghost-like, only seen at night, and day-walkers that marry and spawn children, who may or may not be vampires. The undead come in all colors, shapes, sizes, ethnicities and of every possible religious and sexual persuasion. There are many wonderful books and short stories in the undead realm and I couldn't possibly name all of them and in naming a few I risk omitting many fabulous works by incredible authors. But Introductions are not eternal so I will suggest only a few works for novice readers to ferret out. Anyone can begin with Tanith Lee and her exquisite short fiction "Bite-Me-Not, or Fleur de Fur" and end with her *Blood Opera* novel series. The range of vampire fiction is staggering and some classic examples include: Laurell K. Hamilton's *Anita Blake* series; Kim Newman's *Anno Dracula*; Brian Lumley's *Necroscope* series; P.N. Elrod's *The Vampire Files* series; Robert McCammon's *They Thirst*; and too many others to name. In general, I've found that vampire fiction is well written and it's clear that authors find this archetype gripping. In my library, I estimate that no more than 10% of the titles are *not* up to par writing-wise, which isn't bad for any genre or sub-genre.

Today, the vampire offers something for everyone. And the undead are more popular than ever, it seems, with best-selling books like Charlaine Harris's southern vampire series turned into the already-mentioned marvelous TV series *True Blood*; *Dracula: The Un-Dead*, co-authored by Ian Holt and Bram Stoker's great grand-nephew Dacre

Stoker; Stephenie Meyer's young adult *Twilight* and sub-sequent books and the movie series; *The Vampire Diaries* books and TV series, already mentioned; the innovative stand-alone novel *Let Me In* (2007)by Swedish author John Ajvide Lindqvist (the title of the incredibly atmospheric movie is *Let the Right One In*); and outré vampires roaming the steamy gay world as they suck blood and other liquids on the TV series *The Lair*.

Over the years and amongst the many vampire works I have published, I did previously edit an all-vampire anthology back in 1995 for Masquerade Books, a New York publisher of erotic fiction that wanted to try something different. My volume, *Love Bites*, eroticized the vampire in a major way. That anthology ushered in more changes for the undead and popular writers of vampire fiction jumped on board eagerly: Nancy Collins, Karen E. Taylor, Scott Ciencin, David Dvorkin, Ron Dee, Lois Tilton, James A Moore, Kathryn Ptacek, David Naill Wilson and others. I enjoyed editing a book of sexy vamps. That anthology was ahead of its time.

But time does pass, barriers are broken, concepts expanded, and what would have been unheard of yesterday becomes the norm tomorrow. The vampire has moved into the here and now, residing alongside Homo sapiens, beings of this time and place. The vampire has changed from its early roots in mythology and progressed through its illustrious existence in literature, film, television, comic books, theatre, art, music, and every other medium, it has presented us with a constantly evolving creature of the night.

But the obsessed, like me, are never satisfied. We always want to know the future. We're always asking: "What next?" We long to know how the vampire is changing. What will the undead look like as we step into the second decade of this new millennium? Personally and professionally, I wanted a glimpse of the New Vampire.

Life has a way of opening up doors when and where you least expect them to open. In 2008 I co-edited with David Morrell volume number 13 in the *Tesseracts* series for Edge Publishing. *Tesseracts* has always been a science fiction and/or fantasy anthology series of stories written by Canadian authors. That changed with number thirteen when Brian Hades (yes, his real name!), publisher of Edge, decided to do an all horror/dark fantasy anthology and figured I might be a good person to edit it. I asked David Morrell, whose work I've long admired—and who is, in fact, Canadian—if he would co-edit the book with me and he generously agreed to do so.

For *Tesseracts 13*, we read nearly 200 story submissions which came from all over Canada. Edge's mandate is to achieve the broadest spectrum of Canadian fiction in its books and, to that end, work is solicited and representative of the entire country. We received a lot of good stories and a lot of good vampire stories. For a variety of reasons, one of which was how the anthology was shaping up as we jointly agreed on which submissions to include, we decided to exclude all the vampire fiction. And while this was a reasonable decision, part of me felt badly that some of these stories would not be published. They were too good, too innovative to end up in trunks.

Studying the seven vampire stories (and seven is a significant number for the undead, since in the olden times a seventh son of a seventh son would automatically be a vampire!), I began to see that the motif spoke to the New Vampire. And while stories touched on the vampire we are currently meeting in books and visuals, they also addressed and answered that eternal question "What's next for the undead?" It was clear to me that these writers had a sense of where the sub-genre is headed. I wanted to help them pave the way to the New Vampire because I felt certain that the vampire is, once again, evolving.

I approached Edge Publishing to see if they would be interested in me editing an all-vampire anthology (David wasn't available to co-edit). They were, and I did, and *Evolve*, the volume you hold in your hands, has as its cornerstone seven stories that were originally submissions to *Tesseracts 13*. Complementing them are another sixteen stories and one poem, contributing more pieces to the puzzle of the ever-evolving *nosferatu*. And while the entire country of Canada is not represented in this volume, there's a pretty good cross-section, with submissions from everywhere but the provinces of Saskatchewan, Prince Edward Island, Newfoundland and Labrador, and two of the three northern territories, none of which, unfortunately, submitted material.

Today's vampire takes a lot of forms in fiction, film, television and other artistic arenas. But one thing is certain: characters are no longer saying: "There's no such thing as a vampire!" The existence of Creatures of the Night has been validated. And not only that, but they are often seen interacting with society, being accepted (or *almost* accepted) as part of a world culture that now incorporates both humans and non-humans, living and not quite living, for better and for worse.

In *Evolve* you will find kindly vampires, vicious vampires, helpful and hurtful vamps. Some undead are clearly tricksters. Some seek revenge and others can temper their bloodlust with charity towards us mere mortals. These vampires get along with humans, with their own kind, or with neither. They are users and the used. Hunter and hunted. Dangerous.

But read on. Let the Canadian writers who grace these pages lead you into the shadowy realm between the not quite living and the not quite dead. That dawn and dusk grey area where anything is possible. And as they do so, you'll get a good glimpse of what's to come in the second decade of the new millennium, what the future holds for humankind's favorite predator.

Nancy Kilpatrick
Montreal, 2010

evolve

Vampire Stories of
the New Undead

Let the Night In
By Sandra Kasturi

Shut the night out or let it in,
it is a cat on the wrong side of the door
whichever side it is on. A black thing
with its implacable face.
—P.K. Page, from "Autumn"

Let us go to the moon, he says.
Such a relief to stand on that always
darkened face, cratered imperfect
cousin, beautiful sphere flying
into the celestial darkness.
We tire of the earth-tides, the salt-pull
on your bodies. But these vampires—
they often talk like that, as if every
statement came from a tipped top hat
and poetic frock coat, a white-shirted gleam.
Shut the night out or let it in, you wonder.

Make your mind up, invite him in to stay,
or firm your heart and door
to closing. It's hard—when no one
else has known you, and your house
is empty even when you are there.
But then comes this thing, this strangeness,
with his lack of breath, his words stolen
from centuries, the cool hands
that you have let slip inside
because you yourself have always been
a cat on the wrong side of the door.

The moon, he says, let us fly there,
build our own dark cities on its unseen
face, rest in its comforting shadow.
You think of travelling, away
from the shopping malls and parades,
the smell of fried eggs, all the tickertape souls
that crowd you out of your own head
and you think, yes, let us go to the moon,
sail to its restful silence on a starlight
spaceship, restore this collapsed nova
inside you, this black thing.

We could go to the moon, he smiles,
I would always be awake; no sun could reach
those craters, nor our city with its own
dark cool heart. He has been charmed by the fairy
tale of physics in this century, the clear
voices from between the stars. Hush—he lays
you, bitten, down. The moon, like you,
is turning, its silvered breath stops,
curves to crimson joy, grave-fresh wakening.
Your eyes open—the moon and he both wait,
each with its implacable face.

Learning Curve
By Kelley Armstrong

"I'm being stalked."

Rudy, the bartender, stopped scowling at a nearly empty bottle of rye and peered around the dimly lit room.

"No, I wasn't followed inside," I said.

"Good, then get out before you are. I don't need that kind of trouble in here, Zoe."

I looked around at the patrons, most sitting alone at their tables, most passed out, most drooling.

"Looks to me like that's exactly the kind of trouble you need. Short of a fire, that's the only way you're getting those chairs back."

"The only chairs I want back are those ones." He hooked his thumb at a trio of college boys in the corner.

"Oh, but they're cute," I said. "Clean, well-groomed... and totally ruining the ambiance you work so hard to provide. Maybe I can sic my stalker on them."

"Don't even think about it."

"Oh, please. Why do you think I ducked in here? Anyone with the taste to stalk me is not going to set foot past the door."

He pointed to the exit. I leaned over the counter and snagged a beer bottle.

"Down payment on the job," I said, nodding to the boys. "Supernaturals?"

He rolled his eyes, as if to say, "What else?" True, Miller's didn't attract a lot of humans, but every so often one managed to find the place, though they usually didn't make it past a first glance inside.

I strolled toward the boys, who were checking me out, whispering like twelve-year-olds. I sat down at the next table. It took all of five seconds for one to slide into the chair beside mine.

"Haven't I seen you on campus?" he asked.

It was possible. I took courses now and then at the University of Toronto. But I shook my head. "I went to school overseas." I sipped my beer. "Little place outside Sendai, Japan. Class of 1878."

He blinked, then found a laugh. "Is that your way of saying you're too old for me?"

"Definitely too old." I smiled, fangs extending.

He fell back, chair toppling as he scrambled out of it.

I stood and extended my hand. "Zoe Takano."

"You're—you're—"

"Lonely. And hungry. Think you can help?"

As the kid and his friends made for the exit, one of the regulars lifted his head from the bar, bleary eyes peering at me.

"Running from Zoe?" he said. "Those boys must be new in town."

I flipped him off, took my beer to the bar and settled in.

"How about you try that with your stalker instead of hiding out here?" Rudy said.

"That could lead to a confrontation. Better to ignore the problem and hope it resolves itself."

He snorted and shook his head.

The problem did not resolve itself. Which was fine— I was in the mood for some excitement anyway. It was only the confrontation part I preferred to avoid. Confrontations mean fights. Fights mean releasing a part of me that I'm really happier keeping leashed and muzzled. So I avoid temptation, and if that means getting a reputation as a coward, I'm okay with that.

When I got out of Miller's, my stalker was waiting. Not surprising, really. We'd been playing this game for almost two weeks.

As I set out, I sharpened my sixth sense, trying to rely on that instead of listening for the sounds of pursuit. I could sense a living being behind me, that faint pulse of awareness that tells me food is nearby. It would be stronger if I was hungry, but this was better practice.

Miller's exits into an alley—appropriately—so I stuck to the alleys for as long as I could. Eventually, though, they came to an end and I stepped onto the sidewalk. Gravel crunched behind me, booted feet stopping short. I smiled.

I cut across the street and merged with a crowd of college kids heading to a bar. I merge well; even chatted with a cute blond girl for a half-block, and she chatted back, presuming I was part of the group. Then, as we passed a Thai takeout, I excused myself and ducked inside. I zipped through, smiling at the counter guy, ignoring him when he yelled that the washrooms were for paying customers only, and went straight out the back door.

I'd pulled this routine twice before—blend with a crowd and cut through a shop—and my opponent hadn't caught on yet, which was really rather frustrating. This time, though, as I crept out the back door, a shadow stretched from a side alley. I let the door slam behind me. The shadow jerked back. So the pupil was capable of learning. Excellent. Time for the next lesson.

I scampered along the back alley. Around the next corner. Down a delivery lane. Behind a Dumpster.

Footsteps splashed through a puddle I'd avoided. Muttered curses, cut short. Then silence. I closed my eyes, concentrating on picking up that pulse of life. And there it was, coming closer, closer, passing the Dumpster. Stopping. Realizing the prey must have ducked behind this garbage bin. Gold star.

A too-deliberate pair of boot squeaks headed left, so I ran left. Sure enough, my opponent was circling right. I grabbed the side of the Dumpster and swung onto the closed lid.

"Looking for me?" I said, grinning down.

Hands gripped the top edge, then yanked back, as if expecting me to stomp them. That would hardly be sporting. I backed up, took a running leap and grabbed the fire escape overhead. A perfect gymnast's swing and I was on it. A minute later, I was swinging again, this time onto the roof. I took off across it without a backward glance. Then I sat on the other side to wait.

I waited. And I waited some more. Finally, I sighed, got to my feet, made my way across the roof, leapt onto the next and began the journey home.

I was peering over the end of a rooftop into a penthouse apartment, eyeing a particularly fine example of an Edo-period sake bottle, when I sensed someone below. I glimpsed a familiar figure in the alley. Hmmm. Lacking experience, but not tenacity. I could work with this.

I leapt onto the next, lower rooftop. Then I saw a second figure in the alley with my stalker. Backup? I took a closer look. Nope, definitely not. We had a teenage girl and a twenty-something guy, and they were definitely *not* to-gether, given that the guy was sticking to the shadows, creeping along behind the girl.

The girl continued to walk, oblivious. When she paused to adjust her backpack, he started to swoop in. Her head jerked up, as if she'd heard something. He ducked into a doorway.

Yes, you heard footsteps in a dark alley. Time to move your cute little ass and maybe, in future, reconsider the wisdom of strolling through alleys at all.

She peered behind her, then shrugged and continued on. The man waited until she rounded the next corner and slid from his spot. When he reached the corner and peeked around it, I dropped from the fire escape and landed behind him.

He wheeled. He blinked. Then he smiled.

"Thought that might work," I said. "Forget the little girl. I'm much more fun."

He whipped out a knife. I slammed my fist into his forearm, smacking it against the brick wall. Reflexively his hand opened, dropping the knife. He dove for it. I kicked it, then I kicked him. My foot caught him under the jaw. He went up. I kicked again. He went down.

I leapt onto his back, pinning him. "Well, that was fast. Kind of embarrassing, huh? I think you need to work out more."

He tried to buck me off. I sank my fangs into the back of his neck and held on as he got to his feet. He swung backward toward the wall, planning to crush me, I'm sure, but my saliva kicked in before he made it two steps. He teetered, then crashed to the pavement, unconscious.

I knelt to feed. I wasn't particularly hungry, but only a fool turns down a free meal, and maybe waking up with the mother of all hangovers would teach this guy a lesson he wouldn't soon forget.

"Die, vampire!"

I spun as the teenage girl raced toward me, wooden stake on a collision course with my heart. I grabbed the stake and yanked it up, flipping the girl onto her back.

"That's really rude," I said. "I just saved your ass from a scumbag rapist. Is this how you repay me? Almost ruin my favorite shirt?"

She leapt to her feet and sent the stake on a return trip to my chest. Again, I stopped it. I could have pointed out that it really wouldn't do anything *more* than damage my shirt—vampires die by beheading—but I thought it best not to give her any ideas.

She ran at me again. I almost tripped over the unconscious man's arm. As I tugged him out of the way, she rushed me. I grabbed the stake and threw it aside.

She lifted her hands. Her fingertips lit up, glowing red.

"Ah, fire half-demon," I said. "Igneus, Aduro or Exustio?"

"I won't let you kill him."

"You don't know a lot about vampires, do you? Or about being a vampire hunter. First, you really need to work on your dialogue."

"Don't talk to me, bloodsucker."

"Bloodsucker? What's next? Queen of Darkness? Spawn of Satan? You're running about twenty years behind, sweetie. Where's the clever quip? The snappy repartee?"

She snarled and charged, burning fingers outstretched. I sidestepped and winced as she stumbled over the fallen man.

"See, that's why I moved him."

She spun and came at me again. I grabbed her hand. Her burning fingers sizzled into my skin.

"Fire is useless against a vampire, as you see," I said. "So your special power doesn't do you any good, which means you're going to have to work on your other skills. I'd suggest gymnastics, aikido and maybe ninjitsu, though it's hard to find outside Japan these days."

She wrenched free and backed up, scowling. "You're mocking me."

"No, I'm helping you. First piece of advice? Next time, don't telegraph your attack."

"Telegraph?"

"Yelling, 'Die, vampire' as you attack from behind may add a nice, if outdated, touch, but it gives you away. Next time, just run and stab. Got it?"

She stared at me. I retrieved her stake and handed it over. Then I started walking away.

"Second piece of advice?" I called back. "Stay out of alleys at night. There are a lot worse things than me out here."

I spun and grabbed the stake just as she was about to stab me in the back.

I smiled. "Much better. Now get on home. It's a school night."

Keeping the stake, I kicked her feet out from under her, then took off. She tried to follow, of course. Tenacious, as I said. But a quick flip onto another fire escape and through an open window left her behind.

I made my way up to the rooftops and headed home, rather pleased with myself. We'd come quite a ways in our two weeks together, and now, having finally made face-to-face contact, I was sure we could speed up the learning curve.

The girl was misguided, but I blamed popular culture for that. She'd eventually learn I wasn't the worst monster out there, and there were others far more deserving of her enthusiasm.

Even if she chose not to pursue such a profession, the supernatural world is a dangerous place for all of us. Self-defense skills are a must, and if I could help her with that, I would. It's the responsibility of everyone to prepare our youth for the future. I was happy to do my part.

Chrysalis
By Ronald Hore

The first rays of sunlight crept through the narrow shifting crack between the Venetian blinds and the sheer curtains, tracing a flickering picture against the wall. She opened one eye and watched as the breeze drifting in from the open window altered the image from a fluttering butterfly to something resembling a fading crucifix. In the distance a raven complained, the leaves in the neighbour's oak rustled, and then, downstairs, the sound of the front door opening. Father was home. She stretched, pulled the covers over her head, and groaned.

"Daylight already." Eyes closed, she checked off a mental calendar. "Damn, it's a school day."

She heard the scurrying on the stairs; that would be Mother rushing down in floppy slippers to make breakfast, and counted to ten.

Right on cue: "Lucy, are you awake? Time to get up!"

A normal mother would have called to her daughter from right outside the bedroom door, not waited until she was in the remote reaches of the kitchen, but then, Lucy doubted Minnie was all that normal. She flung feet first out of bed and rolled to stand, staring into the mirror perched at a dangerous tilt on her dresser. Critically she arched her eyebrows, puckered, made a face and examined her teeth. Definitely her best feature, she thought, now those baby teeth had been replaced.

"Lucy, breakfast!"

She shook her head, letting loose the rat's nest of coal-black strands that settled as they pleased around her thin face. Lucy squinted. Minnie always said she took after her father. Where Minnie was fair and blonde, Father had the traditional Hardkin narrow face, thin nose, and shaggy ebony hair. At least he said that was traditional; she'd never met any of her paternal relatives. Of course, Mother's family seemed to avoid them too, now that she thought about it. Lucy idly wondered what her father had ever seen in Minnie. Perhaps years ago—

"Lucy!"

Of course breakfast wasn't really ready, she knew that. Minnie just expected her daughter to spend some quality time with her father before he turned in to sleep the day through.

Lucy threw on her T-Rex-print robe and headed down the stairs. Today they creaked louder than usual.

"Have a seat. Breakfast will just be a few minutes."

"I'm not hungry." She knew well enough to sit.

Father raised his eyes from the *Free Press*. "Don't talk back to your mother."

Lucy kept quiet. His eyes were a piercing ice-blue today. He'd changed his contacts again. She remembered coming across the containers of different coloured lenses one day rummaging through his dresser. Lucy also vividly remembered the night, when she was six, opening her parent's bedroom door because she thought she'd heard a cry. Father's head jerked up, startled, from where he lay sprawled across her mother, and glared at her through scarlet eyes, brilliant as twin suns. She'd run screaming, and it took Minnie all night to calm her down. Some things you don't forget.

"By next week we will have you registered at a different school."

"But I just started this one."

She could feel the glacial chill across the table.

"We have discussed this. You will be attending a private school. A girl's boarding school."

She smothered the urge to mutter, "Whatever." Actually, they hadn't discussed it. She never *discussed* things with her father. He could be as persuasive as melted butter over fresh hot popcorn, or as rigid and cold as an iceberg at forty below. She glanced across to where her mother, back turned to them, worked furiously at scrambling eggs as though they might try to escape the bowl at any moment.

Don't worry Minnie, Lucy thought, I won't set him off. Besides, I know it was mainly your idea. Lying in her room one night last week, staring at the ceiling, she had overheard them talking downstairs.

"She's getting to that age; she's almost grown up." Minnie trying to maintain a calm voice. "She should be with girls her own age."

"Are you certain that's the only reason?" Cold as the mythical witch's tit.

"And we move around so often. It would be better if she could stay in one school for a while."

Yes, they had moved a lot. Lucy remembered asking Minnie "Why?" one afternoon when she came home to find her mother sitting in the darkened family room, staring into space. The TV flickered silently, showing a black and white movie with the sound muted. A half-empty bottle of red wine graced the table beside her. After a minute, Minnie looked up at her daughter standing in the doorway.

"Why do we have to move again? It's your father's work. It's time to relocate."

"But why does the whole family have to move? It's not as though he can't take a plane or a bus or drive himself."

"The company prefers he doesn't have to go too far from home when he's on business."

Lucy took advantage of her mother's abstract gaze that drifted somewhere beyond the TV. "Just what does father do again, sell refrigerators, or used cars?"

"Don't be silly dear," Minnie whispered, "he has an important position, does important work."

"He works for *The Bay* or *Sears*, right?"

"No dear, he works for *The Service*. You know, the one we're not supposed to talk about. He does things for them, and he does them very well." Minnie's voice had faded to somewhere below a whisper. "Don't want to know what he does for them, never ask, don't talk about it."

Then Minnie had turned slowly to stare up at the silhouette of her daughter in the doorway. "Lucy! You startled me. What are you doing home at this hour?"

The rattle of his newspaper brought Lucy back to the present. She toyed with her spoon, thought just for one reckless minute of suspending it from her nose, and then her survival instinct took over. Minnie approached with a pot of black liquid.

"Everyone for coffee?"

His hand extended a cup without ever looking up. Lucy sighed and shook her head.

"You know I don't drink coffee, Mother."

"How about some freshly squeezed orange juice, dear?"

Lucy waited for a reaction from across the table. When none came forth from behind the newspaper, she nodded. He was having his regular glass of tomato juice from his private stock. She decided to give a break for freedom one more try.

"I just signed up for the school soccer team."

He didn't bother to look up. "They will get along without you. I'm sure there will be extra-curricular programs in your new school, although, looking at your last grades, perhaps you should concentrate on academics instead."

"Lucy is a growing girl. She does need her exercise." Minnie's soft tone barely topped the sizzling eggs.

She glanced at Minnie hoping for more support. Three schools since January, move in the summer, register at a new high school, then this new nonsense about private schools. Her eyes narrowed. They were trying to get rid of her!

Lucy noticed the familiar red silk scarf around her mother's neck. Silly woman, she wore the thing everywhere in the mornings. It really highlighted her pale skin. This morning Minnie seemed even paler than usual. Lucy felt her father's eyes appraising her over the sports pages. She concentrated on the orange juice. When he looked at her like that it gave her the willies.

It reminded her of last March when she'd brought home a friend to spend the night. She'd only known Suzanne for a month, but the girl was new at school too, and her parents were going away for the weekend. Father turned on the enchantment, dripping with pleasantries, treated her to the full blast of his charm. Suzanne couldn't stop chattering that night about how wonderful he was, how lucky Lucy was to have an understanding parent like that. Foolish girl, and wouldn't you just know it, Suzanne picked that weekend to have her first period. Lucy thought Minnie would throw a fit, calming the silly girl down. For a change father hadn't gone out that evening. She could hear him roaming around, and then Minnie kept peeking in all night, checking up on them. It had been a disaster as far as sleep-overs went.

Lucy caught a whiff from the frying pan, heard the sizzle. "Sounds like fried blood pudding, can I have some?"

"No, you may not." Minnie scraped a mass of scrambled eggs onto her plate. "And I wish you would wear something different to breakfast. That old robe is not very ladylike."

Lucy patted the T-Rex stalking across her tummy and ran her finger over the frayed cotton fangs. "It's my favourite."

"You are too old for that sort of thing. Your mother will take you downtown after school and get you something more suitable." He looked at her over the edge of the entertainment section, as though daring her to speak. "You will need it for the boarding school anyway."

This time the "Whatever," escaped her lips before she could snare it.

Steel-blue eyes narrowed. "Speak proper English, young lady. We respect old-fashioned values in this family. Don't you forget it."

His breakfast arrived and he set down the paper and ignored her.

Lucy downed the orange juice, inhaled the eggs, and hurried upstairs. Her stomach felt like goblins inside were practising knitting and poking her with their needles. The sensation passed and she threw on an outfit from her closet and then stood thoughtfully examining a zit in her mirror.

"Speak proper English," Lucy snarled, making a face. She knew why they were sending her to boarding school. They never wanted her in the first place. She knew that. She had the proof: the Saturday morning she'd come downstairs to find Minnie at the kitchen table with a bottle of cooking sherry was burned into Lucy's hard drive. Father hadn't come home that night, probably out on one of his *business* trips. It was her seventh birthday. Minnie looked up at her through red-rimmed eyes.

"You weren't supposed to happen," she said.

Lucy froze, her hand on the refrigerator door.

"Said you were an impossibility. Later, he said it must have been because he died in the throes of passion. Did you know that? All those years, he carried the seed." Minnie took a long sip right out of the bottle. Some of it trickled from the corner of her mouth and across her chin. "Said there'd always just be the two of us, then you had to come along."

Lucy had blinked, trying to change the image.

"Lucy! I didn't hear you come down. Would you like me to make you some breakfast?"

"Don't bother, I'm not hungry."

Lucy tossed her head to break up the painful remembrances. She wondered whether to highlight her eyes in black, decided *they* wouldn't approve. "I'm still not hungry," Lucy muttered, abandoning the bedroom mirror. "Not anymore." Her stomach seemed to be churning. Must be nerves.

Someday she'd escape this weird family. She recalled the night she'd been poking around under her parents' bed. The sitter thought she was asleep. Lucy knew her mother's wedding dress was stored in a box under the bed and just wanted to have a quick look. She found a flat wooden box and dragged it out to peer inside. No dress, just a layer of dirt. Dirt! What kind of people keep a box of dirt under their bed? She did finally dig out a cardboard box holding a black silk gown, but by then it was anticlimactic.

She'd waited a whole year before asking Minnie about the wooden box. Minnie had muttered something about it being an old family keepsake, and then grounded Lucy's computer usage for a week. Weird parents, no wonder she didn't have any friends!

"You'll be late for school!"

He was speaking with Minnie as Lucy headed for the door. "I have to leave tonight for Ottawa and I'll be gone for a few days. The President and First Lady are coming for a State visit and I'm on assignment."

"Going to interview him?" Lucy asked, struggling into her backpack.

He gazed at her for a moment. "No. I will be working the night shift." Shaking his head he ascended the stairs to his room. At the top he turned and for a minute she almost believed he was going to smile. "I don't do interviews, I interrogate." Then he disappeared and the door closed.

"Would you like a ride to school?" Minnie said brightly.

"No, I have time, I'll walk." She needed to burn off some frustration.

Lucy paused on the school steps and watched, irritated by the mindless herd flowing around her. Sheep, she thought, a whole flock of sheep. Weak sheep, all dressing the same, trying to sound the same, look the same, baa, baa, baa. After surviving being the new kid at schools, and tip-toeing around her weird parents, weak was not in her private vocabulary. She narrowed her eyes and growled under her breath. *I'm more like a lone wolf.* The cramps hit then, painful and sharp.

"Shit, what the hell was that?" She almost doubled over with the sudden pain. Minnie must have used rotten eggs!

By mid-morning the aches had eased and she got ready for soccer practice; ready to take out her growing bad mood on the first person who dared cross her. That happened with five minutes to go. Lucy had been tearing around the field, trying to drive her foot through the ball, and running over anyone who got in her way. The ditsy teacher's aid in charge of the class had warned her once, then, just as Lucy was closing in like a rogue missile toward the net, Mary-Beth Johansson tried to block her. That was Mary-Beth's first mistake; the second was not ducking when Lucy elbowed her in the nose. Crimson blood spurted like a broken water main. Lucy pounded the ball past the cowering goaltender, then turned and grinned down at Mary-Beth.

"You did that on purpose!" Mary-Beth screamed.

"You, whatever your name is, go to the showers. Now!" The teacher's aid pushed Lucy back and knelt to examine the victim.

For a minute Lucy looked at Mary-Beth sprawled on the grass, stared at the blood spilling across her chin, watched the teacher's aid trying to staunch the flow. For just a minute Lucy imagined she could actually smell the sweet, rich stream, see it pulsing to the beat of Mary-Beth's heart.

"My nose! It's broken!" Mary-Beth screeched.

Lucy turned and pushed her way through the growing crowd. She was enjoying the luxury of being the only one in the showers when she felt something warm on her leg. A tiny stream of blood mingled with the water then trickled across the floor to escape down the drain. She stared at it.

"You've got to be kidding me! Just what I need. Something else to hide from Minnie."

Outside she could hear the excited chatter of the other girls at the outer doors; practice was over.

Lucy shook herself free of a growing numbness and grabbed her towel and a tampon from the dispenser. She dressed and was leaving as the others poured into the change room clucking like a flock of chickens.

"You're screwed. Wait 'till her brother hears about this!"

Lucy almost knocked a skinny redhead over as she escaped. Fortunately, most of these girls were not in her next class; unfortunately, it was English.

"Students, I want you to write me a two page essay on the topic, "My Summer Vacation", Miss Deavor said, beaming. "You have the rest of this session to complete it. Start now."

Lucy mentally groaned. They didn't really want to know about her summer vacation. She was still trying to forget it. After much whining they had gone to the beach and

rented a cottage for a week. What was the use of living near
a lake if you couldn't go sit on the sand and enjoy the sun?
Lucy could have died at the sight of her father, after much
prodding, sitting on a blanket, under an umbrella, wearing
a large straw hat, and clothed from fingertip to toe. He even
wore gloves. She knew he always used the highest SPF
rated sunblock he could find, but this was ridiculous. Lucy
wouldn't come out of the water until he had gone inside.
She had avoided her parents for the rest of the week. Now
she was expected to write about her summer vacation? She
clenched her teeth and lied.

Science class had that young teacher, Mr. Deed. Lucy
listened to his voice. She'd never noticed before how pleasant he sounded. He had a nice smile, too. Instead of staring
out the window, or listening to the two girls in the next
row dissing her, as if they didn't think she could hear them,
she focussed on Mr. Deed. He was wearing some blended
essence of spices. When his lips moved, so did the vein
in his neck. There was a rhythm to it. She felt very relaxed.

"Lucy, are you falling asleep?"

"No...sorry...just resting my eyes."

"Well then, could you explain to the class just what
Darwin meant when he was talking about how a species
might change? What would a creature need to become
successful? How would new adaptations help?"

She squirmed in her seat, trying to remember the class
discussion. "He meant...that...um...in order to succeed,
an animal would do better if it had some advantage over
the rest of the other animals."

"But how would a new adaptation give it an advantage
within its own group, eventually cause it to change?" He
stared at her.

Lucy suppressed a sudden urge to give him a sly smirk.
Instead she calmly gazed into his eyes, caught his sudden
start as though seeing her for the first time.

He blinked and looked out over the other heads in the
room. "The main thrust of what Darwin was saying is that
a species begins to evolve when a member of the group
possesses a new adaptation that gives it an advantage over

other members of the same species. Because it is successful, it is more likely to breed, and that new adaptation is then passed on through its children. The end result is a new species."

Lucy's mind drifted away from Mr. Deed's smile to the conversation of the two girls at the back of the room. They were discussing her and what Mary-Beth's brother was liable to do when he found out about his sister. She shut them out. After class she lingered by Mr. Deed's desk but he appeared in a hurry to leave.

"I had some questions about Darwin and species," she said softly. His eyes were a deep brown.

"Sorry, I have to leave right after school." He fumbled with his books.

"Maybe later?"

"Just pay attention in class." He hurried out.

Lucy had a sudden urge to purr but she suppressed it, along with a giggle. Strangely, she wondered what Mr. Deed would taste like. Probably salty, with a hint of spice, she thought. Grinning, Lucy headed for her locker.

David Johansson was waiting for her; so were a gaggle of girls lurking at the far end of the corridor. He leaned casually against an adjoining locker, watching her approach. She squared her shoulders and pressed on, ignoring him as she spun the combination.

"I hear you messed up my sister, bitch."

"She got in the way of my elbow."

"That wasn't nice."

Lucy turned and looked up at him. Her first urge was to blurt out, "So, what are you going to do about it?" Instead, she let a slow smile spread across her face. "It was an accident." The voice didn't sound like her. The pitch came out lower than expected and sort of left the words vibrating in the air. She trapped his eyes in her gaze.

He looked confused.

"Well...don't do it again."

Lucy tilted her head. David Johansson had an interesting face. She had the feeling if she reached up and took him by the nose she could lead him down the hall.

At the end of the hallway the group was making bets on whether he would just threaten her or slap her around right there. He had a reputation. She patted him gently on the cheek.

"I promise to be good."

Amazing. She held him with her eyes and he was tongue-tied. Lucy studied David's face as if it were a frog she might have to dissect for a school project. Her hand stroked his stubble, and then she ran her finger tips down along his neck and felt veins beneath throbbing faster and faster. She could smell his perspiration, actually hear the irregular beating of his heart. The whispering at the end of the corridor continued at an increased pace.

"What does the slut think she's doing?"

"Why doesn't he just bang her stupid head against the wall?"

"I say we beat the crap out of her the next time we get her alone. Put the boots to her."

Lucy resisted the urge to stare down the hall and stick out her tongue. She gently pushed David back against the lockers.

"Do you have a car?" That didn't really sound like her. Did your voice change too when you had your period?

"Yes." Now he did sound like a frog.

"There's a movie on at the Multiplex I want to see. You want to see it too, don't you?"

"Yes."

She had an urge to tell him to speak up so the spectators could hear him, but decided against it.

Lucy stood on tip-toes, whispered in his ear, left the damp imprint of her tongue. "Meet me at seven in the lobby tonight. You will, won't you?"

"Yes."

"See you later, Davey-boy," she said, gently shoving him away.

He stumbled into the centre of the hall, looked as though he was going to turn and stare back at her, and then hurried off, pushing through the flock of chickens waiting by the exit.

"Watch out ladies," Lucy murmured under her breath, "the fox is loose in the henhouse. Or is *vixen* the proper term?"

She walked out through the main doors and paused at the top of the school steps. Lucy could hear children talking in a playground a block away, smell the bread baking in the plaza down the road, taste the fear in the little dog passing on the sidewalk, knew that someone out back in the schoolyard playing football just split his lip—red blood oozed onto the grass. She turned and gazed down at the janitor lurking at the foot of the steps who had stopped gathering the litter and now leaned on his broom, gawking up at her. Her gaze changed to a glare; he quickly turned his head and shuffled away. Lucy watched him until he disappeared around the corner. Amazing; in that brief moment she had caught a glimpse of his most unsavoury thoughts. The sun burst through the clouds.

Lucy surveyed the street. She was the queen of her jungle. Life would be very different at school now, and just maybe, at home. *I doubt if Minnie will be any more difficult to handle than Davey*, she thought. *But Father...* He would be a different matter.

She tried to picture the scene, the first time she'd dare stand up against him. Would it be better to be subtle, try to persuade him, gently at first, that a private school was not for her? When Lucy thought of his stern face, sarcastic tone, and the burning eyes behind the contact lenses, she felt a sudden chill. But, then she shook her head and smiled.

It wasn't just the exiting feeling of strength flowing through her veins, or the blood pounding in her head. There seemed to be a dozen random thoughts trying to break out all at once. Lucy suddenly knew she would never again be seen as weak or confused like her Mother, but in that same moment she also felt a flash of pity for Minnie. Life with Father cannot be easy, she thought, especially if he's anything like me, like I have become.

Lucy started to giggle: Perhaps it was time to sit down with Father and have a long talk, about going to private schools, and other things. That would be a test of wills!

There couldn't be many fathers who had to face discussing certain *unusual* facts of life with their teenage daughter.

She stretched out her arms and let the heat and light caress her, soaking her face, all of her skin with a radiant feeling of power. Her entire body tingled, as if a jolt of electricity was continuously passing through her, with not even a hint of pain. She took a deep breath. Suddenly, Lucy felt like a goddess, invincible.

She started down the steps, wanting the whole world to know the truth: "Now, there is *nothing* I can't do!"

Mother of Miscreants
by Jennifer Greylyn

"Hello, Mother."

She was not surprised to hear those words emerge from the mouth of a man who looked too young to be her son. Standing in front of her polished wooden table, flanked by a stand displaying many copies of her book on one side and a glossy blown-up poster of its cover on the other, he was tall and lithe, with a handsomely proportioned face and elegantly tousled hair. He seemed the very embodiment of youth, but he was more likely to be taken for her brother, perhaps even her older brother. The truth was quite different.

He'd joined the line after the initial crowd waiting for her had thinned. She'd noticed him right away even though he was dressed similarily to many other people. The goth tones of ebony and amethyst that he wore were popular among her fans, but few could afford the rich silk and lush velvet of his attire. Still, that wasn't what made him stand out. A number of those in the bookstore were much more distinctive than him—the girl with piercings almost everywhere, the businessman in a tailored suit, the grey-haired couple in matching jogging outfits.

She saw him because she was looking for him or, rather, those like him. It was the main reason she held all her signings at night, midnight to be precise. She'd told her publisher, Ishtar House, that it would be a good marketing strategy and they believed she badly needed one because she refused to promote her book in more traditional ways. She wouldn't make TV appearances or let herself be filmed or photographed. She insisted on meeting people in person.

Lionel, a wispy man hovering beside her table, had started out as her editor and then become her liaison with the publisher. She'd given him no choice but to back her strategy and he'd gone almost bald, constantly running his hands through his grey-blond hair as he fretted about all the money Ishtar House spent on TV, radio and newspaper ads. It had almost bankrupted them, but they'd been repaid a hundredfold. Just as she'd known would happen; her midnight signings had become a sensation and her book took off.

"I need a little break," she told Lionel, rising gracefully from her chair and glancing meaningfully at the young-seeming man who'd called her mother. Lionel nodded faithfully, accepting without truly understanding. She had him well-trained. He was used to her taking 'breaks' at her midnight signings. He had no idea the signings were just a cover for her real agenda.

Discontent began to sizzle in the line as people realized she was leaving. She tasted it and silenced it before it could transform into angry whispers and jostling, exerting just a little of her will through a warm smile that made them all feel like they'd come inside from a cold winter day to sit next to a cozy fire. It left them calm and they all drowsily beamed back at her.

This was why she shunned all forms of the media. It tempted people to come and see her for themselves. In person, enthralling them was easy and her reputation spread by word of mouth.

The young-seeming man wasn't among her fans, however. Instead, he was watching her with a faintly quizzical expression that disappeared the instant he sensed her gaze. Then his attractive face took on a less-than-attractive domineering look and she knew he wouldn't be easy to influence. She wondered if he called himself master or king, as the mortals fantasized in their vampire fiction. She didn't particularly care, but she didn't want to embarrass one of her children either. She gave him a mild look in return.

His brows pinched once more and she felt his confusion clearly, a cooler emotion than what mortals typically exuded. It suggested that he couldn't sense her emotions at all and then she knew it for sure when, apparently reassured by her demure manner, he gallantly led her to the coffee shop that was attached to the bookstore. It was run by a mediocre chain she'd become quite familiar with and didn't especially like, but she was trying to be polite and it offered the most privacy. Only a few of the tables were occupied. Everyone else was out in the store, either discussing her book or waiting in line to talk to her.

Her self-proclaimed son continued to take charge, choosing a table for them in the furthest corner. It wasn't a location she would have picked, but it suited her aim and so she said nothing. She did appreciate his manners in holding the chair for her and it gave her hope their meeting might be cordial.

While he was busy seating himself, she frowned over his shoulder at the two other men who'd followed them into the coffee shop. They had the ever-shifting eyes of bodyguards and they were also her children, but she didn't want to talk to them right now. She preferred her first conversation with any of her newly-found children to be one on one. They felt the warning heat of her gaze and froze.

By then, her son had noticed their absence and glanced back to see them hesitating just outside the entrance to the coffee shop. The frown that crossed his face was disapproving, but then he motioned toward the other customers. To her, the bodyguards radiated relief at having to come no closer to her, an unknown quantity, and gladly took to their comparatively simple task of herding away the mortals. It seemed that her strong-minded son was taking no chance of the two of them being overheard.

When he finally turned his attention back to her, in keeping with his earlier, if somewhat heavy-handed, gallantry, she was expecting an exchange of pleasantries or an offer to get her something to drink. Instead, he lifted the object he'd been carrying under his arm and demanded, "Mother, what is the meaning of this?"

She sighed to herself in disappointment. So much for good manners. What he held up was a hardcover copy of her book, *Mother of Vampires*, by Lilith Adams. The publisher had insisted on her using a surname and it did give her a twinge of perverse pleasure to claim it even though her first husband had rejected her. The cover showed a silhouette of her against a purple sky, crowned by dark clouds. It was as close to a photo as she'd allow. There wasn't one inside, not even a provocative bio, although she'd considered it. She wanted her work to stand on its own and, besides, the less people thought they knew about her, the more eagerly they turned out for her signings.

A little of her hope trickled back when she saw the book in his hand wasn't a copy he'd bought tonight. The cover was rather battered and the pages looked well-thumbed. It would seem he'd obtained an advance copy from somewhere and had simply wanted to meet her. It helped her to forgive his peremptory tone. A big part of why she'd wanted a book tour was to reconnect with her wayward children.

"Would you like me to autograph it for you?"

His response wasn't a positive one. His eyes flashed like moon on ice, as if he thought she was mocking him. She told herself not to be offended and kept the fire out of her own gaze. It was hard, however, when he said, even more sternly, "No, I want you to explain it."

She sensed that he was genuinely upset. Although his expression was cool, almost remote, he was holding himself too still, so still that he'd stopped breathing. It wasn't a good look for him because, unlike a mortal who'd go crimson in the face, it just accentuated his unhealthy pallor. But it did remind her why her book was so important.

Before she launched it, she'd thought the legends surrounding her children were just stories they'd made up to take advantage of the gullibility of mortals or maybe were stories the mortals had made up to scare themselves. She hadn't believed any of her kind could take the legends seriously. Since then, though, she'd met many who did. The man in front of her was plainly one of those unfortunates. She should be patient with him.

"It's quite self-explanatory. It tells my life story. How long ago I was born of wind and fire and then given in marriage to an ungrateful man who blamed me because

I couldn't conceive. He spurned me and told many lies about me to make himself look better. To get back at him and have a family of my own, ever since then I've been transforming his children into my children."

"How could you tell the world all those things?" His emotions had become an angry maelstrom hidden by his glacial exterior.

"Are you worried about the risk to us? There is none. Vampire fiction, in fact paranormal fiction of all types, has never been more popular. That's all the mortals think my book is. They're very good at deluding themselves. But I know my children will know better. That's why I wrote it. To set the record straight about my life and to expose all the misconceptions about our kind."

Disbelief made him even paler. "*Misconceptions?* Is that what you call them?"

"Of course. They're not true." When he didn't say anything, she patted his hand. It was cold. Hardly unexpected but another sign that he was an unfortunate one. "I know this is hard to understand. You're not the only one who—"

He jerked his hand away. "*Hard to understand* is putting it mildly, *Mother*."

There was no respect in how he addressed her now. The lack of it strained her patience. She knew she was partly to blame for not keeping a closer eye on her children. She considered them all that, even though most of them were the children of her children of her children. There were so many of them that she'd lost track. She'd hoped they'd come to her midnight signings and she could get to know them. She'd hoped they'd read her book and want to talk about it. But she'd never imagined so many encounters with them would be like this one.

Struggling with her own temper, she didn't notice the change in him right away. She only sensed it when he reached for her hand again, very unwilling but overcome with sudden wonder. "You're *warm*. How's that possible? I've been watching you for the past couple of hours and I know you haven't fed."

"I'm feeding all the time, my son," she murmured, keeping her voice low and unthreatening. She didn't want to frighten him when they were just beginning to form a connection. Maybe this could be cordial after all. Maybe she could make him see just by talking to him. "I feed on emotion. The way our kind is meant to. It's easy and the mortals can't detect it. It's also natural. Everyone feels, even you."

Disgust and alarm, warring with each other, cracked the frigid mask of his face and spilled out like black polluted water. He dropped her hand as if it tainted him and he looked like he wanted to get far away from her. "You mean...you're feeding on me? You're doing it even now?"

"As you could feed on me, if you wished," she confirmed, saddened by his reaction. "I can't say I like the flavour of your emotions at this moment. I do have my preferences. But I'm not harming you. I'm simply making use of what you naturally produce."

Pride seemed to be the only thing keeping him in his chair. He was visibly fighting to control himself. "But it's obscene...impossible..."

Her own pride seethed at how he insulted her, her way of life, her sincerity, but she knew it was unintentional. She stuck to her soothing tone. "Many of your siblings have felt the same way. They—"

He found strength in his anger and foolishly cut her off again. "I've heard from them. I couldn't believe what they told me. But a number of them sent me copies of your book. This was just the first one I received." He slapped the hardcover on the table. "I read it. I just don't believe it. How can you say we're meant to feed on emotion? How can you say the way we live is wrong?"

"I didn't say *wrong*," she corrected him, still softly, but there was no softness in her voice now. It was rather the echo of a gale, heard from a great distance when one might still safely escape its wrath.

Her son, if several times removed, heard it and quickly, if figuratively, tucked his head down. The respect was back, but it was grudging, a thin skin of ice over his temper. "Mother, help me to understand."

She was annoyed at herself. She hated having to frighten her children. But that was the price she paid for not having seen so many of them for so long. They knew of her but they didn't believe in her. She was one legend they dismissed when they shouldn't.

In an effort to be conciliatory, she chose her words with care. "I've never said how you live is wrong. I've simply said it's *unhealthy*. You've picked up bad habits over the centuries. Habits that put you in danger."

Sensing he wasn't convinced but was too wary to say so, she directed him, "Look out the window." He turned toward the two long panes of glass that met in a corner where they were sitting. Only darkness punctured by the white streetlights of the parking lot and the occasional set of headlights looked back at him. "You have no reflection. Tell me how that's a good thing."

He twitched self-consciously and scanned the restaurant. His bodyguards had cleared out all the customers and were dutifully blocking the entrance, yet they hadn't done anything about the girl behind the counter. She seemed absorbed in polishing the coffee machines, but he still glared at his two men. They snapped to attention and one moved toward the counter.

"There's no need," his mother informed him. "She hasn't heard or noticed anything. I'd have felt it. She's simply exhausted and looking forward to the bookstore closing."

He studied her for a moment, uncertainty wafting off him, before he waved the guard back.

She nodded in approval, preferring not to interfere with mortals if there was no compelling reason. It only complicated matters. She resumed where they'd left off. "So you know your lack of a reflection is conspicuous. Why do you allow it then?"

As he fixed his gaze on her, a little of his insolence slipped back in. "You make it sound like I have a choice."

"Of course you do. Look at me." He followed the movement of her hand and saw her replicated in the dark glass.

He opened his mouth, made hesitant by wonder again. "But... how?

"A misconception, as I told you." She hooked his gaze with hers. "You, like so many of my children, seem to be even better at deluding yourself than mortals. Bram Stoker popularized the idea that our kind has no reflection and now many of you don't."

"But we've always been this way..." His voice trailed off as his eyes slid back to her reflection in the glass, apparent proof that he was mistaken.

"You haven't always looked the way you do either," she continued, pressing her point now that he was actually listening to her. "Mortals once thought our kind should be red in the face and plump from all the blood they believed we drank. If they saw you, they'd think you were one of our victims, thin and pale. Look up Voltaire's *Philosophical Dictionary* sometime. He blamed us for consumption or tuberculosis, as the mortals say today."

"What happened then?" her son asked, half challenge, half true curiosity.

"The perception the mortals had of us was reversed in the nineteenth century. The consumptive look became fashionable. Our kind did too. You can thank the Romantic writers for that. Mortals like Lord Byron, the poet, and John Polidori, his friend and doctor, put the two things together and the mortal fascination with our kind began."

He was shaking his head vehemently. "No, I can't believe it. It makes no sense."

"Yes, my son, it does," she replied, just as forcefully. "You, like many of my children, have changed depending on what the mortals believe. It's a consequence of taking their blood."

He tore his eyes from the window at last and barked a humourless laugh. "I knew it was going to come down to this. You're going to tell me drinking blood is wrong. The others warned me about it."

"Not wrong," she repeated firmly, "just unnecessary. It's not healthy for you."

He forgot his fear of her in a rush of cold anger. "How can you say that? It's what we need to live."

She felt like he hadn't heard anything she'd said and it shredded her patience. "You only think that because you're born of blood. It's not how I intended my children to come into this world."

"I read about that in your book," he acknowledged, but was still scornful. "You claim you made the first of us with your 'breath of fire'. It sounds like what a mortal has after eating too much spicy food."

She narrowed her eyes at his tasteless joke, but refused to react any further. She sensed he was baiting her as a way of avoiding having to think too deeply about what she'd said. She'd shaken him. Her words *had* gotten through to him. That realization made her keep talking. "It's your heritage. It's how you should have been transformed. Instead, you were born in blood and so you crave blood. I thought that was a mere superstition of mortals until I began this tour."

"What's wrong with blood, *Mother*?" He was openly sneering at her now. She couldn't really blame him though. She was questioning his birth and, as he saw it, slighting it. This would be so much easier if he could sense her emotions. Then he would know she was only trying to help him.

"Because you don't just get the blood, my son. You get everything that's in it. I don't mean potential disease; obviously, you're immune to that. What I'm talking about is a taste of the mortal soul. The flow of blood binds a mortal's soul to his body. His blood is thus influenced by his soul. What he feels but, more significantly, what he *believes*. I suspect this is how and why the misconceptions about our kind have spread."

"What do you expect us to do," he demanded, "stop drinking blood?"

"It would be better for you, yes. You don't need it. Emotion is purer and safer. You've just become dependent on blood. You'll realize that if you let me help you—"

"What about sunlight?" he asked suddenly. "Are you going to tell me that's yet another *misconception*?"

She paused, tasting something sharp and bitter in his abrupt change of subject. It made her respond carefully. "Yes, a rather recent one. Stoker only had his vampires weakened by sunlight, not harmed by it. We have the movie

Nosfertau from 1922 to thank for the idea that sunlight can kill us."

If she didn't know what he was feeling, she might have thought he was considering what she'd said. As it was, she tensed when he went still as ice again and braced herself for the explosion that was coming. Shards of his anger stung her when it did. "You call it an *idea*! A *misconception*! As if we believe sunlight can hurt us so it does. Mother, it's not like that. It's real."

She almost embraced him with her will. It would have made things simple. No more arguing, only acceptance. But she'd vowed she wouldn't use it on her children except as a last resort. She thought they'd suffered enough because of her not being there for them. "Now, my son, listen to me. I know this is hard to accept—"

"No, *Mother*, you listen to *me*. Some of my people have accepted what you say. They've read your book and taken your words to heart. They've stopped drinking blood. They've gone out into the day. I tried to tell them you were the first of us and maybe the same rules don't apply to you. But they didn't believe me. They believed you."

He stopped and stared at her with agonized eyes. The despair his anger had been concealing rose like a wave from the sunless depths of the ocean and broke over her. "You have no idea of the chaos your book has caused. There have been *deaths*, Mother."

She sat back in her chair, stunned. Now she understood why he'd been so stubborn, so resistant to her words. "I didn't know. I've met with skepticism before. Anger. Even hate for my neglect. But I didn't realize anyone had died. I've never wanted to see my children hurt."

"Then you don't want us to starve? Turn to ash? Die out as a race?" He leaned forward, as if to give her a better taste of his sarcasm.

"Of course not!" she snapped and then forced herself to be calm. "It seems I may have presumed too much."

"That's what I've been trying to make you understand." he said emphatically, meeting her gaze. "You need to stop selling your book. Publish a retraction, even. Then I can tell my people you were wrong and they'll believe me."

"But I'm not wrong." She held his gaze and let him see her eyes flame. "My children still need to know the truth. I was intending to write about the lives of my first children in my next book. But I can see I should write something else. A book of manners. It'll tell my children how to free themselves from their bad habits."

"But, Mother, think about it," he pleaded with her, clearly feeling the heat emanating from her but not backing down. "That'll only make things worse. My children will believe you and even more and more of them will die..."

The bleakness in his tone touched her heart and she knew then he cared for his children as much as she did hers. Ultimately, it was what she'd been hoping to learn from their meeting. To know he was worthy of the gift she had to give.

"You may have been born in blood, my son," she whispered, "but you are a true child of mine." Then she cupped her hand around his head and pulled him close to her. She opened her mouth over his and gave him the breath of fire.

He shuddered as it scorched through him, hot as a desert storm, and almost fell off his chair, spasming violently as the fire merged with his body.

The girl behind the counter looked like she was about to scream. One of his bodyguards took her by the arm and kept her at their end of the coffee shop. The other guard rushed toward his employer—*his father*, she realized—and wasn't stopped by the warning hand his mother raised. He only stumbled to a halt when he felt the heat flowing off her son, her true son now.

Her kiss would complete his transformation, but it wouldn't be easy for him. It should have been done when he was a child, a baby even, before his body had become accustomed to what it was. But it was never too late. She regretted the pain he had to go through, but it was his birthright, well-earned, the immortality of wind and fire.

Although it probably seemed like an eternity to him, the first phase was over in seconds, so quickly the girl behind the counter was blinking, uncertain of what she'd seen. The bodyguard released her and joined the other, both hovering close to their father to protect him from the girl's curious gaze.

He straightened in his chair and the guards gasped, shocked by the faintest of colour seeping into his face. He saw it in their eyes and turned to the window. A reflection gazed back at him, still blurry with his disbelief, but much more than he'd had before.

He seized a breath and let it out slowly. Then his eyes widened as he had his first taste of the emotions all around him. He turned to her, his mother, sensing her pride and her love. She smiled back at him.

"It'll take time for you to adjust, but you will," she assured him. Then she rose smoothly to her feet and he tried to follow her, only to find his legs too weak. Without a word, each of his sons took him by an arm and gently helped him up.

She smiled at them too but brought her eyes back to him. "I should be finished my signing soon. Then I'd like to come home with you and meet the rest of your family."

He nodded in perfect compliance. "Yes, Mother."

Resonance
By Mary E. Choo

Peg stared through the peephole in the front door, watching as the local Health Officer retreated down the sidewalk and terraced steps to the street. When he started his car and eased it into the road, she let out a slow breath.

"He's gone," she said.

The slap of papers on the living room coffee table startled her. She turned to see Mark stuffing documents into his heavy briefcase.

"You're damn lucky he didn't raise other issues," he said. "If you'd control yourself and stop doing such stupid things, our group wouldn't have all these problems."

"So some of the neighbours don't like my feeding the wildlife!" Peg countered, stung. "So what? It's none of their damn business!"

"*Wildlife*? Come on, Peg! It was the rats that did it. You can't blame people for being upset! And you really don't want any kind of official nosing around here—they might start digging deeper—you're jeopardizing all of us!"

"The Health Officer didn't find any fault with the house—he just said to stop feeding the vermin!"

Peg saw the unfortunate glimmer of red that still lingered in Mark's eyes when he was really angry. She was well aware she'd gone too far. He snapped the locks on his briefcase shut, turning it over roughly on the table.

"Be careful!" Peg said. "The table's antique—Chinese—you'll ruin the finish!"

Mark ignored her. "It's all settled then, except for the casket. What would you like? Marble? Rosewood?"

"Silver," Peg said. "It'll be small, as it's a cremation, so it shouldn't cost too much—considering what we all are, silver's *somewhat* appropriate, don't you think?"

"Wrong species," Mark said, sarcastically. "Besides, it would have to be custom, and we haven't time."

"Oh, so we're a *species* now?" Peg said. "I didn't know we'd acquired such status. Anyway, a silver casket might be seen as relevant in a roundabout way, symbolic—a tip of the hat to our werewolf friends. What do you think?"

"Stop it, Peg! You know all this is necessary. Anyway, you brought this mess on yourself."

"No, Mark," she said quietly. "Not altogether."

The sound of birds squabbling in the garden outside broke the silence between them. Mark yanked his briefcase from the table and started towards the kitchen and the back door.

"Someone will pick you up tomorrow, first thing."

Peg followed, watching him through the screen as he navigated the broken pavement. Keeping to the shade, he brushed aside low branches on his way to the lane. His sleek German sports car was parked carefully at the edge of her property. He always came and went from the back, to avoid notice. She smiled bitterly—that was Mark: designer suit and sunglasses, custom Italian-leather shoes— all the trappings of a successful company director. He worried about drawing attention in the suburbs, but not enough to change his clothes or drive a less conspicuous vehicle. The car engine started smoothly.

"Tomorrow," he called through the open car window, pulling away.

Always his way, Peg thought, struggling with her anger. She couldn't—wouldn't—think of tomorrow right now, or the unhappy changes it would bring.

She blinked as the sunlight shifted through some branches and into her eyes. Her special lens implants were largely successful in blocking the sun's rays, but she still felt more comfortable wearing sunglasses in bright daylight.

Peg took her spare pair from the hook by the door and put them on, making her way out and down the steps into the overgrown garden. The sun block she'd applied earlier should last two more hours at least. Her skin had adapted enough to do without for brief periods anyway.

Peg hated Mark's manipulative ways, especially as he was the one who'd duped her into her current lifestyle. Her condition might be permanent, and she knew she needed the support of the Group to get by, but her resentment over their control ran deep. Worse, her latest escapades had pushed their patience to the limit.

She'd maintained the house meticulously since her parents left it to her. The garden ran wild, but she loved the creatures her unkempt lot attracted. And if a few rats and crows had benefited from the food she'd left for all of them to enjoy, so be it. She was sorry her neighbour's dog had been bitten by a rat that strayed into his garden. She'd paid for the veterinary costs, and apologized repeatedly. As for her more serious transgression in town, recently, well...

Pushing her way into the riot of flowers, she began to pull weeds. She studied the small birds that flitted from branch to branch, listening to their intense chatter. One good thing about being a vampire—or having Changeling's syndrome, as it was now known—was the ability to sense the essence of all living things. The birds' excitement over finding a food source was palpable; it sang across the air with frenetic joy. Peg felt it in her head, heart and bones. For a moment, the sun, the scent of flowers and the warm breeze seemed to fill her weary soul to the brim.

"Hello, little ones..." she breathed, pitching her voice just so, and following with a low, trilling whistle. Several of the birds answered her, and she was rewarded by the bright images that flashed from their minds to hers.

Strains of sound carried on the breeze from further up the lane: violin music, flawlessly played. It was Mendelssohn's Violin Concerto in E Minor, a favourite of Peg's.

Sophie was out in her garden.

Bending, Peg plucked flowers rapidly: daisies, bachelor's button, some re-growth Canterbury bells.

She left the garden and started up the lane, grateful for the shade of intermittent cedars. She'd been part of the committee that fought to save the trees, to the anger of those who wanted the view.

When she reached Sophie's small gate, she rang the garden bell. Sophie didn't pause, so Peg opened the gate and descended the winding stone steps to the path.

I won't tell her about tomorrow right away, she thought.

Peg left the path and found her way along the large stepping stones to the corner of the garden. The pride of Sophie's late husband, Jeff, the space harboured every conceivable kind of local plant.

Sophie sat on the bench by the river-rock wall. The light filtered through the overhanging perennials, dancing all about her, emphasizing her slender form and pale hair. Peg sat down quietly in the willow chair opposite, as Sophie continued to play.

Sophie's phrasing sustained the sense of melody well through the silences the orchestra normally filled. Peg listened, breathless. She was sorry when the movement came to an end and Sophie lowered her bow, placing it carefully with the violin in the cushioned corner of the bench.

"What do you think, Peg?'

"Wonderful, as usual."

"The orchestra doesn't think so. They're replacing me for the Saturday concert. I messed up badly at rehearsal. Jeff loved Mendelssohn, and I got part way into it and I just...God, when does it end, Peg? When does it *stop*?" She began to cry.

Peg was used to Sophie's passionate bursts of grief. Since her husband's death over a year ago at the hands of a drunk driver, Sophie was inconsolable.

"For you," Peg said gently, handing Sophie the tousled bouquet. Sophie's garden was well-ordered, but she loved more wayward flowers. Drying her cheeks with the backs of her hands, she embraced the bundle.

"Thank you. They're so wild and bright and...*free*."

"Not any more," Peg teased, breaking off a loose root. "It's a vase on your kitchen table now, for all of them."

Sophie laughed a little. "Silly thing to say, I know." She started up from the bench. "Tea? Japanese, yes? I've some almond biscuits, too."

Peg studied Sophie as she went up the path and back steps into her house. She'd lost more weight, which was worrying.

The house was charming—renovated early fifties. Sophie kept the place obsessively intact, leaving Jeff's things exactly where he'd placed them last.

Her talent had seemed boundless before Jeff's accident, yet now she struggled with work she'd once handled with ease. On her own, Peg knew, Sophie's playing was as enchanting as ever, but when it came to performing, her tendency to falter and freeze was destroying her promising career.

When Sophie returned with a pot of Japanese green tea and almond cakes on a tray, she was smiling. Placing the tray on the table, she poured the tea, handing Peg a porcelain hand-cup.

"Tea's just right," she said. This was a familiar ritual, agreeable to both women. In the real-world sense, Peg was approaching middle age, the theatre makeup she applied each day supporting this image. She'd wanted children, before Mark changed her life so cruelly. If she had a daughter, even a niece or companion, she'd want her to be like Sophie: artistic, independent.

"I love our afternoons," Sophie said after a moment. "You'll stay for supper, of course?" This, too, was accepted practice, though often if Sophie stopped in, Peg would play host. Peg had adjusted to the point where she could nibble a little at meals, but mostly she toyed with her food or covered it with a napkin for quick disposal later.

"I couldn't have survived this year without you, Peg—no, no protests! You've been such a great friend." She poured herself another cup of tea, reflecting. "You know what really gets me? I heard the bastard that hit Jeff could be out in seven months. *Seven months!*"

Peg reached out and patted Sophie's hand. The urge to 'hunt' Sophie had passed long ago—Peg couldn't do that to someone she cared for so much. Yet sitting here, with the sweet scent of Sophie's blood in her nostrils, it was impossible not to feel the finer impulses of that primitive instinct. She could sense the pulse of Sophie's arteries and veins, her heart. Images of Sophie's emotions—complex, coloured patterns—played across Peg's mind. There was a sound, too, a mingling of things physical and spiritual, like an eerie kind of music. In her mind, she could see Sophie's heart beating, appreciate her sadness on so many levels.

"Peg?" Sophie was looking at her, puzzled. "Supper? You'll give me a hand?"

Peg nodded, and Sophie returned to the house with her violin. Peg loved the way the sun filled her with warmth recently, a welcome change to the deep chill that had been with her since her initiation. She tuned in briefly to the wild creatures in the garden. One of the birds was old and sick, and Peg felt his distress, tuning into his grey-green flashes of fear. To think her kind had used this instinct to 'hunt'...

She pushed herself to her feet and went to help.

Sophie's kitchen was a pleasant place, filled with jars of herbs and spices. After a time, the two women sat enjoying their supper on the back porch. Sophie ate well when Peg was around. They chatted afterward, in the waning light. Peg grew uneasy, wondering how to break the news about tomorrow, but Sophie provided the opening.

"You know how we talked, a few weeks ago, about taking a holiday together? Peg, I think it's a great idea—if we could find a reduced fare—"

"Sophie, wait," Peg broke in. Damn, she was bad at these things.

"What?" Sophie's expression changed. She appeared wary in the lantern light. Her hair, skin and eyes seemed to be the same shade of gold, and she looked thin and vulnerable.

"Something's come up, problems..." Peg blundered on. "I need to have things...done. I'll be out of touch, for a few days—"

"You're sick, aren't you?" Sophie pounced, agitated. "Oh Peg, I knew it. You've been looking so drawn, and those friends of yours are in and out so much."

"It's complicated," Peg finished lamely. She wrestled constantly with whether or not to tell Sophie about herself. With all her peculiarities, she wondered that Sophie had never guessed—others had, and had shunned her, as most did her kind. But the longer she sat here, waffling, the worse she'd make things. She stood, unhappy.

"I'm tired—I need to get up early. Thanks for supper."

The two women climbed the steps to the gate in silence, Peg clutching the lantern they shared back and forth on any nocturnal visits. Sophie pressed Peg's arm. "I hope the results are negative," she whispered.

Peg couldn't bear to look back. She hurried down the lane, oblivious to the growing night. A car approached, and she stepped to one side.

"Coffee, Friday morning," her neighbour Madge called from her open car window. Peg nodded and waved; it was just easier. She closed her gate and made her way around to the front, sitting on the bench by the steps.

This would be one of the last nights she'd spend here. The thought filled Peg with anguish. She loved this house, perched on the hilltop, with its coved ceilings and leaded glass windows. She'd maintained the place in period, and in keeping with the other houses on the street. The view was the best part, at dawn, and at night when the lights of the greater suburbs below performed their magic, or the moon came up.

Peg had hurt Sophie, would hurt her more in the coming days. The edicts of the Group were cruel and absolute. Yet she had to go through with things, for now, until she had a set plan.

The sound of a car pulling up to the curb below roused her. She recognized the vehicle at once. A woman got out and made her way up the steps.

"Hello, Nel," Peg said. "Come with my death warrant, have you?"

"Nope," the other answered, sitting beside her, smoothing her crisp, light business suit. She fished in her briefcase, bringing out papers. "Just paperwork for the condo purchase." There was an awkward pause. Nel brushed her

brown hair from her face. A fellow Group member and a
real estate agent, she was originally from back east, from
pioneer times, and her accent reflected that.

"I'm sorry Peg," Nel said. "A lot of us don't agree with
the way these relocations are handled—we've talked about
some of the things you said at the last Group get-together,
and we want you to know you have friends."

"Thanks," Peg whispered. The papers lay on the bench
beside her long after Nel had gone. Peg couldn't bring
herself to look at them.

The terrace vista of mountains, inlet and metropolis was
postcard perfect, Peg thought.

Mark came up behind her, placing an arm around her,
and she willed herself not to flinch. "Twenty five stories
up, over two thousand square feet and designed by the
best architect in town."

"People are homeless, down there," Peg said, obstinate.
Mark sighed.

"Peggy, I only want what's best for you. This is better
than the suburbs." There it was again, that tone, paternal,
patronizing, full of the old possessiveness. Peg shrugged
his arm away, crossing the large terrace garden and entering the penthouse.

At least a hundred of the Tyme and Nevermore Investment Group were enjoying wine, fellow-sufferers celebrat-
ing Peg's 'move.' That she hated this large, glossy condo
with windows that looked out on every aspect of the city
was irrelevant.

It was hers, and an expensive punishment. Relocation
was traumatic. Change of address and identity, a false death
certificate and new papers for every contingency, even
surgical enhancements...

She'd made a serious slip, this time. She should have
persisted with her medication, as others did, even if it made
her emotions flatline. 'Hunting' that young man a few
weeks ago had been stupid, especially since the Group had
banned the activity. It was a minor nip, but still assault,
and though the police hadn't got to her yet they were
assuredly closing in.

"Peg!" Nel called, waving Peg over to a group of people by the galley kitchen: Len, Donna, Carlos and a few others, the caterers moving among them. Company brochures were scattered over the marble counter top.

Tyme and Nevermore Investment Group, Peg thought. Few caught the literary allusion in the name, as Poe wasn't widely read any more.

Peg glanced at the young caterer next to her—blood scent, pulse, skin temperature, and something else, hard and aggressive... *a tumour!* Peg was shocked. *And she's so young!*

"You should get a mammogram," Peg blurted. Taking a glass of wine from the startled girl's tray, she turned to greet her friends.

"Just forming your defence," one of them, Len, quipped as she approached.

"Thanks," Peg grinned in spite of herself. "It is a bit like a public execution."

"And all the judges," another man, Carlos commented. "Our Board of Directors—so smug! They've no right to do this to you, Peg, not in law."

"The attention's put all of you at risk," Peg conceded.

"And so the Board decideth," Nel giggled. Peg wondered if she was drunk.

"The Board 'decideth' a lot," Len said. "How we live, who we see, where our money goes."

"That part's interesting," Carlos, a chartered accountant, ventured. "With Nel's help, I've done a little hacking into their records."

"Carlos, for God's sake be careful!" Peg was alarmed. "I broke the rules, and look at me. Forced to relocate, to purchase a place I loathe, and I don't know my forfeit yet."

"You can afford this," Len said. "We all could. It's just *their* damned, galling—"

"Easy," Nel cautioned. "They're looking."

A small, well-dressed group of men and women gathered by the long glass dining table, studying Peg and her company with disapproval. The Board could make things so much worse—they controlled what the public knew, managed the company investments and branches, and the clandestine blood bank. Many had special and historic power reserves, personal and frightening abilities the newer members lacked. One of them, Fiora, brazenly held up a glass of what was surely blood—Peg could smell it from here.

"Perhaps we should play our part—you know, indulge in the time-honoured cliché," Len said. He was a handsome man, and looked in his late thirties. "*Good evening*, my dear," he said to a passing caterer. "Or perhaps I should say *good afternoon*." Curling his fingers and baring his teeth, he produced a loud, hissing "KKKgh!" While this perplexed and amused the catering staff, the Board observed stone-faced.

It occurred to Peg that her friends were drunk. To make things worse, Mark was headed their way.

"Peggy," he said, taking her aside. "You seem so unhappy." She glimpsed the old Mark for a moment, before the darkness and desolation in his soul resurfaced.

"Yes."

"You could try a little harder, for me. We go back so far. It took a lot to set this up."

"I can see that."'

"My new place is nearby—we could see more of each other."

"I don't think so." Peg pulled away.

"That's too bad." Mark paused, looking out and down at the windmills in the distant inlet. To Peg, they seemed like grounded birds. Most vampires were like that too, now, though they'd once flown with ease, if in a different form. "I met Sophie, at last, yesterday, in your lane," Mark went on suggestively.

"Leave Sophie out of things!" Panic seized Peg. Mark knew it, and took cold delight in it.

"Mark." She tried to grab his arm. "Mark!" Sunlight caught his fair hair as he passed into the crowd. Peg took slow, deep breaths. Another night, that was all. Tomorrow it would mostly be over. She'd find some way to protect Sophie; she could persuade the others to help watch her place, tonight.

I've had too much wine, Peg thought, and with that came the drunken, primitive urge of her kind to 'hunt'—in broad daylight this time. She felt the stinging in the front of her mouth, her nostrils—the young caterer with the tumour would do...

Peg came sharply to her senses. She couldn't remember if she'd ever loathed herself this much, or when she had hated Mark more.

Peg disliked the cloying scent of the big, white lilies all around her.

She sat towards the rear of the funeral chapel. With no theatre makeup, she was recognizable now as the Peg of long ago. Still, she was cautious. She watched as the Board members arrived, along with a number of others from the Group. It was a private funeral, the home owned by a Tyme and Nevermore member. Most didn't bother to come, as it was both a sham and an unhappy obligation. Peg's attendance was part of her punishment.

She wondered where they'd obtained the cadaver for the coffin. It was a closed-casket service, but the Group always purchased a body just in case there were questions. There were always 'friends' willing to swear to the deceased's identity. Wheels within wheels: a death certificate, brand new persona, and everything from a legitimate source...the Group reached deep into the community.

I'm dead, Peg thought, stifling a growing hysteria. *I'm someone else, now...*

Organ music played softly as Len and Nel entered. With a nod to Peg, they went through a door near the side of the coffin and altar, where Mark had gone earlier.

What a joke that we were once called 'the undead', Peg thought. *We are dead, all of us. Worse, those of us who belong to Tyme and Nevermore are trapped, manipulated...*

It wasn't like that everywhere. There were other organizations in Europe that were far more liberal, and better at gaining public support. Peg's frequent trips to France had garnered her many friends, both in and outside her afflicted community.

More Group members came in, and soon the generous chapel was full. Peg was surprised by the numbers.
The nods and half bows of respect the newcomers gave
her were both moving and disconcerting.

Peg grew restless when Len and Nel didn't return. Nel
had promised to sit with her during the service, which
was about to begin. Peg rose, adjusting her veil, nodding
here and there as she made her way to the front and the
door behind the altar. Turning the doorknob, she slipped
through.

The passageway beyond led to the basement work and
storage area. Angry voices carried up from below, and
Peg hurried across the hall and down the narrow stairs,
turning right onto a wide landing. Nel, Len, Carlos and
several others were engaged in a heated debate with Mark.

"Come on, all of you—is this any way to behave at my
funeral?" Peg joked.

"We were talking about that," Len replied. "We've been
trying to corner Mark alone for days. I was just asking
him how many of these travesties he expects us to go
through. Tell me, Mark, do you think you can cover things
up forever? You're good, you and the Board, I'll give you
that. But someday you'll come up against someone who
can't be influenced, and whatever you're up to will be
exposed—it'll ruin all of us!"

Clutching his laptop and a small silver casket, Mark
looked unnerved, though he stood his ground. Peg
couldn't remember ever seeing him like this. She suspected that Mark, roused, could be very dangerous. He
was overwhelmingly strong and could still make his way
through cracks in a wisp of vapour.

"Peg's right," he said. "This isn't the time or place. Peg,
I got the silver casket—our little joke—"

"Don't change the subject, Mark." Len's voice rose.
"Peg's the one who's been talking to us, making us question things—not that we haven't been thinking on our
own. A lot of us are unhappy with the status quo—"

"And I've been digging, Mark," Carlos broke in. "You
haven't been straight with us about the source for the

blood bank—and none of us likes the idea of foreclosing residential mortgages and putting families out in the street—"

"You've been busy, Peggy," Mark said, fixing his dark eyes on her. "I'm surprised and disappointed. You know the rules."

"We *did* just talk, Mark," Peg said. "Most of us think we can do more generous things with Tyme and Nevermore's assets. And there's the ability we have to sense things—that could be put to use in the medical community, and in other ways—"

"As for *rules*," Carlos broke in, "has he told you about your forfeit, yet, Peg? Your *real* punishment?"

Anger grew in Mark's face. "Carlos, that's none of your—"

"He hasn't, has he?"

"What do you mean?" Peg felt a sudden chill.

"You have to sell the Group your family home," Nel said gently. "They've prearranged papers. You must pay the proceeds back into the Corporation. And the Board insists you end all thought of friendship with that girl you're so attached to."

"Sophie? My home? No!" Peg stepped forward, tearing off her veil. She wondered if anyone upstairs had heard the commotion, particularly the Board members who were present.

"I won't do it, Mark." The depth of her outrage surprised her. "And you'll leave Sophie out of it—I want your word!"

She blocked his way, but Mark, angered by her defiance, shouldered her aside. Len stepped in and pushed him. Mark dropped the laptop and suddenly they were fighting.

"Stop it!" Peg cried. The sound, the full sense of their rage half-consumed her.

Both were formidably strong and determined. Peg tried to separate them. Nel and Carlos came to help, but Mark flung Carlos halfway across the landing. Len pinned Mark to the railing; it heaved and cracked, giving way, and Mark went over and down into the darkness below.

Peg heard a hideous, snarling sound. Someone flipped a light switch for the lower basement and Peg raced down the stairs. Mark lay amidst a mass of old furniture and half finished caskets. A sharp piece of scaffolding protruded from his chest; it had pierced him back to front. He struggled to free himself, trying to change shape, his face slipping in and out of focus.

"Help me!" Peg cried to the others.

"Stake's the wrong way 'round," Nel sighed, but she and Len came anyway. When they finally freed Mark, he was a bloodless, shrunken figure, labouring to breathe. He still clutched the small silver casket.

"It's no good," Len said. "Peg, he shouldn't be—I didn't mean to—"

Above them, Carlos had recovered. He seized Mark's laptop, typing frantically. "Lock the door going upstairs, Carlos," Peg called. "*Carlos!*"

It was too late. The faces of Board members and others peered down from above as Mark gave Peg's hand one final squeeze.

"Sorry, Peggy," he said. There was a flash of the old Mark, a softening of his expression and an odd tenderness, and then he was gone.

"I've hacked the database," Carlos shouted up the stairwell. "I've sent information places you really should be concerned about! You go for Peg, I'll make it worse!"

Peg stood up, shaking. "You heard him," she said, not looking up at them. "It's over. You can do whatever you want to me, but others want change too. You can't hang on to the old ways any more."

There was a panicked scuffling from upstairs as they pushed back through the door, doubtless to salvage what they could of Tyme and Nevermore, and what passed as their lives. A few waved approval. Peg stooped and closed Mark's eyelids, gently arranging his arms and pressing his hands around the small silver casket.

"You can have this, at least," she whispered. Nodding to the others, she turned and mounted the stairs.

###

"Your papers—all your ID and everything—Carlos fixed it, got them back," Nel said. "They're waiting in the car, with your passport and travel documents. Len and I will drive you."

"Thanks Nel." Peg squeezed her friend's arm as she started up the dark lane.

"Don't worry about the house—I'll stay in it until you decide what to do!" Nel started towards the waiting car at the bottom of the lane.

Peg swung the bright lantern in front of her, dabbing at her hastily applied makeup. The lane seemed particularly beautiful tonight, though she couldn't linger. She had to get to Sophie. The plane might be a private jet, but time was tight. The media was everywhere, and the troubles of the Group and the sudden disappearance of its director were all over the evening news.

She hoped Sophie would understand. Peg had to get them both away, for now, even if the others wouldn't come. The Board members were dangerous and would surely enact vengeance when they weren't dodging the press. Carlos had picked his targets well, destroying just the right amount of access and information, and creating a superb degree of chaos. The refuge in Paris was a godsend—Peg's friends there, both her kind and those in the general community—would help. Sophie would be put up with a regular family.

Peg knew that if she didn't make this change, what lay ahead was bleak. The appreciation of life that had grown in her this past while would diminish; the cold would creep back into her heart and bones, and she would be more alone and unhappy than before.

She could feel that life about her: soft as sounds that mingled in twilight, yet strong, like some cosmic concert. It was a universal, constant hum, where the essence of every living thing, however insignificant, registered in its own way.

A resonance.

That ability of Peg and her kind to sense what humans could not was rooted in that force. She'd helped the young caterer, yesterday. There was hope. For those of her kind who wanted better, wanted more, there was a way.

Until then, there were her friends in France, and Sophie, if she'd listen. But how should she explain what she really was?

When we're safe, I'll tell her the truth, Peg thought. *Give her a choice. It'll be a shock, but otherwise I'm no better than Mark.*

The familiar violin sounded from Sophie's back garden. Tchaikovsky, played with passionate fury, the bow sawing across the strings. Back doors up and down the lane began to slam as the neighbours lost patience with Sophie at last. Peg laughed and turned in at the gate.

Every lantern in Sophie's garden was alight. She paced the pathway, working her bow ruthlessly, and only stopped when she saw Peg. Disbelief, then joy crossed her lamplit features.

"Peg? Oh my god, I thought—I tried to get hold of you. I went to your house, but those friends of yours were all over—they were so close-mouthed, I thought… you seemed ill, when I last saw you…"

Her own excitement, and the sound of Sophie's heart beating, grew inside Peg. She was on the threshold of a challenging new world. A warning whistle from down the lane— likely Len—told her to hurry.

"I'm sorry you were worried," she said, reaching for the latch. "I should explain. I wasn't at my best, but I'm much better now…"

The New Forty
By Rebecca Bradley

The simple truth is, they lack empathy. Soulless, self-absorbed, prowling the night for good times and quick fixes; nothing in their heads except sucking liquid down their throats and jumping on each other like apes in the zoo. Mindless, shameless. And the vampires are just as bad.

Oh, the young!

But I am not as bitter as I may sound. It is only that, after centuries of observation, I understand them a little too well. These days I observe them on talk shows, the youthful of both species, especially the undead. The rising stars of the new-epoch vampire movies, the super-models of vampire chic, vamp-rock bands with names like *Bloody Waters, Grateful Undead* and *Bled Zeppelin*. How perfect are their cold, shapely cadavers, and how beautifully they match the new tenor of the world. If ever there was an age when my kind could come from the shadows and *blend right in*, that time is now.

My kind? *Their* kind, rather. I have no kind. Even among vampires, I am a freak, a sport, an accident. A common slattern the first time around, spawned into a class and age where women did not give birth so much as whelp litters of unplanned annual brats, whose short lives and hacking deaths recapitulated those of their ancestors. Not mine, though. My father died when I was small, my mother when I was perhaps ten; whereas I survived two husbands and all seven of my own poor whelps, and plodded on dismal and solitary to the extraordinary age of sixty-four.

Then I became a witch, by definition, and through no true fault of mine. In those times, it was enough to be beyond the menses and to live alone, to have wrinkled flesh, grey hair, gaps in one's jaw, and a reputation for wisdom. Perhaps I should have known better than to be wise. They took me for torture, and cast me between-times into a cold cell with vermin for company, and my own bodily effluents, from blood to puke, for what is now called interior décor: colour-coordinated wall- and floor-coverings that reflected the inner me and gave the place atmosphere, in the language of the home-renovation shows to which I am now addicted. One day, they tossed me a cellmate.

We exchanged no words. I never properly saw his face. The mob had beaten him bloodily enough to kill a Christian outright, so his very survival proved him to be a creature of the devil and fodder for the stake. After they clanged the door shut on us, I crawled across the cell to steal his coat and check his pockets, on the chance of a crust of bread. He was sprawled motionless on his belly, but when I turned him over, he struck like a snake out of his swoon, straight for my gullet, biting so deep I heard his teeth click together inside my flesh. I think I bit him back, since the taste of his blood was in my mouth when I woke up; or maybe he bled into me from his many wounds. At any rate, by then he was gone from the cell and I was a twice-born accident, who barely knew my father and never knew my sire.

I knew about the devil, though, and how his minions could come to even virtuous old women in the night to tempt them into vile congress. This, I assumed with shame and fear, was what had happened to me. And it also appeared that the devil took care of his own. Just as the prison door had opened for the Apostle Paul in Philippi, the door to my cell swung obligingly off its hinges, and no living thing stirred in the gaol. I ran out and into the dark wood and away from the sleeping town.

So there was I, a babe again, new to the ways of a strange new world—but a babe in a withered body with deep fissures in its face. Yes, I felt a difference as I ran. For the first time in twenty years my hips and back did not hurt me, my old bones moved easily in their sockets, my breath did not wheeze in my throat. Even the welts and breaks from my torture were miraculously painless.

How I ran! First from fear, later from the joy of running freely under an icy moon, setting the farm dogs whining and cringing as I passed. I outran a deer in the king's forest and—on fresh instinct—caught it with a strength that was novel to me, twisted its beautiful neck, and drank from its throat. So now I was not just a witch but a poacher, eligible for the rope as well as the stake; but I was also a small mewling child overcome with the newness of everything.

Back to the talk shows.

"Look, Oprah, we've got feelings too. We're very sensitive, very nurturing with our young. For us, newborn vampires are like newborn babies. We stay close, we do everything we can to help them through what is often a difficult, highly emotional transition. We teach them—"

"...to kill?" says Oprah, with the frown that signals she is asking a hard-hitting question. The audience cat-calls and applauds.

"Hey," says the strikingly handsome young man. His pale marble skin glows under the studio lights. "I find that remark both vampirist and personally offensive. You're thinking of the bad old days, when we did what we had to, just to survive. That doesn't mean we liked it."

Liar. He'd rip her throat out now if a half-billion people weren't watching, and he'd like it very much. Mortals haven't known us long enough to read the body language. And as for *sensitive* and *nurturing*, I saw little of those qualities during my own difficult, highly emotional transition. There were many things I had to discover painfully for myself, starting with the fatal nature of sunlight.

It was only by luck I did not immolate myself out of sheer ignorance when my first post-mortem sun rose. I hid whimpering under the bracken and dug myself my own little grave in the forest dirt, among the worms and moles; and at sundown, I clawed my way out again with still-smarting hands.

Beyond a vague theory that I'd accidentally sold myself to Satan, I had no idea of what I had become. Not even the sudden attraction to blood—several moles and a badger had helped me pass that first long day—felt out of the ordinary. Later that night, when the nest tracked me down, I knew only that I should be afraid of them, deathly afraid, yet somehow I was not.

Three handsome youths and two beautiful maids surrounded me among the trees, luminous in the moonlight, richly dressed—quality folk they looked like, such as I'd seen before only as passengers in liveried coaches, holding their noses as they were whisked through the stinking streets of our town. They stared at me with surprise and all-too-evident distaste. Much later, I wondered if one of them was my sire. At the time, I did not even know enough to ask the question. Then one of the youths laughed harshly.

"God's truth, who'd have thought *that* was worth turning?"

"You have to admit," says Oprah coyly, "that you're all— how shall I put it—a little better-looking than the average human. In fact, I'd say you're all drop-dead gorgeous, no pun intended. So, is becoming a vampire like having a beauty treatment, or what?"

"Oprah, modesty forbids my answering that." He laughs, oh so decoratively. Oprah and the audience laugh along. "But to be perfectly honest, appearance doesn't matter much to us. We can't help what we look like."

More lies. Back in the shadow days, only the young and beautiful were candidates for turning. The old, the ugly, the worn, the imperfect, were simply dinner. And now I know how lucky I was, that long-ago moonlit night in the king's forest. Under a different alpha, they might well have torn me to shreds, in the same spirit as humans once exposed nonstandard babies on hillsides. But all I knew of them then was that they were neither gamekeepers nor inquisitors.

"Help me," I said to them, holding out my sun-blistered hands. "Take me with you."

The lad snickered. "Why should we? What use would you be to us?"

"I know things," I faltered. "I'm good with herbs, and helping at childbirth. Women come to me for counsel."

Judging by their laughter, they thought that was hilarious. I can see why, in retrospect, but at the time I was stung to anger. I snapped at them, "You could show respect, then, for my grey hairs, and some pity for a poor old woman in distress."

"Grey hairs?" cried one of the girls through her laughter. "Your age is *nothing* to us, hag. Why, I could be your three-times-great granddam—though I dearly hope I'd never have a grandchild as ugly as you." Then she lifted her head to laugh more freely, giving me a much better view of her teeth.

That is how I learned I had joined the legendary undead. I recognized *her* for what she was. I ran my tongue around the inside of my own mouth: no teeth had grown back, but the remaining stumps had become long, strong and sharp. The beautiful ones found my howl of discovery very amusing indeed. But when they tired of teasing me—those youths and maids who were old before I was born—they ran off on a further merry chase and left me alone. That was more dreadful to me than their derision. I ran after them.

"So you see it as a kind of liberation? An empowerment of the vampire community?"

"Absolutely, Oprah. An end to centuries of discrimination and ostracism. And—yes—a long-overdue end to the victimization of a misunderstood minority. Believe me, we welcome the opportunity to become full, productive members of society."

"And do you see that as a challenge?"

"Absolutely, Oprah."

I am tempted to throw something at the screen. How well they have learned their lessons, these vampires-for-the-twenty-first-century. And how they adore being a demographic. But I could tell them a great deal they don't know about being a minority, a demographic of just one, and what always set me apart from the others was not just my raddled face. I gained the first inkling of this truth on that first night, when I ran wailing after the beautiful ones and caught up with them just after they downed their prey.

He was a lad I knew, one I had helped deliver into this world some sixteen years before. A good enough boy, hardworking and honest, perhaps a little lumpen. He was courting, I knew that too, and in my opinion it was well past time he should be decently married to the smith's middle daughter.

When I crashed through the brush, all five of them were suckling at him, fastened to his body like piglets to a sow, but he was still alive and conscious. His eyes widened when he saw me. Hope? Appeal? Or did he see me as one of *them*, truly a chattel of the devil, just as the witchfinder had said?

The next moment, the alpha made the question moot by biting into the artery at the base of the boy's thick peasant neck. "Here, granny," he said, grinning up at me, "I'm of a generous disposition tonight. There's a mouthful or two left in the beast—come see how fine it tastes. And then go away, because the sight of you offends us."

"The beast's name," I said, "was John." I turned and walked into the darkness, and never once looked back.

"But you have killed people, right? How do you feel about that now?"

"That's an excellent question, Oprah. Sure, we've had to kill people in the past, simply to survive. Does that make us evil? I don't think so. It makes us no different from any other nation or ethnic group in the history of the world."

For once I agree with my good-looking colleague, whom I last saw in London wearing a fashionable swallowtail coat and chowing down on a thoroughly Dickensian street urchin. The fact is the youthful of my species are no more evil than the human young they used to be. They are no more than Peter Pan with fangs, butterflies in amber, trapped forever in the borderline psychopathy of youth. They are the ultimate expression of neoteny. Life never gets the chance to knock the stuffing out of them.

But life had already left me with very little stuffing by the time I was turned. I never could bring myself to prey on humans—too much damned empathy to start with, too liberal a schooling in the sharing of mortal pain.

After parting from the beautiful ones, I became the terror of small forest creatures as I worked my way slowly across the wilderness of several southern counties. In London, I took a new name and became a poor widow from the country—who would notice another ravaged beldame among so many? In fact, it was not a bad choice of what is now called 'lifestyle'.

For many years I supped handsomely on the vermin of Whitechapel and Lambeth, and slept in safety in the great underground palace of the London sewers. Plagues and fires came and went, fashions changed and changed again, generations of mortals flowed past me, but the rats and the sewers went on forever. Early in the regency, I conceived a bright idea: why not dress as a man and work for the borough as a rat-catcher? Why not get paid for what I was already doing? The bounty on the barrow loads of bloodless vermin I delivered became the foundation of my later fortune, now nicely diversified in a number of offshore investment banks.

Naturally, I saw others of my kind in London's rich hunting ground. They rarely saw me, though, since I preferred to observe them discreetly from a distance. Their ethnology became a hobby of mine: their feeding and mating habits, pecking orders, kinship patterns, ritual behaviours. I could write a book on them, and probably will. On the few occasions when they recognized me as undead, they reacted much as my first vampires in the forest had done, with a mixture of amusement and distaste.

"Now, can I ask you something personal, something that literally millions of women out there are just dying to know?"

"Certainly, Oprah."

She leans forward to an intimate closeness. In the audience, and presumably all over the television-viewing world, many other women lean forward as well. "Do vampires—fall in love?"

The vampire closes the gap even further. "Yes, Oprah, we totally do fall in love. And we are perfectly capable of forming stable, loving relationships."
"Do you, er—go out on dates?"
"We most certainly do."

Dates? Hunting parties, in the shadow times. Nowadays, courting vampires dance the night away, or go out to dinner in one of those new specialty restaurants. The first cross-species marriages are being watched closely by sociologists and tabloid journalists. Romance is in the air—and not just for the young.

I had long thought I was beyond all that. I was *old*. Average life expectancy for mortals did not go much beyond fifty until well into the twentieth century, and persons of my apparent age were both rare and hopelessly over the hill. I began to dress better and more expensively as the nineteenth century wore on and my pest-control business expanded into a small commercial empire, but I did not dress to attract lovers. Who, apart from the obvious fortune-hunters, would want to court such a withered old crone?

Then a curious thing happened. For whatever suite of reasons, the brief lives of mortals began to *stretch*. More people began to live beyond their fifties, and then their sixties; more and more began to outlive the biblical three-score and ten. Suddenly, I was surprised to learn from magazines that life began at forty; and then, not much later by vampire standards, that fifty was the new forty. And then it was sixty. Clearly, the boomer generation was starting to catch up with me. As the new millennium approached, I was amazed to find I was a relatively youthful and potentially attractive woman.

"Yes, Oprah, I think you can safely say the world is seeing a new breed of vampire. And I have high hopes that a brighter future lies ahead for us all."

Amen to that. The face-lift did not take, alas, but the dentures make a remarkable difference. Then there is the transforming power of makeup, a clever stylist, and a personal shopper with a taste for good labels.

The roses are from a virile gentleman of seventy-six who is happy to give up golfing in the sun for my sake. Tonight, we shall make a little champagne ceremony of his turning. And why not? Immortality, like youth, is wasted on the young.

Red Blues
By Michael Skeet

Your hand closes around the neck. Just for a second, you let your slender, grave-cold fingertips caress the gentle curve. Long since a stranger to the subtleties of tactile sensation, you nevertheless rejoice in the smoothness of the back of the neck, in its slender vulnerability. Then you press those fingers down, firmly but not too hard.

You begin to play.

Fingers flying over the strings of your vintage Gibson, you give them your twenty-seventh variation on the verse of "They Can't Take That Away From Me." It's your tenth night of a two-week gig in this club and the tenth time you've played this song they think they know. No one in the audience, though, has heard it the same way twice. You've memorized a lot of different versions of this song.

As Garrett and Holman join in for the chorus, you switch to variation one thousand eighteen. The two fit well together: their tempos match, and the flourish of sixteenth notes you've crammed into each bar of the chorus gives the impression of furious improvisation. After two choruses of this you head into the bridge, keeping the tempo but dropping back to an earlier variation on the tune, with more eighths than sixteenths and a couple of strategically placed discords to give the punters the impression of something new going on. Then it's back into the chorus—a different variation again—and as you head home you begin scouting the audience, looking to see if she's here tonight. It takes one more chorus until she drifts into view through the smoke and by then you've already caught her scent. As you scatter a series of eccentric chords through the final bars of the song, you're already planning tonight's conquest, with the same thoroughness you've planned tonight's set.

When you look up to begin the next number, though, she is gone. You could make her stay, could weave a web of pheromones and waking dreams around her until she has no more will than your Gibson, but you have rules you follow in cases such as this. There will be no coercion; she invites you in, or you wait another day and try again. You wait.

Most people misunderstand the beauty of jazz. They revel in its unpredictability, its scattershot virtuosity and the emotion with which their favourite practitioners approach it. For you, though, jazz is complex mathematics, a poetry of numbers. Improvisation is what people resort to when memory fails them. You have built a house of memory over hundreds of years, and in the last six decades, since you took up this music as a distraction, your memory has not failed you once.

You are in mid-set on the eleventh night when you detect her presence, then see her sitting down with a group of friends. She brushes her hair behind one ear as she orders a drink. You're playing "A Shine on Your Shoes." You've kept the sprightly tempo of the original, but from the bridge you set off into an extended solo that quotes from just about every Dietz-Schwartz tune on the sound track of the film *The Band Wagon*. None of your audience recognizes the gesture, but they appreciate the overall effect, and that's enough. You're surprised for a moment when Garrett, on bass, actually matches you note for note during your two-bar segment of "Dancing in the Dark", but you recover quickly enough and return his smile with a nod. The intuitive pattern-matching instincts of human beings can still, it seems, take you by surprise.

Instinct is no substitute for experience, though. As Garrett takes a verse, you fix your gaze on her. She has given you a good chase, but she will weaken in the end.

They always do. She knows you are watching her, and fights against the hold of your eyes. When she wins, you concede gracefully. There is no hurry. You are never in a hurry.

You isolate her scent from amongst the charred nicotine and oxidized alcohol smells even before you begin playing on your twelfth night, and that knowledge brings you one step closer to conquest. She still resists your eyes, but you can smell her growing interest as easily as you can see the small shift of her shoulders and tilt of her head as she begins, mid-way through the set, to isolate herself from her companions. It's time to focus the music directly onto her, and to let her know what you are doing. "Drop the next one," you say to Garrett on your right. He passes the message to Holman behind his drum kit, and you forget about "I Got Rhythm", swinging directly into "How About You?"

The music is light, fanciful, and the version you've chosen to remember has plenty of airy frills at the end of each line of the chorus. It's appropriate to your mood, now that you've seen her, and you know that before the night is over she will be yours. In a gesture that echoes your mood, you let Garrett have two choruses to himself; you actually enjoy the fat, staccato thumping of the bass as his thick, calloused fingers fly over the strings. Garrett looks like an old man, but is in fact only thirty-eight. You've appreciated the irony since you've known him: you look like you're not a day over thirty, when in fact you're about fifty-five thousand days over thirty. He's been a heroin addict since the evening of his first professional gig sixteen years ago. In a sense that has made him a good partner. You don't bother him about what he puts into his veins and he doesn't bother you about what you take out of theirs. There is no feeling between you—there could never be—but you look out for him, do what you can to keep him alive in spite of himself. Consistency in companionship is something your kind is drawn to. You used to tell yourself that it was the heroin that kept you from deepening your relationship with Garrett, but in the last fifty years you've made a habit of keeping your professional and private lives separate. Good sidemen may be easy to find, but understanding ones aren't.

Your private life is beginning to intrude now, the hunger demanding your attention before you're ready. She's brushing her hair back behind one ear, drawing attention to the pale band of her neck; the gesture almost causes you to miss your entry for the final chorus. Not for the first time you wonder if this one is aware of her effect on you, has been playing you over the two weeks you've been hunting her.

"Savoy Blues" is next, the first song you learned. Chess had been your distraction of choice before then, its multiplicity of potential moves appealing to the strong sense of memory that develops in the living dead. But after a century chess was losing its appeal, and the first time you heard Lonnie Johnson play—1926, in Chicago—your mathematician's soul was somehow able to discern from a single two-minute performance the infinite potential jazz might have to an undying intellect. Through Johnson you met Eddie Lang, and it's not entirely your fault that Lang died so young—nor can Charlie Christian's death a few years after that be laid solely at your feet. At least a part of them lives on in you.

That part emerges as you begin "Seven Come Eleven". You are no fan of bop, but enough of Christian's blood continues to mingle with yours that you are almost compelled to echo the scatter-gun single-line riffing, the eccentric chords and rhythms of the pioneer of bebop guitar. The audience loves it, too. Their desire for novelty overrides all other considerations; it's one of the things you dislike about bop. The precision of swing demands more of both performer and listener. Nobody has time for that any more, not even here.

Now she is leaning over her table, transfixed as your fingers fly over the strings, her desire to unite with the music so strong you can taste its musky flavour on your tongue. She is yours, now, captured by the music. You do not have to guess: you know it in your blood, your skin.

Nevertheless, when you pack your guitar at the end of the set, she is nowhere to be seen. Somehow, she is breaking free of the music's spell.

Tonight, the last number in your set is "The Red Blues". The lyrics—and the musical for which it was written—hardly represent Cole Porter at his best. But Porter was a great tunesmith, even in his declining years. This tune is superb raw material. You have an affinity with this song; playing it allows you to project into the mind of each member of the audience something dark but compelling, an emotional thunderstorm. Every entity has a piece of music to which it resonates; "The Red Blues" is yours.

Is it hers? She has come late, settling into a seat alone only a few minutes before. At least she is here. You have only one night after this song and you are loath to degrade yourself by forcing her into your grasp. You're going to have to do something, though.

What you decide to do is to put more than your memory and technique into this song. It's what you've seen humans do and though the prospect is distasteful, you are willing to try it. There are limits to patience, after all.

You don't look at her as you start playing; it requires all of your concentration to do this. Fingers flying over the strings, you make the music black with night and eternal despair, letting it fill you until the hairs on your neck are standing erect with it. Then you pour out of you all the fear and rage and power of the night, sending them splashing into the club and willing the listeners to soak it up, drown in it.

Then you sit up, the strings still vibrating with the final notes. The room is silent. Even the wait staff is immobile and voiceless. No one looks at you; they are all wrestling with themselves—some in tears, some struggling to suppress cries of horror or triumph according to their natures. Feeling uncomfortably numb, you wonder if this phenomenon is repeatable, if someday you'll be able to study the impact you have on your sidemen.

And on her? You smell a hint of fear; has some primitive part of her brain warned her that she has been the target of your play? She is still here, though.

Now the spell breaks, and the audience is on its feet. You are calm as you put away your guitar; you've heard the shouts and applause too many times over too many years to care much anymore. You play for one person a night these days.

It's time. You wish Holman would take the equipment home with him tonight, and he does. Garrett has already disappeared into the dark and the smoke, looking to mingle neurochemical salvation with his blood. Your blood demands satisfaction too, but even though it's been days and your hunger is frost-sharp and desperate, you will not spoil the hunt by breaking the rules.

You look up after locking your Gibson in its case; she is no longer in the club. Even as you rub your eyes, your nose tells you that she's gone. Another twenty-four empty hours, then, and one last chance. There are plenty of hangers-on clustering around the front of the stage and it would be easy to take any one of them. Once you would have done that, if only to fill the emptiness. But, as your years have run into decades, you have come to believe that emptiness can be more meaningful than most of the things you've tried to fill it with. You let yourself melt into the gloom and slip out the back door, to a dust-blown alley and a bone-dry basalt sky.

She's not there. You admit that a part of you had been expecting her to be waiting for you. Perhaps you're not what you once were. After so many unchanging decades, contemplating deterioration is an unfamiliar sensation.

At the end of the alley, though, a figure is waiting. She's downwind, you realize; that's why you saw her first. "I was hoping you'd waited," you say.

"I wasn't going to," she says. "That last song was for me, wasn't it?"

"They all were," you say, struggling to control the excitement rising in you. "If only the last one actually got through, that's all right. Most people don't even hear that much."

She is walking, you note, on your right side; the guitar case is between you, your hand occupied in carrying it. "I don't usually…go out with musicians," she says.

"I'm not like other musicians," you say, and it is mostly true.

She doesn't answer that, but she continues walking beside you. Under the streetlights her soft, pleasant face looks more drawn, pale; her eyes when she looks at you are black and endless as your nights. When she sees you watching her, she self-consciously brushes her short dark hair back behind her ears. She smells of partially oxidized alcohol and burnt tobacco, but these are veneers only; her true scent is there too, under her white t-shirt and worked into the fabric of her jeans. Her throat is smooth and pale as polished chalcedony. No veins are visible, but the blood is there; you can almost taste it.

"Why do you play only the old songs?" she asks, destroying the pleasure of your contemplation.

"As opposed to what passes for pop music today?" She's probably only asking to be polite; you try to be polite. "The older songs are more conducive to jazz," you say. "They allow changes in key that give me more patterns of notes to choose from when I play."

"I've always wondered how jazz musicians improvise," she says. "I've been in the club for just about all of your dates and I've never heard you play a tune the same way twice." She mistakes careful selection for improvisation, you think. You are not really offended, though. Everyone makes that mistake; they've been making it for nearly eighty years. And each year it grows easier to fool them as your store of knowledge grows. Teaching yourself new permutations of old songs is the only thing that gets you through endless days in darkened basement rooms.

"It must be a bit frightening, I'd think," she says after a moment's thought. "Not really knowing what you're going to play next, and if it'll work? I know I'd be scared."

"It's not really that bad." There are plenty of things that frighten you—loneliness, the bitter taste of so much that you used to enjoy—but being on stage is not one of them.

"Besides," you say, "the excitement more than compensates."

"Oh, yeah. I was in my high school band. I was always afraid I was going to throw up before concerts, but once they started I loved it."

The excitement you feel is the excitement of the hunt, but perhaps at some level she knows what you're talking about. Her face is animated now, her eyes glinting with reflected mercury vapour light. Her breathing is more rapid, and you can feel the flush stealing into her cheeks and throat. Her growing awareness is exciting her, and you are in turn feeding on that excitement.

It has been your intention to take her home first, but the blood rising to her skin is beginning to inflame you. You remind yourself that, after a few weeks of waiting, a few more minutes shouldn't be all that much to deal with.

A dark alley beckons, though. You pull her in, turning so that your black leather blocks any street view of that white t-shirt. "Hey," she begins, but her lips stay parted and her eyes are shining as you lean the guitar case against a wall and place your hands on her neck, cup her face in your hands. "Not here," she protests, but her face tilts up to yours. Now your cold hands are absorbing her own heat, sending it back to her, and when you press your mouth to hers you are warm enough that she does not start at the sensation. She can taste your desire, and though she does not understand it, she responds to it. One hand stroking her neck, you move the other down to a breast, brush against it until the nipple stiffens from the gentle pressure. Then you shift your hand lower. There is no pleasure for you in this, but you want her blood suffusing her skin and your weeks of observing have told you that this is the variation to play on this particular tune.

When you lower your lips to her neck, she throws her head back. "Ah," she says.

Her skin tears easily, onionskin paper under a quill pen.

She tenses briefly as you begin to drink, but makes no sound beyond a soft moan; and not for the first time you wonder if you have found something more than a victim here. Her hands still grip your shoulders and briefly your spirit soars as you try to make yourself think about sharing yourself, your everlasting life, with her.

But her blood is spicy and hot with the sharp odour of dust on hot metal and it has been days since you last fed. Before you are aware of what you are doing, her hands have released you and her arms have dropped limply. There is still plenty of blood, but it cools rapidly. For a moment you pause, bitterly chastising yourself for your lack of feeling, of restraint.

Then you return to feeding. You will have to start over again because of this, and it may be some time before you eat again. And what is the point of chastising yourself, anyway? You are out all night, you have no real friends, and you cannot maintain any kind of relationship. How does this make you any different from any other musician?

You let the body drop into a pile of empty boxes then pick up your guitar case. As you walk out of the alley, you brush your hair back behind one ear.

The Drinker
By Victoria Fisher

I remember my first.

I was poor, unemployed and desperate. I had a basement apartment with rusting plumbing that dripped noisily into a bucket. Somehow along the way I'd left most of my friends behind and counted my greasy landlady among those I still had.

I'd taken to going to bars. I didn't drink much—never liked alcohol, never had the money—but I'd sit at the bar, my hand resting on a glass of whatever was cheap. I'd watch the people come and go and came to recognize the regulars and know their life stories and sorrows without counting myself among them. Nobody took much notice of me and I was okay with that. I hated everyone for their successes, and hated myself for failings.

She wasn't a regular. She was in her thirties, too old and well-dressed for the usual crowd, her black hair cut too severely for her round face and soft features. She sat beside me at the bar without ordering anything. She sat there for a long while without speaking at all.

I watched her out of the corner of my eye. There was something odd about her skin: her round cheeks seemed grey and matte instead of pink and shiny. She'd put on blush to hide it, but so close to her I could see her pallid colour. She wasn't wearing lipstick and her lips were as ashy as her face.

The barmen didn't bother her, although she wasn't ordering. She sat silently watching the people, like me.

"Fuckers." I don't know what made me say it.

She looked at me for the first time. She smiled and her teeth were pure white.

"Want a taste?"

Somehow, in the way she said it, I knew she didn't mean her, or drink, or drugs. She meant the people. Did I want a taste of them? It made perfect sense.

I hesitated.

"Just a sip," she said. "If you don't like it, it's just a sip. Fuckers, like you said."

"Okay," I said.

She put a hand on my shoulder. Her little fingers on my collarbone seemed to push downward through skin, bone and muscle until they touched my heart.

"Pick one," she said into my backbone. "Pick the best one."

I picked. He was blonde, tall, and laughing and drinking beer with friends on a Saturday night. He was tipsy and his shorts pockets bulged with a wallet, cell phone and iPod.

She laughed, delighted, and the sound slipped down my spine like ice. "Take a sip."

I sipped at him. He sat across the room, facing away, but somehow I tasted blood and then I tasted success. It was sweet, musky and warm. Success: I swam in its milky depth, allowed myself to drown there until the light dwindled to blackness.

When I opened my eyes, the bar was all but empty. The girl was gone, but I could still feel her hand on my heart, the tips of her fingers gently digging into the delicate flesh. The barman was already closing and he didn't give me a second glance as I walked out.

The next day, I got a job. I bought a cellphone, and iPod and those plus my wallet made my pockets bulge.

Everywhere I went I felt her little fingertips against my heart. Just a sip. Just a sip. I wanted more. I laughed it off. And I tried—I *tried* to resist.

Just a sip. I sipped from the manager when he left work early to drive home in his Jaguar. I sipped from the police

officer who pulled me over for speeding. I sipped at base-
ball games and from people who talked at the movies.
I drank from people I disliked. I gulped from my enemies.
They disappeared soon enough.

Each time I drank, I drank more. I took people's success
and then I took their hope and then I took their lives. I
took them all. I travelled the world, seeking out my victims
at the opera, in court, on the street, in hotels and motels;
the distinguished, the abusive, the rich, the poor. All the
fuckers of the world never knew I was there until their
lives twisted out of shape and petty arguments became
blood feuds, anger became self-loathing, battles became
wars. Fuckers.

All the fuckers in the world were never enough.

"Are you feeling alright, sir?" my assistant asked one
morning, after I'd returned from a long absence. "You look
pale."

I felt fingers grip my heart and laughter trickle down
my spine. I didn't answer. I was thirsty. I'd not tasted
anyone since my flight the night before. I went to the
bathroom and locked myself in before turning on the
lights.

My skin was grey and unreflective, my hair cut in a
style too severe for my unremarkable face. I grimaced and
my teeth were pure white. Whiter than any dentist could
make them.

And still I was thirsty. So thirsty. My ugly, bestial thirst
viciously hounded me like desire or pain that I couldn't
shake. I tried, for the first time in years, to resist it. I had
my assistant bring me coffee, tea, wine, beer, but none
had an effect. When she brought the whisky I took a sip
from my assistant instead of from the glass. And then I
took a gulp. Then I drank as I had never drunk before,
soaking up success and vitality and life.

I woke hours later. It had grown dark. I fumbled for
the desk light and turned it on. My assistant was still there
in the office, lying on her back by the door, one knee bent
with her leg strewn out sideways and a graceful arm flung
over her head, as if she were dancing. Burnt into the

wooden floor, ringed around her hair, were black scorch marks.

She was the first one I'd killed.

I left the office and drove across town. The bar was still there. I don't think I really needed to be there, but something poetic drew me back. I was already thirsty when I arrived.

I sat down at the bar, watching the people. The barman ignored me as if he didn't see me and I didn't order anything. The guy beside me ordered another beer with a wave of his hand. He was watching a girl laughing as she tried not to spill her drink. The despair in his blue eyes and pale face was clear. I could see the grey just beneath the surface of his skin.

He saw me looking. "What you want?"

The laughing girl turned her head, and her dark hair swirled out. I felt the familiar need. Just a tiny sip...just a little tiny sip. A last sip.

"Fuckers," he said.

"Want a taste?" I said, and the question rolled off my tongue as if I had put it there.

He agreed quicker than I remembered agreeing.

I put my hand, flat, fingers splayed, on his left shoulder. My hand slid through his leather jacket as if it were melted butter and the skin and bone with little more difficulty. I touched his heart, hot and wet and pounding away under my fingertips. I felt him flinch as I gripped.

"Take a sip," I said.

I saw through his eyes, felt though his teeth, tasted through his tongue. I coaxed him into reaching out, stretching across the room towards that dark-haired girl. He sipped her. I felt him taste blood, felt his pleasure, and felt him faint as I pulled out his heart.

It sat in my hand, a smooth, misshapen stone. It was scarlet, dripping blood and still warm from his body. I left the bar by the back door and entered the alley where the darkness was deep and I was hidden.

I touched the bloody stone to my tongue, expecting to savour blood but tasting only water. Convulsively, I swallowed and choked, slamming my body backwards against the brick wall. I arched my neck and back. My chest blazed with fire and my head was crammed with ice. I scratched my hands raw on the bricks behind me. The world turned red, black and white.

A couple came out of the bar and walked past without seeing me. I was alone. I fell to the ground.

"Hey," said a girl, leaning over me, "are you okay? Do you want us to call you an ambulance?" Her long dark hair hung down over me—it was the girl from the bar. Even in the shadows, I could see in her eyes the piece of her soul that was missing, how her life would slowly become twisted and broken.

I felt fine. I told her so. She and her friends helped me up and she brushed off my expensive jacket. I gathered my belongings from where they had fallen—my cellphone, my wallet, my iPod; my sunglasses sat in a ring of scorch where my head had lain on the concrete.

"I'll call you a cab," she said, taking out her cell phone.

"Don't worry. I feel fine." But I still felt a hard lump in my throat and knew it for what it was: remorse. I felt a terrible, dark remorse still choking me.

"Are you sure?" she asked.

"I feel fine," I said again, and as she smiled I reached out and touched her hand and gave her back what I had taken from her, and more. She glowed from the inside. "Don't worry, I'll walk," I said.

She smiled again and turned to go. I watched her walk away, surrounded by her friends, laughing once again.

Suddenly, the back door of the bar banged open and a blue-eyed man came out. He burned so black and hollow I had to look away. I was standing right in the light of the open door, full of horror and fear, but he didn't see me at all. He disappeared quickly into the night.

The girl waved at me as she went around the corner. The last I saw of her was the flip of her hair and the sound of her laughter.

She was my first and, although it was a very long time ago, I remember her well.

Sleepless in Calgary
By Kevin Cockle

"I'll be damned," the vampire said. "You *do* see me."

David didn't know what to say. Looking up from his seat on the side-bench facing the rear exit-door of the Calgary Transit bus, he felt like he might pass out. Back at the last stop, as the bus was pulling away, he could have sworn he'd seen a man coalesce out of a sudden swirl of blowing snow and what looked to be tendrils of fog. Could have been the pattern of white snow against the dark brick backdrop at first—suggesting an outline in the way of an optical illusion. But then the illusion had smiled, revealing its vicious, trademark incisors, and returned David's gaze with a mix of surprise and delight.

The vampire regarded him now with a slight frown, right hand securing the overhead bar for balance as the filled-to-bursting bus lurched its way forward on rutted winter streets. The creature was pale, appearing to be a man in his early thirties, long-faced, not quite gaunt, but certainly lanky. He was dressed in a good wool long-coat—black—with black dress trousers and white sneakers for sensible traction on the treacherous city sidewalks. His cerulean eyes seemed set in a permanent scowl, blazing as though just on the edge of true fury, but his aspect was more curious now than threatening. He ran his left hand through long, wiry black locks, considering David as one might stare at a Rubik's cube, as though staring alone could solve the problem.

David swallowed, cleared his throat to speak, but the vampire interrupted him. "Don't. You'll look like an idiot, talking to yourself. I'm a vampire...but you know that. I *am* here, but these folks aren't registering, if you know what I mean. Listen: you've got questions, I've got questions—we should talk. I'll look you up later when it's not so crowded. I gotta say...it's good to see you, brother. It's good to be seen."

The bus pulled over and the vampire moved to disembark. David blurted out "We..." and then caught himself, covering his mouth as though shielding a cough. The vampire stepped off the bus, put his bare hands in his pockets and walked off into the night.

David sat back in his seat, blinking in stupor. He glanced around, checking the reactions of his fellow passengers—but all seemed to possess identical 5:30 PM glassy-eyed mirror-gazes. Anyone who took mass transit with regularity developed the capacity to un-see anything he or she might have to. Maybe they'd seen the creature and were ignoring it; maybe not. It was impossible to tell the difference.

Breathe, David reminded himself. *In through the nose...count of seven...out through the mouth...count of eight.* He focused on that: swelling his belly with intake, counting slowly in his head. But he cringed at every single stop for the remainder of the trip.

After a forty-five minute commute of breathing and terror, David stood in his grey overcoat in front of his bathroom mirror, staring at himself for nearly five minutes. A puffy, pale face; round, brown, basset-hound eyes; unkempt brown hair starting to turn grey; stubble—he'd forgotten to shave again, a sign of slipping discipline. And sadness: frantic and increasingly undisguised in the eyes and in the set of his thin lips. *Either that thing was for real, or I'm working too hard,* David thought. And then, out of the blue, he said aloud: "Happy birthday." He had suddenly remembered it was his fortieth, and his reflection appeared to age right before his very eyes.

The birthday grounded him, replacing gut-clenching fear and confusion with the fatigue and resignation with which he was much more familiar. Finally removing his coat, David changed into sweats-and-slippers, pulled some leftovers together and sat himself down in front of the television.

Somewhere between the meatloaf and the chocolate ice cream, David let his mind begin to turn on him. A tightening in his chest; a quickening of the heart—the tell-tale signs of rising anxiety. Waves of worry were starting to build and he knew from his stress management courses that he needed to break the negative momentum. *Better get the bike*, he thought, glancing over at the exercise-cycle in the corner. He hadn't used it in weeks. He pulled it across the hardwood floor, positioning it in front of the television. He flipped channels until he found mixed martial arts in progress.

His thighs and tendons were stiff, but riding the bike helped with his deep breathing and started burning off some of his excess nervous energy. He watched the fights as he rode, trying to distract himself, but it wasn't working: turning forty and seeing a vampire apparently trumped ground-and-pound.

The birthday started to nag at him, made him think of other birthdays, happier times involving cake with baked-in dimes, and neighbourhood friends, and sleepovers. The contrast was heartbreaking, and he winced at the memory of a childhood that seemed so distant and alien to him now.

Anxiety-waves were building, growing in amplitude. He glanced at the clock near the television set—7:10. Only two more hours until bedtime and the question of whether or not he was going to sleep began to quicken his pulse. He shouldn't have thought about that, but it was too late now. Wincing, he pushed harder at the pedals, trying to escape on the spot.

Birthdays made him think of Christmas and how, because December was also the important financial year-end, he had gradually made the choice to work through the month rather than taking his holidays at that time. It was all too much: getting the time off; arranging coverage; arranging a flight down east at the busiest time of the year. Like many long-distance relationships, his family in Ontario started failing to make his priority list. Eventually they caught on, sending cards and Christmas letters with no expectation of receiving anything in return. With the holidays phased out of the picture, it became easier to dedicate more of his time to work throughout all parts of the year. People came to anticipate his answers and stopped extending invitations.

"Stop!" David said aloud, exhaling as he did so. The technique calmed the storm for a moment, but the waves immediately regrouped to pound at him anew. "Stop!" he said again, but he heard the desperation in his own voice this time, thereby undermining his efforts.

Things were really rolling tonight—worse than they had been for some time. Before he could stop himself, he saw that the clock showed 7:32.

He was breathing too hard, unable to keep time: he was out of shape. Dismounting, David paced the main floor of the condo, hands on hips, feeling the sweat on his neck and back. Walking the main hallway, he stopped and stared at a sight that took him aback. The mail—days of it—was piled haphazardly in a shallow box near the front door. Most of his bills were auto-debited, so he wasn't afraid of the power cutting off, but Jesus: *you gotta get at that stack*, he chided himself.

And then he remembered why he'd started leaving it unopened in the first place.

The bill from the nursing home. The warehouse he kept his parents in. The sight of that pale brown envelope was enough to get the tension-ball rolling all by itself.

"Ah, Christ," David said, looking away from the mail and fighting down tears. A big, crashing wave hit the surf of his frontal lobe at the thought of Mr. and Mrs. Moore sitting in numb oblivion in that place with the television on but no one watching. They'd be in the common room now, after dinner, each locked in their own private little world. Cocooned: like passengers on a bus that never stopped.

Both parents—not just one, but both—had been stricken with premature dementia. What were the goddamn odds? They'd become gibbering, staring shells over the last few years, but they were still relatively young, still needed to eat, still needed to be housed and cared for. Paid for. David made damn good money as a Registered Investment Advisor Assistant, but keeping both his parents in long term care was a hell of a monthly nut.

Breathing out through his mouth, David climbed the stairs to his bedroom, turned on the computer. He thought idly of the web-cam girl he used to visit, but he'd found the practice counter-productive. Visiting and paying by the minute for the view had only made him feel lonelier, more nervous. He winced the thought away and opened a file entitled "Good Memories".

His therapist had suggested this: build a file of happy memories and accomplishments, and review it during times of stress. David scrolled through the fifty or so points, trying his best to relive them.

A spelling bee he'd won in the sixth grade. Province-wide in Ontario.

Moving to Calgary on his own; his first apartment.

Buying the condo with his own money. He hadn't always felt so...overwhelmed.

Lola.

Had she been a girlfriend? David still didn't know for sure. He'd met her at work—one of the few work relationships he'd ever had that transcended the office. He'd invited her to lunch, then drinks after work, then dinner. After a few weeks, she made the first move when he hadn't. They'd had a few...moments—David couldn't call the sessions "lovemaking" exactly, but he'd gone at the task with enthusiasm and what he hoped would be perceived as passion. But all that aside, she'd said something once that had always stuck with him. Something that had gotten her onto the "Good Memories" list.

"David, you're cute."

"Right," he'd said, looking down and away in that way that he had. "Moving on."

"I'm serious. I don't know what you see in that mirror of yours, but you're hot, mister. You are. It's crazy that you don't go out more. I mean...you're distant—I kind of get it now—but when people look at you—when girls look at you—they don't see what you do. Believe me. All you'd have to do is show up."

He hadn't believed her, but he'd always thought it was a nice thing for somebody to say to somebody else, for no money down.

A Tsunami crashed home, drowning out the memory of Lola, swamping the last of his fragile defenses.

The job kept his parents alive—killing David in the process—but nothing else he could do would come close to covering what he needed. And worse, the workplace also offered him escape. Like it or not, once at work, he could get overwhelmed with administrative trivia and for a few precious hours keep the anxiety at bay. And if a little work was therapeutic, then a lot of work could be downright anesthetic.

The math was inescapable.

I can't get on top of this, David thought. The computer clock told him it was 8:15, and his heart began to hammer. *That's it: I'm not sleeping tonight.* A heavy gust of wind rattled his windows, announcing one of Calgary's famous Chinooks. If it kept up all night, that would make achieving unconsciousness even harder.

Rising from his chair, David padded down to the kitchen, poured himself a glass of water and took a sleeping pill out of the cupboard. He didn't want to take it—was afraid to take it—but he had no choice. He needed to be up at 5:30 and catch the bus by 6:15. Calgary was two hours behind New York and that was just the cold hard truth of working in finance.

He swallowed the pill with a grimace and then reached for his gumshield. He was a terrible night-grinder, had had to have a special shield fitted for his teeth. Suddenly, David thought of the vampire and wondered what the hell *he'd* do in this situation. "Guy would bite the shit out of himself," David chuckled, thinking of the inconvenience of fangs.

Feeling like he'd diminished the vampire somewhat with the mouth-guard observation, David headed back to his E-Z chair in front of the television. He pulled a blanket over his legs and reclined, feeling his heart-rate start to ease. The TV would help: often he'd doze off in front of it when sleeping in his bed proved impossible. It was just enough distraction, just enough input to allow him to sidestep the worry.

Idly, David began flipping channels, lingering at something about sharks; moving on to black and white World War II footage; drifting past current news. He didn't want to fall asleep here, he just wanted to lull himself, trick himself into a peaceful state. When his attention wandered, that was good: he let it. He refused to look at the clock, so he was uncertain of exactly when it was that he first caught himself nodding...

That fog and snow, swirling at the bus-stop.

People rushing to-and-fro, even as the vampire emerges from the background with a weird sort of...refocusing. Like he's somehow been hiding in between those big, soft flakes of snow, there all along, in the gaps.

That smile. The blazing recognition of mutual perception.

The vampire reaching out with one arm, clothes-lining a man who doesn't seem to see the creature in front of him.

A succulent bite into the neck from behind, taking the man above his right shoulder. Lips forming an air-tight seal on skin.

A woman with astonishing, straight-backed posture talking on her cell phone as she walks not two feet past the scene, eyes never leaving the horizon.

The hideous gulping: David hearing it, somehow, from his seat inside the bus. Smelling the coppery tang of flowing blood.

The man sinking to the sidewalk—steam rising from the wet neck wound in the cold night air.

The vampire lifting his gaze from victim to David, slowly smiling once again, displaying sharp teeth cherry-coated in blood.

A banging as the bus pulls away from the curb.

A banging, and a tapping.

David awoke with a start. The windows were rattling in the wind as the Chinook pulled at the condo shingles, threatening to rip them out. He blinked in confusion, squinting groggily at the TV set.

What the hell? He thought.

That's not what happened.

That's not what happened, but...

David struggled to regain the images, sorting out what was real from what had been dream. The strange thing was that the dream imagery felt somehow stronger than what had actually occurred. Everything he'd dreamed seemed more vivid, more graphic, harder to dismiss as simply the effects of over-work.

As he sorted the images, categorizing them and reviewing them, he also tried to gather in the fleeting emotions he had been experiencing. Terror, certainly, when the vampire had acted with such ruthless efficiency.

But not terror alone.

Threading in and out through the terror was something like...excitement. Almost elation. A voyeuristic thrill—like seeing a webcam girl for the first time, only much more intense.

That didn't happen...but did I want it to? David thought.

I think I wanted it to.

I think I wished that's the way it had happened.

Because if the vampire had killed—made me hear the slurping, smell the blood—then that vampire's real.

And if vampires are real, anything's possible.

Anything is still possible for me.

David glanced up, accidentally catching sight of the clock: 9:45. "Shit," he said to the television set. It was definitely going to be a two-pill night.

David's first couple of bus-rides after the event were nerve wracking—anticipating another visit from the creature—but it didn't happen. By Wednesday morning he no longer flinched when the front door swished open to allow new passengers on board.

Work piled up as it always did, and David was thankful for it. The sheer weight of labour and time-pressure helped push thoughts of non-mission-critical monsters onto the sidelines. By Wednesday afternoon he knew he'd be staying late just to keep himself afloat. It was always the same calculation: work enough nights during the week and you might get the weekend off. More often than not, he worked the nights, and came in Saturday anyway. But the plan always worked in theory, and believing in the plan got him through to each Friday, week after week. Month after month. Year after year.

Thursday night, after the cleaning staff had come and gone, David ground out the paperwork his broker needed for the client meeting the next day. Opening brokerage accounts these days—in the wake of increasingly sophisticated criminal and terrorist activity—was no joke: serious preparation in advance needed to be done. This particular client had a family trust, and a corporate account to open as well—both tricky structures with plenty of complexity built in. David would be lucky to get out of his cubicle by nine o'clock.

He glanced through the doorway to his broker's office and saw that snow had begun drifting down outside the office window—stark white against the black night sky. He mumbled a curse, praying that it wouldn't turn into a blizzard: finding a cab was hard enough downtown.

His phone rang. On the display, he could see it was the hall security phone from the 16th floor elevator lobby, just outside the brokerage offices. Frowning, David picked up and said by rote, "Sanderson Advisory Group, David Moore speaking."

"David," the voice said. "Right. Buzz me in."

"Who..." David began, even as realization dawned.

"You know who. Or better yet, tell you what: bring your coat. Let's go for a walk."

"I'm...I'm going to call security. Right now."

"Do that. Then, after they grill you for the false alarm, get your coat. C'mon—take a break. Christ, if I was going to hurt you, you'd be hurt, brother. Seriously, take a look at your desk; what's there that can't wait thirty minutes while you chat with an honest-to-God vampire? Where the hell are your priorities?"

David hung up the phone, feeling nerve-endings tin-gling all over his body and sweat breaking out on his arms, legs, back. He swallowed, licked dry lips. Then he reached for his coat, heart drumming.

"It's beautiful, isn't it?" The vampire—who's name was Karl—said as he looked up.

They stood beneath a large monument that had been set up on Calgary's 8th Avenue outdoor mall. It was a bone-white, abstract tree design that reached almost two stories in height and fanned out to produce an alien-looking arboreal arch over the walkway. For December, an array of lights shone green, violet, crimson, and gold in slow procession, illuminating the ivory boughs. With the large flakes of snow drifting down through the gaps between 'branches', and the sky-scrapers on either side of the mall framing the scene, David had to admit that it was indeed beautiful.

"So. How long you been seeing vampires, David?"

"Umm...I...really, you're the first."

"Wow. You know what it means?"

"What? What does it mean?"

"Means you're just about ready to come over."

"Come over?"

"Come over. Be one of us. Means you're close—you just have to take the next step. You know, if you want."

"Are you going...?" David paused, throat suddenly constricted. "Are you going to...?"

"What? Turn you? David, vampires don't make vam-pires: people make vampires."

"What?"

"You choose. It's up to you. I'm just saying that for whatever reason, you're close enough now on your own that you can see us, talk with us. The rest is up to you."

"But why would I...why would anyone...?"

Karl chuckled, tilted his chin down into his scarf. "Let me guess, kid: you've been at your job since you got out of school. You had friends once, but they've drifted away, and anyway, you wouldn't have time—or wouldn't make

time—for them now if you had them. No girlfriend. No
boyfriend. You get to work in the dark; you go home in
the dark. You're too old to start over, too young to retire,
and you've built up too much momentum now to change,
so they've got you. Twelve, thirteen, fourteen hours a day?
Then you go home, drug-up, try to get some sleep before
the sun rises and then you do it all over again? Jesus, David,
you're more undead than I am."

"But...but how, Karl? How is this done? I don't
understand...and why here?"

"What, instead of some Romanian castle?" Karl snorted.
"Far as I can tell, Calgary's the perfect town for this to
happen. City never ages—nothing's older than 1970—
everything gets rebuilt every ten years. There's nothing
to remind people of any other era or reality, nothing to
distract them from the 'now' of their mortgages and their
jobs and their lives."

Karl began to pace, gesturing with his right hand, squinting as he gathered his thoughts. "It's more than that,
though. It's almost like...like it's the shape of the buildings
here—the rushed-up glass and steel; the vibrations the
Chinook wind sets up blowing through the streets; the hiss
of the C-train at night; the pace and rhythm of life here,
tapping and banging out some kind of code. It's almost
like the city's set up to sing us into being...or something.
Generate us, somehow. Maybe before now vampires were
just myths; maybe we can only be real right here, right now.
I think the seeds may have been planted hundreds of years
ago and thousands of miles away, but it's only now that
those seeds can bear real fruit.

"But I don't know—I'm no scientist, kid. All I know is
people don't see us because they can't see us. Not until
they get tired, David, lose their focus. And even then, not
everyone sees what you can see. We're free, brother. There's
no Van Helsing, no rules, no rhyme or reason. No one
knows to come after us. Freedom. That's why you do it.
Or, you know: stay at your desk, hope for a stroke to end
your misery suddenly before too many more years pass...
Whatever you like. Ask me, it's not much of a choice, D."

David stared at the snow on the ground, listening to the traffic in the distance. "What would I have to do?" he said quietly.

"Blood, baby. You know what vampires do: you got to do it to be it."

David felt the cold reaching through his coat, finding him as the breeze picked up. After a moment, he said, "I've got to be getting back."

"Yeah," Karl whispered. "That paperwork ain't going to do itself."

Friday went well.

The client and his wife came in, got their personal accounts out of the way, and then dug into the corporation and trust. David had explained the need for the settlor of the trust—a third party who had not attended the meeting—to provide photo ID in this era of rampant fraud, and the clients—much to David's relief—hadn't squawked. They also cooperated when David told them he'd need to see last year's tax return for the holding company—to prove its continued existence. Little details like that could derail a signing and, even though it wouldn't have been David's fault, he would've been held accountable. A multi-million dollar account had hinged on the unpredictable reactions of clients who didn't understand legalities and didn't care much about them. David had been burned by irrational reactions before, and every complex account held the potential for such setbacks; every new relationship introduced variables beyond his control, putting David on the brink of catastrophic failure.

Hence the sleeping pills.

But Friday had gone well. At least until 2:33 PM, when David's boss shot him an email:

"i just talked to stela jonson she says she didnt get her monthly eft amount yesterday???????? how the fuck does that happn. get yr head out of your ass......send the money"

David stared at the screen: *how the fuck does that happn.* how the fuck does that happn?

It happens because I'm fucking exhausted, you illiterate bastard, thought David.

David's cubicle was a few feet away from his broker's office and the open door. They could just have spoken, but they rarely did: all communication was via email. David had long since stopped saving the abusive emails with an eye towards launching some kind of complaint: assistants never won those battles, but they could—and did—lose them big. David breathed in deep through his nose, counted to seven.

And Karl came around the corner.

"Jesus!" David said aloud. Behind him, one of the other assistants glanced up from her computer screen, confused by the outburst. "What're you...how did you get in?"

"I waited at the door, somebody let me in. You don't look so hot. Late night?"

"You know it was."

"So. What do you figure?"

"David?" The girl behind him spoke up. David ignored her as though she was the thing no one else could see.

"What do you mean?" David said, his mouth suddenly dry.

"Come on now. Blood, baby. Blood."

David swallowed. In his peripheral vision, the white wall to his right seemed to flex and warp, then snap back into place with an un-wall-like plasticity. Glancing at his desk, he saw a large, polished granite paperweight that held two pens and a brass-plate inscribed: *DAVID MOORE, COMMITMENT TO EXCELLENCE AWARD WINNER, 1999.* Karl saw the glance, lifted his eyebrows.

"That would do," Karl said quietly, eyes blazing. "For a start."

David stood and picked up the paperweight. The wall bowed again, and his desk seemed to ripple, momentarily disorienting him. His face felt hot—almost feverish. He braced himself on his heels, uncertain of his balance. The paperweight was heavy, broader than his palm. He hefted it, breathed in deep through his nose. Then he left his cubicle, crossing the few feet to his broker's office.

Mr. Cavanaugh looked up from behind his desk with a scowl. To his right: his computer screen; beside that: a classy black and white headshot of his much younger wife. "Not now..." he snarled, but David never broke stride.

Rounding the desk, David took the granite plank in both hands, raised it back behind his right shoulder, then swept it down and across, shattering the orbital bone of his broker's left eye with the crisp wet crunch of snapping celery. The man rocked back in his swivel chair, whining as blood bubbled from the vicious gash.

Karl came to the doorway, crossing his arms, and leaning against the frame.

David pulled his arms back then struck again.

Then again.

Mr. Cavanaugh slid from his chair, sprawling on the carpet as Cindy Carswell began to scream.

"Better hurry, David," Karl said. "Drink and cross over. They're coming."

David reeled, feeling the room swaying around him as though the ground beneath his feet was shifting. He could *feel* himself crossing; it was happening. The world was tilting.

All he needed to do now was drink.

David knelt—his knees sounding out with a loud, sclerotic popping—and got down on all fours, straddling Mr. Cavanaugh's hips. The man's eyelids twitched, and his breath came in rapid, panting gasps. David hesitated, hearing the sound of running footsteps, and then leaned in closer, pushing his face into Cavanaugh's throbbing neck.

I don't have fangs, David thought as he fixed mouth to throat and realized how difficult this would be.

"They're coming, D. Choose."

David bit as hard as he could. Then he started working on the area, gnawing at it, because chewing through raw, living flesh was not easy. He went at it with persistence, with grim determination—the same traits he had once employed in an attempt to satisfy Lola. She may well have been faking her reaction, but Mr. Cavanaugh wasn't: David tasted blood and swallowed, then began gulping as the horrid wound pulsed with flow.

Men rushed in, grabbing at David's shoulders and waist, heaving him off.

Blows fell, kicks were delivered: David was pushed onto his back and held down; familiar, but terrorized faces loomed above him as screams filled the office.

"They still see me!" David bellowed. He felt the wet warmth upon his face, knew he must look a sight—worse than forgetting to shave. "They still see me! I drank! I drank! You said I would cross over!"

"I did say that, didn't I?" Karl called out over the shrill sounds of rage and panic. "Yeah...what I really meant though, I guess, is that *I* would be crossing over. Listen, David: you've been a big help—*huge!*—and I'm not going to forget this. This blood sacrifice here? I can almost taste it myself David—I'm stronger for it. These clowns all gaping at you now? They're all thinking the word 'vampire', and that word is making me stronger. You're gonna be in all the papers buddy—helping to shape people's minds for a new reality—and when enough people's minds are the right shape? I'm coming on through, D. Believe it. And when I'm all the way real, I'll come back for you. I will. Your despair has not been in vain, brother. No pun intended."

David's shrieks grew incoherent as he struggled against his captors. Karl stepped backwards out of the office, straightened his scarf and watched as David was secured then roughly hoisted to his feet. Karl glanced to his left— across the expanse of cubicles—then did a double take.

One of the assistants was staring at him; directly at him. She could see him.

Her name was Ellen Anders; she was thirty-seven, and already a little tired. Not as tired as David had been, but she'd do.

Karl smiled, and made reassuring eye contact.

Outside, a strong Chinook blew a hard, hot wind down 8th avenue, and the city purred as though caressed.

Come to Me
By Heather Clitheroe

The thought comes to her so suddenly one day that it's painful even to think it. But gradually, she comes back to it, turning the thought over in her mind and gently probing it, as one might touch an aching tooth. Tentatively, carefully. Half expecting it to hurt, yet shocked at the white hot flash that lances through everything. Even good intentions.

I am going to walk into the forest, Jane thinks. *And never come out.* The voice is, at the same time, not her own and only her own. She does not know where it has come from. Only that it is there, in her mind, and she cannot forget.

It's simple to say these words to herself, simple to feel them just below the surface of the monologues that run through the days. *Running out of orange juice. That man smells bad. I miss Vauxhall. I want to walk into the forest and never come out.* And she stops, startled and surprised, jarred out of complacency and half-stunned by the force of it. *That's a stupid thing to think. That's just stupid.*

It returns to her, again and again, and she finds herself saying the words to herself as she walks from her apartment to the little office where she works during the day. *I am. Going. To walk into. The forest. And never. Come out.* The words flutter against her consciousness in time to the click of her heels on the sidewalk, and she tucks her head down, blinking her eyes furiously. *Never come out. Never come out. Never come out.*

She leaves for work early in the mornings, before the neighbours start to leave for their own jobs. Early in the morning, with the sun just rising, she can lengthen her stride and almost imagine she is back home instead of in a country where courtesy demands smaller steps, with arms held to one's sides so they won't swing freely.

...*into the forest*...

She remembers that there was a time, once, when she loved Japan. She brought her well-worn copy of *Neuromancer* with her, and revelled in the frenetic pace of life, the crowd, the exotic smells from the little vendors lining the streets in Shinjuku. She imagined herself in the pages of the story. Those days, she was glad to leave tiny Vauxhall—the short main street with the farm supply store at one end and the fire station at the other, the flat horizon that stretched out and away until it met the sky. She was glad to go, leaving for university; she studied languages. As many as she could. French. Russian. Chinese. And then Japanese. The Japanese department helped her find the job in Tokyo, and she left the skies of Alberta behind her. Long behind her.

...*and never*...

She remembers that Japan seemed so exciting. She took a flat away from the usual ex-pat haunts, choosing to live in a tiny room above a smoke shop, smiling to herself every time she passed under the large sign that read *tobaccoo*. Mr. Narita, her boss, was what she expected...so typically the salaryman. She still enjoys the work, translating legal documents into English, and the English into Japanese. She makes enough to pay the rent, to buy a bicycle, and to take trips to the countryside on her days off. She learned Japanese folk tales, developed a taste for manga. For a few years, she knows, she was young and Japan was exciting.

She remembers these things, but vaguely, as she recalls a film she watched the week before.

She thinks she might have been happy once. Not now. She has come to see that the polish wears thin. She developed asthma. Gained fifteen pounds. Mr. Narita started to drink in his office, barking orders to the staff and then began to drop hints about the economy and money.

The sky is overcast, and the wind is dull; she misses the biting cold of the prairie winters and the vivid blue skies, when the air is so icy it stings the eyes and freezes tears. Jane knows she could go back to Vauxhall...or

Calgary, maybe. Toronto. But the defeat she'd have to admit feels too great to even admit to herself. *I'm not tired of living in Japan*, she thinks. *I'm just tired of living.*

And then she stops herself. *That's no way to think.*

The days seem so dull now that she feels immersed in a monochromatic world, one that always smell of cabbage and vomit, and where she is always too tall, too gawky. Too different. *I want to walk into the forest.*

She walks a little faster, her heels now stomping against the pavement that has been hosed down in the pre-dawn light so that the noise of her feet on the cement sounds fake; altered. *A Foley track.*

And then she sees something. Something makes her lift her head and look sharply to the left where she is suddenly quite certain…it's a fox! There, yes…a small fox, running swiftly through an alleyway, richest red, and black whiskered. It stops to look over its shoulder at her. A fox with amber eyes that could know her, she thinks, could know her aching emptiness and the dullness. *There are no foxes in Tokyo.* No, but she's so certain, so filled with a longing to get closer to it.

She changes direction, turning down an alleyway and breaking into a run, her breath catching in her throat until she is forced to stop, coughing, bent over with the exertion. *There are no foxes in Tokyo.*

She is standing in front of the train station. The wise thing to do—the proper thing to do—would be to turn back down the alleyway and go to work. Mr. Narita won't arrive until eight o'clock, at least, and he'll be so hung over he will hardly notice if she's a little late. She has work to do; legal contracts for an offshore client that are due…due when? Soon. At the end of the week.

For a moment, though, the veil lifts, and the words swell inside her. The train station is in front of her, and it is hammering away at her soul. *I will walk into the forest, and I will never come out again.*

She buys a ticket for Otsuki, gets on the train, the orange train. The one that will take her west, out of the city and away from the cramped apartment, the drunken boss, and the crowds.

She changes trains in Otsuki, this time the Fujikyuko Line heading west. West, west, towards Mount Fuji. The sun has risen now, and the trains that pass, heading east, are full and she turns away from them, looking instead at her hands in her lap. *What am I doing?* But the veil has settled over her again, and she is looking through gauze, a sour taste in her throat. *I'll be fired for sure.* She does not care.

In Kawaguchiko Station, she stops a moment to look at the sky—the wide open sky—and the thought is so overpowering that she barely hears herself asking to buy a bus ticket for the forest. "One ticket, please," she says. "For Aokigahara."

The trees here mass together, so that when the wind blows, they move as one. In this sea of trees, this *jukai*, all drops away: the sounds of the world are swallowed up, the air is thick and heavy, the silence unbroken but for the gentle murmur of leaves and the creak of branches rubbing one against the other. It is dark, always, in this forest. They say it is haunted. They say it is where people come to kill themselves. They call it the suicide forest.

She has heard this before, on the late night variety shows that turn to the supernatural. Spirits walk in this forest, she knows, or at least that is what she has heard. But the words are still pulsing in her, and through the indistinct fog that she finds herself in, she is walking behind a group of tourists into the forest. They are stopping, taking pictures of the signs along the path. *Don't do it*, one reads. *Think of your parents and your family. Try counselling first. Please reconsider.* She gazes at the signs dully, and walks on, past the tourists and into the forest, stepping off the path and disappearing into the black, silent wood.

As she walks, she tries to think. She tries to reason with herself, but her thoughts are half-formed and clumsy, as though she has had something strong to drink. She pushes on, through the beech trees, her clothes soaked with dew. She shivers, but does not stop. She is searching for the fox, turning her head this way and that, peering through the undergrowth and looking beneath the masses of tree roots that cause her to stumble.

And then, in the shadows, she sees it. The fox, running lightly along a fallen tree. She stops and watches dumbly as it turns to look at her. She catches her breath, afraid to cough, to move. In the dim light she can see the fox watching her too, and it stops, settling on its haunches to consider her. It turns its head to one side; one amber eye gazes at her unblinkingly.

Jane takes a step forward before she realizes what she is doing. The words that have been inside her head these many days suddenly rise to a thunderous crescendo, blasting a channel through the fog, and the veil rolls back again. Her nose fills with the smells of the forest: the clear air, the dampness of the earth beneath her, the lush, heady aroma of sun-warmed leaves and the acrid tang of rot. She is alive, gloriously alive in a way that she has not been for the longest time, and the colours around her are vivid and glowing and she feels a fullness of purpose in the words that have plagued her. "I have walked into the forest," she whispers.

She blinks. Where the fox was, a woman now sits. A tall, lithe woman with a long, narrow face and amber eyes, with blackest hair hanging loose about her shoulders. The kimono she wears is old, mouldering, but...beautiful. It cannot be described as anything but that, for it is the richest red that Jane has ever seen. Spun silk glints and ripples, shot with gold and embroidered with white flowers. The woman stares at her with her head cocked. "So you have," she says.

Again Jane steps forward, again her body moving ahead of her thoughts, a vessel empty of will. "I..."

The fox woman sighs. "I called you," she says.

"Why?"

"I live here." Simply, as though nothing else matters.

"I heard in my head," Jane says. "To come. Then I saw a fox."

"You saw me."

"I saw a fox. In the street. Nobody sees a fox in the street. But then I wanted...to come here. And walk into the forest.

This forest...they say this forest is haunted. They say demons walk among the trees."

The woman rises, stretching, and cocks her head to the other side. "They are not so very wrong about that."

"But you are not afraid?"

"I am not afraid."

"This makes no sense," says Jane, and she takes another step forward. Now that she is closer to the woman, she can see the jewelled pearls in her hair winking in the weak light.

"Even the bravest do not care to walk into this forest alone," says the woman. "And so I call."

And now the woman is smiling, and Jane can see that her lips glisten, that her teeth are white and even, glowing as the pearls glow, with a lustre that would sound like a tinkling bell, were there to be a sound at all.

"There was a time when I searched, when I walked the streets of Chiba. They called me a demon even then." And she laughs. "I made myself to be a whore." And now she reaches out a hand, adopting a hungered expression, lips parting slightly, her head bending forward so that her hair falls forward to cover her cheeks. "It is easy enough. I had no need to call except with my body." And she straightens, haughty and proud once more. "But I tire of the city. As you tire of the city."

Jane is aware of something else now—that her heart is thudding very fast in her chest; she feels its frantic, squeezing beat.

The woman is standing in front of her, touching her face, and Jane lifts her chin to look up into the woman's eyes. She smells perfume: a woody musk, sweet and threaded with the scent of freesia and white lily.

"I come here instead," the woman says. "I was nameless once. Before I was *kitsune*, I had a name. I remember it—how can a creature forget her own name? The sound of it on my lips is alien to me. Only sounds. Not a true name. But when the hunger took me, and I was scalded by the daylight; I came to think of myself as the fox. And before long, I *was* the fox. My nature, known only to me."

The woman leans forward to whisper in Jane's ear. "I am the fox demon."

Jane's body is not her own. It will not move. She stands very still, even as her memory recalls the stories. First of the fox, the demons of Japan, the demons that take the soul and feed upon it, and she thinks *but it was only a story, stories aren't true, they never are.* Then she is thinking of the forest where...where people come to kill themselves. They walk into the forest. *That's what they say.* Even as she is thinking this, the fox woman, the *kitsune,* has let the kimono fall from her shoulders, and within Jane there is a rising fear, a terror mounting itself as she feels the woman tugging at her jacket, pulling it open.

"I call for you," the fox woman breathes. "I possess you, Jane, your soul. Your body. You come to me."

She is touching Jane now, first cupping one breast and then the other with cold hands, and Jane cannot move, cannot breathe, can only watch the fox woman bending down, the pearls in her hair glowing all the brighter as she kisses her chest. Within the terror, there is more. Gone is the apartment in Tokyo, the sour smell of Mr. Narita as he tries to brush up against her, the overcast skies and the rain. All of it, gone.

Her heart beating, she stands in the forest—the sea of black trees where men come to kill themselves, and she knows in her heart that they do not come except as they are called, and she imagines them standing naked in the darkest wood in front of the fox woman, as Jane stands now, bound and unmoving.

The fox woman lifts her head to gaze at Jane once more, and Jane is filled with longing, and a desire that cannot be her own, must not be her own, and yet...

And now her arms, freed, are her own again, and she clings to the fox woman, wanting to draw closer to her, wanting to shout with desire and frustration, but only a whimper and a whisper in her throat. "*Onegai shimasu,*" she whispers, "*dakishimetai.*" *Please. Hold me.*

And the fox woman smiles in triumph. She presses her cold lips to Jane's, and Jane can feel the fox woman's hands on her stomach reaching for her. With the pleasure, there is more—so very much more—and again Jane thinks she would shout with desire in a way she has never shouted before, but she is so very tired, so tired…and then there is pain, and now the fox woman is kissing her neck—*kissing my neck, not kissing but biting oh I want you to kiss me but not like this oh no not like this but please don't stop…*

The fox woman lifts her head. Jane can see the blood on her lips, and now, finally now, she can give herself to the desire, for the fox woman has returned desire to her, as she is taking her life from her. "I have you," she says, and her amber eyes catch the light. "You have come to me."

It is in these last moments that she dreams of the prairie winds. *I would have liked to feel them just once more,* she thinks. *Just once more.* And she wavers. Then, she slips quietly beneath the surface of the sea of dark trees, dragged down by the weight of the *kitsune,* the smell of the damp, decaying wood engulfing her, entering her, filling her.

There is a last, fleeting memory of a bright, wide sky; of racing down the highway in an old pickup truck to catch the sunrise on an endless horizon; of canola and wheat fields nodding under the August sun; of the clean smell of new snow… And then—the stink of rot in the darkness and the whisper of leaves, the fox woman's mutterings.

Come back, Jane begs, desperate to hold onto the distant call of the prairie…*please, come to me…*

An Ember Amongst the Fallen
By Colleen Anderson

Shadows fluttered from the corners as Buer bit in just above the fine lines of the wrist and sucked. Only five swallows. No overindulgence before the dinner party, but that was much later. The blonde male, lightly haired and slim, twitched but held still, his blood warm and slightly tart. Buer avoided the bull's stare and looked around the pen at the other beasts. He liked to keep the cattle clean and ready to drink at any point.

Some liked the taste better when the cattle fought but Buer found it made the blood acrid, sour upon the tongue and sometimes it stung going down. He preferred them docile, easy to subdue. The *Book of the Fallen* expressly forbade cruelty to or treating cattle as more than the meat and blood for which they were bred. Unpredictable, they could turn suddenly. Yet, if it wasn't for their musky smell and the rhythmic thump of their speedy hearts, they could almost pass as vampirii. It was their gazes that bothered Buer most.

He shuddered and licked the wound to help it close, then dropped the arm, smelling the tang of oniony sweat. He checked the other stock in the wood planked enclosure, the skylight now closed. The cattle liked sunlight and earthen tones and it was the one area of his condo that was not sleek metallic with black and blue accents. A plump white female steeped with red wine; every half hour a cup of pinot dripped into her bowl. A slimmer male paced in front of his white wine bowl. Buer pulled the list from his pocket and checked the time. He'd have to order the rest of the stock while at work. One calf still needed for the scotch. A fresh brown female raised on grains and exotic spices for the dinner. Oh yes, he had better grab a few rabbits for Jeanine. She was still adhering to her distasteful fad.

As he rolled down the sleeves of his white shirt, he locked the pen behind him, then looked in the fridge. There was enough cattle feed for later. Some flowers, an extra bottle or two of wine and he'd be set for the party. He pulled on the encompassing coat, the leather gloves, his shades and the wide-brimmed fedora.

He hated this season. Even with the protective clothing, he often itched at high summer. But it couldn't be avoided if he wanted to keep his job. Squinting, he hurried into the late afternoon sun and off to the lab.

Ronobe and Sammael barely noticed when Jeanine arrived, their hands entwined like hibernating snakes. Mystery slithered and slid about them, but Sammael only looked up long enough to accept the bloodwine that Buer offered.

Jeanine kissed Buer's cheek and handed him a bottle. "Hello, my dears. Here, pour me a pure glass."

Buer took the bottle as Jeanine turned to Ronobe and Sammael. "Honestly, you two act like you just met. What's with you?"

Buer shook his head as he went to the kitchen. The troughs held the white, freckled cow and a pale bull slumped and tethered beside each other on a large Naugahyde pad. He found Arkon drinking white bloodwine from the wrist of the bull. Arkon raised a black, winged eyebrow at Buer and smiled. "Sorry, I just wanted to see what you had on tap."

"Riesling from the Alsace region." Buer held up a bottle of sauvignon blanc. "I could pour you a glass of pure that Jeanine brought, or you could wait twenty while it decants." He popped the cork onto the mottled grey marble counter and tilted his head at Arkon.

"No, go ahead and decant it. I'll take a glass from this one." Arkon reached for a goblet on the counter and with an elegant, sharp nail punctured a vein in the male's arm; bloodwine dripped into the glass. The pale skinned bull rolled onto his side, snoring. Arkon licked closed the wound and watched Buer open the enclosure door and hook up the IV to a mesmerized calf in the first cage inside. The calves never liked the alcohol but their smaller bodies distilled it faster.

Buer checked the main course and the desert. The cow— exuding enough pungent cardamom, cumin and anise that it wafted off her sweating body—was riding the plump male bull. An astoundingly beautiful cow with long coils of honey gold hair stood nearby sipping from her bowl of port and watching wide-eyed. Buer had picked her and the port up as a last minute item to complement dessert. The pen would be well stocked for the next month. He had always found rutting cattle disconcerting but it kept them content. The hominid similarity was evident. Sometimes the Fallen didn't seem much different from their distant cousins.

Arkon said over his shoulder, "Do you really think you have a chance with her?"

Buer started, then turned and shut the door.

He put a pale hand upon Arkon's shoulder and walked back with him into the living room done in black with brushed silver and blue trim. "I haven't been able to forget about her for ten years. I have to try one last time."

Arkon just shook his head. "Give it up, my man. There are plenty to choose from. Besides, we're not meant for lasting relationships."

Jeanine, short spiky hair, model-poised in lavender, stood at the window staring into the night. She was as pale as the moon's face. Buer handed her a glass of pure wine as the buzzer sounded.

The last guest called out as she entered in a swirl of emerald silk. "I hope you weren't waiting on me." Where many of the Fallen were willowy, she was all curves. Petite, with long, straight auburn hair, she had caught Buer's eye and heart the first time he saw her. They'd spent fifty years together, thirty of them tempestuous, but in the end her restlessness and his timidity had pushed the wedge between them. Like many vampirii, they learned to live with past loves being underfoot. There were always exceptions though.

Buer smiled and drew Camiel to the kitchen. "Not at all, my dear. We're just settling in. I'll bring out the main course soon. White or red?"

"You should know." She smiled at him and he punctured the freckled cow's wrist holding a goblet under the drip. The bloodwine slowly flowed in as Buer asked, "How are you? I haven't seen you in quite a while."

Camiel had opened the door and peeked into the pen. "Oooh, that looks delicious." She turned back, smoothing the green dress that outlined her exquisite body. "I'm good. Busy. Been flying to Paris and London a lot."

Buer had to look away, feeling his desire tighten his scrotum. "That's good. You still like the job?"

She shrugged. "So far. I think I'm good for another twenty before I'll try a new career. Still, I like the benefits of free travel."

He handed her the glass. "Go ahead. I'm going to get dinner ready."

As Camiel walked into the living room, Buer stepped back to the pen and found the cow sleeping. He unlocked the cage and picked her up. She stirred but didn't wake. Laying her in the center trough of the table, he took a moment to clip her black hair short so it wouldn't get into the food. As he walked into the dining room he called, "Dinner's on."

They took their spots around the table, each person sitting into the scooped out spot that allowed close proximity to the hominid. A shallow blue porcelain bowl, with knife, spoon and fork sat beside each plate. Jeanine, so pale her blue veins threaded beneath her skin like lace, hung back, a look of disgust crossing her face.

Arkon rolled his bright blue eyes. "Don't tell me you're still on with this nutty thing about not eating hominids."

"It's not a fad, Arkon," she snapped back. "Can you say there is any difference between one of these and us?"

Camiel said softly as she sniffed the cow's arm. "Hmmm, they smell tastier. And it's brown."

Janine sat near the cow's feet, pulling at her sleeve. "Buer's wine vessels are as white as you and me."

Even Ronobe pulled her gaze from Sammael's angular face and dark intense eyes. She turned, solemnly saying, "Well, let's see, my dear. They lead short lives if left to the pasture. They can tolerate daylight. They don't seem to be able to talk—"

"That's not necessarily true. Primate studies have shown that they can be taught rudimentary language, even make some sounds amongst themselves. All primates show an understanding of sign language, and hominids can be taught simple tasks." She sipped her wine.

Ronobe laughed. "Until they turn on you. They're unpredictable."

Jeanine's lips thinned as Buer handed the long curved knife to Arkon. "Would you do the honors?" To Jeanine, he said, "I don't know, even dogs growl at each other. That doesn't mean they're intelligent. Besides, it doesn't seem right."

Arkon stood and the scraping of the chair awakened the cow. She looked around and started to sit. Buer grasped her head between his hands, staring into her wide eyes. She subsided again, looking dazed. He laid her back in the trough and sat between Jeanine and Camiel. The cow stared at the ceiling, mouth slack and open like a roseate flower. "All right," he said.

Arkon deftly cut into the jugular. The cow twitched and blood pulsed out of her gaping throat while she thrashed weakly. She gurgled for a few moments as blood threaded into the trough. Arkon had already sliced from belly to ribcage as she shuddered her last. "Preferences? Camiel?"

"Oooh, how sweet, first choice. I'd like the heart please." She dipped her finger in the trough and licked some of the blood from her finger. "Delicious."

Arkon deftly skewered the heart and put it on her plate. She ladled some blood onto her meat. He continued to cut the delicacies for each person: tongue, liver and eyes for Ronobe and Sammael.

The fad of the century was to eat meat with the blood, for its nutritive properties, but the lovers immediately played a game of passing an eye back and forth from mouth to mouth, kissing until one of them bit down, filling their mouths with juices as they both laughed. They looked like children with the red smears over their mouths and chins, which they licked away.

Buer went back to the kitchen and returned with a calmed rabbit. As he handed it to Jeanine, he said to Ronobe and Sammael, "What's with you two? You're acting as giddy as kids."

Ronobe, her hair a froth of wheaten curls, smiled as she chewed a piece of tongue, wiping at the blood that dribbled from one corner of her mouth. She pointed the fork at Buer and said, "Can't tell. Well...maybe at dessert."

Arkon, sitting across from Jeanine, made a show of eating the brain, smacking his lips and slurping blood noisily, but he spit the meaty bits out, having never been one to follow the current fad of eating flesh. "Hmm, are you sure you wouldn't want a piece of this? Very tasty. Spicy, hint of sweet. That mangy animal can't possibly taste good." Jeanine had broken the neck of the rabbit and delicately scooped only the blood with a teaspoon.

"I made my choice, Arkon. I'm happy with it. I can't drink hominids anymore. It's like eating a crippled cousin."

Buer sighed and shook his head as he cut into the thigh. She'd always found causes but had stayed with this the longest. "Next thing you know you'll be dressing them up in cute little suits and taking them to market with you. It's unseemly." Buer sipped the thick, heady bloodwine. It was a good mix, the fine wine and the pedigree of the cow. The bull with the white bloodwine had come from the same ranch.

Jeanine shook her head, her hair making her look a bit like a sunburst. "Please, Buer, there are limits. Some day, they may evolve into intelligent creatures. They do like to cook their food and use tools, and have been trained to work the fields in the last century. The anthropologists think we may have a common link."

"Sure," white-haired Sammael added, playing with Ronobe's curls. "If you believe the *Book of the Fallen*, then God sent Lucifer and his kind here where these hominids already lived, made in his image. But if that's the case, does God also look like a snake, a cat, an elephant?"

Jeanine shook her head. "You have to separate myth from scientific fact. Studies in language and primate behavior show similarities between vampirii and other hominids. Besides, God is known as the Great Deceiver."

Camiel's feral smile showed the tips of her fangs as she chewed through another chunk of heart. Of all of them, she took the greatest delight in eating as much meat as blood. "Be careful, my dear. Next thing you know you'll want to fuck the beasts."

Ronobe choked on a mouthful of liver. Silence fell over the table and Buer gulped down the rest of his bloodwine. Even Arkon had stopped chatting, staring wide-eyed at Camiel.

Jeanine sat as still as an ice sculpture, her spoon in hand as her face suffused with a pink luster. Then she turned toward Camiel and growled. "You have always been a self-indulgent bitch, Camiel, but I never thought you'd stoop to such horrific thoughts. Are you really so base as to not be able to discern the difference between an animal that shows possible forms of communication and intelligence and having to smear it with insinuations of bestiality? You disgust me."

Buer stood suddenly. "Ladies, please. This is supposed to be a pleasant dinner among friends. Does anyone want more? If not, I'll clear this away and bring out the dessert. Ronobe? Sammael? No. Anyone else?"

Jeanine still glared at Camiel who smiled and ate the rest of her heart. Camiel wiped her lips, which remained a deep lustrous red that Buer desperately wanted to kiss, working his way to her ample cleavage with love bites. He could still taste her cool, porcelain flesh after all these years.

He cleared his throat and unlatched the center trough, pulling the leftover meat into the cold storage pantry. There was enough for tomorrow's lunch. He drained the blood into containers, which he stored in the refrigerator. Then he brought the plump dessert bull from the pen. Mesmerizing it, he laid it in another trough and brought it to the table. Camiel had cleared the plates and filled two decanters of bloodwine.

Buer went back and tapped the vein of the calf for the rest of the white wine, and then brought out the cow filled with port. She meekly followed him and he tethered her in the living room near the gas fireplace, her amber skin shining in the fake firelight. She sat on the cushion and he left one of the others to mesmerize her while he went back for port glasses. "Help yourselves," he called into the icy silence still pervading the room.

He sighed and took a shot of scotch off of the other calf in the pen. Closing his eyes, he let the fiery drink singe him. Camiel always caused cold wars. But it was that coolness that had drawn him. How he wanted her.

Back in the living room, Ronobe and Sammael clasped each other's hands, sitting tensely on the edge of the sapphire blue couch, too wound up to taste desert.

Arkon bit into one of the fingers, while Camiel fed on the opposite arm. Jeanine just sat back nursing her pure wine. Buer tasted from the bull's ankle and then poured port from the cow for everyone. She lay on her side as if asleep. He had to remember to feed the cattle the iron rich paste before he went to bed. But later.

"Okay," Buer said. "What is it?"

Sammael glanced at Ronobe and nodded. Ronobe bit her lip, uncharacteristically hesitant. "Well, we know you might find this a shock, but we've been talking about this for years now." She paused as everyone sat looking puzzled. "We've decided to have a baby."

"What!" Jeanine blurted, looking even paler. "But—"

"Yes." Lean Sammael smiled. "We'll die."

Camiel shook her head, her brow creasing. "But why? Don't you enjoy life?"

Sammael smoothed back his nearly white hair. His unwrinkled face was as ageless as always. "When you have lived as long as I have, it...pales after a while. I have wanted a child for the last century."

Ronobe smiled. "I wasn't ready then. But we've activated our cycles now. It's exciting. The future has suddenly taken on a more intense hue."

Arkon just shook his head. "But your child won't get a chance to—"

"To what?" Sammael asked. "Our child will get a chance to continue the line or live forever, whatever it chooses."

Ronobe replied, "You forget. We all forget. Our parents did the same and were around for as much as a century after our births. And the sex is somehow...stronger."

Buer shrugged, looking at Camiel. Would she ever want a child? Ronobe and Sammael each had to trigger their reproductive tracts, which would kick in the aging genes: Nature's control over the vampirii. Only an idiot started the process without a willing mate. Buer swallowed his bloodport and poured another, thick and purple.

Camiel glanced over and licked the rim of her glass. "Well, I wasn't going to announce this now but I can't let you two have all the fun." She pulled out an intricately carved silver moon on a chain. "I'm engaged."

Buer didn't hear the rest. The walls and chairs sucked away the sound. Everyone in the room seemed to recede. Mouths moved, motions slowed. What now? Camiel had been his beacon. She must care deeply if she was willing to marry whoever it was. Few vampirii bothered anymore. He would have bothered. Should have.

Numb, Buer saw Jeanine to the door, followed shortly by Arkon. He grabbed Camiel's arm as she swirled toward the door. "Are you sure about this?" At her look he elaborated. "I mean, I was hoping perhaps we could try again."

Camiel's laugh was more a short bark. She ran her fingers over her jaw. "It was fun, Buer, but you're too tame. You always follow the rules." Then she was gone. Out of his life.

He downed a couple more glasses of port and then shooed Ronobe and Sammael out, saying he'd clean up, congratulating them one more time, trying to smile before he locked the door.

He turned back and surveyed the room. The limpid sun was rising, its weak light barely penetrating the darkened glass of the apartment. In the light of the flickering flames, Buer flopped onto the couch. The bull still slumbered on the desert table, and the cow was sprawled to the right of the fireplace. He drank the rest of his bloodport. What would he do now? Follow more rules?

Buer stumbled to and fro from the kitchen, clearing glasses and dishes. He entered the pen several times and poured several large shots of bloodscotch until the calf showed signs of convulsing if he drained any more. He put the bull back in the pen and left some food for the animals.

Stumbling back to the living room, he pulled the curtains closed, took off his shirt and lay on the couch, every once in a while lifting his head enough to swallow more bloodscotch. When the glass was empty, he let it tumble to the wood floor as he rolled off the couch. He crawled over to the cow and bit into a limp wrist.

His mind fogged. He flipped over and found his head on a thigh. Kneading it, he bit into soft inner flesh, his fingers working upward. A quiet gasp reached him. Encouraged him.

Sucking some heady port blood, he closed his eyes and lapped, moving up to the juncture. With a moan, small hands grasped at his hair.

Camiel, always so lovely, so cool. He'd show her he could break rules!

But now she was heated. Her legs spread. He slithered up, his pants being pushed off. Nuzzling her neck, he bit lightly and slid slowly into her. She responded, moaning, wrapping her hands in his hair, her legs about his back, pulling him further in.

Buer groaned. "Camiel." His hands cupped her breasts and he moved rhythmically. As the pleasure built, his head filled with pressure as if his whole being was need and heat. Unexpected, fire flared almost painfully. A thrill of fear that he would burst into flames pushed him over, coming as she convulsed and bucked around him.

Buer groaned and threw an arm across his eyes, snaking his dry tongue over gummy lips. He stumbled off to the bathroom, scratching at his balls. Just as he began to piss he stopped, looking down at his sticky pubic hairs. A spear of ice lanced through him. Shaking, he finished, then turned and stumbled back to the living room.

Lying where he'd left her was the hominid cow, staring up at him. She raised her pelvis to him. Buer ran back to the bathroom, spewing gory chunks of meat and blood into the toilet. Even after his stomach was empty, he heaved and gagged.

Shuddering, he rinsed his mouth. Pink pearls of sweat beaded his brow, rare for any Fallen. Lead filled his stomach as he clutched the edge of the sink.

What had he done? No. Maybe he had dreamed it. A nightmare. But staring at his come-sticky genitals he knew the terrible truth. The one taboo. Never to have sex with an animal, especially a hominid; punishable by death. He climbed into the shower and scrubbed himself clean until his skin shone pink.

He dressed, then reluctantly went to the living room, untethered the cow and put her back in the pen with the others.

Dusk set sullen and cloudy. It was early but he had to get away. Hunger knotted his stomach; he ignored it and hurried from his apartment.

Buer walked the streets, pacing up one and down another, disregarding direction or emerging shoppers. He rubbed his chin and hands, muttering, sorting out what had happened. His mind skittered away from the abhorrent until he convinced himself of the alcohol's influence, the shock of Camiel's engagement. He couldn't bare the thought of going back to his apartment and the thought of meeting friends later for drinks made him squirm. Would they be able to tell what he'd done? Would the hominid smell still be on him? He sniffed at his hands, imagining he could smell port and the musky odor of female primate.

Eventually he wandered into an unfamiliar bar at an hour frequented by perpetual drunks. He glanced around at the lowest blue collar types one step above the gutter. He sat at the bar and asked for a Glenfiddich but had to downgrade when they had nothing of that caliber.

The bartender drained a shot from the wrist of a young bull and put it on the counter. For a moment Buer stared at the row of cows and bulls, labels around each neck indicating the type of drink. Then he closed his eyes and shot it back, asking for another.

A scruffy, black-bearded fellow sat beside him, sewer tang wafting off him. He eyed Buer who ignored him, sipping his second bloodscotch.

The guy's gravelly voice rolled over Buer. "Looks like someone died the big death."

Buer just drank.

The guy leaned over, giving a quick glance at the bartender. "Hey, you interested in some Flare? Good stuff. Big rush. High lasts six hours, makes the world look like daylight."

Buer glanced over at him, shaking his head. "What...what would you do if you'd committed the unthinkable?"

The man's pale skin was pocked and his cheeks dimpled oddly when he laughed. "Like what?" At Buer's look, the guy stood and backed away. "If you're a meat mater?"

Buer swallowed. "No. No, no, not that. I mean...cheating on your partner. Drinking too much." He broke into a sweat again, wiping it quickly away.

The guy laughed nervously. "Man, besides that, nothin's unthinkable. All been done before."

Buer heard nothing else and eventually the guy wandered off. After a couple more shots he left, but somehow the bloodscotch had not blurred his mind. The clarity of thoughts jabbed him. His stomach clenched at the idea of eating and yet he had remembered the warmth of the cow as she had enveloped him. A heat Camiel had never had. A fire that burned and soothed him. But then he'd been drunk. A terrible mistake. A nightmare. He would make sure the cow was used up by the next time he saw his friends. No one would know.

By the time he returned to his condo, it was almost daylight again, bloody tinges in a lightening sky. Buer hesitated outside the pen door. He pressed the button to delay the skylight's opening so he wouldn't be burned, and grabbed vegetables and beef from the fridge. When he entered he heard whimpering and looked down. Cursing, he knelt by the calf he'd left hooked to the IV for too long. Her red hair twisted in wet tendrils and she shivered. Pulling the IV gently from her bruised arm, he picked her up and unlocked the gate to the larger hold.

Staring at the two females and two males, he calmed them as he set the calf in. They would nurse her back to health; if nothing else, hominids always cared for their calves. Then he put their food and the iron mixture inside.

He looked back and met each gaze, releasing them. The port cow was last and Buer flinched from her gaze. When he released her, she started to come toward the bars, hand raised. Buer backpedaled. He slammed the door shut and hit the skylight button.

His eyes squeezed tight; his heart seemed to twist. She was meat. It was revolting to do such a thing to a creature. Buer lurched to the cupboard, pulling out a bottle of pure scotch and sloshing it into a glass. He took two large gulps that burned their way to his belly but he could not dull the edges. Everything remained crystal clear. Rubbing his face, he staggered to the bedroom and dropped onto the bed.

The alarm had been buzzing for long minutes before Buer awoke, realizing he might be late for work. He had time to gulp down two glasses of cold blood before he left.

He immersed himself in his job, staying late each evening for several nights in a row, reluctantly returning home to feed the cattle and sleep.

Three days passed and he found himself drawn to watching the hominids as they slept and ate. The one female and the two males rutted often. The other, with long curls of amber gold hair sat alone, but once was forced to mate with one of the males. She screamed and clawed until Buer intervened, mesmerizing them all before pulling her out.

She tilted her head, looking up at him, a tiny smile playing her lips. He stared into her eyes as they glazed over, then leaned down and kissed the unresisting lips. Once Buer had laid her in the trough on the table, he went back and poured a glass of pure wine. Then he opened a vein on the cow's wrist and dripped the blood into the wine, watching the drops swirl and spread.

Taking two swift gulps, Buer stood with the sharp curved blade and leaned over her throat. She was truly beautiful, for hominid or vampirii. The knife clattered to the table as he admired the gentle curves of her body, the full breasts. Before he knew it he had reached out to stroke a breast. Buer gasped, pulling back, watching the rise and fall of the cow's chest.

This was taboo! There were rules, laws. The *Book of the Fallen* was explicit. Do not raise up the lesser creatures. Yet, the heat had been wonderful, soothing. Buer hadn't even realized he was stroking the warm flesh again. It was more than the yearning for the beautiful vessel. It was more. Far more.

He took her off the table and laid her on the floor as she slowly emerged from the mesmerism. "Aurora. Like the dawn." And Buer was as naked as the cow when he crawled over her, letting his cool flesh heat against her skin, his erection growing.

As he entered her, he felt the steady fast beat of her heart, his thrusts matching it. The cow gasped, moving beneath him.

Conflagration, of all-consuming heat that threatens to boil brain and eyes, evaporate flesh to papery ash. The contrast of fire with the moistness that whetted him brought Buer over the edge, gasping as his heart thumped two bass beats.

He pulled away from the cow's grasping fingers. The realization that his resolve had melted away sent him hurtling away to be lost in the warren of streets and bars.

Eventually he had to return home, only to find that he had left the cow loose.

"Aurora." He stood in the doorway watching her glistening flesh as she ran her hands over his art works, paintings, the couch, feeling textures. She turned and smiled shyly, then moved toward him. He held her at arms' length, looking through her, knowing now that when the Fallen had left God's light for darkness that the fall had not been complete. Buer was still falling.

She had lit a fire within him and this path would lead to dissolution. He knew now what the Fallen feared, what the *Book* forbade.

He took Aurora again, right there on the couch. She gave willingly and as he violently rammed into her, he tore her neck, drinking deep.

Her hands fought weakly against him and her death throes made him come hard.

He cried then. But survival mattered. Fires had been lit that could not be quenched. He stared at the gore of the ravaged cow as he changed clothes. He had broken the unbreakable rule, changed the stakes.

Buer unlatched the pen door, gathered his coat and left, walking into the dawn.

Mamma's Boy
By Sandra Wickham

"Get back," she said, one hand on her swollen belly, the other holding the dinner knife in front of her.

He smiled, the same smile he had used to win her heart many years ago. The same smile she knew now to be an illusion.

"Ruthie," he said, hands outstretched in a gesture of peace, "you really are amazing. That is why I picked you."

Sweat soaked her forehead and ran under her arms as labour pains shot through her like lightning bolts. She stumbled slightly and fought to take deep, slow breaths. She raised the knife higher as he continued to approach. She had to stop this child from being born.

"I said stay back, Christopher." Christopher was not its real name, only part of the human façade she had fallen for. She had been fooled all through their courtship at university, a three year marriage and the first eight months of her pregnancy. Then she woke up a prisoner here and he had revealed his true form.

He smiled again as she doubled over from another contraction.

"There is no point in fighting it, Ruthie. My son will be born with or without your co-operation."

As soon as she could straighten up, she grabbed the knife with both hands and turned the tip of the blade towards her belly. It might only be a table knife but she hoped with enough force she could kill herself, the baby or both. Christopher laughed again but stopped moving forward.

"It would take more than that to kill my son. He would survive, but you probably would not. We cannot have you dying yet. After all," his smile widened, "my son will need to feed when he arrives."

Ruth cursed him, but lowered the knife. Part of her wanted to have this child. She had spent nine months in anticipation of his arrival, reading, singing and talking to him. She backed up and sat down on the bed. Christopher was at her side and wrenched the knife from her hands before the bed could finish sinking under her weight. Another contraction hit, worse than the others.

"Let me help you," he said as he lifted her legs up onto the bed and eased her back against the pillows.

"This isn't exactly how I pictured it," she said as she caught her breath again.

He smiled and for a moment Ruth thought they could have been any ordinary couple expecting their first child. The thought didn't last; the repulsive image of what he truly was brought bile to her mouth.

"I will get the mid-wife," he said as he wiped her forehead with a cloth. "It will all be over soon."

Left alone, she tried to catch her breath and clear her thoughts. Out of habit she rubbed her stomach and sang softly to her unborn child. There was no denying it, this baby was going to come and she could not stop it. She looked around the room for anything she could use as a weapon. But could she *really* kill her own child? If it came out flailing, with sharp teeth and claws, it might not be too difficult. Still, half of it, her half, would be human. She would rather kill Christopher. No part of him was human. But by the time the door opened and the mid-wife entered, Ruth hadn't found anything she could use as a weapon.

"Help me," Ruth whispered to the woman checking her pulse. The mid-wife's expression did not change and she did not speak.

"You must help me. This child," she gasped as another wave of pain struck. "This child cannot survive." The mid-wife ignored her and Ruth cursed again as the door opened and Christopher entered the room.

"How is she doing?"

"It will not be long now, Master," the mid-wife replied.

Ruth only had time to shoot the mid-wife a contemptuous look as another wave of pain grabbed her attention.

Hours passed and Ruth focused only on surviving through each round of pain, growling at the mid-wife's incessant instructions. Drawing on all her hatred for Christopher and the universe for allowing this to happen, with one enormous push she forced the half-monster out of her. As she descended into darkness, Ruth heard the child's first cries.

She woke to find Christopher in the rocking chair, the baby wrapped in the blanket her mother had knitted. The mid-wife was gone. Christopher smiled and brought the child to the bed. Ruth heard a young voice inside her head, disjointed and violent. As Christopher held the baby out for her to see, she was relieved that the infant looked entirely human, although she knew he wasn't. To her surprise he was as large and developed as a six month old. Christopher nodded, as if reading her thoughts.

"He will grow quite rapidly," he said. "That is why he needs to feed, often and a lot."

Again Ruth heard her child in her head, angry and hungry. This time she tried to communicate back, reaching out to him with her mind and heart.

"Could I just hold him for a moment?" she asked.

Christopher hesitated before lowering the baby into her arms.

"You have been an excellent companion these years," he said, as if she should find comfort in that. "It is a shame it must end this way, but this is our tradition."

"Traditions can be broken," Ruth said, then began to sing softly to the baby. He locked his eyes on hers as she sang.

"You must understand," Christopher continued, "it has been this way for centuries. The bloodline is passed to the son; the human mother must be destroyed."

Ruth stopped singing. "Fed to the child, you mean."

The baby squirmed and fussed until she began to sing again, then he calmed and smiled up at her. She smiled back and hid her shock as she heard her child inside her head communicate its intentions.

"It is how it must be," Christopher said and he took the baby from her. He held the infant up in front of him, the perfect picture of a proud father.

Ruth turned away at the first murderous shriek from her child. She did not want to see her baby in its monster form, but when Christopher's screams filled the room, she forced herself to look. Both had now transformed. The child had attached its fangs to its father's throat. The monster that was Christopher crumbled to the floor as blood gushed from his wounds. Ruth had to turn away again as her monster halfbreed child ripped out its father's throat, then continued to tear off and consume chunks of flesh.

When the sounds of feasting finally stopped, Ruth reached down to pick up her son. As she did, the fangs gave way to a toothless grin and the claws shrank to little human fingernails. She scooped him up and headed for the door.

She poked her head out and glanced up and down the corridor. "Still hungry darling?" she cooed at her boy. He looked up at her and from the intensified glow of his red eyes she knew that he was.

"Let's see if we can't find that mid-wife then, shall we?"

Her son gurgled in delight as they headed down the hallway together.

The Morning After
By Claude Bolduc

Translated by Sheryl Curtis

It was so hard, so very hard, to get up from where she lay in the dark. The anguish of looking for something familiar that can't be found, the sense of oppression as your body fights the stiffness that holds it in a vice.

It takes so much willpower, so very much willpower to stand up, while the haze of sleep continues to swirl, carrying with it shards of thoughts and ghosts of confused memories. Deep within her mind, an immense black hole sucks up all the light that exists.

As soon as she stands up, she knows something is not right.

All around, a shell of shadows swallows everything, absolutely everything, including the hands she waves in front of her face. She opens her eyelids as wide as she can. Her entire forehead creasing into her scalp, she feels that she has opened her eyelids too wide, that this is not usual. She closes them immediately. Fingers touching her eyes, she finds nothing but two thin curtains of skin.

There is a sidewalk beneath her feet. She decides to follow it, weeping as she walks, arms stretched out ahead of her like a zombie, bumping into obstacles, stumbling down off the curb every dozen steps or so. Silence every-where. The silence envelopes her in the same way the darkness does, cutting her off from the world, like a night-mare. Suddenly, tenuous, lost in the distance, the sound of a car. The strident shriek of a police siren. *It's night*, a small voice inside her whispers. *Chirr, chirr, chirr,* a nearby cricket confirms. Many noises hide in the silence of the night.

Nothing comes to pierce through the shadows, not the tiniest drop of light, not the slightest reflection, not the most timid star in the sky.

Why walk in that direction? She could have chosen another. Why not turn around, head left? Because it's this way! her instinct replies. Instinct wants to take her to people, where she can find help. Surely, there must be someone somewhere. If there's a sidewalk beneath her feet, she must be in the city. There's always someone in the city.

She reassures herself: Her name is Jacqueline and she has just woken up. She's walking in the dark because she's lost her eyes. They were still there last night, just like always. What happened? How could someone wake up without their eyes?

Walking, walking. In the dark, in the dark. Little by little, a multitude of noises surrounds her. There are cars, voices, music. Downtown. The curb. Be careful! Beside her, a brick wall. She follows it by fingertip. Then, the wall ends. Detour left.

The ground is uneven, as if it were made of cobblestones or riddled with potholes. Take care! Anything can happen, but Jacqueline is no longer as worried. What? She's lost her eyes and she's not worried? It's because there are people around. She's not lost, she'll be able to find help, they'll take her to the hospital to see a doctor, to get treatment for her eyes. There is someone somewhere. She knows that for a fact. But why that way? The noises are all coming from behind her. She's walking away from the main street, where help can be found.

What will people do when they see her? Is her face...? She stops, runs her hands over her clothing. And her...face, what does her face look like? In her mind's eye, she sees eyelids swaying like sheets on a clothesline. It will be better if she doesn't touch her face.

There are obstacles everywhere, debris, garbage bags, invisible things, stacked every which way. Her foot recognizes a cardboard box, her hand a metal garbage can or a plastic bag. The smell of old meat, hot food, cat piss. All sorts of smells. An alley. She's in an alley. Occasionally, alleys lead nowhere. Wouldn't it be better to head back to the street she was on earlier? Here, the noises, the voices, life seems so far away...

But her instinct insists—This way!—driving Jacqueline into the alley, hunting for a noise, a presence, subjugated by the odours that run across her senses one after another. Tap, tap tap! The minute sound of running. She turns her head to the right, where there is nothing but darkness. She thinks of a cat and an image forms in her mind. Yes, it smells of cat piss.

The obstacle catches her off guard. Yet, despite trying to keep her balance, she collapses among the boxes, which scatter through the alley with an infernal noise. The scent of food rises up from the heap. She gropes about, but finds none. It doesn't matter. She's not hungry even though she feels an emptiness within that she's unable to interpret. Once again, something is really not right.

Suddenly, close by, a voice rings out.

"Hey! What's all that racket?"

Jacqueline leaps to her feet.

"Please! Help me!" she cries out, without thinking.

Saved!

She reaches her arms out, stumbles again.

"Who are you?" a man says, hoarsely. "Hoo-ah! I'm not the only one out late! How did you get yourself into such a state?"

She feels him looking at her; like a little spot on the side of her face that itches. The sound of footsteps, breathing, the rustle of fabric advances toward her, moving around the scattered boxes, marking out a darker route in the dark in her mind's eye.

"I can't see anything! You have to help me!"

The sound of footsteps stops. Nothing left in the alley but the sound of panting.

"Well, it looks like you've gotten into something you should have passed up! I only have good stuff. Want some? Hair of the dog that bit you, eh?"

Jacqueline says nothing. The man is very close now. His shoes scrape along the pavement, his jagged breathing produces a small current of air, his voice is...raw with emotion.

"Come on now, I'll give you a line. Too bad, it's not lighter. I'd like to get a better look at you. I just know you're beautiful. In a bad way, maybe, but beautiful. You coming?"

Fabric rustles, the sole of a shoe slides. A foot pushes a box out of the way.

She jumps just as their bodies touch. Because of the contact or rather because of that heat so near, that scent that has suddenly become so intense? The man pushes her up against the wall and then lays her down on a bed of boxes, falls onto her.

"This is fun, eh? Dark little corners like this one? The night isn't over yet, we might as well make the most of it. Whaddya think?"

His breath on the side of her face. The odour of his breath, laced with alcohol, but other scents as well, the smell of his body, something hot and alive, animal. The man's hands race everywhere in the dark. Without seeing them, Jacqueline tracks their slightest movements perfectly.

"You're cold, you know. But don't you worry a bit. I'll warm you up."

The man grabs Jacqueline's clothing. What is she wearing anyway? A dress...yes a dress... And he pulls in one hard tug. The fabric tears. Jacqueline grows tense, feverish as the hands kneed her breasts and fingers wriggle into her vagina. He pants faster and faster, his burning breath caressing Jacqueline's neck, her face, her chest.

The rustling of fabric. A hot appendage on the skin of her belly, slipping and sliding until it worms its way into her like a fiery snake. Salty drops fall on her mouth. An animal pants near her face. His odour overwhelms everything. A whirlpool forms in Jacqueline's mind. Her thoughts collapse in the dark. She can't take anymore, her head turns, she grabs the man around the waist.

"Good! So, your blood is starting to thaw!"

Confused, on edge, as if something is welling up within her, wanting to get out, Jacqueline clasps the man tightly in her arms.

"Yeah, that's it. That's good. You know what to do, don't you, bitch!"

Tighter, tighter, tighter.

"Hey! Take it easy! Are you crazy or what?"

Hold tight, hold tight, hold tight!

"Hey! Stop! You're... Ehhh!"

He screams.

Hold tight, hold the heat close to you, bring the odour closer, until the shriek fades into a squeal.

Eeiiiiiiiii...

Jacqueline holds tighter and tighter, overcome with excitement at this proximity. Crick! Crack! The man is trapped in her arms. Tighter and tighter again, until his rib cage is nothing more than a limp envelope.

Then, the most marvellous thing of all, hot and thick, flows down Jacqueline's face. The odour is so intense that, deep within her, it soothes the unpleasant sensation she's experienced since waking. She opens her mouth, places her lips over those of the inert man. More, more, more! Lost in her fever, she bites. Then she allows herself to be carried away in the maelstrom of sensations, while flashing stars pulse in her mind. It's like coming back to life. Remembering, the painful memories pour in as the vital liquid flows into her, images of a past so near and yet so far...

With small, hurried steps, tap, tap, tap, like the invisible cat earlier, Jacqueline walks. She can walk now because there are eyes in her face, real eyes, her own eyes, but they're worried since she shouldn't be here, not in this magnificent park where they look at everything the moon deigns to show them. Her big beautiful eyes are worried since Jacqueline is no longer convinced she has made the right decision. With them, there's no law, too bad for the unconscious, the fearful, the suicidal.

Before she feels like turning on her heel, a rustle makes the leaves shiver, somewhere in the dark—dark so deep she sees nothing. Then, stepping out of the forest, that man, his face as white as the moon, smiling, stepping ahead, attractive, magnetic... Afraid? Is she afraid? Before the answer comes he's there, so very close, self-confident, his arms draped over Jacqueline's shoulders, his lips—so cold—on her throat.

And life ebbs away, drop by drop.

As the vision gently wanes, Jacqueline pushes the body she has just crushed aside. She stays on her back for a minute, facing a sky she can't see.

It doesn't matter when, it doesn't matter why, it just happened. The impression of knowing a terribly unhappy fate then, during that final second... And then...

A smile pushes the flesh from her cheeks up into her hollow eye sockets.

The limp curtains of her eyelids hang in front of her sockets. Paradoxically, thanks to her eyelids, she can see much better inside herself. Revived, her mind continues to wake and organize the memories of a life that was once something other. And as she thinks, analyzes, makes connections, the fog that has enveloped her lifts. She finally understands how they were able to steal her eyes.

She has no one but herself to blame for this overwhelming misfortune. For reasons as grotesque and futile as altruism, good intentions and so many other things that now seem void of meaning to her, people sign that form, year after year, then go on with their lives without a second thought. And if, by chance, they're victims of an accident, a disease, a murder, when they do die, their organs are harvested without further ado. Too bad for those who are called to come back.

The unpleasant sensation Jacqueline felt within has completely gone, making way for a gentle shiver that runs over her skin. She's surprised at how calm she feels. And it is this very calm that gives her time to consider the issue of her blindness.

She'll never be able to manage without her eyes. In one life much as another what can you hope to do without eyes! Help! She needs help! Not here, not in some back alley, not here, not among men, where she no longer has a place. She has to go back there, to the park where it all started, to *their* place, to her place. Such a long way to go. She has to start. She listens: over there, in the street, the music from the bars has fallen silent, but there's something good about the car noises; there seem to be more cars.

As for the man that now lies inert near her... Perhaps he's part of the solution?

Once again, using her fingertips, Jacqueline maps out a face. Like ants, her fingertips trace the contours of two small globes well encased behind their curtains of skin. She presses two fingers down, one in each corner of a socket. All it takes is a little pressure and, slowly, her fingers dig in, fold under the small globes. Then she hears it. Pop! And, all of a sudden, hot, round, wet, they spurt out of their nests. Wet, like the cold lips that, one certain evening, in a certain park, ran up and down her neck.

How can she release them? If she pulls too hard she might damage them. After stretching out over the man's body, she takes the first eye into her mouth and, using her tongue as a guide, starts to nibble at the nerve that holds it prisoner. A few seconds... a few delicious efforts... and both eyes are rolling in the palm of her hand. Invisible, yet she can finally caress them. And use them.

Jacqueline lifts the two little globes up to her empty sockets and then pushes, pushes, pushes until they fit into their new nests. But she still can't see anything, apart from the images in her mind. What does she have to do now? Does she have to connect the eyes to make them work? And, what if that's not the solution? And what if what she so desperately needs is her own eyes? The eyes they took from her because she signed some stupid paper? Her beloved eyes, that turned opaque in a park, one evening...

The noises of the city are there, waiting for her, and beyond that, the territory of her kind. One hand, sliding along a wall, Jacqueline walks down the alley until she reaches the street where she will find her way, stumbling over obstacles, kicking away debris and waste. She has to pick up the pace, leave this place. A sense of urgency pushes her faster. She's almost running. Her fingers grow hot as they race over the rough brick.

Then, the wall on her right disappears. Carried away with her momentum, Jacqueline trips and crumbles to the ground. And, suddenly, the pain explodes, with lightning power, piercing through her very being.

She screams.

Fire, the flames of hell, plunges her into the boiling lava of a volcano. She presses the palms of her hands against the sidewalk in an effort to push herself up, but her arms break like straws and her face crashes against the concrete. Jacqueline raises her hands to protect herself, but there's nothing there. Nothing but fire, burning, annihilation.

And the screams of a few horrified, early morning passers-by.

All You Can Eat, All the Time

By Claude Lalumière

So, like, my hair is freshly dyed, as black as I can get it. All the clothes I'm wearing are black, too: scarf, leather coat (with a lacy bustier underneath), leather gloves, skirt, fishnets, and boots that go mid-calf. Then there's my skin. I mean, I'm, like, pretty pale to start with. But I smear white makeup all over my face and glam it up with white glitter. It makes my skin almost glow in the dark. Last touch: white eyeshadow, plus some black eyeliner and glossy blue lipstick. I am, like, stunning. Out of this world. Otherworldly.

I mean, really, it's time I got laid already. I'm in Montreal, for fuck's sake. Sin city of the East Coast, blah, blah, blah.

I mean, it's fucking great here. The nightlife. The music. The bars. The cute girls. The hot boys. The even hotter men. It's, like, all you can eat, all the time. But I haven't brought anyone home yet. And I haven't let anyone take me to their place, either. I mean, I'm no prude. In rural Manitoba, where I'm from, there's nothing to do except sex, even if, like, there's no selection to speak of. So you do it, because it's marginally better than not doing it.

But here it's overwhelming. Paralysing, in fact. With so much to choose from, how do you choose? Plus, the truth is, before tonight, I wasn't sure that I was ready. I mean, I'm not entirely sure even now, but enough is enough, you know? There's so much to take in, living in the city on my own. I don't want to lose myself in anyone yet. I just want to find out who I can be in all this wonderful, beautiful noise happening all around me. But I'm beginning to feel like a nun or something. So tonight is the fucking night.

Sometimes, sure, I let some boys and girls kiss me when I go out. Even feel me up a bit if I'm really into them. But I've never let it go farther than that. Not yet. Especially, I've never let myself get within grabbing range of the men. You know the ones I mean. The ones with the irresistible wolf eyes; the ones who move like they own the space around them without being arrogant about it; the ones with the strong hands you know would just make you willingly submit.

No, them I've stayed away from, because I know that's exactly where I could lose myself the most, the deepest.

So, like, almost everyone I see is out in groups, laughing and chatting it up and shit. Me, as usual, I'm wandering through all this solo. It's like I'm a spectre—an undead shade haunting the Montreal nightlife.

I, like, go to my favourite club, BizBiz Bizarre. It's in the Plateau, not too far from where I live, and the people there tend to dress up in all kinds of weird funky ways. But I look so amazing right now that, even among that crowd, I should stand out.

But, for some reason, it's totally boring tonight. The music is, like, totally 1990s. I mean, Red Hot Chili Peppers—really? The crowd is kinda thin and so obviously straight. What is this—like, frat night or something?

Suddenly, there are three guys dancing around me. They keep bumping into me and laughing. They're all of them freaking tall and buff. And the cookie-cutter way they're dressed—they're so obviously rich kids. The type who become doctors or lawyers. Their laughter gets meaner and meaner. I try to wriggle away from them, but they're fucking herding me, slowly boxing me in tighter and tighter. Aside from that, though, they're, like, totally ignoring me. But they know I'm there, alright. I can feel their boners when they grind into me.

Enough is, like, fucking enough.

I, like, scream my fucking head off—loud enough to be heard over the music. Like a fucking harpy from hell. It creates enough distraction that I manage to escape. I don't look back. I'm outta there in a flash, out on the street, just running away as fast as I can.

So, like, I'm an idiot. I could at least have been running toward my apartment. But, no. I was too, like, flustered. A fucking helpless, hysterical victim. This is so not right. Anyway, I'm not that far away from my place.

Fuck. Walking home alone. Fucking alone. Again. I am such a wimp. Such a loser. What a fucking disappointment tonight was. I mean, I'm totally disappointed in myself. I know it wasn't my fault, but, fuck, this is so not what I wanted.

Suddenly I feel the hair at the back of my neck rise, and a shiver goes down my spine. And I'm hemmed in again. It's those same fucking guys from the club. They shove me into an alley, behind a dumpster. Invisible from the street. Yeah, a cliché, but fucking scary nonetheless. I know better than to wait. I make to scream right away but, before any sound can escape from my lungs, rough, stinky hands cover my mouth. I try to bite at the flesh of the dude's palm, but my jaw is immobilized. This guy is way too strong for me.

Shit. Shit. Shit.

I struggle—this can't happen; I am not a victim. I refuse to become a victim. But I can barely breathe and I'm too fucking weak.

Shit. Shit. Shit.

Then I hear a few strangled gasps... I feel a sharp burst of wind, like a mini-hurricane or something... Followed by a few hard thuds... And I'm free.

I should run while I can, but I feel safe. And curiosity wins over caution. I look around. All three guys are on the ground, on their backs. At least two of them are, like, totally dead, their throats slashed, their chests and bellies ripped open. There's a figure hunched over the third guy. A man with his face buried in the guy's neck. Like he's eating or something.

I really should get the hell out of here, but I'm, like, totally mesmerized.

I don't want to make a sound, but, just like a stupid little girl, I gasp.

The man turns to look at me, and I, like, totally recognize him. Before I can say anything, though—poof; there's this dark mist, and he's gone. Like he hadn't even been there in the first place.

But I'm not the one who tore open the bodies of the three dead guys who are still right there at my feet, with their insides oozing out.

I am so outta there.

So, like, men? Older guys, right? Stay away from them. Especially the one who lives across the hall from me.

I don't know his name. Don't know anything about him. No, that's wrong. I know two things. One, he's way too fucking sexy for my own good. I mean, fuck. His eyes are so dark and strong that I swamp up my panties every time I get even the merest glimpse of them. Plus, he's freaking tall. Like, close to seven feet or something. His long hair is the colour of a particularly dark red wine, with only a hint of grey. And he moves like a panther. Quietly, confidently, but ready to pounce at any moment. Also, I know that he can kill and disembowel three buff guys in the space of a few seconds.

Shit. Shit. Shit.

So, like, it's a week later. And in that whole time I haven't seen him once. Not a single time. I know he's there, though. Because he, like, listens to music 24/7. And the walls here are shit. Good thing I don't ever have anyone over, because, like, everyone could hear the sex show.

The old dude's got weird taste. One minute it's hardcore punk rock, and then some avant-garde clangy shit, or like really melodic chamber music. Often he binges on crap like Anne Murray or Barry Manilow.

Why the hell am I scared, though?

I mean, he saved me, right? If he'd wanted to, he could have had me as dessert. I'm sure I taste way better than those frat dudes did. Maybe he's just into guys?

For the, like, gazillionth time, I stand in front of his door, my finger millimetres away from the doorbell. But I chicken out and run back into my room. I always do.

So, like, I go to work. Boring. I go out. Boring. I stay out all night long. Boring. I get drunk. Boring. I get high with anything I can get into my mouth, my lungs, my nose, my veins. Boring. People flirt with me. Boring. Movies. Please—so boring. Everything is boring. Even eating is boring.

And when I masturbate?

What do you think? I see one thing and one thing only: that man from across the hall, blood and gore dripping down his face, looking at me. Seeing me. I replay that over and over again. And I know what I saw then and can still see in my mind: concern.

But why the fuck should he care?

And I come so fucking hard.

So, like, I don't usually follow the news. I don't even have a TV. But somebody left this newspaper on the table in the lunch room at work. And the headline says, *Woman in Wheelchair Saved. Assailants Brutally Killed.*

So, of course, I know right away. I read the whole article anyway. It mentions other incidents suspected to have been the work of the homicidal vigilante: a little boy rescued from a limousine (three men dead); an old man saved from a drunk driver (only one death that time); a twosome of armed robbers eviscerated while threatening a cashier at a convenience store (but the cameras only picked up a blur); a gang of teenage boys who had been torturing and killing neighbourhood cats were torn to pieces. According to the paper, my own trio of would-be rapists seems to have been the first incident. I never reported anything, but of course the bodies were found.

But this time, for the first time, they have a description. This idiot in the wheelchair, like, rats on him. She's a little vague, but it's close enough. Does she want the police to find him? I mean, he saved her. People can be so fucking ungrateful.

So, like, this time, I'm so determined I don't even hesitate. Not for a nanosecond. I press the buzzer for the third time, but still he doesn't come to the door. I know he's in there. I can hear the music. (Although I wish I couldn't. I mean, the Carpenters—really?)

I bang on the door. I'm not going to let him ignore me. Finally, the door opens, and there he is. The sight of him—my first glimpse since that night—hits me hard.

"Hello, Jenny." The dude knows my name! He looks even taller than I remember. Like a fucking towering inferno of primal power. And his eyes, holy shit. That's some deep darkness, there. I feel like a tiny little speck of a girl, barely worthy to be in his presence. And I'm fucking terrified. In awe. Is this what it's like to be in the presence of a god? Fuck. And my panties are, like, soaked. I'm just aching down there. Aching for him.

But, fuck, he's not a god. Why did I even think that? Then the obvious question finally dawns on me, what the hell is he? I mean, I've been so tied up with lust it never occurred to me to ask myself that very basic question. I mean, he's clearly not an ordinary person. Maybe he's an alien, or an escaped government experiment (do we even have weird shit like that in Canada?), or I dunno the fuck what.

As if he could read my mind, he says, "I believe the best word to describe me is *vampire*."

Okay. Vampire. Right. So he's a deluded psycho. What the hell am I doing even talking to him? But say, for argument's sake, that, yeah, maybe he's the real thing... Then, I should really run for my life. Either way, time to run—like, now.

Except I can't budge. I feel his eyes on me—like, physically holding me down, preventing me from moving.

He says, "Come in."

And, like a fucking mindless puppet on strings, I march right into the darkness of his apartment.

I hear the door close behind me.

So, like, the next thing I know I'm lying down on an unfamiliar couch, relaxed as all shit, with this strangely pleasant pain on the inside of my left wrist. I try to get up, but, even though I don't see him, I feel the old dude's gaze, his will, holding me down, keeping me calm. I even try to force myself to panic, but instead a wave of, like, serenity washes over me. So I just give in to it. I'm totally floating in a sea of delicious numbness. It's like after a really amazing orgasm. Only without the sweat or the chafing.

I have no idea how long I've been here. The lights are dim, but my eyes gradually adjust. At least the old dude's music is turned off. Finally, I regain enough presence of mind to sit up and check why my wrist feels different. And there are, like, these two tiny puncture marks along one of my veins.

"Welcome." His grave voice echoes like it comes from deep inside some damp underground cave. It's meltingly sexy.

Again, a part of me knows I should be afraid for my life, but my body refuses to acknowledge those feelings.

That voice again: "If I wanted to hurt you or kill you, don't you think I would have done it already? I couldn't resist having a taste, though. And you are indeed delicious."

By now, my panties must have, like, totally dissolved.

"I'm sorry. I can't fulfil those desires." Again with the mind-reading. Shit. And then he steps into view. And I fight this almost uncontrollable urge to fall on my knees. No, not that way (well, not just that way), but to worship him—'cause I really do feel like I'm in the presence of a god.

"I may look human, but I am not. I look upon you as you would upon a cherished pet or farm animal. You may be pleasant company or be a good source of food, but I would not, cannot, engage in sexual congress."

I manage to say, "Some people really, you know, love their cows." Great. I just compared myself to a cow. Way to go. I am, like, so seductive.

"I do not have to explain myself to you, but you amuse me. It's all moot: I have no sexual or reproductive urges. I simply exist."

I'm not that stupid. I know about vampires. I've seen a few movies and shit. "But when you, whaddaya call it, turn someone into a vampire—" (and it just dawns on me that he might have that in mind for me; and then I realize that, as freaky as it sounds, I now believe that he really is a vamp) "—isn't that, like, satisfying a reproductive urge?"

He sighs. "That's just folklore. Myth. Fiction. I cannot turn a human into a vampire any more than you can turn a cat into a human. I've tried. I've tried every way I've read about or could think of. It's all nonsense."

"Then how does someone become a vampire? How do you make more of yourselves?"

Again, a sigh, but this one is deep and sorrowful. "As far as I know there are no others. There is only me. There has always been only me."

Hey, I know that feeling. *Only me* is, like, the story of my life.

I ask, "Like, dude, how old are you?"

He sits next to me and clasps my hand between both of his. The way my whole hand can be cupped inside his palms makes me feel even smaller. "I wish I knew. My memory is unreliable. Sometimes, in my dreams, I think I recall the distant past, as far back as before humans evolved. Sometimes, I think I remember not always having this humanlike shape. I have dim memories of once having journals, of reading about my past in them, but I lost them in a fire in the late 1800s. That's my earliest firm memory. A fire in London. Some days, I feel that memory starting to slip away, but I try to hold on to it. I remember that, even after the fire, I had other, earlier memories, but they have since eroded away. My mind can only hold so much time, and so my past eludes me, disintegrates with age. I call myself *vampire* simply because nothing satisfies my hunger quite like human blood, and other elements of the myth seem to apply to me as well."

"So, like, you run away from crosses, you can't stand the sun—shit like that?"

"Religious icons have no effect on me. More superstition. Though I am vulnerable to sunlight, albeit much less so if my hunger has recently been sated."

Why the hell is he telling me all this? He's just taunting me. He's gonna kill me as soon as I totally relax and trust him. Just to satisfy some perverse, monstrous kink.

He laughs. And I remember: he can read my mind. "What gave you the courage to ring my doorbell was concern for my welfare. Why shouldn't I trust you? Why are you so suspicious of my motives?"

I almost believe him. Or is he somehow forcing his will on me, mesmerising me in some way to trust him?

"Oh, and I can't actually read your mind. But, like many humans, you broadcast your thoughts and feelings more overtly than you believe. Your smell, your posture, your face, your pheromones...it's all quite transparent. But, yes, I can exert some control over your will. It would do no good to either of us if you were to scream or do something silly like that. But I've been gradually lessening my hold over you. You are grudgingly starting to accept the truth."

I blurt out the question that's been nagging at me most: "So, like, why are you playing hero and saving people?"

"I saw those boys threaten you, and I recognized you as the girl who lives across the hall from me. I was hungry anyway, so I attacked them. Fed on them. But then, as I rescued you, I felt something...something...good. I tried it again, saving other people. Alas, it never gave me the same sense of satisfaction as that first time with you. So I've stopped playing vampire hero. What matters is that you're here now. That we are connected. Isn't this what you want? What we both want?"

What he just said makes me feel all tingly, but I struggle to stay focused. "Well, that's all nice and shit, but now the police might find you anyway, even if you're giving up the vigilante thing. They know what you look like now. We gotta do something about that."

"*We* should?"

And just like that I see how my whole life can change.

"Yeah. *We* should. You want me around just as much as I want to be around you. You may be some way-old bad-ass vampire and shit, but you're not exactly subtle. Maybe we want different things, but maybe we can come up with a plan that'll let you feed, preferably on, like, bad people who don't deserve to live anyway, while you stay hidden from the cops. I mean, you need to eat, right? You might as well do some good at the same time. I'm already involved, you know. I want in." What I don't say, but he probably knows anyway, is how much I need this. Something that no-one from my family or my town could ever even imagine. Something so out of this world that I'll be able to forget all about where I come from. "Now... Tell me: exactly what kind of powers do you have? And weaknesses. Your history. Your name. Whatever you remember. All that shit. Tell me everything."

And, like, his deep, deep dark eyes light up, and he says, "You're right. I do...I mean, *we* need to make sure I cannot be recognized." Without asking, he plunges his teeth into my already punctured wrist.

So, like, he stops sucking on me and then smiles affectionately at me. He likes me, I can tell. Shit. *He likes me?* What am I? A puppy dog? I guess, to him, that is what I am. Beats being a pig in a slaughterhouse. I mean, I'd rather be his pet than his next full-course meal—the occasional nibble and suck notwithstanding.

As soon as the thought crosses my mind, he takes my other arm—the one he hasn't bitten yet—and he bites me again. But he gives in return, too: the whole time he's sucking, I'm, like, coming. Not a big, wild, scream-your-head-off orgasm, but a slow wave of deep pleasure. Whoa! Close enough to sex for me.

Still, I can't help but worry about all these holes in my skin. I mean, I won't exactly be inconspicuous at work tomorrow.

Withdrawing from me, he licks his lips and says, "Don't worry; the wounds will be gone by sunrise." Then he grins,

like a little brat. "Oh, and that little extra I gave you—"
He, like, fucking actually leers at me. What a hypocrite!
Farm animal, my ass. But I'm not complaining. "—I can
control that. I don't give that to my victims. And you are
no victim." Gotta say, dude knows the words to make this
girl feel special.

He opens my blouse, and his teeth fasten onto my
shoulder. And it's, like, bliss. Heaven.

So, like, did I black out again? I'm so fucking dizzy. The
vampire is holding my hand. It's kinda cute.

"So, dude, fess up. We're a team, now, you and me. Tell
me all your shit." I so need for him to open up to me. Like,
I let him open me up and feed on me. Seems only fair. "If
we're gonna be in this together, there needs to be, like,
mutual trust."

He smiles knowingly and takes my arm, running his
sharp fingernails over my skin. It makes me shiver. He
knew it would. He says, "I, too, want to learn everything
there is to know about you." With that, he plunges his teeth
into my shoulder again. As my blood flows from my veins
and into his mouth, I feel the weight of my worries slip
from me. I feel like it's not just my blood, but my self that's
seeping away into him. That numbness is so freaking
fantastic. Like nirvana. I almost forget who I am.

Taking his mouth away, he says, "All these months in
this building, and never have you brought any friends here.
Never have I heard you speak to anyone on the telephone.
You are so conveniently alone."

Shit. All of a sudden I start crying. Shit. I've been in
Montreal for, like, three months. And I have no friends to
show for it. Not that I had any friends in my hometown,
either. And my family? Screw them. Shit. I promised myself
I would never get weepy about being alone. It's my choice.
I am not sad about it, and I am not one of life's victims.
I'm not. I'm not. Fuck. Fuck. Fuck.

The vampire cradles me while I cry. This is so fucking
embarrassing. His teeth tenderly pierce my throat, and he
sips a little more of me.

Taking a break, he says, "Earlier, you asked what my name was. If I ever had one, I've long since forgotten it. This likeness, though, was called Randolph. But it's time for me to shed this old skin and evolve."

Randolph? The sound of the name makes me giggle, and I, like, totally sound high. Like I just smoked a bagful of spliffs or some insane shit like that. I wipe the rest of my tears, touch the little holes on my neck, and continue giggling like an idiot.

His strong hands squeezing my shoulders, Randolph plunges his teeth into my throat again. This time it doesn't feel so gentle. But that's okay. Again, he drinks. It's starting to be hard to remember stuff. Like, fuck, what's my name? Shit like that.

And it's starting to not feel so pleasant, all of this. Like my bones are starting to ache. And I can't see too clearly anymore. My mouth is, like, totally raw and parched. My skin feels dry and cracked, like, all over.

I peer at him, and I, like, totally hallucinate. I could swear I was looking right at myself.

Who the fuck is he, again? Or is it she? What am I doing here? Where am I?

I feel him/her take my clothes off, run his/her fingernails all over my wrinkled skin. He/she bends down and bites into my thigh. And he/she drinks from me. I, like, feel myself flow from my body into his/hers.

So, like, I ache all over. I am so fucking old, so tired. But why does it feel so wrong being old? I mean, everyone gets old. That's life, you know? I just wish I could remember my life. Did I have children? Were my breasts pretty when I was younger? What did I accomplish? No use...it's all gone.

Who is this young girl sitting next to me? She does look familiar, but I can't exactly remember her... Why is her mouth so bloody? And why are we both naked?

She bends down and—oh!—bites down hard on my belly. It should hurt, but instead it feels like a release. It's so good. Like floating numbly on a sea of pure pleasure. Letting go of myself. Letting go of everything...

#

So, like, goodbye Randolph, hello Jenny. Jenny is dead. Long live Jenny.

So, like, I just chop up what's left of the old Jenny and put her in little bags. Then, I put on her clothes. But, really? This is, like, nowhere near slutty enough for what I have in mind.

So I go to my new apartment—Jenny's apartment—and I, like, totally dress up. Vamp it up, so to speak.

I dye my hair as black as I can get it. Then: a lacy black bustier; black leather gloves; black skirt; black fishnets; black boots that go mid-calf. And there's my skin. I mean, I'm, like, pretty pale to start with. But I smear white makeup all over my face and then glam it up with white glitter. It makes my skin almost glow in the dark. Last touch: white eyeshadow, plus some black eyeliner and glossy red lipstick. I am, like, stunning. Out of this world. Otherworldly.

On my way out to the downtown clubs, I drop the little bags of leftover Jenny in public garbage cans, but none close to home.

This is fucking great. The nightlife. The music. The bars. The cute boys and girls. The hot men and women. It's, like, all you can eat, all the time. It's almost overwhelming. So much to choose from. I let some men and women grope me, some boys and girls kiss me. Until I find just the right one for tonight. The one who will taste just right. Then I'll let them take me to their bed, and it'll be my turn to kiss them.

Alia's Angel
By Rhea Rose

I tried to say no, as Alia tipped the dirty Dixie cup to my mouth. Some of the blood it contained ran down my face and into my ear, but most of it went into my mouth. I swallowed.

She kissed my face like she always did, licking off the runaway blood. *No, Alia, don't do that.* Many times I'd warned her not to touch the blood, but she always said she wanted to be like me.

Alia usually came here alone. This time I heard a voice I didn't recognize, a young boy's voice.

"What's that in her hand?" the boy asked her.

I tried to open my eyes and lift my head, but I could not. Until Alia arrived with the full cup, this was the longest I'd ever gone without the blood-drink. But even with her meagre offering, another hour would pass before my wretched condition would allow me to get up from the rough, dank floor boards I'd collapsed onto.

"Don't talk. She needs to rest," Alia said to her friend. She crawled over to me; her warm fingers gently pulled my own thin weak fingers away from the book I held.

Without the weight and comfort of the book, my spirit separated from my body and floated upward. My soul was accustomed to performing this manoeuvre while waiting for my body to recover from lack of drink. My disengaged spirit was stopped only by the silent, rusted fan hanging from the ceiling. From there I surveyed the room below. The two children sat beside my crooked body; their clear, soft voices sounded as if they spoke directly into my ear.

"What is this?" Alia asked the boy, as she shuffled through the book's pages. "It's like looking through a window when the sun's shining," she said.

"It's called a picture book," the boy responded. He looked and sounded older than her. "Let me see."

"I won't!" Alia pulled the book away.

"Do you wanna give the angel another cup of blood?" the boy asked.

"I don't have any more."

"I can get some," he said, and retrieved the crumpled Dixie cup as he left the room.

The first cup of blood Alia gave me had started to do its work; I lost track of the children then. The nourishment coursed through my body like a mouse gone crazy. I could no longer concentrate on conversation, even if it had continued below me.

As I gazed down, I studied my own still form. My body lay on its back separated from my soul. One knee and elbow bent awkwardly, and my long dark hair became lost in the darker shadows on the floor. My white dress spread up and behind my head like a halo. I was a broken angel lying there. Alia's unsteady hand had spilled a trail of red across my skirts.

My condition was recent. According to the ex-lover who passed the disease on to me, it was the latest in uber sexually-transmitted diseases; unlike the STD's that had come before, this new virus enhanced my immune system, denying all illnesses access to any vulnerable bodily systems. The malady would add several centuries to my existence, but it had its drawbacks.

This evening at the bookstore, as I selected the story book for Alia, a long, thin man accidentally walked through the store's plate glass window. Blood spurted from him, like a burst boil. I gagged and ran from the store, the unpaid-for-book in my hand as I fled the scene.

I started flying to escape both the sight of the blood and the desire to lap it up like a thirsty dog in the street.

In the sky I became lost inside a choking, industrial cloud of darkness and the terror of the hydro lines and the tall buildings buried in the fog numbed my brain. I don't know how I was able to fly. When I've been most desperate the ability to fly just comes to me, and somehow I always end up here, through the window of this dreary, brick warehouse. I'd crash onto the oily, damp wooden floor, an old place used a hundred years earlier for storing grain until the trains no longer came to load and unload.

The empty windows held pieces of board like broken teeth; arched night holes gaping like the mouths of dead men who'd uttered their last cry.

Sometimes, at home while I slept in my clean bed, I dreamed of the arched windows. They became my mouth sucking, and my eyes, black and empty of any light.

The building and the people inside it were condemned. For decades, the shuffling, sighing shadows of street refugees, who had boarded out most of the light, found shelter in the ruined place. Human rats.

But as foul as they'd become, they were not like me, a creature unworthy of the sun. Daylight made me weak. The same light would make them strong if they cared to stand in it for any length of time.

How much longer must my body lie down there? How much longer must I float up here?

Then I heard Alia and her friend.

"I want to give it to her," the boy said.

"No. No one goes near her but me." Alia took the fragile paper cup from his hand, pressed it to my lips. The blood filled my mouth, pooled, and very slowly dripped down the back of my throat. A soft gurgling sound escaped me.

"She's not drinking it," he said.

"Shhh," Alia replied. She pushed my head and the blood spilled from my lips. Catching the flow with her small hands, she smeared my face, attempting to push the slippery red fluid back into my mouth. "Drink it, Angel. Please, Angel, this is good for you. Angel, Angel. Wake up!"

"She's dead," the boy pronounced.

But he was mistaken. My soul sank slowly like damp eiderdown into the body to which it belonged. I knew I was back when I smelled the coppery blood—old, nearly dead haemoglobin. I inhaled my own fetid breath. Garlic and Feta. I loved salads and old blood.

"Look, she's alive!" Alia said excitedly. "Angel, you're okay."

Her arms wrapped tightly around my neck. She helped me sit. "Tell him, Angel. Tell him you're from heaven."

Yes, once I told her that I'd come from heaven. But truly it's Alia who is angelic, though unkempt. I'm certain that if I poured a bucket of warm, soapy water on her, she would appear golden and cherubic.

The boy stood beside her, defiant, doubting; he'd guessed that, though I'm from the clouds, I am not from heaven.

"Alia," I whispered. "Alia, you've saved me, again."

"I love you, Angel."

"Who's your friend?" I never took my eyes from the boy. He was afraid, but assured by Alia's familiarity with me. He held my stare, and I realized he knew about me, about my kind. He'd seen someone like me before!

"People call me Peer," he said. He stood taller than Alia and his brown hair was fuzzy at the back where he'd slept on it.

"Pierre?"

Alia laughed. She broke into a fit of giggles and Peer smiled. All of his teeth were brown. "P—ear," he said. "Can you read this?" he asked me, and he pulled Alia's book out from under his jacket.

I looked at Alia with undisguised disappointment. She'd given him her new book!

"For more blood," he said, as if he'd read my mind. He stepped toward me with the book. I took it and he sat in front of me, legs crossed. I sat too, and Alia sat in my lap. I wondered that they didn't shiver in this cold, dark place, but this was their home and if they grew cold they knew better than I how to make themselves warm.

It was dark outside, but by now my eyes were so sensitive to light that I could see the insects that scrabbled in the cracks searching for anything to eat. For the children it was difficult to see.

I waited for the clouds to blow away from the moon. In that quick light we flipped to the pictures and studied them. I slowly and carefully read the story to its end.

Alia had fallen asleep. Only Peer and I continued to look at the pictures.

"You're a real monster, not like the funny one in this book," he stated, somewhat randomly.

"Yes," I said, surprised by my own admission.

"My mom used to be like you."

"Really?" Many questions welled inside me. My head ached with queries, but I didn't want to scare him away.

"You haven't killed anybody yet, have you?" he asked.

"No," I said as gently as I could.

"You're going to kill Alia."

"Never! I love—"

"I know. My mom said she loved us, too. But she killed my sister and my older brother."

"What?" I was stunned, barely able to comprehend what I was hearing. I never dreamed others like me lived, others who murdered their own families to satiate themselves. Whole families lived somewhere in this old building. But I didn't care to explore and find out what the inhabitants were about. At least those who exhausted themselves here could find comfort in death. I wasn't sure that I could die. Alia, I knew, took the blood she fed me from the addicts housed here. Peer, I was certain, got my second cup from someone recently dead. I hadn't killed anyone yet, but I knew one day I might kill to get my drink.

"Mom belonged to a group of people like you. She told me she had to wear white, like you. When you finally kill, then you can wear any colour, even red," he said, matter-of-factly. "White's the only colour you can stand to have rubbing on your skin until you kill to drink. Mom said the other colours hurt, especially red."

I stood mute, riveted. I drank in his words like another cup of blood. When he paused, I wanted to shake him, *tell me more about the others*.

Then Alia stirred, waking up, and I wanted her to go back to sleep.

"Angel, Angel, hold me," she said. I picked her up. "Can I fly with you? Can you take me to heaven and show me the clouds?"

I looked at Peer.

He shook his head.

"No, sweetheart, I don't even know how I fly." But she'd already fallen back to sleep.

"She's why you come here. Eventually you'll convince her to let you drink from her," he said.

"Why didn't your mother kill you, Peer?"

He stopped talking then and looked to the floor. I mistook this for fear. Maybe he thought I'd take his information and use it against him. But when he looked back at me, a strange smile lit his face and the light from that smile flicked into his eyes. He had a secret. A secret I would never learn from him, at least not like this, not by straight-forward questioning.

"What do you want, Peer?" I asked. I knelt in front of him. "How can I help you?"

"Don't hurt Alia. Don't come here."

I shook my head. *No, anything but that.*

"I want my family, but they're dead. Alia's not. Not yet."

Peer's pain and his courage touched me. He and I and Alia were the walking dead. They had more life in their veins than I, but they walked in this tomb under the cover of death and darkness. I clung to a tiny bit of life. Somewhere in me, cells continued to exchange gases that kept me partially human. I was a monster and yet I walked and worked among the living, a place these two had more right to.

"Don't take Alia," he said.

"I won't, I promise."

He shook his head. "You promise but you can't keep it. Take me. I want to live with you. You can buy more books and read to me."

I cried. Yes, I'd take him from here. I'd read stories to him for as long as I could. But how could I not come back here when the drive came upon me? I'd be back because Alia knew what I needed. How could I abandon her? Her angel, gone forever.

"What will happen to Alia? I can't leave her," I begged.

"She's happy. When you don't come back you'll turn into a dream for her. She has lots of dreams and many pretend friends. She'll forget."

Forget? I searched him with my eyes. I looked for a selfish motive. There wasn't one in him. I rejected what he said about Alia and yet his words bit deeply. What did I know about her? Alia's parents were still alive, living somewhere inside this broken castle. She told me about them. I told her that I needed blood. But what did she need?

Peer was alone.

Perhaps the only good thing I could do was take Peer, read to him, and maybe he would see that though I was a monster, I wouldn't hurt him, or Alia. I wanted to believe that about myself.

I looked over my shoulder at Alia. She lay sleeping on an old blanket she'd pulled out from somewhere.

I walked to the crumpled Dixie cup, put it to my nose and smelled the remnants, ran my tongue along the cup's rim.

"It's diseased," he said.

I shook my head and smiled gently. Though I knew little about my condition, I was certain that I'd drunk every disease on the planet by coming here and accepting Alia's offerings.

"Doesn't matter. It can't affect people like me."

"This one does."

His tone stopped me. He cried softly as he said, "My dad made mom drink blood like that. One day she wasn't there anymore and he told me he got rid of her. He told me he took bad blood from a foreigner who lived in this building and he gave it to her. He knew she would die from it. You get sick first and then diseased and then you die."

"How long do I have?" I asked him, confident that this tiny amount of diseased blood would do me no damage.

Peer shrugged, stared at the floor. "I don't know." He wiped his tears on the wrist of his sleeve.

"Why do you want to kill me, Peer?"

He looked so vulnerable and frightened. Coping the only way he knew how with a situation beyond his years, defending his friend Alia with a story meant to frighten me away.

"I don't want you to hurt Alia, but I like you," he said in a small voice. "Sorry," he sniffed through his tears.

Maybe the blood would kill me. In that case Peer would have done me a favour. But I was sceptical and wondered how Peer's father had actually rid the boy of his mother.

I didn't want to frighten Peer by insisting that his small "dirty" blood offering wouldn't harm me and very likely hadn't killed his mother. So, I played along. "If I survive the blood you gave me tonight, promise me that when I get thirsty, really thirsty, and I cry for Alia, you'll bring your dad around to me." If I ever hurt Peer, or Alia, I'd visit the man who could possibly kill me.

He nodded. "I hate him for killing my mom."

Peer gave me a sense of purpose. Many like Peer scrambled around, neglected, shivering in dark holes like this. Maybe I could help some. I hoped to make a new life for him.

I took his hand. He stood up. I pointed to the story book. He kissed the sleeping Alia goodbye and tucked the book under her arm.

"I don't know how to fly when I'm not thirsty," I said.

"It's okay." He sniffled. "We can take the stairs."

He pulled me toward them. All my visits and I never remembered the stairs. But then I'd always been in the throes of withdrawal, or high on blood. Suddenly I wasn't afraid to live; for the first time the thought of carrying on intrigued me.

In the time I had left with Peer, I was happy to hold his warm hand and have him lead me down.

When I'm Armouring My Belly
By Gemma Files

Much later, he would recall the exact moment when he finally forgot his own name: Face-down on a bumpy mattress smelling of semen and Vick's, with Goran pushing and biting into him at once—dry drag and relentless ache, icy and burning in equal amounts, the full Isobel Gowdie daemon-lover treatment. Wasn't like it'd never happened before, and yet, *that* particular time…something broke, never to be repaired. He felt it run out of him like the blood itself, greedily lapped and savoured: Waste not, want not.

When they flipped him over, meanwhile, Cija came settling onto him from above like Fuseli's nightmare or Munch's red-headed whore-dream, her teeth almost meeting around the bed of one nipple—with him in too much nethermost pain even to fuck forward 'til she *made* him, reached back to dip her too-sharp thumbnail right into the seat of his deep, laid-open hurt and *pressed* inward. His hips bucked in a jerky frenzy, and she just laughed to see it; that same laugh they all had, a rippling silver-glass trill, delighted most by the spectacle of damage. Her insides milking him hard enough to bruise all the while, wet and tight and numbing-cold as a close-packed box of snow.

They gave him a bath that night, let the grime and blood soak off in rivulets, exposing all his wounds—healed and unhealed alike—to their careless exploration. Cija ran some sort of hotel shampoo-packet through his hair that smelled of sage and lemon, and exclaimed in surprise at the result:

"Ver-y pret-ty," she said, her 'outside voice' (as he'd come
to call it in his own mind, to distinguish it from either the
half-glimpsed roil of thought or that off-putting sub vocal
communication they used amongst themselves) just a bit
too rough, too slow, still tinged with whatever original
accent she'd had, even after being run through their million-
year proto-tongue Creole as a filter.

Combing her claws carelessly outward from the roots
of his overgrown mop, bangs drooping almost to his lower
lip now, and scoring away a bit of beard as she did; he
damn well knew he'd looked a whole lot pret-ti-er a half-
year back, 'round when he'd first started his tour through
the circuit—before he'd stopped bathing, or shaving, or
talking to anybody he could tell had a pulse. And complaining, as she did: "You *smell* like us, but you *taste* like
them. It's very confusing."

Goran shrugged, licking his fingers clean. "Smells like
us, specific, 'cause we just got done rubbing ourselves all
over him. He's not a toy, Cija," he warned.

"But he could be."

And: *Yes*, he wanted to say, *yeah, I could. I can be anything you want. Let me, please. Let me.*

Please.

But it hurt too much, and he didn't know who he was
anymore, and then he was gone for a while—extinguished,
snuffed out, like a black wax Sabbat candle. He'd been up
for what seemed like months, always in transit, passed like
a party favour from pride to pride; his fever for assimi-
lation through emulation had spiked at last, and he slept
well, dreamlessly. Cradled between corpses.

That first bunch of 'em he'd met in an all-night highway strip-mall drugstore, somewhere considerably closer
to home. He'd seen them coming from a literal mile away,
knowing in his gut how they could see him, too: Not just
background noise, potential prey. That he stood out to them
in some way which intrigued, itched at them the way scar
tissue did—some frequency they were all tuned to, him
and them alike, though he only got the fuzz and the beat,
most-times. Static and hiss, lost between stations.

"You smell like us," the first one to look directly at him said, words echoing magnified through his skull's orbit, in-mouth/in-mind. And: "I *dreamed* of you," he replied, eagerly. "Knew you was gonna be here."

"Of vampires? Not so special. Many do."

"No, I dreamed *you*: Saoirse, Owain, Chuyia. Y'all met near the Black Sea, on a pilgrimage to Chorazin, right? 'There to salute the Prince of the Air.'"

The first one (Owain) simply kept on looking at him, blinkless eyes almost all-white between slitted white lashes, with a faint black ring 'round each iris and pupils like chips of ice. While the second girl, Chuyia—chai-scented hair in a braid to her waist, one gold strand fringed with small coins linking nostril to earlobe on the left-hand side—cast her red-tinged gaze down at her bare, clawed feet, and murmured: "...perhaps worth examining at...closer quarters..."

Saoirse tittered and stroked his cheek, her own eyes eight-ball hemorrhage black, each twisted nail frosted a different, inappropriately candy-bright color. "He's certainly warm enough to seem edible, at least. Whatever *else* he might turn out to be."

Owain shrugged the idea away, like someone ugly-drunk was trying to feel him up. Said: "Just another bug-eater, another would-be tool. There's a new one every mile in this damn country."

"No, I ain't like nothin' you seen before—nothin' like *them*, anyhow. Never have been. But I *am* like you. I mean..." Adding, desperate, as they just kept on staring, fixedly: "Why would I dream you, your names and lives and all, if I wasn't?"

"Why indeed?" Chuyia murmured, as Owain hissed, dismissively. But there was just enough room for one more in the van, as it happened—and after all, they *were* already hungry.

Their nightside existence turned out to be built far less on glamour and magick than on endless boredom, constant flight. Enabling it was steady yet stultifying work, almost as brain-dead as any other crap job he'd ever had—all but the blood part, coming hand-in-whatever as it did with sex parts of every possible combination. Though even that wasn't exactly the way the books and movies had warned it might be: They needed far less than anyone seemed to think in order to keep going, far more often. Five small meals a cycle, just like that Caveman Diet the girls' magazines kept talking up.

So he settled into the routine, head-first. Drove during the day, when they were asleep, booked the rooms, rented storage spaces, made sure the windows were well-taped over by the time they woke and the evenings well-stocked with a steady stream of treats—hookers fresh enough not to be too diseased, experimenting students, runaway junkie-wannabes who hadn't quite connected with the habit that'd kill 'em yet. And now, never would.

He healed fast, thought on his feet, made a nice chew-toy—and he could at least *pass* for human, still, which none of *them* could. Once they'd all done him enough in enough different ways, though, that really was it; they were done with him, and made it more than plain, no matter how he pleaded. The most (and least) they could do before leaving was throw him to a new pride, so he could at least try getting what he wanted out of *them* awhile.

But the next bunch didn't come across either, in the end—nor the next, nor the next after that. And slowly, he came to recognize that whatever mild affection any of 'em might eventually develop for him was entirely predicated on points of difference rather than shared similarities, equally disturbing as they were on both their parts...that what had driven him towards them, in the first place, was exactly what inevitably drove *them* away in the opposite direction. That they liked him as he was, all (comparatively) weak, confused and buzzing with random pain—strong enough to take their abuse and live, to heal, but not scar-free. And never quite strong enough to stop them doing any damn thing they wanted with him, even if he'd thought to try.

Oh, they could enthrall, all right; he'd seen it done, on more occasions than he could count. But he was not *in* thrall to them, and never had been. What he did, he did with a clear mind and an even clearer conscience, willingly, in sure and certain hope of due recompense to come. Of the Resurrection, and the Life.

What remained to be seen, however, was how many times a man could be lied to and still keep on believing; much like any other faith in that way, he guessed, which he had to admit wasn't really enough to keep him from being at least a little resentful.

Backsliding, his Momma used to call it, way back when—*you KNOW how to do right, just don't wanna, do you, boy? 'Cause there's something in you that don't fit with this world, something mean and dead and rotten to the core…and I'm gonna have to beat it from you like a damn rat-killing dog, ain't I, so's you'll get at least a little better. Or so's you won't get no worse, anyhow…*

Ignorant swamp-French bitch.

Momma kept Daddy in the old fall-out shelter under her own Daddy's house, locked down fast, while her and him slept in a trailer in the front yard. At first, growing up, he'd thought it was some game they played between the two of 'em, like other people's parents did—but it went on far too long, never stopped. And one time she'd dragged him down there by the hair, twisting and kicking, with a cat she'd found him playing with hanging slack from her other hand: *Let's make this Daddy's supper!* Threw it in, then, and slammed the door again real quick. Made him watch what happened, after.

Holding him still all the while, his eyes peeled open with a thumb jammed in either corner 'til stars bloomed at the limits of his vision, and whispered: *This is why. Why you are the way you are. Why I gotta do like I do. 'Cause you don't wanna end up like THAT, do you, boy?*

Nobody left alive could tell him *exactly* what had happened, though some certainly speculated (outside his earshot, as well as in it). Seemed fairly common knowledge how Daddy and Momma had married while still in school, Daddy swapping a low-grade sports career for injury and addiction, while Momma waitressed or hooked just enough to keep them both in generic prescription drugs. How he'd went out to score one night and came crawlin' back at the crack of dawn, burned lobster-red, almost smoking; knocked Momma down when she answered the door with a slap that unseated her left upper bicuspid, opened a wound in her shoulder, and got busy.

And nine months later, in a sanguinary haze of emergency transfusions, that's when he was born—with a full set of teeth, already snapping.

When he was old enough to make the highway on his own recognizance, he ran away; authorities brought him back real quick, so he just did it again and so on, 'til she beat on him like he was a rug hung up to dry; daily, habitually, offhandedly. Like hurting him was her hobby.

The last time, he made sure to wait 'til she was asleep (roofies stirred in her beer, when she wasn't looking), then set the house on fire. Tried to get Daddy to come with him when he saw him peering out through the shelter grate, but he just spat and yowled, and then it got too hot to stay. So either he survived or he didn't, and then maybe they were back together in some better world, or at least well out of this one; he sometimes mused on how maybe he'd run across him on the circuit, one of these nights, so high he wouldn't even remember how they were related.

Monsters are defined by what they prey on, what they hunt, Chuyia told him, once, in a quiet moment. *In the jungle, the most fearsome killers are those who know how to hide, to wait. To pretend. Because the best mask of all for strength is weakness, do you know that? Like Saoirse, with her I'm-lost, I'm-scared, Mister-help-me-please game; you've seen how efficient that is. And you would know that better than most, I think, at any rate: Little trap-door spider, so expert at concealment...do you even remember who you used to be, earlier that same night? Before you found us?*

He hadn't wanted to agree with her, then; just shook his head and looked away, agonized, as she picked his half-healed neck-scars open again and bent to lick the blood surface-wards. But now, trapped in Cija and Goran's diffident embrace, he knew at last how right she really was...how nice she'd been trying to be, in her own way. The way even he (most-times) was to those tricks and treats he brought Chuyia and the others, not because he *had* to, but just because he could. 'Cause it cost him less than nothing.

He couldn't feel *anything* for 'real people', not at all— never before, probably not in future. But at least he felt an attraction, one-sided and screwed as might be, for things like them; that had to count for something, didn't it?

So: *Thank you,* he'd told Chuyia, as her teeth slid out. And felt her nod against him in reply, ever so slightly, as the pain washed back up over him like a black wave, tinged with red: *Oh no, thank YOU...*

Kissing the whip-handle, the branding iron. Kissing the hand that stroked his hair, stroked *him* to full attention then slid down even further, all the better to slit his pulsing throat.

"Bad teeth," Cija said, examining them closely, running her finger over their ragged grey edges—a dirty old snow bank to her fresh salt-ice, opaque as hematite. "Do they pain you? They must."

"Naw. They come back in like that, after my Momma took a hammer to the first set."

Cija, to Goran: "A joke?"

"Have you known him to?" They both turned to look at him at once, this time with slightly more interest. "So. Not a fanatic, after all—a dresser-up, a...poser? Is this the word?"

"It's one. But no, I ain't that, just like I keep on tellin' you. *Jah sh'te oupir, kom toy.*"

"*Oupir? Necht, merkecht.*" Goran paused. "*Dhampir,* perhaps. You know this word?"

"Means—halfbreed? Born, not made. But not like—"

"Us, no, never. Not even if we drain you dry. But if your father was *very* fresh when he got you, this might explain; dead man's sperm lives for some time after, viably. Why is it you want this so badly, though? You're *not* them, born meat, so find your own way, *your* desire. Hunt accordingly. Why be hyena if you can be wolf? Don't have to eat our leftovers forever..."

Cija: "You don't have to let us hurt you, either. But maybe you like that."

"Maybe I do."

"Then it's settled. It's what he wants, Goran—you heard him. So very little, really."

"No, I think not. Do you even remember their names, who had you last?"

"Why should I? They didn't want me. Passed me on to you. You even remember *my* name?"

"Benjamin Boucher. Says so, on your driver's license."

He looked down, oddly shamed. Muttered, resentfully: "Y'all say it boo-SHAY. 'Sides...I know *your* names."

"Mmm, no doubt. But, as I say: We leave tomorrow, travelling fast...so fast, you cannot keep up. This is goodbye, little virus. You are...too much work."

"How? *How* am I? I do *everything* for you. Everything! Y'all don't do nothin' for yourselves—"

Cija: "But we don't *have* to, Ben-ja-min, not while we have you. Or someone like you. They are so easy to find, too, always—"

—YOU know that.

"We can of course pass you on again, if you want. There are more coming always, even now: Mortlake, Hu-shien. Marival, and her get..."

Despair welling up in him, sharp yet removed as the sight of someone else's tears: "But *you* won't, that it? Never? Not under no circumstances?"

Goran just shook his head—not unkindly, if not exactly kind.

Which only made him snarl, already near weeping: "Well, why the God shit Hell fuck *not?*"

(And Cija, cutting in subvocally, from what seemed very far away: *Oh look, he's CRYING!* Such pure wonder in her voice, such a depthless, awful joy. As though his pain was the sweetest thing she'd ever seen.)

"Because..." Goran said, eventually; a pause, long even for him. And then—"...I don't know what you would become, after."

Which, he could only think, put pretty much forever paid to *that*.

Goran looked away, pointedly, while Cija kept on grinning, her blank eyes ravenous-covetous. He took a long, sobbing breath, into great silence.

"Then kill me," he said, finally. "Just kill me, right damn now. I *want* you to."

Goran nodded. "All right."

But when Goran's eyes were already rolling back and his own pulse was racing shallow, dying away, he suddenly thought: *I ain't gonna die like this, not after all I done. I deserve more.* Thought: *Who the hell are you to take my life away, anyhow? Even if I did give it? Fuck YOU, dead man. Fuck the pair'a you, and not like I usually do...*

So he turned and bit deep into the neck of the monster who had him pinned, instead—battened on like a tick, held fast and didn't let go, not even when a howling Cija ripped his ear off at the root; something inside told him it'd probably grow back, especially if he finished what he was doing. Just kept on drinking 'til Goran groaned into coma, free hand shooting forward to choke Cija silent with abruptly vampire-grade strength before finally turning on her as well. Strength on top of strength flaring to life inside him, like a double-twisted halogen coil: The wily parasite whose contaminant touch alone had been enough to bring a lion— *two* lions—down.

That was the thing, with vampires: All the ones he'd met, anyhow, before or since. So old, so arrogant. So utterly convinced they'd seen everything there was to see, so sure they knew it all. They never saw it comin'.

It tasted good, too, damn good. And when he caught sight of himself afterwards, shaving dry with Cija's black-handled knife as a haphazard razor, he found he shone so brightly he could hardly bear to look at himself at all— a bleak halo of stolen light all 'round him like some eclipse turned inside-out, Goran and Cija's long, shared midnight ramblings instantly translated to a full-body crown whose crenellations made one point each for every soul they'd ever taken, in turn.

When he finally tracked down Owain and the others, nesting in Montreal, they only had one thrall left between 'em—made him think maybe they'd come down in the world a little, just for a moment, 'til he recalled how they'd always liked traveling light.

Owain opened the door, frowning when he saw who it was. "We told you not to come back," he said, warningly.

He nodded. Told him: "Goran and Cija said 'hi'."

And again, no immediate warning bells seemed to go off—Owain just turned his back, sighing disgustedly, head cocked at a perfect angle for the upswung axe to connect with; it left his slippery hands with a slight, odd 'pop', lodged deep in the parietal lobe. Owain went down, seizing, and he saw Chuyia's blood-dimmed eyes widen from across the room, (pleasantly?) surprised, her mouth moving silently, words booming through both their synapses at once: *Little spider, my born-again jungle creature. Oh, you treasure, you.*

Then she was on him from one direction, Saoirse from the other, tag-teaming him both at once. Not that it ended up doin' either of them all that much good, in the end.

The thrall was just a girl, meanwhile—maybe sixteen and deep-tranced, so much so she beat at him 'til they were all dead, then hugged him tight and cried into his neck: *You're not another one of THEM, are you? Oh God! ARE you?*

And: "Naw, not hardly," he answered, hugging her back. "Me, I'm somethin' else."

Thought about killing her too, little as she and her kind still meant to him. But he forbore instead, for now, knowing full well how she'd be good help and better bait once he moved on to richer hunting-grounds: First in a long line of leech-traps, soft skin over hidden teeth. Another potential predator's predator, one he could teach the true value of pretending to be born prey.

He caught his own glance in the bedroom mirror, eyes like peridot set in gold, and smiled a jagged black pearl smile. Thought: *My Christ but I'm handsome, all of a sudden. Must be the light, the angle—something I did. Something I am. Something...*

(Someone)

...I ate.

They spent the rest of the night dismembering their former masters with all the skill taught by long experience, stopped off at a local hospital to use the biohazard incinerator, slept 'til dawn. Then loaded up the van, him and his new apprentice, and headed for fresher pastures. And every time she glanced at him, all worshipful-drunken, he knew just what it was would keep the vampires flocking to 'em: That endless lust to see your reflectionless self cast back from others' eyes, mirrored a thousand times normal size. Demigod promoted to full God status, if only for the length of time it took to make your victim's gaze fix, dim, cloud over with dust and dreams...go out, entirely. After which you moved on, and on.

...you, or someone like you. For they are so easy to find, always...

Well, yeah. But what went around came back the other way 'round, too, that was for damn sure; just as fast, if not faster. And twice as hard.

Because: He could still hear them, blaring behind his eyes even as he drove—all those pirate dream-broadcasts spilling out into the night, calling to him. That was how he navigated down this particular lost and endless highway, knowing full well they'd never even think to hide.

And when they finally fucked for the first time, him and the girl, it was in yet another motel, on yet another dirty bed—the old familiar pattern, varying only in how he deliberately forced himself to be gentle with her, pay attention to her pleasure, like he was breaking her cherry for real this time, with all the traditional attendant joys on tap: Physical show of affection, give as well as take, mutual orgasm, 'love' (or something like it...'cause what did she know, anyhow? Sixteen. What *she* understood about love would probably fit on a sleeveless baby tee, with room left over for two whole additional rows of dirty jokes and Internet quotes).

He slit his wrist open with Cija's knife at the height of it, too, and let her drink from him 'til her lips were crimson, 'til she shivered, blinked and near passed out from the desperate jolt of it.

Thinking: *Won't make you LIKE me, I reckon, but it's good enough to keep you mine…and that ain't too bad, is it? Considering how I'll for damn sure treat you better than any of those fuckers ever treated ME.*

So. Because he *wasn't* them, he finally knew, not really; never had been and never would be, no matter what. But he wasn't nobody, either—not nothing. Neither wolf nor hyena but something new, something *other*, entirely: A chimera, of sorts. A victory of half-life over half-death, made unexpected flesh.

The flesh, the blood. The dark and sparkling Life. The Resurrection.

A Murder of Vampires
by Bev Vincent

Strains of "Highway to Hell" brought Vic out of a deep slumber. One eye popped open, then the other. It took him a few seconds to realize where he was and what was happening. Glowing red digits swam into focus.

2:17.

Operating on instinct, he grabbed his cell phone from the nightstand, flipped it open, and pressed it against his ear, hoping he had it turned the right way around.

"Yeah," he said.

"We've got another one," the voice on the other end said. The man then delivered an address on Uniacke Street, which Vic repeated to confirm that it had registered.

"Right. Fifteen minutes." That was his stock reply, no matter how long it would take him to get to a location.

Olivia rolled over. Another night of disrupted sleep for them both. Why weren't more people murdered in the daytime? he wondered, then brushed the thought aside.

Olivia sat up and waited for him to lean over to be pecked on the cheek. "Sucks to be you," she said. He returned her kiss with a smile she would sense even if she couldn't see it in the dark. Yeah, sometimes it really does, he thought as he rolled out of bed and lurched toward the bathroom.

It was closer to half an hour before he reached his destination. Finding a place that served brewed tea in the middle of the night was getting harder all the time.

Cars and emergency vehicles clustered in the middle of the street, lights flashing, creating an eerie kaleidoscope against the dark walls of nearby buildings. Klieg lights mounted atop portable towers illuminated the surreal tableau.

Vic pulled into the first available parking spot. Car radio chatter filled the night air. Vic noticed several figures lurking along the periphery, clinging to the shadows.

The North End had always been one of the roughest parts of the city, with a long history of violence, but a mass exodus began five years ago, after *they* started moving in. It was a sure sign that a neighbourhood was going south when even the crack dealers and the homeless packed their bags. Now, although the main station was located less than a kilometre away at the south end of Gottingen, the police rarely patrolled this area, responding only to reports of major crimes.

The previous killings had been mentioned briefly on the inner pages of the *Chronicle Herald*, but there wasn't much public pressure to close the cases. Few people cared what went on here, especially if it only involved *them*.

At their mandatory cultural sensitivity classes, members of the Halifax Regional Police had been advised to treat *them* as they would any other minority. "Imagine what it would be like if gay people had been the villains of horror movies for decades before we found out they were living among us," the perky instructor had said.

Sensitivity be damned, Vic thought. Someone was breaking the law and he wouldn't stand for it—even if he would rather be back home in his comfortable bed with Olivia. He clipped his badge to his belt and ducked under the ribbon of crime scene tape that had been strung around the entrance to an alley.

"Nice of you to join us," Sergeant Heck Wilson said. He thought people called him that because his name was Hector, but it really was because they couldn't get away with calling him "Hell," which was what he treated everyone like.

Vic looked past the assembled officers and forensics analysts to the focus of their attention. In the wash of white light from the Kliegs, the pool of blood surrounding the body slumped against the rust-coloured brick wall seemed metallic. The victim was a male, maybe twenty-five years old. His skin was ghostly pale. His hair was a stylish mess, his three-day beard carefully groomed. He wore faded jeans and a grey t-shirt under an unbuttoned black-and-white checked shirt. A wooden stake jutted from his chest.

The only difference between this scene and the other five Vic had been summoned to over the past two months was the blood.

From the way Heck was looking at him, Vic suspected the sergeant was waiting for him to state the obvious, so he did. "The killer got it wrong this time," he said. "Any idea who this is and what he was doing in this part of town?"

"I.D. says his name is Roger Patterson." Heck held it up. "Address on the Northwest Arm."

"Who called it in?"

"Anonymous tip on a disposable phone."

"Any of *them* see anything?" Vic asked, indicating the loiterers. He tried not to over-emphasize the pronoun, but it was a hard habit to break.

"No one's talked to *them* yet," Heck said, not holding back at all. "We were waiting for you."

"Thanks," Vic said.

As he ducked under the crime scene tape again, Vic wondered if there was a collective noun for *them*. A 'murder'? That was an apt description of what had been happening lately but, no, that was for crows. A coven? They hadn't covered that topic in sensitivity training.

This was the first time *they* had congregated at one of the crime scenes. Maybe the freshly spilled blood had attracted *them*. Or, perhaps, the even fresher unspilled blood coursing through the police officers' veins.

Maybe the dead guy in the alley was the vampire killer and his intended victims had caught up with him. The stake in his chest would be irony, then. Since *they* had signed a pact with the government, promising peaceful coexistence, there had never been a documented case of *them* attack-

ing a human, but that didn't mean it couldn't happen—
or that it hadn't already. A lot of crimes went unreported
in a ghetto.

"I'm Detective Newman," he said, trying to keep his
voice steady. Could *they* smell his fear, the way dogs sup-
posedly could? A couple of *them* shuffled *their* feet, but none
spoke. When Vic took another step forward, *they* moved
back as one. This was something he'd learned about *them*.
Proximity to humans was a delicate issue. It was best to
respect *their* boundaries.

"Anyone see what happened?"

A murmur rippled through the assembled group like
a wave. There were no words, at least none that Vic could
understand, but he sensed *they* were conferring. "Does
anyone know the dead man?" He consulted his notes.
"Roger Patterson?"

"Wannabe." In the uncertain light, Vic couldn't tell which
one had spoken.

"Huh?"

"A human who wants to be one of us," another one said.
It had scraggly black hair and dark sunken eyes. Its face
was pudgy, its skin as grey as wallpaper paste.

"Who would want that?" Vic asked.

"You'd be surprised," it said. "Impressionable teenagers.
Lonely middle-aged women."

"Fat!" the first one said. Vic picked it out this time, a
tall, lanky creature wearing a perpetual smirk. Its face
looked like a cadaver's. The pudgy one gave it a sharp look.

"And do you ever—?"

"Convert them? You humans think that's all we want,
isn't it? To convert you?"

"Well—"

"You've seen too many movies. We have no use for your
kind."

"Food!" the lanky creature said with obvious delight.

"Ignore him," the leader said. "He likes to antagonize
humans." It paused. "We just want to be left alone."

"Someone's been killing your kind lately. I assume you
know that. You watch the news?"

"We have our own way of distributing information," it said. Another murmur rippled through the crowd. "But, yes, we know that one of *your* kind is pursuing us."

Vic indicated the alley. "Not him, though."

"Wannabe," the lanky one interjected.

"Not him," the pudgy one said. "Wrong place, wrong time. Those who adulate us take risks. Come out here when it isn't safe."

Vic let that sink in. "Have you seen anyone suspicious hanging around lately?"

"Everyone who comes here looks suspicious to us. And nervous." The pudgy creature fixed its eyes on Vic. "Like you."

"I, uh—"

"Now *he's* antagonizing you," a new voice interjected. It sounded like a woman, but these were creatures, not people, Vic reminded himself. They might look human, but the resemblance ended there.

It took a step forward, until it was bathed in light from the Klieg lamps. Vic's breath caught in his chest. It was...pretty. Its long dark hair hung loose around its shoulders. Its skin was as pale as the murder victim's, but it wasn't repulsive. "We haven't seen anyone who looks like a slayer," it said. "But how would we know? They don't carry signs—most of them, anyway." It smiled and batted its eyelashes at him. "If you saw me on a street corner on a sunny afternoon, would you know what I was?"

Taken by surprise by the creature's appearance and forwardness, he didn't answer. To mask his discomfort, he held out his card. "If you see someone suspicious, please call this number." No one took it. Thinking that *their* un-responsiveness had something to do with *their* aversion to proximity, he bent to place the card on the curb.

The pudgy one said, "We know how to contact you if necessary."

Vic nodded and took a step backward before turning away. It went against every instinct to turn his back on *them*, but he wasn't about to back up all the way to the crime scene. He'd never hear the end of it if he did.

He was about to step under the crime scene tape when something grabbed him by the shoulder and spun him around. He reached for his pistol, but stopped when he heard laughter. The sound was not quite human, as if it had been learned through imitation, yet it had an irresistible allure. A skilled actor, perhaps, displaying an emotion it had never experienced.

"You have no reason to be afraid, you know," the female creature said—the one that had batted its eyes at him. She seemed to have no issues with proximity.

"You surprised me," he said, his heart still pounding. "Not a smart thing to do to an armed man. What do you want?"

"You asked if we'd seen anyone suspicious."

"I thought you hadn't."

"I travel when the others don't." Vic waited for her to continue. Her eyes were wide and deep. A man could get lost in them, he thought. "When the sun is high in the sky. Did you know we could do that? Most simply choose not to."

"Just about everything we think we know about you is based on fiction. Bad fiction, mostly. So you've seen someone hanging around. In the daytime?"

She nodded.

"Not another wannabe."

"This human doesn't want to be seen by us. That's why he comes when he does. He drives a black car. He parks over there." She pointed to a spot near where Vic had left his car.

"You didn't happen to notice the license number?"

"I notice a great many things," she said, raising an eyebrow. "Not that. He is a young man, younger than you, at least, though not as tall. Thin. Dark." She paused. "Full of blood."

"What does he do?"

"Sets traps."

"What sort of trap does someone set to catch...?"

"One of us?"

"Yes," he said, fascinated by the way her eyes gleamed in the faint light. *Her* eyes—when had he started thinking about her that way? He couldn't remember, but at that moment, if she had asked him to step into the shadows so she could show him something, he would have followed. She was close enough that he could see the features in her skin, the places where there should have been veins, but weren't.

She smiled at him again. Her teeth were neat and even, just like Olivia's.

"I don't know," she said at last.

"If you did, would you tell me?"

"Perhaps," she said. "If I believed you wouldn't use it against us." With that she faded into the darkness, gone so quickly that she might simply have vanished.

He pressed his naked body against hers and wrapped an arm around her to cup her breast.

Olivia awoke with a start and twisted to face him. "My, aren't you up early?" she said groggily, reaching between them until her fingers found him, hard and ready. "What's gotten into you?"

He lowered his mouth to her neck and nuzzled the spot that almost always got her motor running. Mere fractions of an inch below the surface, her lifeblood flowed. So much vitality brimming under the surface, and we're barely aware of it, he thought.

Olivia sighed. He moved his mouth lower until he found her hard nipple and sucked it between his lips.

For a few seconds, in the darkness, he imagined another face, another body.

"Anything new?" he asked when he arrived at the Homicide Unit the next morning.

"Forensics is analyzing some footprints that might have come from our perp," Heck said. "Or from anyone else who walked along that sidewalk in the past few days."

"So, we've got nothing."

"We got a headline," Heck said. He tossed the *Chronicle Herald* onto Vic's desk. NIGHT STALKER, the headline read in large type. Five other cases, but it took the death of a poser from the posh end of town to garner media attention.

"Who talked to his family?"

"Dees. His report's on the computer. Nothing much of interest. It seems *they* were right about his obsession, though."

"I'm going back to canvas the neighbourhood."

"Now?"

"We've got nothing else to go on."

"Who will you talk to? *They* only come out at night."

"That's just the name of a record album," Vic said.

Heck shrugged. "Suit yourself."

"I always do."

Vic spent the morning covering a four-block radius around the latest crime scene looking for dark cars or a man who fit the vague description he'd been given. He was hard pressed to find anyone of any description. Heck had been right about that. He wouldn't have been surprised to see tumbleweeds rolling down the street, carried by a cool on-shore breeze. He was reminded of one of those post-apocalyptic movies where the living dead emerged from the gloom to hunt down the survivors and eat their flesh.

Three nights later, he was again awakened by a phone call.

"Yeah," he whispered, trying not to awaken Olivia.

"He got it right this time. Another one of *them*."

"Where?"

"A block from the last one."

"I'll be there in fifteen minutes," Vic said.

It was the tall gangly one he'd encountered a few nights earlier. The one that liked to antagonize people and uttered phrases like someone suffering from Tourette's syndrome.

A wooden stake protruded from his chest like a flag-pole. There was no blood, of course. His eye sockets were empty, as if a vulture had savaged the body. Another few hours and his cheeks and chest would collapse. By daylight, only a yellowed skeleton would remain and by noon it would be as if he had never existed.

"This one was here the other night," Vic said.

"How can you tell?"

"I recognize him."

"Him?" Heck grunted. He turned around to survey their surroundings. "No audience tonight."

"Maybe they're in mourning," Vic said.

Heck shrugged, as if he thought that unlikely.

Vic canvassed the streets for over an hour, but if there were witnesses to this tragedy, they were making themselves scarce.

"Newman. You've got a call," the desk sergeant said the following afternoon. "Line two."

"Who is it?"

"Didn't give her name, but she says you know her."

Vic punched a button on his phone and picked up the receiver. "Detective Newman."

"I saw him again," the voice on the other end said. Female, but low. Sultry.

"Saw who?"

"The human. The one who sets traps for us."

"Where?" he asked, remembering the alluring way she had looked in the shadows, and in his fantasy.

"I will find you if you come here," she said, and the connection broke. Vic tried to trace back the phone number, but the display told him it didn't exist.

"I'm going out," he told Heck, who waved a hand to acknowledge that he heard him without looking away from his computer.

He wasn't sure how to track down a vampire, especially in the daylight. She would stand out in a crowd, no question, but there was no crowd. Should he expect to find her waiting on the sidewalk, or skulking in a dark alley?

He drove up and down the street a few times, but didn't see her, so he pulled into an open space near where she had indicated the suspicious dark man liked to park. He got out and strolled to a spot on the sidewalk halfway between the two most recent crime scenes. Strands of yellow tape fluttered in the breeze, the only sign that something untoward had happened here recently.

A few cars were parked along the curbs, and several apartment windows were open, but no sounds emanated from them and there was no sign of motion to indicate that anyone was home. There weren't even any pigeons on the ledges. This truly has become a forsaken place, he thought.

"I was just about to eat," a female voice said from behind him. "Care to join me?"

Vic spun around. She was standing a few feet away, though he would have sworn she had just whispered in his ear. Despite what he thought he knew about *them*, she wasn't bursting into flames or dissolving in the sunlight. Her skin even seemed to have some color, as if blood was pulsing beneath it. Her long purple dress clung to her chest and her slender hips. She was beyond pretty—she was...sexy. *Dangerous.*

"Eat?" He was still taking her in, observing the way the breeze billowed her dress and played with the ends of her long dark hair. She had doubted that he would recognize her for what she was if he saw her on the street. Well, here she was, and she was right.

"There's a place over here," she said, pointing at a dilapidated storefront.

"You said you had some information for me."

"Yes. Follow me." She turned and started across the street, covering ground quickly, as if she were gliding instead of walking. She entered through the front door without waiting to see if he was following. No sign announced the name of the establishment. Vic wondered if he was signifying something by accepting her invitation. He shook his head. More movie mumbo jumbo. He followed her inside.

It was a restaurant, or at least it might have been at some point in the past. Tables with checked cloths were scattered throughout, devoid of cutlery, condiments or napkin holders. The air smelled of ancient grease, stale cigarette smoke and something else, a mildly rancid odour that made Vic queasy. She went straight to a corner table, as if she came here all the time. Maybe she did. Vic had no idea what *their* lives were like, or if vampires could even be said to have 'lives'.

He sat across from her, placed his elbows on the filthy table and waited, surreptitiously checking out her chest to see if it rose and fell, but she didn't breathe. When she glanced at him, he looked away, shamefaced, like a teenager.

Though the place seemed abandoned, another one of *them* appeared from a back room carrying a covered serving dish. It approached without a word and placed the dish in front of her, removing the cover with a flourish. It then retreated to wherever it had come from.

Vic tried not to gape at what was on her plate. It looked like raw meat. Not a prepared cut with edges trimmed by a butcher, but a jagged clump that might have been ripped from the belly of some unidentified creature. Blood pooled around it.

She raised an eyebrow at him.

"Go ahead," he said, struggling to maintain control of his stomach.

She picked up the meat in her bare hands and stuck one end into her mouth. Instead of biting, she sucked, extracting blood from tissue and muscle. When she was through with one section, she rotated the clump. Finally she ripped the meat in half with her fingers and repeated the process. When she was done, she tossed what looked like freezer-burned remnants onto the table next to the plate. She then licked the plate clean, as if missing a single drop of blood would be a sacrilege.

While his stomach settled down, Vic wondered how many humans had witnessed this ritual. It seemed like a performance for his benefit, as if she wanted to shock him. He waited until she was done licking blood from her fingers, a sight he found disturbingly erotic.

"You said on the phone that you'd seen the man again. The one you thought was setting traps."

"He is close," she said.

"Right now?"

She nodded, and tilted her head back, as if listening for something. "Yes. Follow me," she said, moving so quickly that Vic had to scramble to keep up. A moment later they were back on the street, the sun so bright that it took a few seconds for his eyes to adapt. She didn't seem to suffer the same problem, or any problem with sunlight, that he could see. There's so much about *them* we don't know, Vic thought.

She held up a hand and Vic stopped. "Here," she said, leading him into the recessed entrance of an abandoned building. They retreated far enough to monitor the street without being seen. As they waited, he acknowledged to himself that he was entrusting his life to her. She could sneak up behind him and sink her fangs into his throat and no one would ever know what happened. His eyes would open some time later and he'd be one of *them*. He started breathing through his mouth.

"You humans are so nervous," she said. "What must your fragile lives be like?"

He could have said something about how it was *their* fragile lives that brought him here, but he didn't.

Seconds later, a black Lexus came into sight. Because the neighbourhood was deathly quiet, the purr of its engine and the whisper of its tires against the pavement were audible from their vantage point. It pulled in behind Vic's car.

The thin man who emerged was dressed in dark clothing and wore a baseball cap. He surveyed the street, and then headed into the blind alley across from them, the one where Patterson's body had been found. He carried something in his hand but, from this distance, Vic couldn't tell what.

It was Vic's turn to lead. As they crossed the street, he felt exposed, as if everyone behind the windows facing the street was watching. He kept one hand on his holster, in case the suspect reappeared.

When they reached the sidewalk, Vic pressed his back against the wall while he debated whether to summon assistance. Any backup was a long way off. Even in the daylight, there were no patrol cars in this part of town. The man in the alley was their only solid lead in Patterson's murder, and the deaths of six of *them*.

He withdrew his sidearm and took a deep breath. "Stay here," he said. "I'm going in." He stepped around the corner with his weapon in one hand and his badge in the other.

The man was bent over, poking around among the debris that lined the alley walls.

"Freeze!" Vic shouted, holding out his badge. "Show me your hands."

The man flinched and looked up. He withdrew his hands from the rubbish and held them flat and extended away from his body.

"Straighten up."

The man complied. As Vic approached, he observed that the man's hands were covered in what looked like blood.

"What are you doing here?"

The man started to reach for his back pocket.

Vic waggled his gun. "Keep your hands where I can see them."

"I was only going to show you my wallet, officer."

"I asked what you were doing."

The man shrugged. "Hunting for buried treasure," he said. "You never know what people leave lying around places like this." He cocked his head. "That's not a crime, is it?"

"Why do you have blood on your hands?"

The man looked at them as if he was surprised. "I must have cut myself." He wiped them on his pants, leaving crimson palm prints on the dark material. "If you would just let me show you my wallet, we could clear this whole thing up."

The man suddenly crouched, moved to his left, reached behind his back again, and produced a gun.

Vic fired once, missed, and rolled to the side. He heard the other gun go off. A split second later, something punched his left shoulder. He only realized he'd been shot when the pain kicked in. Crouched behind a cardboard box, he pressed his hand against the wound. Blood seeped between his fingers.

Something fluttered past. Then there was a rustling sound and a muffled thud. "Hey, what?" the other man said. Then he was screaming. "Get off me. Get it off!"

Vic emerged from cover.

The man was flat on his back, with the female sitting astride his chest, her hands at his throat. His weapon was on the ground, out of reach. His voice reached a fever pitch. "Help me. You've got to help me. It's—"

He fell silent.

Vic approached, his gun extended and his finger on the trigger, ready to shoot. His left arm dangled uselessly at his side. He forced the burning pain from his mind.

She stood as he drew near. Her eyes locked onto his shoulder. Her lips parted.

The other man didn't move. His eyes were open as if he were transfixed by the sky.

"What did you do to him? Is he—?"

"The last thing in the world we want is a creature like him among us. We have more to fear from your kind than you do from us." She was still staring at his shoulder. "He is in a trance. He will return to normal soon. When he does, he will tell you anything you want to know." She looked away at last. "It is good that I fed," she said before bending down to where the man had been rummaging. When she straightened up, she held a bloody chunk of meat in her hands. "This would have been a difficult prize to ignore otherwise." She held it to her nose. "It's human."

"Human?"

"A heart. Bait. We don't kill humans, but that doesn't mean your blood doesn't tempt us." She set the organ down on the alley's tar and licked her hand clean. "You would do well to leave here. Soon," she said, nodding at his injured shoulder.

Vic holstered his gun so he could extract his phone from his pocket and call for reinforcements.

"You are not like the others," she said when he was done.

"What do you mean?" He almost added that he had been thinking the same about her.

"They don't care what happens to us."

"It's my job to catch criminals," he said.

"I'm not sure that your friends agree that he committed a crime. At least, not until he killed a human." She turned and started toward the back of the blind alley.

"Where are you going?" he called after her. "You can't leave—you're a witness."

"Goodbye, Detective Newman," she said. "Thank you for your help. I could not deal with him alone. Because of the pact." She stepped into a shadow and vanished.

Vic followed her. When he reached the end of the alley, he found no doors or windows. No way out—and yet she was gone.

A siren approached in the distance. He returned to the suspect and checked his vital signs. The man blinked. Vic wrestled him onto his stomach with his good arm and handcuffed him.

While he waited for the other officers to arrive, he removed his hand from his shoulder and stared at his own blood, wondering how hard it had been for her to walk away.

The afternoon was growing late. Soon it would be dusk. Vic regarded the windows in the surrounding buildings and thought about all the other creatures behind them that might sense the bait and the blood seeping from his wound.

She was right. He would do well to leave here soon.

The Greatest Trick
By Steve Vernon

Let's get one thing straight.

We don't turn into bats.

Why in the world would we want to?

But, because they saw that trick in a movie, people believe it must be true.

That's just how it is.

People believe exactly what they expect to see and people's expectations must always be met. For example, if a man sits down to watch a Three Stooges movie, sooner or later he expects to see a two-finger poke in the eye.

He doesn't expect high art. He expects a poke in the eye. Anything else is a lie. Mind you, there are some of us who have raised the act of lying to a state of high art.

If you tell it right, a lie can be immortal.

And some of the most immortal lies in history began with those three magic words—"If I'm elected..."

Jessome invited me inside his office. He began our first meeting by informing me that he had a crucifix in his pocket and he wasn't afraid to use it.

Things went uphill from there.

"Nobody is going to vote for a vampire," Jessome said, after I explained what I wanted of him.

"They voted for Schwarzenegger," I pointed out. "And he married one."

"Shriver?"

"The cheekbones are a dead giveaway," I explained. "I thought you had a better eye than that."

Jessome sighed, a long resigning exhalation. That was his strength. He was a thin-blooded man who had smoked too much and hadn't eaten enough red meat. Those who took him on in full-out debate were inescapably handicapped by the growing sensation that they were listening to a dying man's final declaration.

The word was will-power.

"People have a picture in their minds when they think of vampires," I explained. "I need to get elected in order to dispel that illusion."

Jessome knew about illusion. The man was a guerrilla in velvet gloves. He fought by ambush, diplomatic guile and misdirection.

In short, he was the perfect campaign manager.

"You're a man with a cause," Jessome said.

"Yes I am," I said, overlooking the fact that I really wasn't anything close to what you'd call a man.

"I'm not in the cause-fighting business," Jessome said.

"That isn't all that I am looking for," I said.

Jessome considered that. "Convince me," he said.

"They voted for Ronald Reagan," I noted. "They voted for Clint Eastwood. They voted for Sonny Bono. Hell, they even voted for Jesse freaking Ventura."

"Were the four of them all vampires?"

"They were images," I said. "That's all the general public is looking for."

"I thought vampires didn't cast images."

"No, but we can project them." I said. "Larger than life."

"Do you figure you can fool most of the people enough of the time to count?"

"All I have to do is tell enough lies to sound like it's the truth," I said.

Jessome thought about that.

"It's just not going to happen," he said. "America will not elect a vampire."

"You don't think so?"

Jessome shook his head with authority.

I was patient. I needed Jessome on my side. It was his clout and his know how that would open doors that I would otherwise not be invited to enter.

Politically speaking, invitations can be awfully important, especially when you're a vampire.

"All it will take is a matter of votes," I said. "I've got
a platform. I've got charisma. And I've got a gimmick."

"Sure," Jessome said. "It's a hell of a gimmick. What
other candidate sleeps in a coffin?"

"Listen," I told him. "When the pot boils down to dry,
politicians are nothing more than a pack of slimy leeches.
Everybody knows that politicians suck. I just intend to be
honest about it."

Jessome still wasn't listening. He needed some convincing. So I played a vampire's ace-in-the-hole and looked
him squarely in the eye.

"Political promises go in one year and out the other,"
I told him. "The important thing is to keep a straight face
when you're making them."

Jessome kept listening. I could not tell if my stare was
working.

"What most voters are looking for is a candidate who
is a natural leader," I explained, attempting to enforce my
will upon him. "Bluntly put, they want somebody to lead
them."

I kept looking him in the eye.

He didn't blink.

Agree with me, I thought.

I waited for that blank nod but Jessome was two steps
ahead of me.

"Don't bother trying any of your Jedi-Lugosi mind
control tricks," Jessome said. "I'm wearing a set of contact lenses that have been blessed by a bishop, a rabbi, and
an Alabama telemarketer who caught me by cell phone at
a weak moment."

I smiled at that. I shouldn't have, because a vampire's
smile is anything but encouraging. Still, I had to give him
credit for surprising me. I had fully expected the crucifix.
Everybody knew that one. However, I hadn't expected the
thrice-blessed contact lenses.

"I don't imagine you've ever had any weak moments,"
I told him. "Not as far as I can see."

Jessome almost smiled. "Every week or so I allow myself at least one moment of weakness," he bragged. "How else do I stay so humble?"

"So, can I count on you?" I asked.

"You're determined to do this?"

I nodded.

"Determination is a key factor," he said. "I wouldn't do this if I thought your heart wasn't in it."

He let that sink in.

Finally he said, "Let's do this."

I grinned. To hell with the image.

My idea had just evolved into a plan.

To be completely honest, the original idea had risen up in my imagination shortly after the launch of the reality television show, one year ago.

Do you remember that show? Just about three years after the great coming out of the undead? The show hit the air waves and Survivor was promptly voted off of the island. Trump fired himself and American Idol grew tone-deaf.

In short, the show was a phenomenal success.

In my opinion whoever thought of the original concept for the show ought to be slowly turned on a rotisserie spit over one of the hottest pits in perdition. I mean, can you believe the title they came up with?

Who Wants to Be A Vampire?

What I would like to know is just who in the hell sat up at night for at least three and a half minutes of an existence that they will never successfully retrieve, dreaming up that particular title?

As banal as it sounds, the title worked. The ratings soared as people tuned in—despite the fact that a rumour was hastily released by a high-ranking executive employed by a competitor network. The rumour hinted that some form of over-the-air vampiric mind control was directly responsible for the show's immediate success.

In response, the ratings soared even higher.

The executive responsible for the release of the rumour promptly disappeared.

Further rumours hinted that perhaps the legions of the undead were responsible for the executive's mysterious disappearance.

Like that bat that glued himself to the space shuttle, the ratings hit the freaking moon. From one side of the country to the other, contestants battled for the opportunity to join the ranks of the undead. They bleached their skin, endured painful dental implants, learned to sleep comfortably in a coffin and cultivated a taste for human blood.

The entire phenomenon was a pure and undeniable affirmation of the power of the wanna-be—the same driving force behind hair dye, pectoral implants, Viagra and air-brushed photography.

We all want to be something we're not.

After years of coveting the lives of movie stars, rock singers, professional wrestlers and long haul winter truckers, a new yearning had emerged from the shadows. A brand new age-old creature, coaxed out of the darkness and into the daylight, thanks partly to the development of powerful 1000+ SPF sun blocking agents developed in order to counter-act the increased UV radiation that was no longer being filtered by the dying ozone layer.

Life as humans knew it was undergoing an unexpected change. They were learning to hide from the sun.

A kinship was evolving.

It was time for the vampire to take his rightful place on the center stage of this planet.

Three weeks into the campaign the struggle began to heat up as we got down to brass coffin nails.

"You've got three men to worry about," Jessome said. "Samuel Garton, Nelson Hackle and Harold Lee."

"I'm not worried about Samuel Garton or Nelson Hackle," I said. "They don't really seem to be paying much attention to my campaign."

"That is in your favour," Jessome said. "Because you're a novelty act, they don't take you that seriously. You're coming in under their radar of credibility, but if you want to be taken seriously, you need to take them both very seriously."

"Seriously?" I quipped.

Jessome didn't like that one bit.

"Did you hire me as a campaign manager or a straight man?" Jessome wanted to know.

"Both, actually."

Jessome refused to grin. As far as I could tell the man had all of the *joie de vivre* plus the sense of humour of a four day old ripening cadaver.

"Samuel Garton has maturity and experience on his side," Jessome went on. "He's in office already, so he just has to keep his balance and he'll beat us. We need to push him off balance."

"Any ideas on that?"

"I have some photographs that will wobble his platform nicely," Jessome said.

He showed them to me. They were definitely thought provoking. I didn't think one man could successfully satisfy so many leather-clad women. I wasn't sure what to make of the Doberman.

"That's the advantage of being a vampire," I said. "We're paparazzi proof."

"Exactly," Jessome said.

"I think I recognize one of these ladies," I said.

"It might be he wasn't wearing a set of thrice-blessed contact lenses when he laid eyes on her," Jessome allowed, tapping a finger beside his right eye socket. "You aren't the only vampire on our team, you know."

I hadn't known.

I wondered what else I didn't know.

And then I decided that ignorance was bliss.

"Well I hope he had fun," I said.

"What he remembers of it," Jessome allowed.

"And Nelson Hackle?"

"Don't worry about Nelson Hackle," Jessome said. "Plans are already in motion."

"Anything I ought to worry about?"

"Deniability is an asset."

I could take a hint. Politics was a dirty business—a profession that made mass murder and habitual exsanguinations appear immaculate by comparison.

"That leaves Harold Lee."

"Harold Lee sees you as a threat. He's already launched a smear campaign centered on the slogan—*DO YOU WANT TO LET THE LIFE BLOOD OF THIS STATE BE SUCKED OUT BY VAMPIRIC GREED?*"

"Catchy."

"We're countering with *SAY HELLO TO THE NIGHT LIFE.*"

I groaned.

"Vampires don't appreciate puns?" Jessome asked.

"Not puns as bad as that."

"Don't sneer," Jessome said. "It isn't becoming."

"Hello to the night life?"

"There is a direct correlation between the number of words in a political slogan and its ultimate effectiveness," Jessome explained. "Simply put, the American populace has a low tolerance for word-windy bastards."

No wonder Jessome had never run for office.

"Or perhaps they've just got a short attention span," I said.

"I'm sorry." Jessome arched one eyebrow in as close an approximation of wryness as his inner reserve would allow. "Did you say something?"

The first vampire came out to the world on a late night talk show, hosted by an interviewer who looked a little like a genetically modified clonally tri-hybrid of the worst features of Carson, Leno and Letterman combined.

Between the thick layer of mega SPF sun block and the added layers of make-up that were required to actually allow the vampire to appear on television screens, folks who unintentionally channel-surfed into the broadcast thought that they were either watching an interview with the latest member of the *Blue Man Group* or a promo for the upcoming *Watchmen* part six—Doctor Manhattan: Bigger, Bluer and Uncut.

In spite of the indigo misconception, the word got out.

Vampires were real.

The media was crammed with government-sanctioned leech-hunts and good old-fashioned home-grown vigilantism. The price of garlic hit new world highs. Local churches did a booming business in blessed crucifixes and vials of holy water. Synagogues sold the Star of David. Bram Stoker's *Dracula* hit the bestseller list and Stephen King announced that he was working on a twelve-book sequel to *Salem's Lot*.

The increase of public pressure gradually brought the rest of the vampires out into the daylight. Whether they liked it or not, the vampire race was suddenly newsworthy. A combination of spin-doctoring, big budget advertising, talk show appearances and random drive-by *Youtube* shootings accomplished what years of Christopher Lee, Anne Rice and Stephenie Meyer had never dreamed of.

I don't believe every vampire appreciated the sudden exposure. A lot of them would have preferred to remain safely hidden in the realm of urban myth, cheap movies and wistful goth fantasy.

Who could blame them?

One lone exhibitionist brought centuries of tomb dust and tradition to a sudden unsanctified kneeling halt, squarely in the heart of a hundred foot-candle spotlight.

As the notoriety of the vampire populace increased, minority activists nobly stepped in to champion this here-to-for unacknowledged group of the culturally disenfranchised. The need for undead rights soon overtook the proactive lobbyists who had previously dedicated their existence and their undeniable need for a stable income towards fighting for the rights of beached killer whales and wartime refugees, AIDs victims and the homeless. Politicians began to cultivate relationships with the ranks of the undead. Photo ops and graveyard ribbon cuttings became synonymous.

As election time drew near, the mudslinging began. Rumours were spread that certain vampire-friendly politicians were nothing more than a pack of Renfield-like pawns of the vampiric race.

Which was exactly where I came in.

Two weeks prior to Election Day, Samuel Garton made a discrete withdrawal from the candidacy race. He blamed it on family pressure and a need to reprioritize his life. He had seen the Doberman and leather girl photos. Scandal and divorce had no place in his plan of action.

Nelson Hackle, on the other hand, was the victim of a mysterious midnight mugging on his way home from the theatre.

"He must have put up a fight," Jessome said. "I can't understand it, myself. He didn't have that much in his wallet."

"Was that in the police report?" I asked. "How could you find out a detail like that?"

"Ways and means," Jessome assured me.

Do you think I was being callous?

Eggs needed to be broken.

Eyes needed to be poked out.

When you enter politics, check your ethics at the door.

"So that brings it down to myself and Harold Lee," I said. "Will he be mugged as well?"

"Now that would be quite an unacceptable coincidence, wouldn't it?"

"Quite," I said. "Only I'm certain I don't believe in coincidence."

Jessome let that comment slide.

"The polls have us marginally ahead," he informed me. "We don't really have to do anything at all."

That wasn't good enough for me. I had come too far to take chances now.

"I don't believe in polls any more than I believe in coincidence," I answered. "And unless you've replaced those blessed contact lenses with a pair of all-seeing crystal balls, I'm not all that comfortable with depending upon luck."

"There's nothing crystalline about my balls," Jessome said. "Politics is always a crap shoot."

"How do we load the dice?"

Wordlessly, Jessome held up a small vellum envelope.

"Are you going to tell me what's in that envelope?" I said. "Or is this the second half of your mind reading act?"

Jessome smiled. "It's an invitation. A *personalized* invitation."

I took the envelope from him.

His smile widened, just a little.

"Enter freely," he said. "And of your own will."

Two nights later I used that personalized invitation to enter Harold Lee's bedroom. I stepped out of the shadows, resisting the impulse to say something corny like *I've come to drink your blood!*

"I'm the Batman," was what I settled for.

Then I had a good long talk with Mr. Harold Lee.

The next morning Harold Lee met with the local Baptist minister and told him that not only was God dead, but He was most likely buried in an unmarked grave. From there, he moved on to insult both a rabbi and a Muslim religious leader, simultaneously.

He ended the day by insulting a Malaysian shaman. Oddly enough, Mr. Harold Lee wasn't even aware that he spoke perfect Malaysian. Following his rain of politically incorrect *faux pas,* he found himself on the receiving end of a sudden boycott, a jihad, a Sunday edition of the newspaper crammed full of abrasive political cartooning and the gift of a cursed Zuni fetish doll.

It was a politician's wet dream.

I was voted in on a mud slide.

A month after my election, the honeymoon was over.

"You can't do this," Jessome said. "Congress will not stand for it."

"This country has a soaring crime rate," I said. "Police forces are seriously undermanned."

"The budget will address this," Jessome said. "It always has."

"Our fiscal budget couldn't address a self-addressed envelope," I said. "We're in the middle of a war on poverty, crime and ignorance."

"I won't deny that," Jessome said.

"A war that we're losing."

"That's debatable."

I wasn't listening. This was what I had fought so hard for. I wanted to get elected in order to make a real difference.

There needed to be significant change.

"There's no room for debate," I said. "You're supposed to be my aide, so aid me."

"And if I don't?"

"Then I'll find myself another aide, more helpful than you."

One more sigh.

"What do you want to do?" Jessome asked.

"I'll talk to Congress tomorrow."

"Do you really think they'll listen?"

I smiled, letting my teeth show. I was the governor now. There was no more need for any false faces.

"Not all of them are smart enough to wear contact lenses," I pointed out.

That summer the first squads of undead police were officially activated.

What better deterrent for criminal activity? At any moment the night might come alive with police who could not be shot or stabbed or escaped from.

In two months the crime rate dropped by twelve percent. After that the situation evolved. By the third month criminals began arming themselves with holy water, wooden stakes, garlic and crucifixes.

"We're not winning," Jessome said. "We're just escalating the situation."

"I'm a vampire," I said. "I have endured a lifelong standing tradition of situations escalating to torch and pitchfork and worse. Besides, if they're carrying crucifixes and holy water, that means they're leaving the assault rifles at home."

"Do you think that's funny?" Jessome asked.

"I'm still smiling," I said, with a shrug. "In fact, we're looking at increasing the percentage of vampires on the various police forces. It's not just major crime that needs to be addressed."

"Are you planning to start taking down jay-walkers?"

"If need be. The populace is ripe for a stronger state of control."

He took that in. "Are there that many of you?"

"It's easy enough to recruit," I said.

Jessome stared at me.

He let the conversation grow cold.

The two of us stood there, alone in the office.

Finally, he spoke. "This isn't going to stop with the police, is it?"

Another shrug.

"The military?" he asked.

"For starters," I said. "We need more men in Congress, as well. The oval office would make a dandy mausoleum."

"You're ambitious."

"Vampirism is a little like religion. It's as catchy as small pox."

I looked out the window. I could see the lights of the city sparkling like so many distant stars. I dreamed of holding them all in the palm of my hand and squeezing down hard.

When I turned, Jessome was holding a very large crucifix in his extended hand. Silver, of course. He wasn't taking any chances on cheap alloy.

"I can't let this go any further," he said.

"You're in bed already," I told him. "*In flagrante delicto.*"

I stepped closer.

He pushed the cross towards me.

"It's funny. After all these years of letting the world believe that we were only fairy tales, of letting the world believe that we turned into bats and lived in coffins, after all these centuries of letting people believe that a holy symbol really had some kind of power over us..."

I stepped a little closer.

"A lie can last a very long time." I stepped even closer. "Looking at the cross, even now, I almost want to flinch."

I reached out and crumpled the crucifix as if it were made of tin foil.

I crumpled his hand with it.

From this close up, I could see the wet glint of Jessome's thrice-blessed contact lenses. I wondered just how much he had paid for them on the open market. I wondered if he had a patent and whether or not I should buy stock in the company.

I kept hold of his fist all the while, crushing the bones as if they were a fistful of impotent wafers.

As he screamed, I made a peace sign out of my index and middle finger.

I leaned in a little closer.

"Hey Moe," I whispered, driving my two extended fingers directly through Jessome's thrice-blessed contact lenses and the salty jelly of his eyes, deep into the truth and knowledge that hid behind the mask of vision.

Soulfinger
By Rio Youers

"He plays the blues."

"Yes he does. Better than anyone."

"So why is he called Soulfinger?"

"You want the quick answer, or the not-so-quick answer?"

"The quick answer."

"Because when he plays, he touches your soul."

"Cute, but is he really that good?"

"No. Whatever you have in your mind, however you determine what is good—it might be fine wine or the memory of your first true love—take that and multiply it by a number you can't imagine. Only then will you be anywhere close to what Soulfinger can do. He is the moon, brother. He is the ocean. The sky can rain fire and the mountains can fall, but Soulfinger will always be playing the blues."

The bar was called The Smokestack—a rumbling blues joint on Whispering Avenue. Blacked-out windows and heartache on the walls. The doors didn't open until ten P.M., and they opened on a long room that was tapered at the far end, like the world's biggest coffin. The air tasted of cigarette smoke and sweat, heavy with woe, something that could tip a scale.

"What time does he go on stage?"

"When he's ready. Soulfinger doesn't concern himself with hours and minutes, with clocks..." The bartender ticked off seconds with his index finger: *tick-tock-tick.* "He has his own agenda."

"A luxury. I can't stay here all night, though."

"The door is right there, brother. No one is stopping you from easing on down the road. Not yet, at least."

"Not yet? That sounds almost...threatening." Peter Hale smiled. Twenty-two years in journalism, the last six freelance. He was used to threats, subtle or otherwise. Both work and curiosity had brought him to The Smokestack; he was researching an article, but Soulfinger had long intrigued him. Stories about the man were legend, wreathed in mystery. He was here to get closer.

"Take it anyway you like," the bartender said. The jukebox flickered into life before Peter could question him further. The sound of the mechanism engaging, of the needle touching down on old vinyl, seemed too loud in the stillness. Hiss and thump, like someone's heart when you have your ear pressed to their chest. And then music. No—the *blues*. A harmonica in the key of C: the reedy push and pull of bruised emotions.

An old man at the bar started to sing along. He mumbled through down-turned lips. His eyes were the same colour as the rum in his glass.

> Lord I swear I'm so beaten down,
> Got nothing left to lose.

The bar was long, subtly curved inward, like a shoreline, endlessly subjected to waves of hardship. Bottles and glasses glittered, a solar system of promises, miracles, and painkillers. There were refrigerators loaded with beer, the usual brands, and one Peter had never seen before: red label on a brown bottle. A home brew, perhaps. Peter was about to ask about it when the bartender threw his towel over one shoulder, held up his index finger again, and said, "One tick, brother. I'll be back."

He walked away to serve another customer, leaving Peter to sip his drink, make some notes, and gaze around the bar. The walls were clustered with dusty instruments—guitars with missing strings; bass skins beaten like planished metal—and pictures of blues legends, some of them signed: *Thanks for taking care of me. We'll roll again...*Big Joe Turner. *For everyone at The Smokestack, best damn blues joint in America...*Muddy Waters. There was another photograph of a young man dressed in cheap, ill-fitting garments, playing guitar in the moonlight while a mosaic of black, timeless faces looked on.

Empty chairs and tables, with only a few old timers making waves at the bar.

> *Pour me another shot of heartache, Lord,*
> *Got nothing left to lose.*

A waitress stood with her back to him, a short jean skirt and slender arms, her skin as dark as her hair. She turned her face and he saw her in profile. His heart was stretched— pulled against his ribcage with a succession of cymbal crashes. He slipped off the barstool and took a helpless step toward her, and when she turned away it was as if some taut line between them had broken. Peter stumbled back- ward, knocking his glass, spilling S. Pellegrino on his notepad. Words ran across the page, stretched like his heart. Words that were crying.

"Jesus." He wiped his eyes, used a napkin to dab water from his notepad, and another to dab sweat from the bridge of his nose. The jukebox whirred, clicked, and scratched. Slide guitar snaked from the speakers. The old man at the bar nodded and looked at his glass of rum.

"Are you here to see Soulfinger?" Peter asked him, but he didn't really care. He was making conversation, hoping to ease the jitters that had suddenly come over him. He glanced at the waitress again. She still had her back to him, and that was a good thing, he thought.

The old man turned to him, his head rolling loosely on his thin neck. His skin was grey. He seemed as dusty as the instruments on the wall.

"Boy," he said. "I'm always here."

The bartender returned, towel still on one shoulder. He was a tall man with sleepy, hound-dog eyes. Those eyes regarded Peter, and then dropped to the words running like blood across his notepad.

"Need another drink?"

Peter nodded. "Something harder."

"Yeah...look like you need it."

Peter pointed at the refrigerator. "What's that? Bottom shelf...red label."

"You ain't ready for that, brother."

"What is it?"

The bartender smiled. "Something special. A house brew."

"I thought so." He balled another napkin and wiped a mist of sweat from beneath his eyes. "Hot in here. I'll take a Jim Beam on the rocks."

"You got it."

"Who's in the picture?" Peter pointed at the man playing guitar in the moonlight. "I don't recognize him."

The bartender measured a generous shot. Ice rattled in the glass. He looked to where Peter pointed. "That's him," he said. "That's the man."

"Soulfinger?"

"The man."

He was leaning over the guitar, head down, fingers dancing on the strings. The people behind him, watching him, were dressed in the same cheap clothes. *Slave rags*, Peter thought. Their eyes were painted white by flash powder, or the moon. Peter had seen enough photographs during his career to be able to date this one to the mid-nineteenth century. The subject—Soulfinger—looked to be about twenty years old.

Peter sipped his drink. His heart eased. "I don't think so," he said.

The bartender smiled. "It don't matter what you think."

"That photograph was taken well over a hundred years ago."

"One hundred and fifty years ago. Taken in 1860 by Mr. William F. Pearsall of the Sipsey River Plantation. *Massa* William F. Pearsall—Soulfinger's owner."

Peter raised one eyebrow. His felt his mouth become a firm line and his eyes glisten with contempt. "Do I look like a fool?"

The bartender's upper lip flickered. Almost a smile. Almost a sneer.

"I have an M.A. from the Missouri School of Journalism; I've written articles for the *New Yorker* and *Rolling Stone;* I've won several awards, including the Livingstone. I am nobody's fool, *brother*. Facts are my trade, and I have no time or patience for tall tales. You want to tell me about Soulfinger? That's fine. I'll listen. I'll report. But keep the fiction in check."

The bartender gestured with his index finger. *Tick-tock-tick*. He smiled, moved along the bar, and served the old man. *Boy, I'm always here*. Shot of something gold. It disappeared between verses. Another shot. The old man nodded, mumbled. The bartender returned.

"Facts," he said, nodding, and the bar lights cast mauve tones on his skin. "I'll give you a fact right now, Mr. *Rolling Stone*: there are things in this world that lie beyond explanation. Magic and miracles. God's work...or the devil's."

"God doesn't exist," Peter said. "Neither does the devil. When you get that into your head, you'll realize that everything has an explanation."

"Then explain love at first sight."

"Like God, it doesn't exist; it's a weak, false emotion attached to perception." But Peter faltered, and he looked at the waitress, her back to him, her raven hair falling to the small of her back, and his heart moved again, almost volcanic.

"You need to open your eyes, brother," the bartender said, then shook his head, corrected himself. "No...you need to open your *soul*."

"Yeah. Okay."

The bartender smiled.

"Tell me about Soulfinger."

"He plays the blues."

"Right. Better than anyone." Peter looked at the old photograph again. "And he's what...one hundred and seventy years old?"

"One hundred and seventy-two."

There was a small stage at the far end of the bar, little more than a step, where the 'coffin' tapered. An empty stool sat in the middle, next to a mic stand and amp. More photographs on the wall. Robert Johnson. Blind Willie McTell. And a simple poster—black lettering on a white background:

TONITE: SOULFINGER

There were more people in The Smokestack now. The empty chairs and tables were being filled. Peter frowned; he hadn't seen anybody walk in. They bustled, laughed, drank: red labels on brown bottles. The jukebox hissed and thumped. "Bad Train Down."

The old man grumbled, mumbled, drooled.

> *All my people get on board,*
> *We don't stop 'til we die.*

Peter swirled the Jim Beam in his glass. Ice chattered like teeth.

"Okay," he said. "Give me the not-so-quick answer."

He plays in 4/4 time, barely touching the strings, easing into those familiar, worn places on the fretboard. The sound that vibrates from the hollow is all pain and feeling. It is his lover's touch, her words and kindnesses. Tears paint his brown skin. The music reassures him.

He cradles his guitar. This is love.

She comes to him, as if responding to the music, to his pain. Her fingers find the tears on his face—silver lines—and as she touches them, breaks through them, he plays the appropriate note. The final tear, the clearest line, is F#.

"Did yo see him?" she asks.

He opens his mouth to reply but his lips tremble and his throat closes. He nods, vaguely, and lets the music answer for him: A-minor to C, and she understands. She touches his hair and kisses his brow, tasting his sweat, feeling his heat. There is a bucket of cold water at her feet, and the softest cloth she can find.

"Tek off'n yo shirt," she says. "I's see to yo a-hurtin'."

He nods and more tears spill down his cheeks. A# and D. He plays the notes, then sets aside his guitar and unbuttons his shirt. His thin brown body is exposed, every rib, the sinews of muscles worked hard, the darker skin of his nipples. His back is red, hashed with more than a hundred fresh whip marks. Blood has soaked his hemp pants. It drips off the stool he is sitting on. He lowers his head and cries the blues.

His name is Abram Wallace. In years to come he will be known only as Soulfinger. He will play his music and gather his audience, searching for what he has lost. But now, hurting and human, bleeding and mortal, his name is Abram Wallace.

"Oh, Lawd," she says. Her name is Charity, his wife and his love. She understands him, like the music. "Deah, Lawd..." Soft cloth, dripping icy water fresh from the well, applied to his wounds. "Oh, Lawd." Her touch is as soft as it has ever been, even in moments of intimacy, but Abram still groans and closes his eyes. The pain is the reverse of love, but her touch, and his expression, are the same.

"No mo' a-hurtin', Lawd," he says. "I's so tired."

"No mo'," Charity agrees. She is crying, too. Her tears are a different music: waterfall of cymbals; raincloud of cellos, a sonorous and labouring sound—the great bow of misery drawn across strings as thick as the lash marks on his back.

"I seen him," Abram says. "He fount me, honeychile. Came a-walking from da darkness. Da ghostie. Da Hoodoo Man."

"Yo stay away from him," Charity says, dipping the cloth in the bucket. The water turns red, but it is still cold, and Abram sighs when she lays it on his back. "He da devil."

Abram nods. "He sets and a-plays his gitta, and dat music sing to me. It's so sweet-soundin', and I's..." His body shudders, sweat gleaming on his brow. "I's so tempted to go to him. I thinkin' dere be no mo' pain wit da Hoodoo Man."

"No pain. No love. Ain't nuthin' in da darkness. Yo git dat thinkin' from yo head." She squeezes the cloth in her fist. Blood drips into the bucket. It is beneath her fingernails. On her wrists.

The Hoodoo Man knows his name, and knows where to find him. He comes when the pain is overwhelming: an orchestra of red; crescendo of hurt...and when life feels that it should slip away, the Hoodoo Man is there, pale and naked, carrying his guitar.

"He dead," Abram says. "Jus' a ghostie. Dat's all. "

Dead...has to be dead. Abram can't read or write—can barely count his fingers and toes—but he knows the difference between living and dead. The Hoodoo Man is whip-thin and shimmering white. His face is a terrible window. No eyes or mouth, only a misty void, and sometimes the mist will clear and Abram will see the night sky there, or fire. His guitar is sublime, though, and he uses it to communicate, strumming and plucking. Abram is drawn to him. Abram understands.

"He da devil," Charity says again, and Abram nods, wincing as the cold water runs over his bleeding back.

"We should stop right now," Peter said. He made a few notes while the bartender talked, but scratched them out and flipped closed the book. "I told you...I'm nobody's fool. I've been commissioned to write an article on the progression of the blues throughout North America. From Hart Wand to Shemekia Copeland. I don't want a goddam ghost story. This is bullshit."

"You asked me about Soulfinger, so I'm telling you." The bartender held his arms wide and shrugged. His palms were creamy-white. "Like I said, brother...some things exist on the other side of explanation."

"Like faceless, guitar-plucking phantoms?"

"All manner of wickedness." He held up one finger. "I'll be back in—"

"One tick?"

The bartender nodded and moved away. Peter put the cap on his pen and clipped it inside his shirt pocket. He swirled the ice in his glass and finished his drink. It was time to "ease on down the road," as the bartender put it. From *The Wiz.* Cute, but it was just more bullshit. The whole night had been bullshit. A waste of time. Peter was beginning to wonder if Soulfinger existed at all.

His gaze was drawn to the picture of the slave playing guitar in the moonlight. He imagined the man tied to a whipping post, an overseer cracking rawhide across his naked back, punishing him until the pain gave way to cloudy patches of delirium and hallucination.

"Ghosties," Peter said. He closed his eyes for a moment. Abram Wallace floated into his mind, sitting in the gloom of his cabin while his wife soothed his wounds with icy water.

He fount me, honeychile. Came a-walking from da darkness. Da ghostie. Da Hoodoo Man.

Poor Boy Cleon on the jukebox. "Stormy Woman Blues."

The empty stool on stage. TONITE: SOULFINGER. And the joint was full, every table ringed with people. They lined the walls and crowded the floors. Peter shook his head. Where did they all come from? The door was behind him; he'd get a blast of cold air every time it opened, and he hadn't felt that but three or four times all night. So where did...?

"I haven't seen you here before."

Peter swiveled on his stool and came face to face with the waitress. Her eyes were like highways, dark and endless, reaching some distant, perfect horizon. He took to the wheel and drove, pedal hard to the floor, giving himself to her landscape. She was not, he thought, so attractive; her cheekbones were too pronounced, almost vulpine, and her mouth too heavy. But there was something—some glimmer—about her that was captivating...enticing, like a perilous height, or broken glass.

> *She took my heart for her own sweet self,*
> *And done rain all over me.*

And he drove. Fast.

"Never been here before," he said. Even his words fell into her, helpless, trailing stresses and vowels like kite tails. He saw her trees and fields, breathed her impossibly fresh air. The road was long and smooth and he purred.

"What brings you here?" She was sunshine in the dark.

"Soulfinger," he said.

She nodded. "You won't be the same after tonight, sugar."

"Maybe." He gripped the wheel and rolled down the windows. She streamed through his hair and over his skin. "Where did all these people come from? Is there a back entrance?"

The waitress smiled and turned away. The horizon disappeared. He felt the cold rain of reality slapping on his shoulders.

"One way in," she said. "One way out."

"I need to go," he said.

"Baby," she said. "You ain't going nowhere."

The overseer's name is Mr. Pride, long in the arms and thick in the neck, his meanness equalled only by his accuracy with the whip. He has a way of taking Abram to the very edge of everything; the edge of life and death; light and dark; pain and numbness. There is a moment in all such things—a sliver of almost nothing at all—where they cease to exist; a turning point, that scintilla between what was, and what is yet to be. This is where Mr. Pride takes Abram. This is the doorway for the Hoodoo Man.

He lies, clutching dusk's ankles, his eyes somewhere between open and closed. The breeze whispers across his lacerated back, but he doesn't feel it. Blood trickles down his arms, down his sides…he doesn't feel it. The darkness flickers, as if it is made of gauzy cloth, twitching in the breeze. Abram knows what that flicker means, but he cannot shudder, cannot scream. The Hoodoo Man is coming, opening the darkness like a doorway, and stepping through.

Abram cannot close his eyes, or move at all. He bleeds. He waits.

White—not like the Massa or Mr. Pride, but like the moon, or the smooth, sun-bleached stones that glimmer in the shallows of the Sipsey. He shines, the Hoodoo Man, and Abram always thinks he should leave incandescent puddles behind him when he walks. But there is nothing, not even a scuff of dust. He steps lightly, carrying his guitar, and stops by the whipping post. Thin as birch, slender shoulders, long fingers. Red flames dance in the window of his face. The Hoodoo Man gathers the guitar to his chest, places his fingers on the fretboard, and strums a most melancholy chord.

D-minor: MoRe paIn, ABRam?

He coughs. Dust flowers in his eyes, clinging to the moisture on his lashes. "Yessir."

A-major to G: You kNow I can helP you wITh thAt.

Abram manages to shake his head. His fingers scrape in the dirt. "Yo is nuthin' but bad. Kep away, Hoodoo Man."

He plays a six note scale: No MOre paiN, my friEnd. Mr. PriDE can neVer hurT You agaIn. No onE will huRT you. All you Will feEl iS bLISs.

Abram shakes his head, but he is tempted. Tears squeeze from his eyes and he listens to the Hoodoo Man play. An inexplicable melody, like earth elementals in musical form: euphony like water; resonance like fire. His heart pounds on the threshold of living. His soul unravels. It falls.

"No, puh-leeeze." *He pulls Charity's face into his mind and tries to cradle it there, needing to feel her strength, but the Hoodoo Man plays and he surrenders to the minor key. His wife cries through his mind, like a shooting star, and is gone.*

"I cain't. Lawd hep me."

E-minor: No paIN, AbrAm. IMAginE.

Abram is lifted to his knees and begins to crawl toward the Hoodoo Man, soul-stretched, piece by piece, like cottons bolls plucked from the shrub.

A7 to D: ThaT's it. COMe to ME. *A pentatonic scale in E:* NO moRe paiN.

"Yessir, but no mo' love."

The same scale, but with a diminished note—the blues note— offering a different intonation. No moRe paiN.

Abram falls at the Hoodoo Man's feet, crying and bleeding and breathing the last few moments of his mortal life. The Hoodoo Man (the devil…he must surely be the devil) continues to play his guitar, making sounds like birds' wings and flowing water. There is a bottle in his left hand, and he slides the neck up and down the fretboard, finding all the right notes. The bottle is brown, like Abram's skin. The label is red, like his blood.

The Hoodoo Man strums one last time. His face is a galaxy.

DriNK witH Me, AbrAM. *He holds out the bottle.*

Soul-shattered, already dead, Abram takes the bottle—so like his own body. He takes it gratefully. He drinks.

I seen that mojo bag,
I seen him laying down tricks,
But Lord he just a heartbreaker.

"Drink with me, brother." The bartender poured another shot of Jim Beam and placed it in front of Peter. "On the house."

"I really have to go."

"Too late. Soulfinger will be here soon." The bartender's eyes flicked to the glass. "You may as well enjoy the time you have left."

"I intend to," Peter said, moving away from the bar. "But it won't be in this dive; I'm easing on down the road, brother."

"Is that what you think?"

"Watch me." He turned toward the door, less than ten feet away. Bodies crowded the floor. Peter tried to push through them but was pressed back. He felt a tremor of anxiety in the pit of his stomach. A skin of sweat had caused his shirt to cling to his shoulder blades. "Excuse me...I'm trying—hey, I'm trying to get through here!" He pushed harder, using his arms to try to widen the gaps between bodies. Nobody looked at him; their dark faces were fixed on the stage, the empty stool. Peter recognized something eerily familiar about their blank expressions. He pressed forward, stumbled, picked himself up, and found himself further from the exit.

The bartender's voice, cutting through the confusion, the music scratching on the juke: "How about that drink, Mr. Rolling Stone?"

He was exasperated. His heart rolled in his chest like a clumsy shape, bouncing off his ribcage, booming. Tears gathered in the corners of his eyes. "I just want to leave," he said, and thought of the old man at the bar, who was still at the bar, and still mumbling along to the juke. *Boy, I'm always here.*

Always here.

Baby, you ain't going nowhere.

He looked at the picture of Soulfinger, at the mosaic of black faces watching him play. He looked at them carefully, studying every one. He looked around The Smokestack and saw the same faces now. Blank and dead. And there, the tall man in back...the clothes were different, but the sleepy, hound dog eyes were the same.

"So how old are you?" he asked the bartender.

"One hundred and eighty-three." The bartender smiled and nodded. "And still so handsome."

Peter wiped his eyes and looked at the picture again, scanning the faces until he found who he was looking for: a young woman with pronounced cheekbones and a heavy mouth. She was standing at the far left of the frame, clapping her hands, the moonlight trapped in her highway-eyes.

"Impossible." He wanted to suspect some trickery, but a deep, moaning measure of his heart screamed that it was real. Everything was real: the picture; Soulfinger; even the Hoodoo Man.

Especially the Hoodoo Man.

"You see, brother..." The bartender leaned across the bar. Peter could smell the age on his breath. "There are things in this world that lie beyond explanation."

"Magic and miracles," Peter agreed.

"God's work," the old man added.

"Or the devil's." It was the waitress. She looped her arm through his and turned him to face her. He took immediately to her highway, racing pell-mell for the mysterious, distant line that was her horizon. He inhaled her, felt her, let his tires roll over her slick black surface. She touched his face and he sensed her endless skies. She opened her heavy mouth: improbable teeth, too long, curved to points. Bones shimmered in her arid landscape. Her face was the moon.

His engine screamed.

She spoke—only three words, but they rumbled in his soul and brought rain. Her voice was the storm.

"Soulfinger is coming," she said.

She hears him approach, dragging his feet, and she lifts a hand to her trembling mouth. The bucket is in the corner, upside down, where she sits sometimes to patch the holes in their clothes. She

knows she will have to take it to the well and pump fresh water to ease his wounds. Mr. Pride has been heavy with the rawhide
again. She can tell from Abram's poorly step, his bare feet scuffing
in the dirt.

"Oh, Lawd," she implores, brown eyes turned to the ceiling.
"Heah me now. Kep him strong, Lawd. I's pleadin' yo. Hep him
so."

But Charity doesn't know that Abram and the Lord have
turned their backs on each other, and that the devil was waiting. She steps to the corner and picks up the bucket, still praying,
asking God to keep her strong while she eases her husband's pain.
The door swings open behind her and she turns. The bucket falls
from her hands and hits the floor with a hollow sound. The prayer
falls from her mouth in the same way, and makes a similar sound
somewhere in her heart. She looks at Abram as he stands in the
doorway—or what used to be Abram—and knows that praying is useless. God has been shamed and He is hiding somewhere,
head down. God won't help her now.

She backs into the corner. "Abram." Her voice is dry cotton,
too fragile to spin. "Yo got da devil in yo."

His skin is a shade lighter, almost mulatto. His eyes are too
big, and she can see all colours in them. Red and orange, purple
and yellow. The colours of fire.

"No mo' pain, honeychile," he says. His voice clangs and
rumbles, like Satan's hammer. It hurts her inside—deep, where
she loves and lives, because it's not his voice at all. She takes
another backward step but can go no further.

His upper body is naked, glistening with the blood from his
wounds. It smears his shoulders and chest. It paints his arms.
He stumbles closer and she can see more blood on his lips.

"I's so thirsty," he growls, although she believes he may have
said soul-thirsty, and the thought of this makes her so cold. It
blows through the vast rooms of her womanhood, banging windows and slamming doors.

"Oh, Abram," she says, trying to squeeze her thin body into
the angle where the two walls meet. The gas lamp flutters and
his shadow flaps across the walls. The door—still open—creaks
on its hinges. Charity looks at it…at the night beyond. Her heartbeat urges her to run.

As if this thought is reflected in her eyes, he says, and with terrible surety: "Honeychile, yo ain't goin' nowheres."

"Abram..."

"He dead. He gawn." The creature that has moved into her husband's body shuffles across the room, but not toward her. He grabs the neck of his guitar and sits on the stool. His eyes dance. They make fire shapes.

Charity looks at the open door again. She has a clear run at it now. Nothing can stop her. She takes a single step toward it, heart slamming, and then another.

The devil flips the guitar onto his knee, printing streaks of blood across the body. Dull tones vibrate from the sound hole. Charity looks at him once, setting his fingers to make a barre chord. She can see the lash marks reaching over his shoulders, onto his upper arms. The blood on his lips is very bright.

Fresh, she thinks, and it is all she can take. She weeps for the man that was her lover and friend, and moves toward the open door. She doesn't know where she will go; she may run through the darkness for hours, but she knows she has to get away from the monster that has taken her husband's soul.

She reaches the threshold—feels the chill night air on her skin—but stops when she hears the guitar sing. A sweet and perfect sound that holds her in place. She feels it in her soul, and the thought that comes to mind is that it is like intercourse; her soul is being violated; pushed open; spread wide. Intense sensation. And the colours in his eyes...she can feel them in her body, flickering hot and tongue-like. She turns around, feeling her soul spool away.

Two staggering, helpless steps toward him and the cabin disappears. The plantation is gone. The world falls away. It is just the two of them, held in some rift of time and space with her soul shimmering in the air between them. She can almost see it: rainbow-coloured and woman-shaped. He plays his guitar and her soul dances, vulnerable, almost sad, like a flower in the sun.

C-major 7 and she goes to him.

A-minor and she falls to her knees.

D-minor to G and her soul is already lost.

He opens his mouth and Charity can see that his teeth, like his eyes, are too big. They are the devil's teeth, inhuman, long and pointed. The part of her that should feel afraid is gone. She feels his hands on her body, his mouth on her heart.

He plays the blues. Her soul fades like smoke.

"Folla me, honeychile," he says.

"Follow me, baby," the waitress said. She took Peter's hand and weaved him through the tangle of bodies crowding the floor. The anticipation was immense: an electric, violent thing that caused the walls to tremble, the pictures to shake. The audience buzzed, shoulder to shoulder, standing on tables and chairs, waiting for Soulfinger. They drank from their bottles, leaving petals of blood on their lips. Their eyes were flames. Their teeth were like needles.

Want...leave... Thoughts in his mind, like shadows. They faded. Gone. He slipped between bodies, moving to the front of the stage. The empty stool looked terrible. It was like a gallows or guillotine. It was doom.

TONITE: SOULFINGER

And there he was, appearing from some dim rip in the darkness, suddenly there. The strength fell out of Peter's legs and he dropped to one knee, still clutching the waitress's hand, which was cold, synthetic. Soulfinger approached, carrying his guitar. Not old, or young; just a man, as ageless as plastic or a sheet of glass. His upper body was naked, dripping red. Peter could see the whip marks tattooed on his shoulders, still bleeding.

No more pain, he thought. *But no more love. No healing.*

Soulfinger stepped onto the stage, still dragging his feet. The audience cried for him. Their applause was blistering. Stomping. Cheering. They chinked bottles. Blood splashed from smooth brown necks, dripping on the floor.

Peter moaned. Thick tears rolled down his face.

Soulfinger sat on the stool. Somebody handed him a bottle and he drank, licked his lips.

"Who got da blues?" he whispered into the mic, and his followers responded. They howled and pushed, spilling blood, like animals.

Soulfinger smiled, showing his teeth. "And who got soul?"

The Smokestack hushed. The silence was immediate and terrifying. Peter felt everything fall on him, as if he had become the gravitational centre of Whispering Avenue. The waitress squeezed his hand. His heart was in fragments. He pulled himself to his feet and looked at Soulfinger.

"Me," he whispered. "I got soul."

Soulfinger nodded. He took another drink from his bottle and a thin line of blood trickled down his chin. He rested the guitar on his knee, placed his fingers on the fretboard, and looked at Peter.

"Dis one's fo' yo," he said, and started to play.

Bend to Beautiful
By Bradley Somer

I sit on a wire stool and beside me is my companion in this foetal hour. He is an angel in the flesh, or so I thought upon first glance when I saw him in the soft glow of the wall lamp, standing near a scar carved into the drywall. Twenty-five years old, if I had to guess an age. He had a sad face, the half that wasn't in shadow anyway, that didn't belong in that underground space. A glass full of amber clutched in his long fingers, his knuckles bulged at the joints where fine bones met, and all I felt was hunger.

I bought him a drink. I talked to him, me eager and intrusive, him reserved and quiet. I invited him back to my apartment, my pulse pounding for fear he wouldn't be with me. Without consideration, he asked for a glass of wine, accepting my company for the evening.

My own angel followed silently from the taxi to an elevator that lifted us to the top of the building. My own angel in my apartment, twenty-eight stories above the dark, early morning street noise. It seemed like an inadequate cage for him, seemed too close to the ugly asphalt and concrete of the city.

With a glass of wine at hand, he sat down, hunched his shoulders and leaned on the counter, fiddling with a lighter like there was something he wanted to tell me. His chestnut hair, cropped short, hugged the arc of his skull. His skin was smooth, which betrayed his thousand-year existence. He looked young, which betrayed his thousand-year wisdom.

"What's wrong?" I asked. I would tolerate anything to taste him.

"You seem like a nice man," he said.

"And that's a problem?" I prompted.

He smiled. A car horn sounded in the darkness. The noise climbed the building and slipped through the open window, which also admitted the cool night air.

"Yes," he said finally. "I have seen too many nice men in my time."

"It's okay," I said reaching out a hand and cupping the back of his head for a moment before letting my hand fall again. I needed a connection so desperately. I never used to know why. I know now. I am old and lonely.

He smiled what seemed to be a patient smile and said, "I'm tired."

"You're avoiding my question," I said.

"I am," he replied, took my cigarette pack from where it lay on the counter. He lit a cigarette and inhaled deeply.

I lit one of my own.

He looked around my apartment and sneered. "You have some beautiful baubles and trinkets in here."

I adjusted the crystal ashtray on the counter, sliding it between us. Crafted in some Austrian hamlet, its only imperfection was a small fault-line along the rim, just to one side of the smooth indents meant to cradle cigarettes. The ashtray refracted the light, bending it into something beautiful where two feathers had been etched into either side with such expertise they seemed to be falling through the air from a great height. A fingerprint obscured one of the feathers. On the counter, beside the ashtray, lay a small pile of ash.

Our cigarettes rested their filters on the edge of the ashtray and cut a pair of flawless diagonal lines. The ends were the glowing coals of a forest fire, the smoke a stream fanning out, lazy where it entered slower water.

A halogen lamp hung from a black wire above the counter. Though small, its light made a sharp cone, confused by the occasional fog drifting from the cigarettes whenever a breeze pleased to push or pull. The lamp was the only thing illuminating the morning's three o'clock air, the only thing between us and the darkness.

"Why did you talk to me?" he asked. "At the bar."

A blush belied my intentions. No, just one facet of my intentions. I shrugged and stuttered out an answer. My words became more composed as I reclaimed my confidence.

"You're beautiful," I said. "Why does anyone talk to anyone? You have a beautiful sadness. That's the first thing I noticed. It intrigued me to know why."

"That would take more than the span of a few drinks."

"Indeed, probably longer than a lifetime."

"You find sadness beautiful?" he asked. "Or did you think I was more vulnerable because of it, so the chance to get me to come home with you was better."

Again, I was taken aback by both the bluntness of the question and the truth of it. It must have shown in my countenance because he smiled briefly, took another pull on his cigarette and tapped the end against the ashtray.

Offset, to either side of the ashtray, were two wineglasses. One was half full, the second empty, save for a deep purple tint which made it look bruised, as if coated in some exotic oil. To the nose, this oil had the sharp tone of apricots. The bowls of the glasses displayed the loving patina of touch, like the windows of a jewelry store or some downtown peep show. Around the rims lingered the wintry remnants of kisses. These small details blurred when a whispered breeze eased cigarette smoke in front of my eyes.

Earlier, I had run my fingers from the nape of the angel's neck to the crown of his head just to feel the animal's pelt. He kept his eyes locked against mine throughout this motion. Then, as I withdrew my hand, his wine-stained lips parted to a smile. The expression pulled his skin up over his cheekbones; taut against his angled jaw. Now, he sat with both elbows on the counter, slightly drunk and watching the smoke curl from the cigarettes.

"Truthfully," I offered the silence, "you're right."

He raised his eyebrows. His forehead wrinkled.

"A bit of both," I continued, "but it hasn't gotten me any closer to knowing about you. I don't know anything."

"You can't know me in one night."

"I have all the time in the world."

He snorted as if I had made a joke.

"All I seem to do," he said after a breath, "is stand in that bar, beside that lamp, drinking that drink, being picked up by the same guy with the same line every week. Can you imagine such a life, one with a desire to do something so different, seeing so much, but not being able to do anything else? So trapped."

"You can do anything you want," I said, trying to satiate the urge to comfort him. "You can—"

"Lies," he snapped. "I've tried and time seems to erase everything. I'm thinking of quitting."

"Why?" I asked.

"I just think it's time for something new," he uttered.

That was the last thing we said and an hour has passed. We have smoked cigarettes and finished the bottle of wine.

I put my hand on his knee. He looks to me, his eyes wandering, drunk. His hand is warm against my chest and I fall backwards as the stool tips. My back lands on the carpet, pain sparks behind my eyes, which look up.

In this light, he is a burning silhouette. Smoke rises into the lamp's air behind his eclipse. He stands and takes off his shirt; the light shines through him. It is muted, his skin translucent like water, transparent like slow light. Under his skin, I see his heart beating, pushing the wine through his veins. His lungs are thick, the spaces between his innards ripple with light.

He reaches back and grabs his cigarette from the ashtray. Drawing the filter to his lips, he inhales and I watch his light dim to black. Inside his body a cloud spreads from his lungs and, as it digests him, he extends his wings. Slowly they stretch, pivoting on a central joint, charcoal feathers laid in an ordered, dazzling pattern. Each feather, coated with fine opalescent oil, catches the simple light from the lamp, twists it into a frenzy, shattering it against the backs of my eyes.

He leans forward, kneeling on one knee and placing a hand beside my head, his teeth bared in ferocious disgust. He brings his face a hairbreadth from mine. I smell wine and, on his skin, something akin to almonds. A static spark stings my lips when his brush mine. Electricity crawls under his skin. He exhales apricot-scented breath, sending images through my lungs to tarnish my mind. They assault in rapid succession.

"I am tired of it," he hisses in my ear, "Organ harvests. Full bellies. Buffet attacks. Closed eyes. Trading up. Broken people. Broken fingers. Penthouse whores. Diamond rings. Crystal Ashtrays. Golf and country clubs. Sport Utility Vehicles. Heated leather seats. Television commercials. Reality TV. Tears and scars. Shit kickings. Shit eating grins. Holy wars. Air fresheners. Fashion magazines. Breast implants. Beauty culture. Professional wrestling. Liquor lullabies. Back lane beatings. Date rape. Oil wells pumping. Unrestrained longing. I have seen it all, the sum of your efforts." He pauses. "In the end, after thousands of years of hard work, what is left but fat comfort and fake fashion, pretentious excess and neighbourly ignorance? I have seen the ways you have let yourselves down."

He kisses my neck; he pierces my neck; I struggle to pull away from the pain. A small, choked whimper escapes as he holds me in place. Flames seem to fester inside of him like some exploding star. Through his teeth comes smoke, a warm, wet blanket on my throat. The last image I see is the burning angel. His tears are not enough to douse the flames.

I am not strong enough for this and he knew it.

I let go, fade and bend to beautiful.

Evolving
by Natasha Beaulieu

He stands near the dance floor but is not attracted to any of the goth girls twirling around. Despite disliking the old-fashion Victorian style as well as the vulgar black PVC skin-tight outfits, he has been hanging around *Cold Hell* for the last few months; the club appeals to vampires. Real ones.

Anton pretends to be a vampire and knows he has the right to do so. He possesses all the potential to become one. Deep in his flesh, awareness in his soul and knowledge in his heart tells him it is true. He is not yet a vampire, but sooner or later he will have the opportunity to evolve.

It is easy for Anton to align with the club's aesthetic code. His tall slim body, naturally pale skin, black hair and piercing blue eyes are classic features. He only had to buy a closet full of black clothes and he became the perfect goth model.

He knows that most of *Cold Hell*'s dark princes are fake vampires, turning back into everyday guys at sunrise. And it's the same with the goddesses of the night, probably wearing jeans and t-shirts all week.

"Your first night here?"

He hasn't paid attention to the girl—well, more a woman—standing next to him, a skinny blond in a shoddy purple dress clutching a bottle of beer in her hand.

"No," he answers.

"I've never seen you before."

So what? He has never seen her either and he has no interest in someone who couldn't possibly be a vampire. The girl has no class. No strength. No power.

"I don't like to show off."

"Of course! That explains why you're about to take root near the dance floor."

She laughs. It annoys him.

"You like to dance?" she goes on.

"No."

"I do."

Then why don't you just go and dance, he thinks. What is wrong with her? Is she mindless? Can't she understand that he does not want to engage in a conversation with her?

"You don't talk too much."

"Should I?" He looks at her with a grim face.

"No," she answers, her smile fading from her lips. "You're a prick, man!"

And then she disappears into the crowded club. Good riddance!

Anton makes his way among the lace, velvet and satin, glancing around, looking for a real vampire. During his weekly visits to the *Cold Hell*, he thinks he recognized a few. Vampires stand, walk and look at you in a special, stylish way. But as those prospects ignored him, Anton decided that they were merely poseurs or wannabes. Had they been real, they would have recognized him as kindred, flesh of their flesh and soul, even if he has not yet fully turned.

He has thought about it often, how a vampire knows he's a vampire: blood is essential to his survival. Anton does not yet need blood to survive. As a child, he enjoyed sucking at his friends' wounds whenever they were injured in play, which resulted in the 'Anton is a vampire' legend. He kept sucking blood because he liked the taste, which, he knew, made him a freak, not a vampire.

There is a free space at the bar. Anton steps into it and waits to order. As he looks around, he catches the profile of a man standing at the opposite end of the bar. The man is much older than most of the guys in the club but good-looking and, if he plans to seduce someone here, it might just work.

A few weeks ago, Anton left with a gothic Lolita. Once they were in his bedroom, he asked her to get undressed.

"I don't like rag dolls. I like flesh," he said.

As soon as the Lolita was naked, revealing her tender white skin, Anton felt desire rising. Her short red hair left her neck fully exposed and Anton had enjoyed kissing and sucking at it while the Lolita writhed in ecstasy.

"A glass of red wine," he orders from the Sweeney Todd look-alike barman.

Anton does not possess a natural talent for levitating and floating in the air, or flying through it. As a teenager, he wanted to know if that potential was within him. Many times he tried to levitate above the ground without any success. He let himself fall from trees, but instead of going up, he just twirled fast to the grass below. Once he went to the public swimming pool's highest diving board and jumped, hoping to defy gravity.

"You know it's closed, kid," said the guard who caught him in the water.

"I needed to do a test," he gasped, half choking on swallowed chlorinated water.

"You can do all the tests you want during the daytime."

But Anton does not like daytime. He covers as much of his body as he can with clothing, but still he hates when the sun leaves ugly red spots on his face, arms and hands that stay for weeks.

He also has a problem with his eyes. When they are exposed to bright light, he tends to lose the ability to focus. To avoid this, he wears dark sunglasses during the day. At night, his vision is very sharp. He doesn't pretend to himself that he can see in the dark, but his vision is definitively sharper in the evening.

"I like red wine too."

The voice comes from a wasp-waisted girl in a leather corset. Another wanting his attention but Anton is not indifferent to this one. Her décolleté flaunts lots of flesh. He orders a glass of red wine for her.

"Thank you. What's you name?"

"Anton."

"I'm Shanella."

Anton glances again to the opposite end of the bar. The handsome older stranger is looking at him. Is it possible?...

"Are you a vampire?" asks Shanella.

Usually, Anton simply answers yes but now he hesitates. How can he pretend to be a vampire when there might be a real vampire a few meters away from him? But the words finally pass his lips, "Of course."

Shanella grips his arm.

"I am so happy. My life sucks the way it is. Please, take me with you. Make me one of your kind."

Anton's eyes lock with the stranger's. Should he go and talk to the vampire or leave with Shanella? Why all of a sudden is the idea of having fun with this girl as interesting to him as the thought of talking with a real vampire? What an annoying dilemma. Still, Anton leaves his half-empty glass of wine on the counter, grabs Shanella's hand and walks with her to the backdoor of the club, thinking that he will come back for the vampire.

The alley is dark and empty on this chilly fall night. Shanella's breasts are covered with goose bumps, but she does not complain. Anton guides his prey into a narrow space between brick walls. She's excited by the idea of becoming a vampire and Anton knows how to make the experience look as real as possible.

He bends over the shivering Shanella and pushes her long black hair behind her shoulders then touches her soft skin with the tips of his cold fingers. She is afraid, he knows, but she is as excited as she is scared.

"Show me your sharp teeth," she whispers.

What a stupid request. He does not have razor-sharp fangs. Well, he had them as a kid. But the teeth combined with the 'Anton is a vampire' legend made his uncomfortable parents have the dentist fix the 'problem' of pointed canines.

"They were filed off so I wouldn't transform anyone."

"Who did it?"

So damned curious. "It doesn't matter. I will transform you anyway."

Shanella puts a hand on her neck. She is not feeling so confident anymore, is she?

"But how?" she wants to know.

Anton does not let the girl ask another question. He puts his lips on the curve of her breast and starts to suck at the skin. He wishes he still had his spiky teeth to bite through her skin and get at the blood. He wants so much to be a real vampire. Why can't he be one? How can he become one?

He goes on sucking the skin. It will leave a big bruise but that's not his problem. She asked for it, didn't she?

Suddenly, Anton has had enough of this game. Shanella is paler than before and indeed there is a huge purple mark on her breast, but she seems to still be in ecstasy while he feels nothing, nothing at all. He thinks of her now as just a naïve girl, not having the sense to be able to recognize real vampires from fake ones.

Bored by her feigned agony that seems like it will never end, Anton leaves Shanella in the dark and goes back into the club.

Before returning to the bar where he intends to have a conversation with the vampire if by any chance he's still there, Anton stops in the men's room. He glances in the mirror, but can't see himself very well. Of course I can't, he thinks, it's fucking dark in here!

And it doesn't matter anyway. Anton knows he looks good. He's always been more attractive than most guys. His parents were annoyed by that too. He remembers hearing a conversation as a kid:

"His beauty will cause big problems," his father said.

"It has already," his mother replied. "He can get all the girls he wants."

"I hope he won't turn out too bad."

"He can't be worst than he already is."

How was he a bad kid? In what way? Anton exhibited vampiric tendencies, but that did not make him a bad child. He didn't kill any of his friends by sucking at their bloody wounds. Maybe it's time for him to ask his mother about that conversation. She should certainly be able to explain to him what she meant.

He takes a breath to get away from the past. Some other time. Tonight, he has another goal.

The stranger has not moved from his spot at the bar. Anton walks in his direction, his eyes focused on the dance floor. Once he is next to the handsome man, he stops. They make a quick eye contact and then Anton pretends he's more interested in the moving bodies. Facing the dance floor, his back to the vampire, Anton wonders how to make a good impression. What should he say? He can't just ask to be turned into a vampire. How silly! How ridiculous that would be! There must be another approach or it might be better to be patient and let the other one make the first move. After all, Anton has been patient for months. What's a few more minutes?

So he waits. The vampire can surely sense him and recognize him as a kindred spirit, not yet fully formed, but not missing much that's needed to be real. Anton only hopes he will be recognized.

Standing nearby, a guy wearing a fishnet shirt starts talking to another guy with blue dreads. Strong garlic breath comes out of his mouth, reaching Anton's sensitive nostrils. He likes garlic but he hates garlic breath.

"Let's talk," he suddenly hears from behind him.

Anton turns so quickly it seems he did not even move.

"Let's go outside," the vampire says.

Anton agrees with a nod. He follows the stranger to the same back door he used earlier when he went out with Shanella. He remembers how the girl's skin tasted: nice, very sweet and fruity due to some cream or perfume she had applied to it. Blood tastes metallic. But Anton enjoys both tastes.

The alley is as deserted as before. Shanella is gone and wherever she went, she left without the gift of eternal life. A gift that Anton hopes to receive for himself.

The stranger stops near a garage door, turns to face Anton and says, "You got another one tonight, didn't you?"

"Well, they ask for it. Is it not the same for you?"

"For me?"

Anton is a bit confused. Has he been mistaken about this man being a vampire? "Why do you want to talk with me?" he asks.

"I'm Rachel's father."

The name Rachel does not strike a chord in Anton's memory. But then, he looks deeper into the man's eyes and he remembers Rachel's eyes, the gothic Lolita he sucked the neck off a couple of weeks ago. What should he say? Act as if he does not know any Rachel? Admit that he took her to his place and pretended to have sex with her but did not because he does not like having sex?

"What have you done to her?" asks the man.

Anton knows there is no point denying that he knows her. He is not in the presence of a vampire but simply facing an annoyed father. He becomes aware of the anger running through his veins. Anger at himself for being foolish and pretentious, for thinking he has been recognized by a real vampire so that he can finally evolve. Indeed, he has been recognized, but not for the reason he wants. Someone probably described him to Rachel's father.

Anton decides that he does not want this conversation to last too long so he goes straight into it. "She came of her own will to my place. We did not have sex, if that's what you want to know."

Indignation blazes in Rachel's father's eyes. "Rachel is dead. What did you do to her?"

Why should the death of Rachel have anything to do with him?

"She died a few hours after coming back from your place," the man goes on. "She was very tired. Her skin grew paler and cooler every hour. Lying in her bed, she told me about you, Anton. She wanted me to believe that you only sucked at her neck."

"Well, that is exactly the truth, so I don't see how it can be related to her death."

The man thrusts his hands deeper in his coat pockets. He looks behind his back as if he wants to make sure nobody will hear the rest of the conversation.

"Are you a vampire, Anton? We all know that they exist."

Anton cannot help his melancholy smile. "I am not a vampire. I wish I was. I pretend I am, expecting to meet one who will guide me into the transformation. I thought you were a vampire. That's why I followed you out here."

Rachel's father is not smiling.

"I think there's something wrong with you, young man. When Rachel died, her body was drained of half her blood."

"That's not possible. I didn't drink her blood at all. I only sucked her skin."

"Maybe you don't know yourself very well. I don't think you need a vampire to help you turn into one. You're already one. Maybe not feeding the traditional way, by biting skin with sharp teeth, but you have the power to suck blood through skin."

What is that man saying? That he, Anton, is a vampire? A different kind of vampire? Does that make sense?

"Have your parents never told you about your origins?"

"What do you mean?"

"I've investigated you. You were adopted. Maybe your real parents had something to do with vampires and your blood is tainted, vampirism transferred to your genes. That would explain what you do, and why you're different."

Of course, Anton knows he was adopted but it never occurred to him to ask his adoptive parents about his real parents. Nevertheless, why is this man telling him all this?

"What do you want from me?"

"I lost my only reason to live. You took her away from me. I could have gone to the police and revealed what I know about you but I did not. People at the morgue probably suspected that Rachel's death was caused by a vampire. But you know, even these days, no one is comfortable with such weird cases. Nobody really wants to deal with that kind of problem. And you know why, Anton?"

Why should he know? But the man goes on without waiting for an answer.

"Because in the old days, vampires could be destroyed or at least kept away by things like a stake to the heart, sunlight, holy water, a crucifix, garlic, and so on. But these don't work anymore. Vampires have evolved and adapted to modern times; vampires are headed into the future. Like viruses and bacteria, they have developed the ability to protect themselves and avoid annihilation. We normal human beings are no longer immune. We don't know how to get rid of the new and different breed or I should say breeds of vampire. Most of them aren't eternal. They live longer than us but only two to three hundred years. And this has been their most significant decline now that human beings are living longer. In a not too distant future, it's likely we will reach a point where vampires and humans live as long as each other, understand each other better and might live together in harmony. Vampires might still have a taste for blood, but maybe they won't need it to survive."

Anton knows he doesn't need blood to survive, but he likes the taste. He cannot fly, but he sometimes moves more quickly than humans. Anton cannot see himself clearly in a mirror; his image is always slightly blurred. Anton likes garlic, is not afraid of a crucifix or holy water. He can't bite skin but has learned to suck blood from under the flesh and up through the pores. He cannot give eternal life. Apparently he kills his prey.

Anton suddenly realizes that he is a vampire. An evolved vampire. He has not been recognized by a vampire but by a normal human being.

"What do you want from me?" he asks again.

"I want you to kill me. I have no reason to live anymore."

"Rachel's mother?"

"She hanged herself after our daughter's death."

The wind is blowing stronger now than when they first came into the alley. The air is colder. Anton does not know what to do. Should he kill this man? He has never sucked a man's flesh. He does not find the thought appealing at all. But if he does, the man will die and it will be the end of the case. The Rachel case. He will release her father from a life he does not want to live anymore. If he does not do it, what will happen? Do vampires who commit murder go to jail? Ridiculous. Stupid. Nonsense.

Anton looks into Rachel's father's eyes.

"I won't kill you," he says.

"Why?"

"Because I don't want to kill you. Even if I might be a real new-breed vampire, I don't need blood. I only like it. You think I need to kill, but I don't."

"Why don't you want to give me what I want? You killed my daughter. You own me something."

Anton takes a step back from Rachel's father. Do vampires have regrets? Does he feel any regrets over the girl? He owes this man nothing at all. He is a vampire of a new kind, even though some elements will always be the same for all vampires. No, he has no regrets.

He turns and walks away from Rachel's father, who has no power to force him to do anything that he, Anton, does not want to do. Anton knows that he is the one with the power.

How foolish he has been in not realizing that he is a vampire! Now that he knows, he will ask his parents about his origins.

Anton decides not to go back into the club. He has nothing more he needs to do there. He will never return to *Cold Hell*. He no longer needs to meet a vampire. He *is* a vampire.

He knows he won't spend time looking for others and yet he hopes that one night he will meet his kindred. Will they be vampires from the same breed, or different than him? He hasn't met any others yet; maybe that means he's the only one of his kind. If he is the only one and yet he cannot turn a human into what he is... He can live with that. For now. Until he evolves again.

How Magnificent is the Universal Donor
By Jerome Stueart

Jacob stumbles from the elevator on the fourth floor of Sanctuary Hospital. He's in a hurry, and feels guilty that he's been detained for three hours at a press conference helping the Deputy Minister field questions. He can still see the lights from the steadycams, purple spots now erasing the hospital walls. The white hallways seem suddenly quiet. His short stride makes it look like he's running, and his beard is hiding clenched lips. At Room 423, he stops at the door. The sheets of the bed are neatly folded. *They moved him.*

Back in the hallway, he breathes in and scans the patient screen, but doesn't find Harlin Moybridge anywhere on the list. It's probably just a mistake. He turns and looks around to find anyone who can tell him what's going on. A blond-haired nurse in a cool blue uniform is standing, leaning over a desk. The desk lamp highlights her neck, and her skin looks like white fire. When he asks her where they've moved Harlin Moybridge, she checks the desk, a flat screen where she moves documents back and forth with the tip of her finger.

"Oh, Mr. Moybridge," she looks up. "Your husband died this morning."

He stares in disbelief. Dead? "He was just in for tests," Jacob says. "Look. There's been a mistake. I would have been called."

She looks hurt, sad for him. She glances back to the desk. "They called you."

"They didn't." His voice is higher than normal.

"It says that you were contacted, and made arrangements to see the body."

"Where's the body? I'd like to see it."

She looks back down at the desk, flustered. "It says... it says you've already seen the body." Now she looks up, as surprised as he is. "You came in at 10 am, two hours ago."

It didn't matter that he insisted he didn't come in. There it was in the records. Harlin always said that when it's in your medical records, it's scripture.

"How did he die?"

She scans the records, tells him, "He tested positive for BBD."

"He didn't," Jacob says evenly.

"You received the letter in the mail and came in for tests for BBD. Obviously there was reason to suspect your husband had the disease. Those initial tests are rarely wrong."

"Rare," he says, "but not impossible."

The Beijing Blood Disease, or Baby Dee as it is popularly known, is not normally fatal. Since more than 40% of the population has it at any one time, it is rampant, but transfusions seem to keep those infected in check. But Harlin Moybridge has the strongest immune system he's ever seen.

"I never been inoculated, never had flu shots, never been sick. I'm fine, and they *hate* that," Harlin once told him. He smiled, arched his back and spread his shoulders. "I'm on a black list somewhere because I don't take their damn shots." No antibiotics, no synthesized medicines ever entered his body. His father made sure that none of his kids got shots. He was a homeopathic doctor, but his children were fine examples of health. The dad faked the shot records himself, enough to get the kids through schooling.

"They don't like people who say they don't need doctors," Harlin said. "It's a scam, you know. To make you need 'em. They want you to need 'em. It's about control. But everybody's smart enough to take care of themselves."

It's that rebellious streak that Jacob loves. And wasn't Harlin proved right? At fifty-six, he was in perfect health, robust, full of life. He could have given any man twenty years younger a run for his money.

"I *don't* have Baby Dee," Harlin said when he opened the letter. "They just want me in the hospital."

Like a subpoena, a summons from the World Health Organization is pretty much unbeatable. Jacob read the letter. It indicated Harlin was a "health risk to society." Baby Dee is contagious. He is to report to the hospital for more tests and possible treatment. "They *loved* my blood. They *envied* it. Dadgum 'em, they'd never *seen* finer blood than mine. The bastards!" When he was angry, his Texas drawl really showed.

Everyone has to give a blood sample, just a tiny needle's worth, at the front of every supermarket. This ensures that on a continuous basis, every person who needs food is screened.

"It's a mistake," Jacob told him. "It must be. We'll go down to the hospital, and we'll retake the test and we'll show them that they got yours mixed up with someone else's."

Harlin resisted. He balled up the letter and threw it across the room. "From now on, *you* buy the groceries."

"Look, if we just go and prove to them that your blood is fine, this will be over."

Harlin growled at him.

Jacob smiled "Let them be stinking envious. You have to clear your name."

The nurse invites him behind the desk, and lets him read the report himself.

Harlin died on the transfusion table. His body is awaiting incineration. They have to burn it. An out of control BBD could infect so much of the population that it would be impossible to contain the spread. No, Jacob isn't allowed to view the body. "Again," she adds. Yes, he will have to be screened as well. Could he stop by the main floor and give a blood sample? He cringes at the lack of compassion.

Looking at the document, Jacob is sure he will sue the hospital for negligence. There on the document is his phone number.

"I never came in to see the body," he tells her again. "I was never called."

She nods.

He walks away from the nurse. She calls after him that there is a chapel and a counselor on the second floor. But he's not going there. Harlin wouldn't be in the chapel.

The elevator doors shut and he's alone. He looks at his blurred reflection in the walls of the elevator. He's angry at the hospital. What man, playing Jacob, came and saw the body? Who would do that? He's angry at the nurse. He's mad at Harlin. How could a man with an "unbeatable" immune system go and die during tests? And finally, as the elevator sinks further and further down, he thinks, *I should have stayed.* Then, thankfully, he finds a way to blame it on the Deputy Minister and lastly, China, and this gets him prepared for the doors to open.

He wipes his eyes with his sleeve. But he needn't. An aerosol antibacterial mists the air. The spray is wet only for a second, but he can feel it on his face, and when it evaporates it leaves his face dry, and the doors open to the basement, the morgue.

"You can pull off anything if you're confident enough," Harlin told him before his first interview for the communications position with the government.

"Yeah, they call that false confidence," Jake said.

"Unjustified confidence," Harlin smiled. "Who knows? You may be a whiz at it. Just act like it 'till it comes natural." Harlin liked that he was transparent. "You're an honest man," he said. "You got no guile. But sometimes, buddy, you have to learn to fake it."

Press conferences are great testing grounds for faking it. And Jacob ended up in more than his fair share as the communications analyst for the Deputy Minister. But even when he learned to hide nearly everything in front of a camera, still Harlin would tell him, passing his hand warmly across Jacob's face, "You can't fool me. This face is a map. And I've got the legend memorized."

On his way to the morgue, he passes three pathology labs, an autopsy room. He walks through the retracting door into the morgue. It is bland, sterile. He expects to smell formaldehyde, but there is no strong odor. A shiver goes through him. *Harlin should be here.*

Silver panels line one wall. He imagines they have bodies tucked away behind them. There are tables with bodies on them in four rows. They are each draped with thin muslin. Should be plastic, he thinks. One table has the muslin, but no body. He looks around first, and then begins to uncover the faces of the different bodies.

They don't shock him. He's so determined to find Harlin, to see that white-haired, clean-shaven face, smiling even in death, underneath the muslin. He does it quickly, a flip off, a flip back on. The faces are peaceful. Nothing in their skin gives it away that they are dead. They're pale, yes, but not blue-lipped. Some women, mostly men. They all have their clothes on. This is not at all what he expected. But he checks each one in turn until he has looked at them all. Harlin is not here.

He looks up. He walks over to the computer controls on the wall. All the silver panels are represented by a green LCD number display. On the main screen is a list of names, none of which are *Moybridge*.

These are all the dead bodies in the room, and all the bodies in the slots.

Where the hell is Harlin?

In the back, he discovers a change room. Lockers. Showers. It makes sense. If the nurses burn their clothes because of disease risk, then he can see why showers for pathologists might be available. He just didn't expect them in the morgue.

He expected Harlin.

But if Harlin isn't in the morgue, where is he?

From the corner of his eye, Jacob sees something stirring.

A body on a table moves, stretches. One of the dead bodies. He sees a hand come from underneath the muslin cloth and pull it slowly down its face then its body. It exhales and then breathes in deeply.

Jacob slips into the locker room. His breath is shallow and his heart races. He hears the squeak of the table where the body was lying, as the person steps down. Jacob remembers the faces of the dead-still and peaceful. He hears them moving and feels trapped. He looks around the change room for hiding places. Lockers are too small, showers too open. And what about a weapon?

He hears another squeak. "I thought Jardin was on today," says a voice.

"Jardin's sick. I'm filling in," says another.

They're conversational, casual.

"He's just a third year."

"Sad, isn't it?"

Jacob takes off his shirt and lays it on a bench. Maybe he can pretend to be someone, anyone, dressing after a shower. Maybe.

He has his back to the footsteps as they enter the locker room. They're talking, hardly noticing him. They pass him.

"I don't want to work today," one says.

"Are you third year?" There's a pause. "Oh. Well, I can understand."

Jacob acts as if he's just putting his shirt back on. He looks at his shoes, trying not to think about *them*.

Two of them stop talking. "Hello?" one says.

He turns slowly. He remembers them from the tables, how they looked when they were dead. One is shorter, blond hair, stocky build; the other taller and lean.

"John Lake," Jacob says, not extending his hand. "From St. Mary's. In Omaha."

They introduce themselves, smiling. They seem to buy it. These dead people. He looks at their faces. He would not be able to tell they are dead. He starts to think maybe they were just asleep. But this is the morgue.

"I'm here on a visit," he adds.

"Oh," they nod. "How are things in Omaha?"

What would they want to hear? He waits. It's always good to wait in an interview to hear a follow up question. People clarify themselves. They do it all the time in press conferences.

These two don't. They shuffle awkwardly. The tall one looks at Jacob's hands as he finishes buttoning the shirt, watching his fingers work the buttons. Will they notice his hair's not wet?

"About the same," he says. "You know how it is."

The short one smiles weakly. "You kind of think it's better somewhere else."

"Especially somewhere more rural," the other one says. He turns and strips off his shirt. "Less people to worry about."

Jacob doesn't say anything back. He's hoping they find him aloof. Maybe they'll shut up. He tucks in his shirt and turns to the door.

"Did you leave your jacket in Omaha?" says the tall one. "You can borrow one here. I'm sure no one will mind."

They both approach him helpfully. They filter through a rack of red coats against the wall. "Jardin's not here," the tall one says, holding out one to size him up. "But you could probably use any that's your size." They are friendly. He doesn't want to touch them. He wants to run, but he nods politely and takes Jardin's coat. It is a bit large; Jacob is a small-framed guy. "This is great. Thanks." His shoulders are swallowed in the coat.

"Hmmm. Try this one. It was Eamer's." The short one gives him another and he slips it on. It fits. They both smile. "He's gone now. It's good to get some use out of it." The shorter man brushes the coat down.

"Thank you." Jacob feels the need to explain himself. "I left mine."

The short one smiles. "Well, I hope you enjoy your visit."

He wants to leave. He thinks he can smell death on them. But they are smiling; they seem sincere.

A door opens behind him at the far end of the morgue.

An older man walks in, already taking off his coat. "We need to wake up the others," he says. "Dr. Esterhazy's found a new donor. Impeccable blood, no impurity."

"No BBD?" the tall one asks.

"No anything. Pure. Almost unheard of."

Jacob feels a lump in his throat. They have to be talking about Harlin.

And donors can't be dead.

The shorter one turns to him. "Good day to visit, eh?" The two are beaming pride as if they are offering Harlin as a miracle they'll be performing in an hour, something to break out the cameras for. Jacob can't help but grin and his eyes start to water. If Harlin's still alive, it *is* a miracle.

The two turn to the older man as he comes into the locker room. "Dr. Lake from Omaha," the tall one says.

Jacob must look ridiculous, about to cry. Scared to death of this man approaching. Of these two *men* that have come from a room full of dead bodies.

"Mercy?" the older man asks. He has thick black hair and bushy eyebrows. You can see the veins in his hands and they look younger than his face.

"Mercy, yes. It's been a day," Jacob says.

"Mercy *Hospital* in Omaha," the older man says.

"*St. Mary's*," the shorter one replies for Jacob. "He's up for a visit."

"St. Mary's?" the older man asks, looking as if he's trying to remember any hospital by that name.

"A small clinic," Jacob says, "big name. We aim to grow into it."

The doctor smiles, extends his hand. "Philip Gontard." Jacob shakes it. It's cold. The doctor seems surprised, holds Jacob's grip, a curious look on his face that fades as quickly as it appeared. "Enjoy Sanctuary. There's a lot to see. I'd suggest Room 710 in an hour." He looks at the other two men, suddenly in a hurry. "We need to wake everyone. Esterhazy wants everyone there."

Jacob fades back through the morgue towards the door, as the men proceed to wake the others. The older doctor moves to the console next to the silver panels and presses a few buttons. Jacob doesn't want to see any more bodies come to life.

Except one.

And he already feels as if Harlin has risen, somewhere.

The Seventh Floor. If you are infected with Baby Dee, you come here. The walls are white. All the doctors wear redcoats, as does Jacob. They are all specialists in blood identification: hematologists, hematopathologists, phlebotomists. The names of their specialties make him queasy. He hated needles as a child. His parents were like most. They believed in the booster shots, flu shots, and in taking their child to the doctor as much as they could. With healthcare free in the country, there wasn't a reason not to. But, if he watched a needle approaching his arm, he fainted. "We got a fainter," the phlebotomists would say, chuckling to each other, as if he was supposed to be okay with people drawing his blood. There was something unnatural about it.

And yet, every time the government issued a health risk warning, his parents got "in line to get in line with the law," as his father would say.

Jacob followed rules, for the most part. But the blood, the needles, the alcohol smell — it still bothered him. Harlin, in some ways, gave him an excuse to run from the whole thing. As if they were playing a game with the medical establishment. "Let's see if they can catch us," Harlin said.

There was a time without Redcoats. Before Baby Dee. Hospitals were scarier then. There was a sense of the unknown, of the unpredictable. Then, after Baby Dee, the WHO appointed all these specialists to treat BBD before it could become a global crisis. Smart-thinking, dedicated Redcoats were credited with averting disaster. "In the war for your life, Redcoats are the front line," went the commercials. Jacob watched TV specials on their procedures — it looked like a common transfusion to him. But the transfusions — the frequency of them — were "the reasons the world stays safe" the nations' Presidents assured their citizens. The Redcoats found new treatments for several more blood diseases, and cured Leukemia. But BBD was a constant threat that the doctors could only contain. These doctors worked as a team, cooperating with hospitals all over the world. They earned the respect of the world, and most people revered them.

Jacob was indifferent. He just wanted to avoid doctors and hospitals. But Harlin was skeptical. And adamant. "It's a show," he said. "Where'd all these specialists come from? Phlebotomists were the low man on the totem pole. Why'd they all of a sudden rise up the ladder? The medical profession is fulla secrets, Jake."

Well, now Harlin knows some of them. And so does Jacob.

On the seventh floor, he sweats nearly through his red coat. He pictures every other doctor he meets lying under the muslin cloth on a shiny silver table. Dead. Or asleep. Who are they? *What* are they?

He feels like a guided missile going through the hallway. He reads the numbers on the doors, smiles at people. He's now past confidence and has moved into determination. Harlin is alive. Or at least he will be for the next hour.

Jacob encounters more and more of them. The hallways are flooding with Redcoats plus a few white coats, floating in among the nurses and general staff. They look vibrant in the over-whitened space. He can't take his eyes off them. They even look back at him as he passes.

"Dr. Lake?" says a voice to his right. It's the older doctor, Dr. Gontard, who now walks beside Jacob, matching his pace. "Could you assist me here?"

The man's eyebrows overshadow the slits his eyes have become. The grin on his face isn't pleasant. He grips Jacob's arm and he can feel small pinpricks.

Dr. Gontard pulls him into a dark room with a central set of lights illuminating a patient on an angled platform. The patient, a man who appears to be his late twenties, looks unconscious; the light creates an impression of rapture on his upturned face.

"Dr. *Lake*." He says the name as if he's savoring it, amused by it. "I need to conduct a transfusion and we need a hand." He indicates another doctor in the shadows in a red coat, operating a tower of blinking lights and some cords, none of which are connected to the patient.

Dr. Gontard walks over to the patient and climbs up onto his body until he is straddling the man. "This man has BBD. If we don't transfuse him, he'll eventually succumb to the neurological side-effects, the tremors, the loss of muscle tissue, the general wasting away of a healthy individual. *As you undoubtedly know*," he turns to look at Jacob, continuing wryly, "transfusion is all that works right now, and this will eliminate 99% of the disease. We've never been able to totally cure an individual. All we can do is keep them as healthy as possible despite the ongoing infection."

The man on the board isn't strapped down except at the waist, to prevent him from sliding.

Dr. Gontard places his hands beside the man's neck, far enough away for Jacob to notice the nails on both middle fingers elongate into needles, the tips sharpening to fine points.

"This patient will eventually die of BBD if we don't do something, but hospitals can't handle the number of complete body blood transfusions, which is why they have relied on us for the past twenty years."

He inserts both needles into the man's neck and cups the chin in his palms. His fingers puncture the skin then the veins. He leans his own head back and sighs. "If only we could keep all the blood for ourselves instead of just the nutrients. But I suppose our job is to purify as much as we can, then return it."

Jacob steps back. The other doctor, the one who has been monitoring the situation at the blinking tower, is behind him.

"What does this have to do with me?" Jacob asks. He has to stop himself from backing further away. Dr. Gontard's fingers are fat sausages, red and flush with blood as the patient's blood transfers through the doctor's body. What *are* these people? He gulps. "I know all this," he says.

"Do you?"

Jacob reaches into himself to pull out as much confidence as he can. "I've performed these transfusions for fifteen years."

"Have you?" says Dr. Gontard. His head turns so that he is peering over his shoulder, his eyes completely blocked by the oppressive eyebrows.

"Well, I think you have this completely under control. As a guest, I do appreciate you showing me your technique; however you didn't need my assistance. I'm not sure your positioning is best for accomplishing a transfusion. In Omaha, we do our transfusions from the side of the patient so as not to restrict blood flow. Thank you for your time, Dr. Gontard. Perhaps we'll... we'll meet again."

Jacob turns to go, and looks directly at the Redcoat who stands between him and the door. The man hesitates but finally steps aside and Jacob leaves the room.

In the hall, he feels sick. Faint. The hallways are filled with Redcoats. He wants a bathroom more than anything else. But instead, he scans the numbers above the doors, counting backwards. He weaves in among the medical personnel, hoping he won't fall. If they've hurt Harlin already, Jacob doesn't know what he'll do. What he *can* do to people like this. If they *are* people.

Finally, he feels a rush of relief as he spots Room 710 and pushes through the door.

There is only a central light above a body on a table.

It's Harlin, flat on his back. A sheet covers him from the waist down. He looks like he's sleeping.

The room is small, empty of people. A little desk that glows from the LCD imbedded in its surface, blinking lights and tower, and rolling silver tray tables against the wall. The room is a circle.

He hurries to Harlin's side to see if he's breathing. He looks so alive. His cheeks are flush, his hair is combed, his lips half parted as if he has just lain down. For a moment, it's as if Jacob has only turned over in bed to see Harlin sleeping. He has done that so many times, just to watch the man breathe. He often thinks of that breath as keeping a rhythm to the night, a way of knowing that everything is secure. Jacob is such a light sleeper, if the breath stops, or if Harlin turns his head, Jacob wakes. Is he afraid of losing the man? Or is he just... afraid?

"Harlin," he says.

But Harlin doesn't answer.

Jacob feels a pulse in his neck and, most importantly, there are no needle holes. No one had gotten to Harlin yet, but there are two lines marked on his neck. His chest moves up and down slowly but steadily. "I got the body of a thirty year old," Harlin often says. "From hard work and good livin'. I'm gonna live to be a hundred and twenty."

"You're gonna live," Jacob says to him now, pats him on the chest.

He moves to the computer on the desk. He saw how the nurse pulled up files, so he searches fast for *Moybridge*, and finds Harlin's records. He needs an ace in the hole. If the Redcoats are afraid of Harlin — if he doesn't have such perfect blood — they won't want him so badly. And they will let him go.

The file opens, and Jacob creates a disease.

It's not so different than a press release, really, just more subtle.

And medical records are scripture. He just hopes that Harlin will forgive him for messing up the scripture as it pertains to him. Muddying up his reputation, his perfection.

Jacob adds a note at the end of Harlin's records, as if a doctor added it. That done, it is time to get Harlin and himself out of there.

Quickly, he reaches the gurney and begins to unlock the wheels. He is covering Harlin to his neck with the sheet when suddenly lights come on all around him.

Jacob finds himself standing in the middle of a surgical theatre. Above him, surrounding him, are windows and at those windows Redcoats. Fifty, seventy five, a hundred. All of them peer down at him, all watch him as if he is a drop of blood on a slide at the end of a microscope.

"Ladies and Gentlemen, may I introduce you to Dr. John Lake from St. Mary's Hospital in Omaha, Nebraska," a familiar voice booms through the speakers. The Redcoats clap. As the clapping dies, Dr. Gontard continues. "We are indeed privileged that Dr. Lake is with us. Today, he is going to tell us a bit about a new donor that we discovered among the pool of applicants that come to the hospital. And, I believe," and here Dr. Gontard smiles, "he is going to show us a new transfusion technique. Is that correct, Dr. Lake?"

Though initially frightened, Jacob suddenly feels at home. This is a press conference. Instead of being the communications man behind the scenes, whispering the strategies, the lines, every second, he is now the Minister himself.

"Thank you, Dr. Gontard," he says broadly, "and to the staff of Sanctuary Hospital for your generosity and the honor of demonstrating to you the Omaha Method of transfusion, popular at our clinic, but also a technique that is becoming more popular in other hospitals."

He stalls, looks around the room. "I wish we had this kind of staff at St. Mary's."

The crowd murmurs their pride and approval. It's a cheap shot, but it gives him time to think. "I would like to tell you about this donor; I'm going to need his records."

Dr. Gontard taps the window twice and small screens appear at intervals around the glass. A projected holographic image, shoulder height, displays in front of Jacob.

The report is two pages, which include his additions at the bottom.

Dr. Gontard begins, "With your permission, Dr. Lake, I'll give an overview of the patient."

Jacob nods, even as sweat runs down his back. He sees the door behind him, and knows that most of the Redcoats are close by, too close; he might have only minutes to escape, if that. He can't be too obvious.

"As you can see," Dr. Gontard begins dramatically, "the patient, Harlin Moybridge, is in peak physical condition. Even at fifty-six years, he is as healthy as a man half his age."

Oh how Jacob wishes Harlin could hear this. It would stroke his ego.

"Harlin Moybridge has never had any man-made chemicals invade his body. He made a point to list on the patient application that he has only eaten organic foods all of his life, drank purified water, that he'd never taken antibiotics, and only employed homeopathic remedies. He is chemical-free and therefore chemically unaltered. His blood cells possess the ability to regenerate at an astonishing rate. He could be a universal donor and could be the answer to our own dilemma, even as we are the answer to theirs."

What did he mean? Jacob suddenly remembers the doctors talking in the morgue. 'Jardin's sick.' Another doctor was 'gone'.

Someone calls out, "What is SVD?"

"Excuse me?" Dr. Gontard asks. There is general curiosity.

"At the end of the record: *evidence of SVD. Patient not safe to transfuse.*"

"But the top of the form has him approved."

Curiosity has become confusion as they each check the records.

"I don't know SVD. And who is the doctor listed? Esterhazy." Dr. Gontard looks up, "Dr. Esterhazy. What do you mean by SVD?"

"I didn't put that there!"

"It's on the records."

"But, I don't even know what SVD is."

There is now rumbling among the Redcoats. Jacob knows he has only seconds to convince them. They are so much like a group of reporters hearing something they can't believe, something they fear... You can calm that fear. Or not. He watches the slow chaos forming, wants to wait until it hits a peak. But, he hears a murmur from behind him. Harlin moves his head and grunts.

"May I address the doctors?" Jacob asks.

They quiet down. "It is what I feared I might find at Sanctuary. Something only recently discovered in other hospitals. SVD or Shanghai Ventricular Disease has started appearing in our patients in the heartland of America. It is not confirmed yet, so WHO doesn't want rumors spread.

"First discovered one week ago, SVD is responsible for three deaths at our hospital, two of those doctors. Harlin Moybridge, it appears, carries this disease."

He keeps his face as straight and convincing as possible. "Which means that anyone who transfuses him will contract SVD."

The silence tells him they are waiting for one last word.

"This man is no longer of use to us." He moves to the head of the gurney and begins pulling it backwards. "Gentlemen, for your own safety, please keep back. I've already been exposed and I will take this man to isolation. Thank you."

He moves quickly towards the door.

"Jake?" says Harlin. "Jake. That you?"

He tries to place a hand over Harlin's mouth.

"Jake," he's slurring. "Got me strapped down, buddy."

"Dr. Lake?" says Dr. Gontard. "Please stop."

The door behind him opens and two Redcoats stand just outside it, blocking his exit.

The gig is up. But the spotlight is still on. What would he say to a Minister caught in a lie? No comment, no comment, no comment. He doubts that will work here.

"It's not Dr. Lake, is it?" Dr. Gontard says. "Convenient that you come on the day we find a universal donor. That the universal donor has a mysterious disease no one else has heard of, and that you are able to, equally conveniently, provide us with a definition, a history of the disease. No, I think not. He called you Jake."

"He said Dr. Lake, but he's sedated and is slurring," Jacob says.

"Jake, where am I? Who's talkin'?" Harlin asks.

"It's okay, Mr. Moybridge," Jacob turns to him. "We'll have you fixed up and back in your room soon. Don't worry."

He places a hand on Harlin's arm. *Not great timing, Harlin.*

"Ah!" Dr. Gontard says, smiling, as if he holds all the cards now. His voice has an uplift, a lilt. "You're listed as next of kin. *Jake Moybridge, husband.* Well, that makes sense."

No comment. No Comment. No comment. These are the rules of politics and media.

"My name is Dr. Lake and I have come from St. Mary's in Omaha, Nebraska."

"Mr. Moybridge... .Jake, there's no need to play any roles now. It's valiant, trying to save the life of your husband. We're doctors. We hold to the same values. We want to save lives. Your husband is a universal donor." He pauses, looking around at the Redcoats.

"Dr. Gontard, we can argue over my identity all you want, but this patient is a health risk to this hospital and I must insist that this be our priority."

Dr. Gontard smiles. "By all means." He waves to the men in the doorway. They step to either side of the gurney.

"No!" Jacob says instinctively. He pulls one of the doctors away, hitting him across the face with the back of his arm.

"See," Dr. Gontard says through the speakers. "The actions of a husband, not a doctor." He waves again and the two Redcoats back away to the door.

"Mr. Moybridge, you are standing at the edge of the greatest opportunity you will probably ever have to make a difference in this world. Your husband has impeccable blood — a kind of blood that will save our lives, even as we save yours. We are filters. We take out disease and give you back better blood. But there are so many of you, so many people with BBD, that we filter too much. We finally succumb to it ourselves. And who is here to save us? No one. We are discovering our own limits."

He turns to his right and begins to walk the length of the circular area, as if he's in a lecture hall and Jacob his only student.

"But Harlin Moybridge has a chance to change that. His blood — with its purity and exceptionally rapid regenerative quality — will give us the ability to transfuse without consequence. We'll save more lives, and be under less risk ourselves. Thousands of people, Jake, will benefit from Harlin's blood."

"You want to do a transfusion of his blood?" Jacob asks.

The doctor stops walking. "Jake, we need *all* of Harlin's blood. We can't give any back. It's not a transfusion as much as a *donation* that we need. A donation for humankind. Harlin's blood, combined with our skills, may mean that we can duplicate his blood type and strength for all the doctors."

"Did you ask Harlin?"

Silence.

"No," Jacob steps more into the light. "You listed him as dead. You didn't consult his husband. Where are the patient's rights, Dr. Gontard? You didn't want to bother with someone saying no. How many people have you done this to already?"

Dr. Gontard snaps, "Don't look at us with disgust, Mr. Moybridge. Surely you can empathize. We were just like you once — a minority no one cared about. We were forced to feed in the dark, forced to put who we were into a back alley. We cleaned up your poor, your diseased, your refuse from your streets. And now we hold respectable positions. We save lives. We don't often take a life on purpose any-more—but we *could*. We could still feed off of you, you know. Be the shadowy scary 'vampires' of legend. But we don't, because society gave us a chance. And we rose to the occasion. The world needs us. And we need your husband. And when you are that badly needed, what is one sacrifice for millions?"

"Then sacrifice *yourselves* if it's that important to you," Jacob says.

Dr. Gontard places his hands against the glass. His fingers elongate becoming needles again. "Who is look-ing out for us, Mr. Moybridge? Can you honestly say that you would sacrifice the lives of other people to save your husband? Can you make that choice?"

Jacob drops his head, feels like his feet are taking root, but it's just because he's pressing them into the floor. "First of all," he says, "you and I have nothing in common. Gays as a group do not kill people, nor feed off anyone. You were a minority that had a skill, and you volunteered that skill. Your choice. You benefited from that skill and from your choice. Second, Harlin Moybridge has a choice to become or not become your saviour. You have to obey the same law that gave you benefit and power. You can't say you're saving lives when you decide who gets to be saved. Hos-pitals are obligated to heal everyone. It's part of the Hippo-cratic Oath to 'Do no harm'—even if *harming* might save millions."

"One interpretation of a law," says Dr. Gontard. "You want to ask Harlin Moybridge? Let's ask him." Dr. Gontard calls out, "Harlin Moybridge!"

Jacob's voice rises. "He's half *asleep*. He's *sedated*. You can't ask him to give up his life for whatever reason if he can't understand the question."

"Harlin Moybridge, would you like to save the world?"

"Harlin, don't listen to him," Jacob tells Harlin. His fear, his real fear is that Harlin would *love* to save the world. It is the kind of question he has been waiting for his entire life. He loves swooping in with a heroic, helpful hand. Sacrifice is something he would do if he had the shot. To be the Messiah... what if he says yes?

"What's he saying? Saving people?" Harlin asks.

Jacob looks up at Dr. Gontard, walks towards him. "You can't believe that his answer is binding in any court of law. He's drugged!"

"Harlin, you have perfect blood," says the doctor.

Harlin smiles, slurs his words. "I know. I got a helluva pedigree."

"Harlin, we need you to help us."

"What? What do you need? Just ask. Jake, tell him he can have what he wants."

Jacob turns to the crowd of Redcoats, pleads with them. "How is this right? *You can't be doing this.* I'll expose you to every news media outlet. I know everyone in the media, everyone." Okay, he's just threatened people with needles on the ends of their fingers. He tries to calm down. "You're still the vampires you were if you're taking innocent lives."

"Harlin," Dr. Gontard continues, "we need your blood."

"You want my blood, don't ya? It's good, damn good blood." Harlin is smiling. Eating up the attention.

"We need that damn good blood, Harlin. We need you to donate your blood for sick people everywhere. Your blood will save millions of people, Harlin. Do you want to save millions of people?"

Harlin grins, looks at Jacob. "Millions of people?"

"Yes, millions of people. But we need all that blood. You have to give us your life, Harlin, for the lives of millions."

Jacob grabs hold of Harlin's bare shoulders. "Harlin, they want to *kill* you."

"Harlin," the doctor says. "We want you to *volunteer*."

Jacob starts to cry. He can't help it. He's powerless. Harlin reaches out and touches Jacob's face, traces his right eye. He cups his chin in the palm of his hand and stares into Jacob's eyes.

Then he turns his head to address Dr. Gontard. "All these sick people you're talking 'bout..." He looks around at the Redcoats standing above. He sounds almost awake, but slightly drunk.

The Redcoats silently wait to hear what he will say. Jacob waits, scared that if Harlin gives his permission, Jacob will have no power to do anything about it.

Harlin frowns. "Why should I give up my blood for them? People don't take care of themselves today." He throws an arm into the air. "Lazy *assholes*. Let 'em get their own selves better. Sheesh! How many times you gonna drain one of us to save one of them? Get your own damn blood! I made mine myself, took good care of it, stayed healthy — and now I gotta die to save millions? You're full of *shit*, that's what you are. And I mean that, from the bottom of my bloody, damn-good bloody heart. You bastards!"

He lolls his head back. "Sheesh. What do they think I am now — a bloody blood bank?"

Jacob smiles, barely suppresses it and looks up at the doctors. "Satisfied?"

The doctors murmur. Someone speaks up. "Mr. Moybridge is right. Perhaps we *should* ask Harlin Moybridge when he comes out of the sedative. I think if he understood the question—"

Jacob laughs a little to himself. They don't know Harlin. And he realizes that, for a moment, *he* didn't know Harlin. He looks at his husband, who is rubbing his eyes, complaining about the strong light in the room. Jacob loves him for being a damn curmudgeon at the right moments.

Jacob glances at the Redcoats standing above at the windows, at the way the doctors are looking at them, at how their fingers elongate, how they sharpen into needles. It seems you can take the vampire out of the alley, but give him a bright room and he'll turn it into a back alley. Now vampires will kill people for the good of the world! If the world knows, will it sanction this?

Jacob reaches for Harlin's hand and holds onto its warmth. Harlin squeezes his hand, using the leverage to sit up then stand.

Redcoats pour into the room through the door, surrounding them; a red river.

"There's only a hundred of 'em," Harlin says. "We can take 'em, buddy!"

The Sun Also Shines
On the Wicked
By Kevin Nunn

I arrived later than expected, about two-ish. When Stefan let me in, he appeared different, but not in a way I could immediately put my finger on.

"I came as soon as it was convenient."

Stefan looked me up and down as if taking a moment to remember why I was here, his light eyes flicking here and there before he snapped his long fingers. "Kenneth; of course! There is no need to rush; all won't be completely ready until seven or so."

"Seven!" I declared, allowing my surprise and irritation to show a little at this ridiculous idea. "I need to be home by then, as you well know."

He stepped aside, waving an elegant hand as if this was a triviality, and I stepped past him. "I have a spare chamber, you can stay there."

"Ridiculous! What is important enough to take such a risk?"

"The sun, of course," he declared matter-of-factly.

"Stefan, you are mad." I declared grumpily. Of course he was mad. Most of us were; it was a risk with our condition.

"I sincerely hope so," he said, striding to an elegant antique cask and drawing me a thick red drink. "Madness is clarity, without the shackles of context."

I accepted the goblet. It was excellent. "For this..." I raised the glass, "I forgive you. You have excellent stock."

He waved his hand dismissively and, now that he was closer to the lamp, I noticed the difference more clearly than I had upon arrival.

"Stefan! Your hand...!"

He smiled, and drew himself another glass of ruby liquid, but played up my observation, holding the glass high before his face with his hand between us.

"Your skin...it's darkened. You have a, oh what's the word...a tan; that's it, a tan!"

He smirked, "Really? And how would I procure one of those?" He asked and took a drink. He licked the thick juice from his lips, not wasting a drop.

"I believe that the common method is to expose yourself to the sun, but what I'm curious about is how you did it. It's not just make-up, is it? That would be very disappointing."

"No, although I have to admit that I did experiment with something called 'liquid tanning', but it is, unfortunately, merely a chemical application. In the end it served no purpose to my line of experimentation." He placed his empty glass on the table. "Follow me, I shall show you the apparatus."

He opened large double doors, thick old wood, quite uncommon these days, and led me into his laboratory.

"You do not wish to find yourself in this room in the morning," he stated plainly, pointing up. "You would find a rather unpleasant surprise."

There, above him, was an accoutrement that one would not find in the abodes of any in our circle of friends; a glass panel in the ceiling.

"A window? No, wait, what is the vernacular?—"

"You really should adjust to these new times," Stefan declared. "It is called a 'skylight'."

"But in the morning the sun will shine through it, *entirely unimpeded*!"

"Rather the point"

I had nothing to say to that. The idea was unsettling and I just stood for a few minutes, half empty glass in my hand forgotten as I gazed at the stars peeking out from behind the clouds in the sky. I returned to myself and drained my glass. It was quite normal for me to stare up at the stars, lost in reverie, remembering clearer stars from less complicated days, and darker nights.

"Stefan, what do you hope to prove, exactly? You are not suicidal—I know you better than that."

"Am I not?" he mused. "Did we not go to death all too easily the first time?"

"Speak for yourself. Like so many of us, I had no choice."

"Like so many of us, you chose to continue nonetheless."

"Don't be smug. I am not suicidal either, and I know myself a good deal better than I know you."

"When did you last see the sun?" Stefan inquired.

"Yesterday. I was unsettled and watched some television," I replied with pique. "It does not have appeared to have changed much, so I hardly imagine we've missed anything."

"Have we not?" Stefan mused, his gaze drawn to, then through the skylight.

I strode to the cask. "You owe me another glass, I think." I turned the spigot to let it pour. "For your over-dramatic presentation, if nothing else. Next we'll be striding around baring our fangs and hissing gratuitously."

He at least had the good manners to chuckle at that. "Let's hope it has not come to that. We'll all be wearing pirate shirts should it end that way. Pour me another as well. We'll see to it that the cask is empty by the time the sun rises."

I obliged. "So tell me, then, when you last saw the fiery orb," I said.

"The last I saw the sun, I lay in the grass of my homeland, arms twined around my beloved. I thought the day, the sun, special then, but have come to revere it even more since."

"Very poetic. I imagine she is long dead, so I don't think you'll be needing the sun again. Leave the past were it belongs."

"I have. A century does wonders to mend a broken heart."

"And your cask does wonders to fill an empty one." I drained the goblet again, savouring the rich flavour. "Your supply is quite robust."

Stefan smiled. "It is rich in vitamin D."

"Spare me the mumbo jumbo of these modern days. Neither of us cares for vitamins."

"I used to think that too..." Stefan grinned at me like the proverbial Cheshire cat. "All I mean to say is that it is rich in sunlight."

I rolled my eyes. "You are a dog with a bone. Very well, I will sit and endure your lunacy for friendship's sake, but try not to drag it out too long." I made myself comfortable on a nearby couch, hoping that he would not spout foolish theories all night long.

"Very well. Observe!" He strode to the corner and pulled a drop cloth off of a large contraption of wood with wheels at the bottom. It resembled a pergola, much as one would expect to see in a garden with vines curling up the edges and grapes hanging down. But instead of leaves and fruit, it bore an arrangement of narrow dangling mirrors in triangular shapes, many six foot strips of them fused together. These triangles were further arranged in slightly overlapping layers, somewhat like Venetian blinds. They covered the length and width of the top, and hung four deep, a web of wires thin as spider webs holding everything in place but allowing each long mirror to sway gently from the sudden removal of the cloth. "Good heavens! Rube Goldberg would be proud."

"Form follows function."

"Blah, blah, blah. An actual explanation would be preferred."

"When was the last time you purchased a mirror," Stefan asked with a smirk.

"Some years ago. A designer felt that it suited the front hall. I kept it; I have a fondness for irony in design elements."

"I use mine to reflect the sun. It certainly brightens up the room. Your designer might have mentioned that particular usage—"

"I believe it was meant to reflect some flowers, however, the lack of natural light tends to limit their longevity."

Stefan smiled. "I keep my blooms under the skylight; they remain quite robust. It's interesting, but did you know that all things on earth owe their life to the energy of the sun?"

"Depending upon your definition of life, no, not everything does."

"You are wrong my friend. All plants and animals would die without the sun."

"Well then, how clever of us to die first and give up the sun second."

Stefan rolled the strange contraption beneath the skylight, blocking it from view. He walked around the structure pushing down levers with his foot, locking the wheels in place before stopping at one of the support pillars. As he spun the ratchet, the mirrors beneath wound down the silver-web cables like spiders descending from the heavens. The mirrors opened, a tumbling waterfall, and all the various corners of the large room jumbled in the panes showing a confused mish-mash of walls and corners as if Escher had gone mad. Almost everything in the room, save only its occupants, could be found at least partially in the images.

"I have now set it," Stefan declared, straightening his shirt as he turned towards me, "at the last setting that I have used. It is as far as I have progressed."

"As far...? So then you brought me as a witness to some final step? Should I be aquiver with anticipation?"

"If it amuses you. However, as the sun rises, you would probably prefer to stand further away. It took me some time to acclimatise to the current setting."

"Current setting...? Are you saying that you have already developed at least a partial immunity? That's amazing!"

"You have seen the affect on my skin already—"

"Then you *are* immune? You may wander freely?"

"I do not believe so. But—"

"But? State plainly what problems remain. I will work with you if it is a problem that can be solved!"

I strode to the device and scrutinised it as well as I could without actually climbing it.

Stefan smiled at me. "So, it happens to you already."

"Pardon?"

"You, who say we don't need the sun, so rapidly offer to help solve the problem."

"It is deadly to us. If we can remove the harm, not doing so would be insane."

"You feel the pull. The desire to walk in the sun."

"And I what…lose control like all the actors wearing cheap fake fangs in low budget films when someone is bleeding? Please, don't insult me."

"I don't. But of course we do not drool and crawl like our fictionalized cousins of the mass media; food is not denied us, we can have it when we will. No, we are denied the sun."

"And we do well enough without it."

"Certainly. Because we must, but not because we wish it."

"Humans can't breathe water. It doesn't mean they miss the womb."

"An arguable point. However, I will tell you this: once I tasted the sun, it pulled me more than ever it had in the days when air was fresh and I bothered to breathe it."

I had nothing to say to that. I searched my own heart, looking to find what I felt about the sun and honestly came up with no real answer; it had been absent for so long that it was like a long buried relative who had died in one's youth, the mysterious subject of pictures and a familiar name, but very little more. Perhaps I, too, was to fall victim to some tragic nostalgia should I be reintroduced.

Stefan pushed a comfortable chair beneath the mirrors that hung like a strange and oversized chandelier.

"When the sun rises, I shall sit here, beneath the sky-light," he declared.

"And the mirrors shall block the sun, and you shall survive," I pointed out the obvious.

"Quite right," Stefan said, and reached out to a lever. "Then I shall do this." Giving a tug the mirrors turned, ropes and pulleys lowering them towards the chair and at the same time dropping them farther apart from each other. I gazed in curiosity, striding around the chair, and finally settling into it.

"And yet, there is still no direct line between the sun and your person. I would suspect that you should still be safe," I speculated.

"I hope so. But since mirrors are of no use to us, it is easy to forget their properties." He pointed at the hanging glass. "As you can see, each apparatus twists as it falls, redirecting the reflection. The sun, as more and more gaps appear, flows from mirror to mirror, like water around stones, eventually flowing entirely through to the underside where I shall sit awaiting its embrace."

"By eventually," I commented, surrendering the seat to him, "you mean essentially immediately. But at no point will it strike you directly."

"That is, of course, why I survive. I would be a liar, however, if I did not tell you straight out that I did not feel it on my flesh."

He looked reflective, as if basking in a memory, but finding the memory itself too weak to take any real pleasure in. He shook his head and continued. "I need you here...out of the light's range, of course. But it has become too dangerous to continue the experiment alone."

"Dangerous? But the light will never strike you directly, it will be diffuse and weakened; surely you do not intend to progress recklessly!"

Stefan smiled, but the sort of smile that was meant to hide doubt. "Of course not. I have taken precautions."

"By which you mean me."

"You shall talk to me, keep me sober."

"I should think that the foolish danger of allowing sunlight to stream through your ceiling would suffice to keep you focused."

He smiled. "Let us not belabour the plan. We both know our roles; let us pass the time until morning speaking of other things."

And so we did. The elephant in the room remained undiscussed, its presence never far from our thoughts, but banished from conversation. Any number of subjects, all light or frivolous topics, were spoken of that night around a steadily depleting cask, but I honestly cannot recall a single discussion, such was the anticipation of the morning's experiment. When the cask was empty, so was our will to blather. We spent the last hour in silent companionship, waiting for an antique clock to chime us into our roles on the stage.

Suddenly, Stefan strode through the doors and under the reflective pergola like a horse quivering to start a race. Perhaps he was drawn towards the gate with a thrill, excited by what lay ahead. Or perhaps he was instead sprinting to hide fear, to overcome some inner resistance.

He stood before the chair and spun gracefully towards me. "Stay well beyond the door, for the light will spill slightly inward."

I nodded, and did indeed stand well back, yet close enough to see the sky lighten above the mirrors, the telltale shade of grey that showed that day loomed.

Imperceptibly, moment by moment, the sky brightened and the mirrors filled with the slow cascade of light tumbling in, reflecting crystal one to another. Soon Stefan was bathed in the yellow sunlight that had bounced through the silvered glass. He stood in front of the chair, eyes closed, breathing in the light.

"Stefan! You are breathing."

"Yes. I can smell the difference in the air, feel the warmth of the sun."

"Ah," was all I could think to say.

He glowed in the sunlight as it drifted over him like a halo. My eyes were no longer used to light of that particular hue. Squinting, I sat sheltered in the darkness watching a golden nimbus settle around my friend like a poison gas that I couldn't approach for fear of my own safety. Slowly my eyes began to adjust and details were easier to see.

Finally, Stefan's hand reached out and touched the lever. And as he did so, I remembered something he said earlier: "And then I shall do this," as he tumbled the crystals down. What I did not remember at any point was him resetting his device to his previous level.

"Stefan! It is at your next level!"

His hand jerked away from the lever, but the mirrors were already dropping in their cascade of light; shards of sun spinning across the walls of the room like daggers slicing into the paint.

I jumped forward, but was immediately repulsed by the line of light that pressed in on the doorway. I could smell the warmth now, and caught the sound of a heart beat. Lurking in the dark, I huddled away from the light like a cornered animal.

Stefan however, stood still, glorious in a halo of luminescence. His hand remained outstretched, reaching towards the lever. His fingers twitched, inches away from the tool that controlled his fate, torn like a man who has been spurned by a lover and doesn't know whether to turn away or reach out to touch her, trying to bring her back.

"Stefan!" I hissed from my artificial cave, "return it! Raise the mirrors!"

He drew in a breath, long and ragged; whether in pain or pleasure I didn't know. "It calls me...it caresses me..." he said.

"Then tomorrow, tomorrow you will meet again; but for now, reset the device!"

"It's been so long." His fingers twitched again, like a man caught in an internal battle. "So long—"

"For the sake of...raise the lever!" I called to him.

He withdrew his hand. The action seemed to calm him, leaving him serene. He raised his chin and closed his eyes as he turned his face upwards towards the falling light.

"Stefan! It is sunlight! It destroys us! You need to begin the experiment anew, under properly-controlled conditions. I will stay with you tomorrow and we can do it again properly."

He laughed. "It really is a shock to the system, Kenneth." He took a deep breath and ran his hand over his face, still turned upwards to the sky.

"Does it hurt?"

"I think it might. But then again, it might not."

"Might not? Don't be ridiculous, you should know. Raise the shutters!"

He raised his hand again towards the lever. "It's overwhelming. There are so many sensations."

"I can imagine. In fact it's all I intend to do. Let's end this for the day, come at it tomorrow after you've rested."

"I've come too far. It's like I have too much sun in me now. I remember so many things that I have forgotten. Like warm grass. I wonder if it is still the same."

His hand jerked out and, with a click, the lever dropped, not just down once, but spastically rocked up and down in place as it ratcheted out its line. The crystals descended, spinning further away from each other as they dropped. They hit the end of their lines and jerked at full extension, bouncing on their wires.

Stefan fell into the chair in symphony with their awkward choreography, his arms hanging over the overstuffed arms. He sat still, not moving at all save for one or two raises of his chest as he inhaled the warm air of the room and bathed in the brilliant light.

He said nothing and neither did I. I wanted to but knew not what to say. I listened for anything, any word, any breath, any clue of what was happening. Perhaps the truth was that I felt disturbing the silence would upset some delicate balance that allowed him to survive. His body neither twitched nor writhed in pain. I saw no smoke, nor smelt burning flesh. There was nothing more to say, and nothing I could do.

And so the silence held through the day, the arc of sunlight tracing a path across my door frame making my room an impromptu sundial marking the passage of time. I huddled in the dark watching Stefan's silent form. When finally darkness fell I emerged and straightened myself out, gathering my dignity as well as I could.

When I touched his skin he was warm, surprisingly, like the newly dead, rather than what we truly were. Yet, he was as dead as the night he had been reborn. I bit my finger and held the blood to his lips, but he had passed beyond the place where even my old blood might reach him.

What to do? Mourn the passing of a friend? Regret the loss of years full of age and wisdom? I didn't know. Death was so easy and familiar, but there he sat, not as dust, or a hunted villain, a bloodthirsty fiend, or a misunderstood monster; he sat propped up just as any dead man might. The most unexpected of all ends.

I turned to the machine and lay my hand on the limp and lifeless lever. Did he let it run on purpose or was this an accident? I will never know for certain. In either case, it was clear that my next action was simply to destroy this device before it did any further harm.

It was the only appropriate response.

Slowly I began to wind the crank, absently watching as the mirrored triangles rose upward like glittering spiders climbing their webs.

Perhaps, as in folk tales of old, they served as the arachnids that ascended and descended their webs again and again, messengers between heaven and earth. Perhaps just as his strange mechanical spiders brought the sun down to Stefan, they carried the pieces of his lost soul up, weaving them into their webs under the purifying heat of the sun.

Just perhaps.

Quid Pro Quo
By Tanya Huff

"That first dose will keep him out for four or five hours and I can safely give him two, maybe three more without ill-effects." Setting the syringe aside, he pulled a key ring from the discarded jacket and passed it back without turning. "Search the house. If you find her, restrain her, and bring her directly here."

"Restrain her, boss?"

"I suggest you use a generous amount of duct tape."

There were people in the house. Two of them. Given that their years together had taught her all the rhythms of his life, Vicki could say with confidence that neither of the hearts currently pounding out barely-contained fear about two and a half meters above her head belonged to Metropolitan Toronto Police Detective Mike Cellecui—which was interesting, because the house did.

As she slid out the end of the packing crate, an alarm went off, freezing her in place. Watch alarm probably. Maybe cell phone.

"Shit! Sunset!"

They were speaking quietly—high emotion but low volume. Not that it mattered.

"So what? She's not in here."

"You one hundred percent positive about that, Steve? You sure that she's not tucked in between the floors or buried in the insulation in the attic or behind a false wall?"

Whoever he was, he wasn't stupid, Vicki acknowledged as she lifted the section of the false wall away and moved out into the crawlspace. This was unfortunate because he headed toward the door as he spoke, his footsteps and Steve's beating a fast tattoo against the floor.

Fast enough to survive?

Good question.

The crawlspace slowed her a little—at just under a meter high it had been chosen for safety not speed of exit. Out into the laundry room. Up the stairs as the door closed. Across the kitchen in time to see Steve and the smart guy throw themselves into the car they'd parked in the driveway.

Also smart. Parking in the driveway made them look like they were friends visiting and gave them faster access to their wheels if, say, they'd stayed a little past sunset and had to haul ass or die.

Vicki'd bet the smart guy wasn't planning on letting Steve drive and was therefore not the short, bearded white man but the taller, clean-shaven black man sliding behind the wheel. She'd have been inclined to say they didn't look like criminals except she'd been a cop long enough, back before it had come down to change or die, to know criminals didn't actually have a *look*.

She could have caught them before they got the engine started. A closed car door would have meant squat to her but the whole sleeping naked thing made her hesitate a moment too long. February in and of itself didn't mean a lot but she could hear Peter Yuen and his sister arguing as they headed up the driveway of the house next door and flashing the neighbor's teenagers would definitely cause trouble for Mike.

As the black Jetta sped away, she considered the few inarguable facts she had. Not only did Smart-guy and Steve have a pretty damned good idea of what she was but also thought they knew where she spent the day and were willing to break into a police officer's house in order to do something about it.

The edge of the counter cracked under her grip.

"Just what I need," she growled, heading back to the crate for her phone. "A pair of fucking 21st century Van Helsings. Like my life isn't complicated enough."

Of the two halves of her life, maintaining some semblance of a normal relationship with Detective Mike Celluci seemed to be giving her the most problems. It required careful socializing with people who'd known them before she'd changed, and a safety net of lies complex enough to give the most jaded politician pause. The creature of the night thing, *that* she had down.

Never growing old had lost a little of its shine as she watched Mike's hair grey and the lines around his eyes deepen but, basically, being stronger and faster, being able to deal with the human and not-quite-human things that haunted the nights of a big city seemed a fair trade for being helpless between sunrise and sunset.

Or had been a fair trade.

Until today.

Still naked, she headed back upstairs, listening to Mike's phone go straight to voice mail. Theoretically, he finished at three and by 5:47 PM shouldn't be doing anything that would keep him from answering. And anyone who believed cops had half a hope in hell of keeping regular hours was in a prime position to buy some Saskatchewan beach front property.

"We have a situation." A *situation*; their personal code for *someone knows*. "Call me as soon as you can. Oh, and I'm heading into the office so you can meet me there."

She couldn't stay at the house. Not and think clearly.

Pausing by the notepad on the fridge, she scrawled down the four numbers on the license plate that she remembered—*AAK, blank, dash, blank, blank 2*—then went into the bedroom to dress. Half her clothes were here, half at her office downtown. She hadn't spent the day there for months but the belief that she maintained two separate residences allowed for a greater plausible deniability when "friends" couldn't find her before sunset.

Smart-guy and Steve hadn't been subtle in their search. Both bed and dresser had been shifted and both closets emptied enough to check the back walls. They didn't bother moving anything too small to hide a body.

"Definitely knew what they were doing," she snarled, yanking on a pair of jeans.

She repeated the sentiment a few minutes later, slamming the kitchen door behind her and locking it. It was the door Smart-guy and Steve had come in through, and they'd taken the time not only to pick the lock on the door but also the lock holding the chain, rather than take a pair of bolt cutters to it. The cold, and the pungent hand lotion used by whichever one of them had actually handled the door, made it difficult to get any kind of a scent and they'd both obviously been wearing gloves while they were in the house. Winter clothes blocked most of the fear sweat.

Scent would have allowed her to pick them out of a crowd regardless of how good a look she'd got at them. As it was, she might recognize their voices, but that was damned little to go on.

Still, she'd found other men with less.

"Picked the wrong damned vampire to stake this time," she growled, forcing herself to relax her grip on the steering wheel before she broke it. Again.

Winter driving in Toronto was never fun. Winter driving at rush hour, Downsview to her office on King Street East, barely maintaining a grip on her temper was less fun by an order of magnitude.

As the door to her office closed behind her, Vicki exhaled what felt like the first actual breath she'd taken since sunset and admitted that just maybe the break-in—not to mention the possibility of true death that came with it— had left her a little tense.

Any lock could be picked but the two heavy steel bolts and the two-by-four slid through steel brackets that secured the office door required an entirely different skill set. And tools. And would likely attract unwanted attention from the other tenants in the building, three quarters of whom ignored the clause in their lease that stipulated studios in the renovated warehouse were not live-in.

She was safer here in the day than she was at Mike's.

She'd given up that safety for Mike.

But then Mike had given up normal for her so if someone, somewhere was keeping score, the game was tied as far as Vicki was concerned.

"By sunrise," she muttered crossing the room to her desk, "I'd like that to be completely irrelevant." Find the car. Find out who owned it. Neutralize the threat. A few months ago, she'd had dinner with a man who designed data bases for the Ministry of Transport. He didn't know it but after she'd fed, he'd built her a back door into the system and set up the search protocols that allowed her to make the best use of it.

With the day denied her, it was nothing more than a way of evening the odds. That said, she hadn't mentioned it to Mike. It wasn't like he shared all the little details of *his* job.

Model and license information had just been entered when her office phone rang. The caller ID showed Mike's cell number.

Speak of the devil.

"Hey. In case you didn't get my message, we have a situation."

"You have more than that, Ms. Nelson. You have one chance to save Detective Celluci's life."

She didn't recognize the voice.

Or her own when she answered, but then her lips were pulled so far back off her teeth that was hardly surprising. "You're a dead man."

"One chance," he repeated. He didn't sound particularly worried about her reaction. "My people will meet you in front of your building and bring you to me."

It didn't seem like she had much of a choice. "When?"

"As soon as you can get out there. Leave your cell phone behind."

He'd hung up without waiting for a response, but she called him a few choice names anyhow as she shrugged back into her coat and pulled her phone out of her pocket.

The black Jetta. Big surprise.

Smart-guy was still driving. Steve sat in the back and held up a phone as she closed the door. "Boss can hear every word. Try anything and the cop dies."

Vicki twisted around and smiled at him, giving the Hunger free reign. They thought they knew what she was. They weren't even close.

There was a sudden, sharp smell of urine and Steve whimpered. He hung onto the phone though.

"Stop terrifying my people, Ms. Nelson." The speaker crackled as they pulled out into traffic, passing under a triple layer of overhead wires. "I can see you, I can hear you, and only your full co-operation will keep Detective Celluci alive."

"If you kill him..." The small webcam had been mounted on the rear view mirror. She turned to stare directly into it. "...I will make you scream."

"I don't doubt it. I am, however, banking on the fact that you will do nothing to endanger Detective Celluci's life. Your phone?"

"In the office."

"Excellent."

"You're going to take my word for it?"

"If I find out you've been lying, you won't be the one to suffer for it. Put the blindfold on. You'll find it on the seat beside you."

She found it on the seat between her and Smart-guy, almost covered by the spread of his grey wool winter coat.

Smart-guy hadn't looked at her once, his eyes locked on the road. At the speed they were traveling along the snow-covered city streets, she could kill him and take control of the car without endangering anyone else on the road. From the trickle of sweat running down his temple to disappear behind his fleece scarf, it seemed he knew that.

"Ms. Nelson?"

The threat was implicit in the question.

"Fine. I'm putting it on."

It wasn't just a strip of black cloth, it was a strip of black cloth that had clearly been designed as a blindfold—thicker where it passed over the eyes, the ends thin enough to tie securely. Whoever this guy was, he probably knew if anal retentive had a hyphen.

"Good. Now, since your hearing is undoubtedly good enough to pick up environmental sounds that may give my position away, Daniel, if you would."

Smart-guy had a name.

Vicki heard the shush as the fabric of his coat brushed against itself, felt the air currents in the car shift, heard the click of switch, the whirr of a CD, and the dulcet tones of Céline Dion at a decibel level that had to be causing as much pain to the other occupants of the car as it was to her.

Unless, of course, her 21st Century Van Helsing had recruited his minions from gay-men-trapped-in-the-nineties.com.

"Couldn't you just distract me by telling me your evil plan?" she muttered, hands up over her ears. A whimper of agreement from Steve in the back but no reply from the big man. "Whatever he's paying you guys, it isn't enough."

It might still have been possible to separate out distinct traffic sounds but Vicki didn't bother trying. She didn't memorize the turns or try to time the sections of the trip. Wherever they were headed, she'd never need to find it again. The moment they'd laid their hands on Mike, everyone involved had died. Steve had died. Daniel had died. And their boss had died. Oh, they were still up and walking around, still apparently breathing, but it was only a matter of time. The only actual question remaining was just exactly how long their deaths would take. And that depended on the shape Mike was in.

Céline slid into *My Heart Will Go On*.

Vicki sang along. No reason they shouldn't start suffering now.

Fourteen and a half songs later, they turned onto what felt like unplowed ruts. Before the fifteenth song finished, Daniel turned the car off and Céline fell silent.

All three of them breathed a simultaneous sigh of relief.

"Stay in the car, Ms. Nelson, until Daniel comes around and opens your door."

By having Daniel do it, both minions were on the same side of the car as she was. Easier for one to react if she killed the other. Van Helsing was wasting his redundancies since no one was dying until Mike was safe.

She stretched as Daniel closed the door behind her.

"Turn to your right, Ms. Nelson."

Vicki turned.

"Now walk twenty paces."

Four paces took her through a doorway and inside an unheated building. Her heels made no sound against the concrete floor. Approximately two meters behind her on the left, Daniel matched his pace to hers while on the right Steve's boots thumped out an arrhythmic beat, the echoes defining a large, empty space. The air reeked of cloves but, sixteen paces in, she caught a whiff of a familiar scent under the spice.

Mike.

He wasn't bleeding.

There weren't spices enough in the city to cover that.

At twenty paces she stopped. Two heartbeats in front of her, four, maybe five meters away. Mike sounded drugged, his heartbeat slow but steady. Van Helsing sounded excited but not afraid.

"You may take off the blindfold, Ms. Nelson." He sounded as calm up close and personal as he had over the phone.

The calm before the storm.

Vicki stuffed the blindfold in her pocket and slowly opened her eyes, her vision sensitive enough that even the low light in the empty warehouse was enough to cause painful starbursts.

When she blinked them away, the first things she saw was Mike. Arms, legs, and chest duct taped to a wheelchair, his eyes closed, his mouth slightly open, a glistening line of drool running down his chin, a small vapor cloud blooming with each breath.

Her would-be Van Helsing stood slightly to the left of the wheelchair, holding a gun to Mike's head. He wasn't particularly tall, with brown hair and brown eyes, expensively dressed and vaguely attractive in a *I'm confident enough to kidnap a decorated police officer in order to get the drop on a vampire* sort of a way. Vicki had to admit she appreciated that kind of confidence—if only on an intellectual level.

She kept a tight grip on the Hunger. As much as she wanted to let it loose, allowing herself to give into blood lust would very likely add Mike to the body count and that was the one thing she wanted to avoid.

"We meet at last, Ms. Nelson." His words created a vapor cloud.

Hers didn't. "You do know that it's entirely possible I could kill you before you could pull the trigger?"

"I know." He seemed impressed. "Which is why my men are also armed. If you begin to move toward me, they will shoot."

"They couldn't hit me."

"They won't be aiming at you."

Although she could smell the fear rising off the two men behind her like smoke, if she had to attach an emotion to this man, she'd say it was anticipation. He was studying her like she was the answer to the only riddle he'd never been able to solve. "You don't want to kill me."

His brows rose. "I beg your pardon?"

He knew what she was. He suspected she lived with Mike—knew about the connection between them at least. He got the keys to the house from Mike when he grabbed him, but finding her there had been incidental to his plan or he wouldn't have waited until the end of Mike's shift and the chance she'd wake. He took Mike because Mike's life was the only thing that would allow him to control her. And if he wanted to control her...

"What is it that only I can do for you?"

He smiled then. "Make me like you."

Vicki blinked. "Like me?"

"Yes."

"You have no idea what I am."

"Faster, stronger, immortal, Nightwalker, vampire." He gestured with his free hand. The hand holding the gun remained rock steady. "A piece of evidence here. A rumor there. A camera you weren't aware of. Oh don't worry, it's all been taken care of."

"If you think this is a worried expression, you're more delusional than I thought."

"Fine. Don't feel you need to start ripping throats out to cover your tracks, it's all been taken care of. The point is, I don't want anyone else to put the pieces together. I assigned Daniel and Steven to you exclusively and I did what research was necessary myself. The only thing I haven't discovered is why."

"Why?"

"Why you would take the risks involved in tying yourself to a mortal life."

She couldn't stop her lips from lifting off her teeth. In all honesty, she didn't try very hard. "There's a lot of back story."

"I'm sure there must be. And it's not really important, here and now. The point is, I know exactly what you are, Ms. Nelson, and in return for the detective's life, you will give that gift to me."

Vicki hadn't had a headache since she'd started walking the night, but the effort of holding herself back and trying to figure out what the fuck was going on had combined to wrap a band of pressure around her temples. "Okay, let's leave your ideas about me for a moment; who the hell are you?"

"You don't know?'

If she had to bet, she'd say he honestly thought she *should* know.

"My name is Damon Shea and I am the CEO and majority stock holder of—"

"Shea Pharmaceuticals, a multinational, multimillion dollar corporation run by a man too ambitious not to cut corners and too smart to get caught."

A dimple flashed in one cheek. "See, you do know me."

"And you want to become a vampire."

"Think of what I could accomplish."

Vicki snorted. "Yeah, I am. You kidnapped a police officer, drugged him, and are holding him at gunpoint—strangely enough, that doesn't say using immortality to work for the greater good." She spread her hands, carefully, aware of the weapons behind her. "But that could just be me."

"Needs must, Ms. Nelson," Shea shrugged. "As long as you co-operate, Detective Celluci will wake up with nothing worse than a dry mouth and a temporary craving for carbohydrates."

"And you'll release him when I agree to change you?"

"I will."

She sighed. "The change isn't instantaneous."

"I said I did my research, Ms. Nelson. While I am changing, Daniel and Steven will keep an eye on your detective, as an insurance policy. You'll have left him a note explaining enough to keep him from searching for you. After the change, you won't be able to kill me because of the blood bond. Neither will I be able to kill you. You'll be free to go and I will then change Daniel and Steven as payment for services rendered."

She wondered if Daniel and Steven actually believed that.

Didn't matter.

"So," he continued, "here's what's going to happen: you are going to sign the note I've already written, you will allow me to secure you. Daniel and Steven will take the detective home and we will get started. There is no way out of this, Ms. Nelson. I've covered every contingency."

The bang of a fist against the warehouse door was so loud and unexpected the shouting wasn't entirely required. "Open up! This is the police!"

One of them—she expected was probably Daniel—kept his head and pulled the trigger as she began to move. The round caught her just under her left shoulder and the pain broke the last of the Hunger free.

Her hand around Shea's hand and the gun, she crushed the bones against the metal.

He screamed.

"A gunshot. A scream. Police'll be breaking the door down." He smelled like terror now. Vicki smiled. "Time to leave."

Flicking the bloody remains of Shea's trigger finger out of the way, she turned just far enough to put a bullet into both Daniel and Steven's heads then threw the moaning man up over her good shoulder and ran for the other end of the warehouse, not caring that blood from his hand left a trail on the floor.

She could have broken the door down but she shot the lock off and shoved it open carefully enough to keep from ripping it off the hinges. Scuffing her feet through the snow to keep from leaving a clear impression, rage keeping her moving at nearly full speed in spite of the wound and the struggling man, she stopped by a set of tire tracks then made an impossible jump across them to a bit of bare rock. Looked down, smiled again, and dropped down into the ravine. She'd thought they were down by the waterfront but, given the terrain, it was more likely they were in one of the recession-hit warehouses on Riverside Drive.

When she figured she was far enough from the warehouse to delay discovery, she tossed Damon Shea down into the snow. He stared up at her, eyes wide and shocky, heart racing, cradling his ruined hand to his chest, not so much holding the gun as unable to release it.

"You... called..."

"The police? Yeah, before I left my phone in the office." One of the benefits of fighting to maintain some semblance of a life with Mike was that she still had friends on the force. She'd reported the threatening phone call and passed on the information about the car she'd seen *lurking* around the house.

"Research..."

"That whole vampires-are-lone-predators thing? That we never share our territory? That we're top of the food chain? That we walk alone? You researched vampires, Mr. Shea." Crouching in the snow beside him, she gave his shoulder a friendly pat. "You didn't research me. And you know what you also missed considering? People in the process of breaking the law tend to overreact when the police show up."

The banging on the door had caused one of the minions to panic, shooting the boss, who shot them both, and ran for it.

There were likely drops of her blood in the warehouse as well as Shea's but, given the way budget cuts had created a massive backlog in the labs and given that the scene was pretty self explanatory, the odds were good they'd never run the tests. And if the scene wasn't self explanatory enough, she'd have a talk with the officers at the scene before they wrote up their reports.

She thought about explaining all that to Shea but the scent of his blood, steaming a little in the cold, loosened the last of her self control.

"They lost Shea's trail for a while but they found his body later down in the ravine. Bastard slipped, cracked his head on a rock and between that and the blood loss, well it was minus 27 when they found him. And there wasn't much left. A pack of feral dogs or maybe coyotes had torn the body apart, probably before it was even cold, but they found his weapon, three shots fired, two into his men and one into the lock on the rear door. Running ballistics is just a formality, really."

"Thank you, Constable." Eyes silvered, she held his gaze with hers. He shivered as her voice whispered across his skin.

"Do you..."

"Shhhh." She laid her finger against the swell of his lower lip. "I wasn't here and you didn't tell me any of this."

When he nodded, she slipped past him and into Mike's hospital room. Although he'd been essentially unharmed, the drugs had left him too out of it to protest a night under observation as vigorously as he could have.

He looked completely wiped but he opened his eyes when she took his hand, obviously having been waiting for her to show up. After a moment, he closed his fingers around hers and squeezed. "What time is it?"

"Five fifty."

"You're cutting it close."

She stayed to make sure that the police who found Damon Shea's body found what she'd wanted them to find. "I've got time. You've got to love a February night."

Mike's mouth twisted into something that wasn't quite a smile. "No, I don't actually."

"Well, maybe not *this* February night."

"Vicki..." He paused and searched her face. Hospital rooms were never entirely dark and she had no idea how much he could see. He often saw more than she wanted him to. If he asked for her version of the story, she wondered what she'd tell him. Finally, he sighed, yawned, and said, "I've been lying here trying to figure out why Damon Shea of all people would grab me. I mean, there's a lot of low lifes out there who might want to get their own back, but Shea? It doesn't make sense." He met her gaze then, one of the very few who still could, and said, "You have blood on your sleeve."

That was impossible, she'd changed her...

When Mike's brows rose, she sighed.

"That's what I thought." And she was just as glad he didn't say exactly what he thought, given the blood that wasn't on her sleeve. "Shea was using me to get to you."

"It didn't work."

"This time. But I'm a danger to you."

"Given that you were the one grabbed and drugged..." Seemed reasonable to skip telling him about the gun to his head. "I'd say I was a danger to you."

"So..." He dragged her hand over onto his chest, "what are we going to do about it?"

She supposed she'd always known it would come to this. It wouldn't be easy finding another territory but she'd have to get out of the city entirely to put enough distance between them.

To her surprise he laughed before she could say anything. "You've always thought too loud, Vic. And you've always been my weakness, from the moment I first met you, same way that I've been yours. And we've always lived the kind of lives where people could use that against us. So, we'll do what we've always done."

His heart beat slow and steady under her hand. "We'll watch each other's backs."

"We'll watch each other's backs," he repeated. With that settled, his eyes started drifting closed.

Vicki glanced over at the clock. If she stayed another twenty minutes, she'd still have time to get to her office before sunrise. As she watched him sleep, she realized that Shea had entirely missed the point. Mike was her weakness, but he was also her strength.

He kept her Human.

And should she ever be threatened the way he'd been tonight, he'd kill to keep her safe. She just prayed he never had to.

Biographies

Artist

Ex-gravedigger **John Kaiine** self trained professional artist/photographer is also the author of the critically acclaimed metaphysical thriller *Fossil Circus* and various short stories, including the now filmed short feature *Dolly Sodom*. He lives in a house by the sea with his wife, Tanith Lee and two black and white cats.

Editor

Nancy Kilpatrick has edited ten anthologies, two involving the subject of vampires. She has published eighteen novels, four of them in her vampire series *Power of the Blood*, and three stand-alone vampire novels. She wrote four issues of the *VampErotic* comic series, and has published two novellas featuring the undead. In addition she has quite a few vampire stories in print, a small number of which are included in her collection *The Vampire Stories of Nancy Kilpatrick* from Mosaic Press. Her most recent vampire short story "Vampire Anonymous" can be found in *The Moonstone Book of Vampires*. Lest anyone think she only writes about vampires, check out her website: www.nancykilpatrick.com

Translator

Sheryl Curtis lives in Montreal, where she works as a professional and literary translator. Since 1998, her short-story translations have appeared in *Interzone*, *On Spec*, various *Tesseracts*, *Year's Best Science Fiction 4*, *Year's Best Fantasy and Horror 15* and elsewhere. Her first book-length fiction translation, *Of Wind and Sand* (*Terre des autres* by Sylvie Bérard) was released by EDGE in 2009.

Authors

Kelley Armstrong is the author of the "Women of the Otherworld" paranormal suspense series, "Darkest Powers" YA urban fantasy trilogy, and the Nadia Stafford crime series. She grew up in southwestern Ontario where she still lives with her family. Armstrong first introduced the character of Toronto vampire Zoe Takano in her 6th Otherworld novel, *Broken*, and has since featured her in several pieces of short fiction.

Colleen Anderson resides in Vancouver, BC where vampires live the high life. "Ember" was a spark on the back burner that came to life—a tale of morality and what happens when a vampire breaks the one taboo. Anderson has published numerous poems and stories, with other vampire fiction "Hold Back the Night" in the Open Space anthology and "Lover's Triangle" in *On Spec* and *Dreams of Decadence*. New work is forthcoming in *Shroud*, *Crucible* and *On Spec*. There are a few more vampires lurking in coffins in her attic, waiting for release.

Montréal author **Natasha Beaulieu** published many short stories before her dark novel trilogy *Les Cités intérieures* (*The Inner Cities*) saw print. The trilogy has been translated into Polish but not yet into English. Her latest novel *Le Deuxième gant* (*The Second Glove*) is still on the dark side, as well as her other projects. Even though there has been no true vampire in her novels up to now, some of the characters share similarities with vampires, like immortality or blood passion. But Anton in "Evolving", is her first true vampire.

Born in Quebec City, **Claude Bolduc** now lives in Gatineau and has been writing horror short stories for twenty years, dozens of which were published in magazines and anthologies in Québec, France and Belgium. His best stories can be found in the collections *Les Yeux troubles et autres contes de la lune noire* and *Histoire d'un soir et autres épouvantes*, the latter winning the Grand Prix de la science-fiction et du fantastique québécois in 2007. He says, "If vampires live among us, why should their existence be perfect? Shouldn't they face the kind of problems any human being might encounter?"

Rebecca Bradley is currently based in Calgary, but gradually shifting to Ootischenia, BC. While living in Hong Kong in the 1990s, she co-wrote *Temutma*, a novel about a Chinese vampire, published by Asia2000. She has also, just for the joy of it, posted a few Buffy fanfics under the name Whinter. Her story is a boomer *cri de coeur*, written as Rebecca contemplates the approach of yet another damn birthday.

Mary Choo was born in Vancouver, British Columbia, and is a long-time resident of the Lower Mainland. The spectacular beauty of the area forms the backdrop for her story, "Resonance", which was inspired by her belief in the ability of all things to adapt in the face of adversity. Mary's dark fantasy pieces have appeared in a wide variety of publications, including two of the acclaimed Canadian *Northern Frights* anthologies, and her work has placed on the preliminary ballots of the Nebula and Bram Stoker awards (poetry collection), and the final ballot of the Aurora Awards. This is her first published vampire story.

Heather Clitheroe lives in Alberta, a part of Canada not generally known for demons or dark, mysterious woods filled with demons. "Come to Me" was inspired by the stories—be they true or urban legend—of the Aikogahara forest at the base of Mount Fuji in Japan where people go to commit suicide, as well as the mythical kitsune. "When they're good," Heather says, "fox demons can be very helpful...but when they're bad, they're very, very bad."

Kevin Cockle lives in Calgary Alberta He is a published boxing journalist and a frequent contributor to *On Spec Magazine*. Combining a background in finance with an education in critical theory, Kevin's work is often concerned with the odd dialectic between economics and the weird. Of his story "Sleepless in Calgary", Kevin says: "Calgary's a fast-paced, forward-looking, well-meaning city with all sorts of potential for accidental horror. What happens when people start to fall off the hurtling pace? At what point do people stop trusting their hopes and instead start praying to their nightmares to save them? Calgary's a good town for vampires; Calgary's ready."

Born in England and raised in Toronto, Canada, **Gemma Files** has been a film critic, teacher and screenwriter, and is currently a wife and mother. She won the 1999 International Horror Guild Best Short Fiction award for her story "The Emperor's Old Bones", and the 2006 ChiZine/Leisure Books Short Story Contest for her story "Spectral Evidence". Her fiction has been published in two collections—*Kissing Carrion* and *The Worm in Every Heart*, both from Prime Books—, and five of her stories were adapted into episodes of *The Hunger*, an anthology TV show produced by Ridley and Tony Scott's Scot Free Productions. She has also published two chapbooks of poetry. In 2009, her short story "Marya Nox" appeared in *Lovecraft Unbound*, edited by Ellen Datlow, while her story "each thing I show you is a piece of my death" (co-written with Stephen J. Barringer) appeared in *Clockwork Phoenix 2*, from Norilana Books. She is currently finishing her first novel, *A Book of Tongues*.

Victoria Fisher was born in England but presently lives in Ontario, where she is a student at the University of Toronto. She is distracted from her studies by a fascination for stories of all kinds: past, present and future. In 2006, her short story "Buttons" appeared in Tesseracts Ten.

A writer for most of her life, **Jennifer Greylyn** has only recently been persuaded by the thoughtful but not very subtle prompting of family and friends that other people might enjoy her work as well. Her stories have appeared in, among other places, Abyss and Apex, Malpractice: Tales of Bedside Terror and Lilith Unbound, which features the prequel to her story in this anthology. "Mother of Miscreants" was inspired by her fascination with history and mythology, particularly the way in which the lore of vampires has changed over time. She lives in Halifax, Nova Scotia.

Ron Hore, from Winnipeg, Manitoba, can be found sailing on Lake Winnipeg when he's not writing or critiquing for an on-line magazine. Two of Ron's short stories and a poem were published in a collection issued by a writer's group and he won first prize in a Canadian Authors Association contest for a ghost story published in their 2006 anthology. Supervised by his wife and a large, demanding cat, Ron has "waiting-to-be-published" novels on topics such as reincarnation, alternate history, fantasy, and a detective who tangles with vampires. "Chrysalis" allows him to practice his vampiric urges in a family setting.

Tanya Huff lives and works in rural Ontario with her partner Fiona Patton, six cats, and an elderly Chihuahua. Her twenty-fifth novel, The Enchantment Emporium, is out in hardcover from DAW Books, Inc. and she is currently working on a fifth Torin Kerr not-entirely-a-Valor book. She occasionally writes essays for BenBella's Pop Culture books and once in a while does a review for the Globe and Mail newspaper. While happy to be back in Vicki Nelson's mythos for "Quid Pro Quo", she has no idea of what inspired the story.

Sandra Kasturi is a poet, writer and editor living in Ontario. In 2005 she won the prestigious ARC Poem of the Year award. She is the poetry editor of ChiZine and the Co-Publisher of ChiZine Publications. Sandra's work has appeared in various places, including *Prairie Fire*, *Contemporary Verse 2*, *TransVersions*, *On Spec*, *Taddle Creek*, several of the *Tesseracts* series, and *Northern Frights 4*. Her cultural essay, "Divine Secrets of the Yaga Sisterhood" appeared in the anthology *Girls Who Bite Back: Witches, Slayers, Mutants and Freaks*. She managed to snag an introduction from Neil Gaiman for her first full-length poetry collection, *The Animal Bridegroom* (Tightrope Books). Sandra has spent entirely too much time wondering where the best place would be for vampires to live, before deciding that the dark side of the moon was a fine idea.

Claude Lalumière is the author of *Objects of Worship*, the co-creator of *Lost Myths* (lostmyths.net), and the editor of eight anthologies, including the Aurora Award nominee *Tesseracts Twelve*. He lives in Montreal. The first inklings of "All You Can Eat, All the Time" came to him, fittingly, at Nuit Blanche 2009, the dusk-till-dawn event of the annual Montreal High Lights Festival. But, as often happens, the story he intended to tell was not the story he ended up writing, so almost all the elements directly inspired by Nuit Blanche were gradually edited out with each new draft.

Kevin Nunn lives in Guelph, Ontario with a supportive wife, son, two dogs and four very unsupportive cats. "The Sun Also Shines on the Wicked" is Kevin's second published story, and his only one about vampires, which is why when he's not stealing time to write, he toils away happily as a tradesman in order to pay the mortgage. This story was written because he thinks that no matter what your state—monster or non—you always struggle to be more than you are. That, and he wanted to see if he could write a vampire story that does not use the words vampire, blood or bite.

The idea for this story came from a nightmare **Rhea Rose** had in which the main character maneuvers at night through smog and clouds, unaware of why she is headed to the warehouse, terrified that she will electrocute herself on a power line.

Rhea is a Vancouver, BC writer and a fulltime teacher. Her stories and poetry have appeared in the *Tesseracts* anthologies, *Talebones* and in other speculative fiction markets. Many of her pieces have been nominated for awards including the Rhysling award for poetry, and two short stories have received preliminary nominations for a Nebula award. A short story appeared in a David Hartwell *Christmas Forever* anthology. Her horror story "Summer Silk" made the 2007 Honorable Mention list in *The Year's Best Fantasy and Horror* edited by Ellen Datlow, Kelly Link and Gavin J. Grant.

Michael Skeet is a writer and broadcaster in Toronto. A two-time winner of the Aurora Award, he has been writing SF, fantasy and horror fiction for over 20 years. "Red Blues" was inspired in part by his career as a disc jockey and jazz critic, as well as his love of movie musicals and the golden age of American pop songwriting.

Bradley Somer lives in Calgary. He has had fiction published in many literary journals including *Matrix, Qwerty, Carousel, Existere, Filling Station, Grimm Magazine, The Scrivener Review, The Nashwaak Review* and in John B. Lee's anthology *Body Language* (Black Moss Press). Several of his works have dabbled in dark matters. "Bend to Beautiful" is his first venture into the realm of vampires—in this case the ancient Roman bird-like vampire strix. He says that this story was inspired by a similar vampiric encounter which occurred several years ago, the details slightly altered to maintain anonymity. Read some of his tales of the urban fantastic at www.bradleysomer.com

Jerome Stueart is a graduate of 2007 Clarion San Diego. His work has been published in *Strange Horizons, Fantasy Magazine, Tesseracts 9 and 11, On Spec,* and other magazines and journals. He has written several CBC radio series, most notably *Leaving America,* about his immigration from the United States to Canada. Currently he writes and reports for the Arctic Institute of North America, and also teaches writing to teens and adults in Whitehorse. About his story, he says: "I hadn't written a vampire story before. But the idea of vampires evolving was really interesting to me. After watching the Swine Flu epidemic mania, and remembering SARS, I started thinking about the power of the

WHO in our lives, the power of hospitals and medicine, really the power of any institution that can convince people it is right, that they must do something. I wondered how vampires might play a helpful medical role in society — and what might happen if their new status were threatened."

Bev Vincent grew up in northern New Brunswick and attended Dalhousie University before moving to Texas in 1989. He has written two non-fiction books, over fifty short stories, and numerous essays, interviews and reviews. The *Road to the Dark Tower*, his authorized companion to Stephen King's *Dark Tower* series, was nominated for a Bram Stoker Award. He is contributing articles to the *Encyclopedia of the Vampire: The Living Dead in Myth, Legend and Popular Culture*. His affection for crime stories inspired him to choose a police detective as the protagonist for "A Murder of Vampires". His web site is www.bevvincent.com

Steve Vernon is a writer and storyteller living in Halifax, Nova Scotia who's been writing horror for over twenty years, with two novels, three ghost story collections, one children's picture book, five novellas, "more poetry than any practical writer ought to write," a radio play, and a lot of short stories to his credit. He wrote "The Greatest Trick" with an eye towards some of the real parasites in this society—those who would run it. For more info check his website: http://users.eastlink.ca/~stevevernon.

Sandra Wickham was raised in rural Ontario and now lives in Vancouver with her husband and two cats. She has been a Professional Fitness Competitor for many years, but is thinking about retiring to start a family. "Mama's Boy" sprang out of the hopes and fears that come along with the daunting prospect of parenthood. Sandra has been a coach and fitness trainer for over ten years and has just recently returned to her love of writing, with this story being her second fiction submission and first publication. You can visit her website at www.sandrawickham.com

The bestselling novelist Peter Straub has described **Rio Youers** as "...one of the most vital, most exciting young talents to come along in this decade." Youers is the author of two novellas: *Mama Fish* and *Old Man Scratch*, and the acclaimed vampire novel *Everdead*. Rio says that "Soulfinger" is inspired by the raw, unforgiving power of music, by his love of the blues, and his fear of strange places. He lives in Cambridge, Ontario with his wife Emily.

Our titles are available at major book stores
and local independent resellers who support
Science Fiction and Fantasy readers like you.

EDGE Science Fiction
and Fantasy Publishing

Tesseract Books

Our titles are available at major book stores and local independent resellers who support Science Fiction and Fantasy readers like you.

Alphanauts by J. Brian Clarke (tp) - ISBN: 978-1-894063-14-2
Apparition Trail, The by Lisa Smedman (tp) - ISBN: 978-1-894063-22-7
As Fate Decrees by Denysé Bridger (tp) - ISBN: 978-1-894063-41-8
Avim's Oath (Part Six of the Okal Rel Saga) by Lynda Williams (pb)
  - ISBN: 978-1-894063-35-7

Black Chalice, The by Marie Jakober (hb) - ISBN: 978-1-894063-00-7
Blue Apes by Phyllis Gotlieb (pb) - ISBN: 978-1-895836-13-4
Blue Apes by Phyllis Gotlieb (hb) - ISBN: 978-1-895836-14-1

Children of Atwar, The by Heather Spears (pb) - ISBN: 978-0-88878-335-6
Cinco de Mayo by Michael J. Martineck (pb) - ISBN: 978-1-894063-39-5
Cinkarion - The Heart of Fire (Part Two of The Chronicles of the Karionin)
  by J. A. Cullum - (tp) - ISBN: 978-1-894063-21-0
Clan of the Dung-Sniffers by Lee Danielle Hubbard (pb) - ISBN: 978-1-894063-05-0
Claus Effect, The by David Nickle & Karl Schroeder (pb) - ISBN: 978-1-895836-34-9
Claus Effect, The by David Nickle & Karl Schroeder (hb) - ISBN: 978-1-895836-35-6
Courtesan Prince, The (Part One of the Okal Rel Saga) by Lynda Williams (tp)
  - ISBN: 978-1-894063-28-9

Dark Earth Dreams by Candas Dorsey & Roger Deegan (comes with a CD)
  - ISBN: 978-1-895836-05-9
Darkness of the God (Children of the Panther Part Two)
  by Amber Hayward (tp) - ISBN: 978-1-894063-44-9
Distant Signals by Andrew Weiner (tp) - ISBN: 978-0-88878-284-7
Dreams of an Unseen Planet by Teresa Plowright (tp) - ISBN: 978-0-88878-282-3
Dreams of the Sea (Part 1 of Tyranaël) by Élisabeth Vonarburg (tp)
  - ISBN: 978-1-895836-96-7
Dreams of the Sea (Part 1 of Tyranaël) by Élisabeth Vonarburg (hb)
  - ISBN: 978-1-895836-98-1
Druids by Barbara Galler-Smith and Josh Langston (tp)
  - ISBN: 978-1-894063-29-6

Eclipse by K. A. Bedford (tp) - ISBN: 978-1-894063-30-2
Even The Stones by Marie Jakober (tp) - ISBN: 978-1-894063-18-0
Evolve: Vampire Stories of the New Undead edited by Nancy Kilpatrick (tp)
  - ISBN: 978-1-894063-33-3

Far Arena (Part Five of the Okal Rel Saga) by Lynda Williams (tp)
  - ISBN: 978-1-894063-45-6
Fires of the Kindred by Robin Skelton (tp) - ISBN: 978-0-88878-271-7
Forbidden Cargo by Rebecca Rowe (tp) - ISBN: 978-1-894063-16-6

Game of Perfection, A (Part 2 of Tyranaël) by Élisabeth Vonarburg (tp)
  - ISBN: 978-1-894063-32-6
Gaslight Grimoire: Fantastic Tales of Sherlock Holmes
  edited by Jeff Campbell & Charles Prepolec (pb)
  - ISBN: 978-1-8964063-17-3
Gaslight Grotesque: Nightmare Tales of Sherlock Holmes
  edited by Jeff Campbell & Charles Prepolec (pb)
  - ISBN: 978-1-8964063-31-9
Green Music by Ursula Pflug (tp) - ISBN: 978-1-895836-75-2
Green Music by Ursula Pflug (hb) - ISBN: 978-1-895836-77-6

Healer, The (Children of the Panther Part One) by Amber Hayward (tp)
  - ISBN: 978-1-895836-89-9
Healer, The (Children of the Panther Part One) by Amber Hayward (hb)
  - ISBN: 978-1-895836-91-2
Hell Can Wait by Theodore Judson (tp) - ISBN: 978-1-978-1-894063-23-4
Hounds of Ash and other tales of Fool Wolf, The by Greg Keyes (pb)
  - ISBN: 978-1-894063-09-8
Hydrogen Steel by K. A. Bedford (tp) - ISBN: 978-1-894063-20-3

i-ROBOT Poetry by Jason Christie (tp) - ISBN: 978-1-894063-24-1
Immortal Quest by Alexandra MacKenzie (pb) - ISBN: 978-1-894063-46-3

Jackal Bird by Michael Barley (pb) - ISBN: 978-1-895836-07-3
Jackal Bird by Michael Barley (hb) - ISBN: 978-1-895836-11-0
JEMMA7729 by Phoebe Wray (tp) - ISBN: 978-1-894063-40-1

Keaen by Till Noever (tp) - ISBN: 978-1-894063-08-1
Keeper's Child by Leslie Davis (tp) - ISBN: 978-1-894063-01-2

Land/Space edited by Candas Jane Dorsey and Judy McCrosky (tp)
  - ISBN: 978-1-895836-90-5
Land/Space edited by Candas Jane Dorsey and Judy McCrosky (hb)
  - ISBN: 978-1-895836-92-9
Lyskarion: The Song of the Wind (Part One of The Chronicles of the Karionin)
  by J.A. Cullum (tp) - ISBN: 978-1-894063-02-9

Machine Sex and other stories by Candas Jane Dorsey (tp)
  - ISBN: 978-0-88878-278-6
Maërlande Chronicles, The by Élisabeth Vonarburg (pb)
  - ISBN: 978-0-88878-294-6
Moonfall by Heather Spears (pb) - ISBN: 978-0-88878-306-6

Of Wind and Sand by Sylvie Bérard (translated by Sheryl Curtis) (pb)
  - ISBN: 978-1-894063-19-7
On Spec: The First Five Years edited by On Spec (pb)
  - ISBN: 978-1-895836-08-0
On Spec: The First Five Years edited by On Spec (hb)
  - ISBN: 978-1-895836-12-7
Orbital Burn by K. A. Bedford (tp) - ISBN: 978-1-894063-10-4
Orbital Burn by K. A. Bedford (hb) - ISBN: 978-1-894063-12-8

Pallahaxi Tide by Michael Coney (pb) - ISBN: 978-0-88878-293-9
Passion Play by Sean Stewart (pb) - ISBN: 978-0-88878-314-1
Petrified World (Determine Your Destiny #1) by Piotr Brynczka (pb)
 - ISBN: 978-1-894063-11-1
Plague Saint by Rita Donovan, The (tp) - ISBN: 978-1-895836-28-8
Plague Saint by Rita Donovan, The (hb) - ISBN: 978-1-895836-29-5
Pock's World by Dave Duncan (tp) - ISBN: 978-1-894063-47-0
Pretenders (Part Three of the Okal Rel Saga) by Lynda Williams (pb)
 - ISBN: 978-1-894063-13-5

Reluctant Voyagers by Élisabeth Vonarburg (pb) - ISBN: 978-1-895836-09-7
Reluctant Voyagers by Élisabeth Vonarburg (hb) - ISBN: 978-1-895836-15-8
Resisting Adonis by Timothy J. Anderson (tp) - ISBN: 978-1-895836-84-4
Resisting Adonis by Timothy J. Anderson (hb) - ISBN: 978-1-895836-83-7
Righteous Anger (Part Two of the Okal Rel Saga) by Lynda Williams (tp)
 - ISBN: 897-1-894063-38-8

Silent City, The by Élisabeth Vonarburg (tp) - ISBN: 978-1-894063-07-4
Slow Engines of Time, The by Élisabeth Vonarburg (tp)
 - ISBN: 978-1-895836-30-1
Slow Engines of Time, The by Élisabeth Vonarburg (hb)
 - ISBN: 978-1-895836-31-8
Stealing Magic by Tanya Huff (tp) - ISBN: 978-1-894063-34-0
Strange Attractors by Tom Henighan (pb) - ISBN: 978-0-88878-312-7

Taming, The by Heather Spears (pb) - ISBN: 978-1-895836-23-3
Taming, The by Heather Spears (hb) - ISBN: 978-1-895836-24-0
Ten Monkeys, Ten Minutes by Peter Watts (tp) - ISBN: 978-1-895836-74-5
Ten Monkeys, Ten Minutes by Peter Watts (hb) - ISBN: 978-1-895836-76-9
Tesseracts 1 edited by Judith Merril (pb) - ISBN: 978-0-88878-279-3
Tesseracts 2 edited by Phyllis Gotlieb & Douglas Barbour (pb)
 - ISBN: 978-0-88878-270-0
Tesseracts 3 edited by Candas Jane Dorsey & Gerry Truscott (pb)
 - ISBN: 978-0-88878-290-8
Tesseracts 4 edited by Lorna Toolis & Michael Skeet (pb)
 - ISBN: 978-0-88878-322-6
Tesseracts 5 edited by Robert Runté & Yves Maynard (pb)
 - ISBN: 978-1-895836-25-7
Tesseracts 5 edited by Robert Runté & Yves Maynard (hb)
 - ISBN: 978-1-895836-26-4
Tesseracts 6 edited by Robert J. Sawyer & Carolyn Clink (pb)
 - ISBN: 978-1-895836-32-5
Tesseracts 6 edited by Robert J. Sawyer & Carolyn Clink (hb)
 - ISBN: 978-1-895836-33-2
Tesseracts 7 edited by Paula Johanson & Jean-Louis Trudel (tp)
 - ISBN: 978-1-895836-58-5
Tesseracts 7 edited by Paula Johanson & Jean-Louis Trudel (hb)
 - ISBN: 978-1-895836-59-2
Tesseracts 8 edited by John Clute & Candas Jane Dorsey (tp)
 - ISBN: 978-1-895836-61-5
Tesseracts 8 edited by John Clute & Candas Jane Dorsey (hb)
 - ISBN: 978-1-895836-62-2

Tesseracts Nine edited by Nalo Hopkinson and Geoff Ryman (tp)
  - ISBN: 978-1-894063-26-5
Tesseracts Ten: A Celebration of New Canadian Specuative Fiction
  edited by Robert Charles Wilson and Edo van Belkom (tp)
  - ISBN: 978-1-894063-36-4
Tesseracts Eleven: Amazing Canadian Speulative Fiction
  edited by Cory Doctorow and Holly Phillips (tp)
  - ISBN: 978-1-894063-03-6
Tesseracts Twelve: New Novellas of Canadian Fantastic Fiction
  edited by Claude Lalumière (pb)
  - ISBN: 978-1-894063-15-9
Tesseracts Thirteen: Chilling Tales from the Great White North
  edited by Nancy Kilpatrick and David Morrell (tp)
  - ISBN: 978-1-894063-25-8
Tesseracts 14: Strange Canadian Stories
  edited by John Robert Colombo and Brett Alexander Savory (tp)
  - ISBN: 978-1-894063-37-1
Tesseracts Q edited by Élisabeth Vonarburg & Jane Brierley (pb)
  - ISBN: 978-1-895836-21-9
Tesseracts Q edited by Élisabeth Vonarburg & Jane Brierley (hb)
  - ISBN: 978-1-895836-22-6
Throne Price by Lynda Williams and Alison Sinclair (tp)
  - ISBN: 978-1-894063-06-7
Time Machines Repaired Whie-U-Wait by K. A. Bedford (tp)
  - ISBN: 978-1-894063-42-5